I0598010

Future Tense

Boson Books by Frank Almond

Future Tense
Tempus Fugit

FUTURE TENSE

by

Frank Almond

BOSON BOOKS
Raleigh

Published by Boson Books
An imprint of C&M Online Media Inc.

ISBN (print) 978-0-917990-77-9
        (ebook)1-932482-10-5

© Copyright 2003, 2011 Frank Almond
All rights reserved

For information contact
C&M Online Media Inc.
3905 Meadow Field Lane
Raleigh, NC 27606
Tel: (919) 233-8164
email: cm@cmonline.com
URL: http://www.bosonbooks.com

Cover image by Joel Barr
Designed by D.F. McAllister

Contents

Chapter 1

I hadn't seen Emma since the night they said I murdered her. But even though her back was turned to me and she was wearing what I can only describe as a Jane Austen dress, I just knew it was Emma standing by that window. Something about her bright brown hair, the way she stood—her whole aura—told me that I was looking at the real Emma Gummer. And it was such a relief to see her again that all the doubts and horrors I had been through simply melted away. At last we were together. I closed the door discreetly behind me—things were likely to get pretty steamy.

"Em?"

She jumped. "Sloane! Would you mind telling me what the hell is going on? Why am I a prisoner?"

I laughed. "You're not a prisoner."

"That door was locked!"

"Was it? Oh."

"Yes—it was! Something very odd's been happening." She pushed up her fringe with her hand, and looked a little lost for moment. "I don't know how I got here—"

"I can explain everything."

"Oh really? This had better be good. Well?"

"You're pregnant, Em."

"What—? How do you know?"

"Believe me, you wouldn't believe me if I told you."

"Try me." She folded her arms.

"Well, I was there when we, um."

"Just tell me how you know—because I certainly haven't told anyone."

"It's a really long story, Em. Can't we just—?"

"I'm waiting." She tapped her foot.

I didn't want to tell her—I knew how mad it was all going to sound. I took a deep breath. "All right—my father's a time traveller from the fourth millennium and he's immortal—it sort of runs in the family—"

"Oh, puh-leeze!"

"No, listen, Em—it's the truth. I swear. The future's controlled by a puritanical police state and they keep sending these—these robot things back through time to erase me—and anyone connected with me—"

She covered her ears with her hands and shook her head. "I'm not listening."

"No, Em—I know how it sounds, but—"

"Sloane, I'm not in the mood!"

"Emma—they know that's my child you're carrying! But there's no need to look so worried—they can't get you here. It's about 1800, I think, and this is my old man's place, Duckworth Hall. His name's Sir Julian Duckworth and he's fabulously rich." I laughed, nervously. I was getting some very strange looks from her. "Yeah, he-he only looks about nineteen—you wait till you meet him, Em. Ah-ah. We call him the Duck because he kind of quacks when he laughs, but his real name's Zebulon Zirconion and he's a Doctor of Temporal Engineering, and, I mean, he's obviously a lot older than nineteen—although, technically, he hasn't even been born yet. Do you want me to go on? What?"

"You must think I was born yesterday."

"No. You won't be born for another two hundred years. You see, as I was trying to explain, this is—"

She pushed me aside and looked around the picture rails.

"All right. That's enough. Where's the camera? This is one of those stupid reality TV shows, right?"

"No. I'm not joking—this really is the past. There's a lot of other stuff I could tell you, but I won't scare you with all that right now. All that matters is you're safe—and we're having a baby!"

"Correction—I am having a baby." She barged past me again.

"Well, that's what I meant." I slumped down on the bed. "Now, do you think you could come to bed, love? I haven't—you know-er-seen you since the third millennium." I scratched my head. "Although, since this is the past, I suppose the last time I actually saw you was the first time I met you. Ha-ha. Remember when we met, Em?"

"I remember when I dumped you!" She was still looking round the room for a hidden camera. She looked behind an old oil painting of a horse.

"Yes, but in view of the circumstances, I thought we could forget that little blip and move on."

"Forget the spin, Sloane—I *have* moved on." She sounded cold and distant, and kept searching. "That's why I'm not playing any more of your little games!" She said it loudly, as though she thought others might be listening in.

"There's no one there, Em." I patted the empty space next to me. "Please come to bed."

"That would be unethical," she said, stooping down to look under it.

"Unethical? You sound like one of them! How long were you in the future?"

She checked behind the dressing table mirror. "It's over, Sloane. Get over it."

"Sometimes a thing has to be broken before it can be mended," I said. I got up and tried to put my arms around her. "Let's mend our love, Em... you're expecting our little baby."

She shrugged me off. "Don't remind me. Now, where's the camera crew?"

"Don't remind—? There isn't one. I've been to hell and back looking for you! The police think I murdered you and my so-called best friend—Matthew bloody Turner—says the kid's his and the two of you have been at it behind my back! You haven't, have you, love?"

She spun round and slapped me hard across the face. All in one swift movement. And it bloody hurt!

"I'm getting a cab back to London!" she screamed—in my face—and stamped towards the door.

I jumped up in front of her. "No—listen, I mean, you can't! The only cabs round here use real horsepower and take three days."

"Get out of my way, or I will kick you very, very hard."

"Emma, please—in that dress?"

"Get out of my way!"

"Just let me explain—"

There was a ripping sound and I felt a sharp pain in my shin.

"Aunt-Blood-y-Nor-a!"

I tried to hop away in retreat, but she hooked her ankle around the back of my standing leg and pushed me over. Then she tore open the door. The Duck, who had obviously been listening through the keyhole, tumbled into the room.

The Duck and I were now both lying flat on the floor, looking up at a startled Emma. She suddenly realized the Duck was looking up her torn dress, and quickly covered the split.

"May I present my father, Sir Julian Duckworth," I said.

"Charmed," smirked the Duck, extending a hand up to her.

Emma was so surprised to see the elegantly dressed youth fall at her feet, that she almost accepted it. She recoiled.

"What am I doing?" She picked up her skirts, skipped over the Duck's legs and fled down the hall. "You're mad! All mad!" she cried.

I tried to go after her, but the Duck grabbed my ankle.

"Let her go, mate—she won't get far," he said. He used my trouser leg to haul himself up, adjusted his big red spectacles and flicked his ponytail straight. "I've told my staff not to let her off the estate."

"Every time you're around, my life goes down the toilet." I rubbed my shin. "Have you noticed that? You're like Elizabeth Barrett Browning's bloody dog!"

"Hey?"

"The mutt was called Flush."

"Charming. But if I know Lizzy she meant a hot flush, mate—not a wet one. Racy filly that Lizzy Barrett. You know, I nearly got off with her once at one of old Coleridge's, er, parties—what a night that was—if those harpsichord strings hadn't snapped, I might have been in there—I was nearly up the pleasure dome."

"Is this leading anywhere? Only I'm in a hurry—I'd like to catch up with Emma and explain why my father looks like my kid brother."

"Ha-ha, no, I mean—we're young—full of high spirits—plenty of time to play the field yet—come here. I want to show you something, Son."

"Can we please drop the 'son' bit?"

He closed the door and led me over to a writing bureau. He pulled a secret lever somewhere in the back of a drawer, and a decanter of wine and two glasses popped out of a hidden compartment. "Glass of Madeira, me dear, uh, mate?"

"You know, this was not the reunion I had in mind," I said, as the Duck did the honours.

"I know what you had in mind," smirked the Duck, handing me my wine, while raising his to his mouth to guzzle it down.

"I'm not talking about *that*, I'm talking about love," I said.

The Duck sat on the edge of the bed and bounced up and down. "Yeah-yeah. This brings back a few happy memories," he laughed. "Anyway, there'll be plenty of time for all that lovey-dovey stuff later—we have a mucho problemo, old son—ah-ah! Old son—get it?"

"Yes, I get it, Father. And you can forget it."

"Forget what? I haven't said anything yet."

"You don't have to. I can hear it coming. The day I go on another one of your freaky little time trips, cuckoos will be crapping from the clouds."

"She'll come round," said the Duck. "Stuck here, in beautiful Georgian Gloucestershire, waited on hand and foot, living in the lap of luxury—preggers. Now, ask yourself: where's she gonna go?"

"I'm not leaving her," I said. "She's confused. She can't get her head around all this. Neither can I." I took a large gulp of wine.

"I'll ask Emily to have a little heart-to-heart with her. They'll have stuff to talk about, what with 'em both being in the pudding club," smiled the Duck.

Suddenly, I felt faint and had to sit on the bed.

"All right, Son?"

"Er, yes, I just felt a bit funny then." I peered into my glass. "Sort of queasy."

"Spot of time lag catching up, I expect," he grinned. "Close your eyes a sec and hold your nose—soon clear it."

I did as he said and when I opened my eyes, the Duck was right, I felt much better. But, strangely, the room appeared to have darkened somewhat.

"Wow, that was really odd," I rubbed my eyes. "Anyway, I'm—I'm, um, staying here," I said, "until you can fix me and Emma up in another time period—a safe one—and then I want you to stay as far away from us as possible. I fancy the 1920s—the Charleston, Scott and Zelda, flappers—"

"And then the Great Depression," added the Duck.

"You're the great depression—that's why I'm off. You can come and visit your grandchild from time to time, but keep it short, and I don't want you turning up every five minutes either," I said. "Has it got darker in here or is it me?"

"It's you," said the Duck. "Remember Jemmons?"

"Of course I remember Jemmons. Why—what's he done now? There's something wrong with my eyes."

"Only got himself nabbed by a Temporal Criminal Pursuit snatch squad—the duffer."

"Well, I can't help that—I've got enough on my plate," I said. I blinked my eyes repeatedly. "It was definitely brighter in here..."

"Oh, that's nice," said the Duck. "That man risked his neck for you, and this is all the bleeding thanks he gets. Remind me not to do you any more favours, mate."

"Please don't do me any more favours," I said. "And consider that a final reminder."

The Duck got up on his high horse and started strutting up and down the room. "You couldn't give a toss, could you, Stephen? There's poor old Roger, rotting away in the worst hellhole on Earth and all you can say is: I can't help that. Well, I just hope you end up sharing the same cell some day, then you can explain to him why you just couldn't be bothered."

"It's not that I can't be bothered. Anyway, I seem to remember it was me who did all the rescuing last time—you both owe me. Big time. I had to save you from getting sent down, while good old Jemmons went walkabout." I got up and walked over to the window to look up at the sky. "Did a cloud just pass over?"

"I explained all that—Rog was arrested and I offered myself up as a sacrifice to save you and the others. Just like whatshisname in that book by whatshisname. If you hadn't interfered we wouldn't be in this mess. Dickens."

"Wouldn't be in this mess? They were about to cart you off to the human vivisection farm! In case you'd forgotten," I said. "Sydney Carton."

"Yeah, that's the geezer. I would have escaped. I had it all sussed," said the Duck.

"I'm not even going to discuss this. If you're so keen, you go and spring him, you don't need me."

"It's a two-man job."

"Well, take Emily's dad with you, he likes a good punch-up. I'm staying here to get my love life sorted. And that's that."

"Roger has been sent to the Castle!" said the Duck. "I can't ask Tree to go back there—the poor bloke did a seven stretch in the place. He nearly has a heart-attack if he sees a sandcastle."

"That's funny, because you told me he's never even been anywhere near the Castle. You said he made it all up." I looked around the room for something to explain myself with.

"Well, I might have bent the truth a bit."

"Yeah, you are to the truth what Uri Geller is to spoons, mate."

"You're coming—I'm your father—you've got to do as I say!"

"Bollocks."

I chose a heavy looking metal clock from the mantelpiece.

"Not that!" quacked the Duck. "It's a Louis the Fourteenth!"

"I want to get it through your thick skull, once and for all!" I said. "I am not going to the fourth bloody millennium!"

I swung it at his body—missed—and it slipped from my grasp and smashed into the wall.

"That was ormolu!" He charged into me, with his legs kicking and fists flailing.

Now, the Duck liked you to think he was an expert in the martial arts, so his assaults were always accompanied by lots of oriental-sounding screams and extravagant posturing. But since he only has the physique of an apprentice jockey, I easily grabbed him by his ginger ponytail and slung him out of my way. And then I dashed out the door to find Emma.

* * *

I didn't have far to look. I found her talking to some bloke at the foot of the stairs, a tall, smartly dressed, foreign-looking guy, with a 'tache. And Emma had changed her torn dress and was looking very fetching in an elegant floral morning gown. She was leaning against the banister, girlishly trying to conceal a blush with her fan, while they shared what looked like an intimate joke. I wasn't a bit jealous, but thought I should break it up before the jumped-up little poser got the wrong idea.

"Em! There you are—shouldn't you be taking your nap?" I called, as I came bounding down the stairs.

I got my body between them, with my back to my rival, completely blanking him, and spoke directly to Emma.

"You know, in your condition, you really should be taking it a bit easier, love," I said.

"I yam sorree—you are not well, Emmeur? I did not meen to tireur you," said the young man, in what sounded—to me, at least—like a phoney French accent.

I turned on him. His handsome—if you like that sort of thing—Latin features were filled with concern. "She's blooming, mate—she's having my baby. That's all. Close the door on your way out."

"Oh, pardon," he said, looking all embarrassed and awkward. He bowed to me and then to Emma. "Forgeeve my clumsee intrushone, Monsieur. Pleese excuse mee, Madame Emmeur. I did not no." And then he backed away and scuttled off.

"That's right—run along," I sneered. I turned back to Emma, who promptly slapped me across the face and swept past me to chase after him.

"Monsieur Travis! Monsieur Travis!"

"Emma?" I said. "I was only—"

"—Wasting your breath, mate," said the Duck, patting me on the shoulder. "I forgot to tell you about my other house guest. He's a bit of a lady's man is our Travis. I should have warned you."

"Who the hell is he?"

"He's on a mission," said the Duck confidentially.

"I can bloody see that," I said. "But who is he?"

"Name's Travis De Quipp. He's from Paris in France."

"I know where Paris is," I said. "What I want to know is—what's a lump of it doing over here? I thought we were supposed to be at war with his lot."

"It's a long story. He just needs a bit of help, that's all," said the Duck.

"Well, he's not helping himself to my girlfriend!"

"Yeah, you want to watch that—the women just seem to fall at his feet, that's why I've sent Emily away for a few days. She's having some retail therapy in Bath. I told her to visit the Pump Rooms. Put it all on my account."

"Hm, very convenient. So, what does this guy want, apart from a smack in the mouth?"

"Now, now," said the Duck. "Travis is all right."

"It's easy for you to say—you've got dozens of women," I said. "What happened to that one you were going to marry—whatshername—the Viscount's daughter?"

"Henrietta? She dumped me," said the Duck. "I need to build up a bit more cred around here before I crack the posh crumpet market. Seems her old man didn't think I was good enough for her. Said I was only after her for her heirlooms. Heirlooms? I said, I've had more heirlooms than you've had hot dinners, mate—you can keep your family silver—I was after your bloodstock!"

"Yes, well, you've still got Emily," I said. "I like Emily."

"Yeah. Why don't we take a turn around the garden?" The Duck put his arm around my shoulder and walked me through to a back drawing room, which led out onto the terrace. "And I can tell you all about it over a spliff."

"I'm not leaving Emma alone with him," I said, holding back.

"Not much of a basis for marriage, is it, mate?" said the Duck, with a lopsided grin. He took out some papers and started patching them together.

"What's that supposed to mean?"

"A serious deficiency in the trust department, if you ask me."

"Well, I didn't. Anyway, I do trust her, it's just—she's acting very strangely. It's as if she doesn't care about us—but I know deep down inside she does."

"You don't think you're being a bit, you know... now, how can I put this, without sounding offensive—pathetic and self-delusional?"

"Do you want a smack in the mouth as well?" I said.

"Face it—she blew you out, man."

"She doesn't mean it—wait a minute, how do you know? You'd better not have anything to do with this?"

"Me? As if."

"If I find out this is all your doing, I'll—" I scratched my ear. "I don't understand it—I'm the father of her child."

"It's not uncommon," said the Duck.

"What isn't?"

"Rejection of the biological father."

"And you'd know all about that, dad," I nodded.

"The mother conceives by mistake with an unsuitable partner, then rejects him and seeks a superior substitute," said the Duck. "Happens all the time."

I grabbed him by the collar of his floppy white Byronic shirt. "If I find out you've been poisoning her mind against me, I'll tear that evil little forked thing you call a tongue right out of your lying mouth!"

"Get off!" He broke free and straightened his matching white silk neck scarf. "You want to watch that, mate. Jealousy is a very ugly emotion. No wonder your bird's playing away from home."

"She is not a bird and she is not playing away from home! We are in love—with each other!"

The Duck nodded through the window. "You'd better tell her that. Doesn't look like it from where I'm standing, mate."

I followed his gaze. My heart sank. There, standing on the terrace, was Emma, in the arms of Monsieur De Quipp.

"What is she playing at?" I gasped. "She's killing me."

The Duck stifled a laugh. "I think we know what her game is, mate."

I grabbed him by his lapels and swung him round to face me. "I don't know how and I don't know why yet—but you're behind this—and when I find out what *your* game is, you are going to be very sorry! And *I'm* not playing games. Got that?"

He shrugged me off. "Charming. I got the blame for everything last time!" He jumped up on a card table and swung his feet onto a Chippendale chair, to continue rolling his spliff.

"That's because you were to blame for everything," I said, not taking my eyes off the loving couple out in the garden. "You're always to blame for everything. I'm going out there."

"You're wasting your time, mate. Besides, it won't last."

"No, it won't, because I'm going to put a stop to it right now," I said, lurching towards the French windows. I lurched back. "You see, once again you seem to know everything—this is how I got into trouble last time. How do you know it won't last?"

"Well, stands to reason, doesn't it?" said the Duck, sealing his spliff with a single lick. "His sort are only after one thing—once he's had his wicked way with her, he'll be off like a shot."

I knocked the spliff out of his mouth.

"Mind the gear, man!"

"Travesty De Creep, or whatever his name is, is not having his wicked way with my Emma!"

"Your Emma? You really are an emotional dinosaur, aren't you, Stephen? When are you going to realize that you can't own people? Emma has free will, if she wants to give you the old heave-ho, you just have to respect her decision, and let her get on with it, mate."

I was speechless.

He picked his spliff up off the floor and inspected it for damage. And then, satisfying himself that it was still intact, stuck it back in his mouth and lit up. "You don't have much luck with birds, do you, Son?"

I pointed at him through the cloud of marijuana smoke. "You're behind this. And I will find out what you're up to. That's a promise. But, right now, I'm going to go out there and give that cheesy Frenchman a piece of my mind!"

"Watch yourself," said the Duck.

"Don't worry about me—I can take care of myself." I reached the glass doors and turned back. "Why?"

The Duck expelled another cloud of thick grey smoke. "Well, he's from the eighteenth century."

"So?"

The Duck sniffed. "Code of honour and all that, innit."

"Code of honour?" I laughed. "Don't give me that. I know his sort—bloody gigolo—he'll probably hide behind Emma when I lay into him." I made for the French windows again.

"Don't say I didn't warn you!" called the Duck.

I swung open the doors and stepped out onto the terrace. Both parties looked suitably compromised and released each other from their embrace. Emma primped her hair. The Frenchman coughed into one hand and looked skyward.

"What exactly do you think you're playing at, Em?" I said.

"We were just—nothing—" she began, momentarily caught off-guard, but then she recovered and her face hardened. "What business is it of yours, anyway? I can do what I like. Travis and I have become—we've become very close and—"

"Very close? You've only known him five minutes—wait a minute!" I took her by the shoulders. "How long have you been here?"

"How long have I been here?" said Emma, looking puzzled. "You know how long I've been here—I just spoke to you a minute ago."

"No. I meant actually staying here, at Duckworth Hall?"

"Three weeks, of course."

"Three week—? Don't move," I said. "I'll be right back."

I stomped back into the drawing room, where the Duck was still lounging on the card table, enjoying his spliff.

"You, have done something!" I said, jabbing my finger in his face.

"Moi?"

I grabbed him by the lapels of his frock coat and shook him. "She has been here three bloody weeks! When we got back from your last little prank she'd only just arrived—what happened to my three missing weeks? I lost them somewhere between here and the bedroom."

He pulled my hand away and jumped down. "Get off me—what're you on about? You're rambling."

"Yeah, I'm not rambling, mate—but you will be in a minute—rambling straight through that window—if I don't get some answers!"

"All right—all right," said the Duck, straightening his coat and then holding up his hands. "I'll tell you the truth."

"And I want the whole truth. Every detail. Not the Duckworth version—with all the dodgy bits left out. I might be able to repair some of the damage you've done."

"All I did was give her a little time to think. I could see she was upset and I just wanted the two of you to step back and have a cooling off period—"

"Cooling off? She's iced over!"

"I was only trying to help."

"Yeah, you helped all right—helped her into the arms of that smarmy French Casanova! I want to know exactly what you did and said—and why—the real reason this time—you scheming little rat!"

"Well, that's the last time I try to play matchmaker. In future, you can sort out your own love life."

"What love life? You have single-handedly destroyed my love life. She's in love with Travis De Generate out there—he's had three weeks to work on her—three weeks to break down her defences and worm his way into her pant—affections. If I've lost her, I'll—"

"You haven't lost her," said the Duck. "Don't be wet—she's expecting your kid. She'll come to her senses. What you see out there is just a—just a wild, passionate fling—the mere overture to a mad sex romp—when the fires of his ardour have been quenched, he'll soon lose interest and move on to the next one. Mark my words. And you'll be there to pick up the pieces."

"Have you finished? I don't want to pick up the pieces—she's pregnant for Pete's sake—what kind of a man preys on a pregnant woman?"

"Some men find it a turn on," said the Duck, suppressing a smutty grin.

"Well, you'd better turn him off, because I know you started all this, you're trying to pull one of your devious little strokes—and you're not going to get away with it!"

I barged him aside and rushed out to rescue Emma from the clutches of her French seducer.

"All right—break it up," I said. "This has gone far enough." I dragged Emma out of De Quipp's arms and pushed him away. "Emma," I said, looking her square in the eyes, "this gigolo is only after one thing, he's getting some perverted kick out of all this, and I am not going to stand by and watch you make a complete fool of yourself."

Emma brought her knee up sharply into my groin and I doubled up and turned away on my toes.

"Bloody Nor-"

"Don't you dare speak to me like that!" she cried. "I don't want anything to do with you ever again—come, Travis."

I shuffled round and saw the disgustingly handsome Frenchman gallantly offering Emma his arm. It was all too much to bear.

"You are the pits!" I shouted. "The lowest of the low. You pervert!"

"What doze hee say?" said my rival.

"Don't listen to him, Travis," said Emma.

"I said you're the pits—you piece of dog turd!"

"What ees thees bitz of docteur?" said De Quipp, with a Gallic shrug.

"Just ignore him, my love," said Emma. "He's only jealous."

To hear her call him "my love" knocked the breath out of me.

"Vous merde de chien!" I gasped, in my best Franglais.

De Quipp merely laughed when he realized what I had been calling him. They both turned their backs on me and walked towards the steps, which led down into the formal garden.

"He doesn't love you, Emma," I called. "He's lying through his teeth, just to get in your bed! He's a dirty rotten liar!"

The Frenchman suddenly froze to the spot and then slowly turned to face me, with an expression of injured disbelief on his face. He retraced his steps the half dozen paces and looked me up and down.

"What deed you call mee, seur?" he said.

"Dog turd?"

"Non, not thee docteur—thee otheur," he said, holding his chin and looking at me sideways.

"The pits?"

"Non-non." He clicked his fingers. "Thees otheur thang."

"Liar?"

"Ah! Mon Dieu! I thought that was what I heurd." He reached inside his little tailed jacket. I thought he was feeling his mortified heart—but he pulled out a card and snapped it against my chest, letting it fall to my feet. "My card, seur! My second wheel call to make the necesseuree aurrangemaunt. I shall have my sateesfaxsheon. Do not disappoint mee, seur."

And with that, he gave me a curt bow, turned smartly on his heels and marched back to rejoin Emma. I picked up the card. There was just his name printed on it.

"Yeah, and up yours!" I said. "I'll be having my satisfaction and all, mate!"

The Duck stuck his head out of the door to see what all the shouting was about.

"What's up, man?"

"That guy's right up his own arse," I said. "One dark night he's going to hear something go bump—right on the back of his head."

"What you got there?"

"His card." I tore it up and threw the pieces down on the ground. "I am going to so enjoy punching his lights out."

"What did he give you his card for?" said the Duck, pulling a face.

"I don't know. The ponce. But I do know he's going to come to a sticky end the way he's carrying on," I said.

"What did you say to him?"

"Oh, I let him know I was onto him all right. And he says: I shall have my sateesfaxsheon, seur—who does he think he is—Mick bloody Jagger!"

"Oh—no!" cried the Duck.

"What?"

"He's only gone and challenged you to a duel."

I laughed—a bit nervously. "You what?"

"With shooters—pistols at dawn, mate," said the Duck.

"Yeah, well, bring it on—that's what I say, I'm not afraid of him."

"Well, you should be, mate. They say he's one of the finest shots in all France," said the Duck.

"Now he tells me!"

"Don't worry," grinned the Duck, "I'll give you some coaching."

"Oh great!" I said. "First I get dumped, now I'm going to get shot. You've done it to me again!"

"Believe me, man," said the Duck, hand on heart. "I had nothing to do with any of this. Honest."

Reader, I hit him.

Chapter 2

"What month is it?" I said, as my father's old butler vigorously brushed down the mourning suit I had been loaned. It was a snazzy little black velvet number.

"March. St Paddy's Day, as it happens. Why?" said the Duck.

"I always wondered what month I'd die in. I mean, it's strange to think, innit? Every year we pass over the exact day, the exact hour—moment of our death, and we don't even know it. It's just waiting there for us. Waiting for the right year. I wonder if it gives us a sign. You know, a shiver up the spine or a sudden flash of light. I wonder if there'll be something to mark my death day…"

"Yeah, a tombstone—the way you're going on. Shape up—you're a Duckworth!"

"I don't wanna die. I'm not ready."

"You're not gonna die. Stand up straight. Be a man."

"I could be a corpse by tomorrow morning. This could be the suit they lay me out in."

"Steady, Bentley," said the Duck, "that frock coat set me back three guineas."

The butler dug a little less deeply into the nap.

"I don't see why I have to wear it anyway," I said, but rather admiring myself in it, in the full-length mirror.

"As I've already told you," sighed my father, who was sitting on a Hepplewhite chair, looking me up and down with a critical eye. "It's in the Duelling Code of Honour: the challenger and challenged shall wear similar apparel and be equipped with matching pistols, so that neither shall gain unfair advantage. And don't get any holes in it."

I shot him a sour look. "This is bloody stupid," I said. "I don't know how to shoot a pistol. I've got no chance."

"Leave us, please, would you, Bentley," said the Duck, looking rather ruffled.

Bentley gave my back one last stroke with the hog bristles and bowed out.

The Duck stood up, tugged his waistcoat tightly down over the top of his breeches, from where it had ridden up, and started strutting. I watched him in the cheval mirror. I hated it when he strutted, with his hands stuck behind his back, flicking his tails up as he talked, like a duck preening its feathers.

"Stephen, I make no secret of the fact that you are not the son I had hoped for—" he began, in a grave tone.

"And you're not the father I'd hoped for," I said, fiddling with my silk cravat. "I thought you'd be taller."

"You will hear me out, sir!" he quacked. "I will brook no defeatist talk in front of the servants."

"Oh, shut up, Shorty."

"Sir, I will not stand for your damn impertinence!" he insisted.

"Siddown then," I said.

"Remember," he said, puffing out his chest, sticking out his chin and gazing off into his own little dream world, "you are a Duckworth, sir. Need I remind you, the family honour rests on your shoulders in this matter?" And then his voice became almost Churchillian: "And never, nay, never, forget the Duckworth family motto: ego amo adversa."

"Yeah, well, let's hope I don't run out of ammo. How many bullets do I get?"

"Ammo? Bullets? I'm talking about honour, sir. We Duckworths thrive on adversity," said the Duck.

"You might, mate. I just want to thrive on," I said.

"It's in our blood," said the Duck, drifting off into that dream realm of honour and noblesse oblige again.

"Just as long as I don't get any lead in mine, I'll be happy," I said.

"Do your duty, sir—that is all I ask," said the Duck.

"I'll do a runner if you don't put a sock in it," I said. "And how come I'm always the one who has to defend the family honour? Why don't you get stuck in for a change?"

"She's your bird!" he cried. "You're the one he challenged!"

"You could have warned me he was the Clint-bloody-Eastwood of Versailles!"

"I tried! You wouldn't listen!"

"Yeah. Right. You're loving every minute of this. If I should die in a corner of some farmer's field, think only this of me: it's all your bloody fault!" I said.

"How the hell is it my fault?"

"It's always your fault."

"Not this time, mate—you got yourself into this one—don't go blaming me."

"Who brought us here then? Who drugged me and stole three weeks of my life?"

"I never told you to insult a bloody French aristocrat, did I?"

"Who invited him here?"

"He invited himself! I told you—he needs my help."

"He must be desperate if he needs your help! What are you up to this time—treason?"

Suddenly there was a rap on the door.

We both stopped arguing and looked at the door and then back at each other. There was another sharp knock. I nodded towards the door and the Duck marched across to answer it.

It was De Quipp's second, a fat French army lower rank, sporting a huge walrus moustache, who had mysteriously appeared at Duckworth Hall that very afternoon, in full Napoleonic uniform, completely out of the blue. He reminded me of someone, but I could not for the life of me think who it was.

I heard the gruff-voiced Frenchman whispering and then the Duck whispering something back. And then the Duck exclaimed:

"Vous plaisantez! You have got to be kidding! Il est un aristocrate!"

More urgent whispers ensued and then their business seemed to be concluded with a curt bow apiece. The French soldier shot me a cursory glance, clicked his heels, and disappeared. The Duck slammed the door.

"Bloody cheek!"

"What?" I said.

"He was only going to call it off!"

"Was?" I said. "You mean you called it on again?"

"What choice did I have?"

"You re-challenged me?"

"I had to! Do you know why he wanted to call it off?"

"Never mind that. Let me get this straight. This guy was going to blow my brains out and then he changed his mind, and then you changed it back again? Is that what you're telling me?"

"You don't understand—"

"I don't understand? Pretty soon I won't be able to breathe, walk, talk, pump blood around my body, or change my socks. What did I miss?"

"Listen. He said De Quipp said he couldn't take to the field of honour with you, because after talking to Emma he realized you were not his social equal."

"Yeah. So?"

"That's an insult. He's thinks you're not good enough to shoot."

"Yeah. So?"

"He's calling you his social inferior."

"Yeah. And?"

"And you're not."

"Yes I am."

"No you're not. You're my son."

"Don't remind me. Look. I don't mind being called his social inferior—I like being his social inferior! Now, go and call Captain Walrus back and tell him I accept De Quipp's withdrawal."

"That will not be necessary," blinked the Duck.

I could see he was about to make some startling new revelation. He tugged the lapels of his frock coat straight.

"Oh, I see," I said. "You've volunteered to fight him."

The Duck closed his eyes and shook his head, patiently.

"Just tell me what you've done," I said.

"You, my son, are his social superior," he announced.

"I work in advertising. I make up jingles for breakfast cereals and haiku about cars. I was brought up in a semi in suburbia. How am I superior to a senior officer in Napoleon's Imperial Army?"

"Because I bought you a baronetcy for your eighteenth birthday—that's how! You even outrank me, mate!"

I was dumbfounded. Now, I would be lying if I said a certain warm wave of good old-fashioned snobbery didn't wash over me in that first instant of my investiture. I believe my spine actually straightened a few notches.

"I'm a baron?" I said.

"Net," corrected my father. "A baronet: lower than a baron, higher than a knight."

"You bought me a title? But—why?"

"Is that all you've got to say, Sir? And that's sir with a capital 'S,' by the way," blinked the Duck, with what I thought I detected as a hint of deference.

My hands automatically clasped together, in a rather Prince Charlesesque manner, as I struggled to find the appropriate words and tried to look humble. "Well, of course, one is always terribly, terribly humbled on these occasions. One doesn't know what to say. One means, one is overwhelmed by one's generosity—but it's not going to do one much good if one is six feet under by tomorrow morning, is it!"

The Duck spread his hands out like a film director, interpreting a scene for his cameraman. "Imagine the gravestone: 'Sir Stephen Gilmour Sloane of Duckworth, Bart.'"

"It might as well say 'fart'—I'll be dead, you moron!"

"You are not going to lose this duel. Trust me."

"Me—trust you?" I laughed. "Satan will be doing the school run in a troika first."

"Listen to me. No way would I let that Parisian peacock take you down."

"Yeah, right. Anyway, I thought I was supposed to be immortal," I said.

"Only if you don't die," said the Duck.

"Duh."

"No, what I mean is: you're not Superman—the bullets won't bounce off your chest—but the gene string I implanted in your foetus will prevent you from ageing beyond normal adulthood. You'll be ever young. Just like me."

"A beautiful corpse, you mean." I gripped my father's arm, suddenly seized by mortal fear. "Don't let me die, Dad."

"You're not going to die. I'll sort it."

"Oh God, I just had a premonition of the cold earth closing over me." I shivered. "The darkness...oh, the darkness...the never-ending nothingness—I can't face it—I'm not ready. I've got a kid on the way I'll never even see. I can't go through with this! Everything's black, black, black—"

The Duck prised my fingers off his arm. "You're sounding like a Morrissey lyric! Snap out of it. Let's roll one and chill."

"Don't say that word!"

"What—Morrissey?"

"No—chill." I grabbed his arm again. "I just felt Death's icy hand feeling my collar!"

He shrugged me off. "Get off! It was just a draught from the door."

"What was that?"

"What?"

"Every noise appals me. I thought I heard something." I raised my eyes to the ceiling. "Up there."

"It's just the wind in the chimney."

"It came from... the attic."

"Er, there's nothing up there, mate."

"How do you know? Something could be lurking in the shadows, something evil..."

"Because I turned it into a bowling alley. Now, pull yourself together."

"A bowling alley?"

"Yeah, it's all sound-proofed. I've got the lot up there—jukebox, beer cooler, automatic set-up and return—"

"You built a bowling alley in your attic?"

"Fancy a couple of Buds and a few strikes?"

"You expect me to go bowling, when all I can think about is death?"

"Have a little faith," sighed the Duck. "De Quipp has agreed to use my boxed set of genuine Robert Wogdon duelling pistols—Robbo let me have 'em cheap—they're a really lovely brace, muzzle-loaders, walnut grips, brown octagonal barrelling—"

"I do not want to hear this!"

"Listen, I'm going to nobble his gun, so it blows up in his face."

"Okay. Let's go bowling," I said.

"Hey?"

"Bowling, a few beers, you said."

"Is that all you've got to say?"

"Don't get the guns mixed up," I said.

"Don't you even want to know how I'm going to do it?"

"No. Less I know, the better. Then I can act surprised. Come on, let's go."

"You've perked up."

"I prefer bowling to death."

"Oh, um, I forgot the pin set-up gear's playing up. Gotta get it fixed. I use a blacksmith in the village—he thinks it's a top secret cannonball loading machine I invented."

"So, we can't go bowling? You promised me bowling. Have a little faith, you said. How can I trust you to fix De Quipp's gun, if you're the kind of father who promises his son bowling and then reneges?"

"Look, I'll get it fixed. I'm still staunch, mate. We can go bowling another time."

"That's what all fathers say," I said. "Don't promise your kid things you can't deliver."

"Yeah, all right. Point taken," said the Duck. "We could do something else."

"Like what?"

"Um, shooting—er, no, not that. Um. Happy Families? No, maybe not. I know, let's do some drawing—"

Suddenly, there was another knock at the door.

My skin goosebumped. The Duck and I looked at each other and both shrugged. There was another knock. Only this time, it was louder.

"Are you expecting anyone?" whispered the Duck.

"Yeah, a hooded guy in a long black cloak, carrying a scythe," I said. "Tell him I already gave."

I scrambled under my bed, while the Duck went to answer the door. I held my breath. I think I actually managed to stop my heart from beating. And then I thought I might give myself brain damage, so I allowed myself a few shallow breaths. I heard Emma's voice and then the Duck's inviting her in. I squeezed myself right under the bed, meaning to come out the other side and pretend I was tying up my shoelace or something. But I got stuck midway.

"Steve? Steve?" I heard Emma calling, close by.

I craned my neck round and saw the bottom of her pretty blue and white floral print dress, and the Duck's yellow-stockinged legs and black patent leather house shoes.

"He's not here," said Emma.

"Well, he was," said the Duck. "Stephen? Come out, come out, wherever you are."

I knew the Duck knew where I was, and that he knew I knew he knew. But there was nothing I could do.

"Where is he?" said Emma.

"He's a bit spooked," said the Duck.

I could have throttled him. I saw her dress sweep away.

"Steve? Steve? Where are you?"

I felt hands grip my ankles and yank me free. The Duck hauled me out and gave me a hand up.

"Duckworths do not hide under beds," he said.

"Why did you have to tell her I was spooked?" I said.

"Steve—there you are!" cried Emma, turning round to see me holding hands with the Duck. "My, you two really are close. Where were you hiding?"

I snatched my hands away from the Duck's. "Hiding? I wasn't hiding—I thought I heard something under the bed."

"Was it a bogeyman?" smirked the Duck.

"No, I think it was a Death Watch Beetle."

"He'll be watching your death if you don't grow a spine," said the Duck, from the corner of his mouth.

"Oh," said Emma, and looked down at her hands.

"Er, would you mind leaving us, Duck," I said.

The Duck remained, grinning at Emma.

"I'd like a word with Emma, Father—alone," I said, giving him a kick in the ankle.

He kicked me back.

"Will you get lost!" I hissed, in his ear.

"You want me to leave you alone with her?" he whispered. "She might be armed."

"Don't be ridiculous—get out!"

"It's rude to whisper, gentlemen," said Emma.

"Yeah, I know, sorry, Em—my father was just leaving." I gave the Duck a shove towards the door.

At last he took the hint, but as he left us he couldn't resist a parting shot at Emma.

"I hope you have not come to mock my son, Miss Gummer," he said.

"Of course not!" exclaimed Emma. "You know I haven't!"

"What *is* your problem?" I said.

"Or question his honour—a Duckworth never backs down," he added. "We Duckworths never waver from the path of honour—our ancestors had more garters than Cheltenham Ladies' College—and they hung onto 'em, too, which is more than can be said for some of those so-called ladies at Cheltenham Ladies'—"

"—Just go," I said. "I'm really sorry about this, Em."

"I'll call back before I turn in, Stephen," said the Duck. "To make sure you're settled."

"Don't bother," I said. "I mean, don't trouble yourself, Father."

The door closed behind him.

"Is that kid really your father?" said Emma.

The door opened and the Duck's head popped back in, before I could answer.

"It's no bother, Son," he said. "I'll just drop by and tuck you in."

"Don't be so bloody stu-pendously considerate, Father," I smiled.

"Are you sure? It's no trouble, Son."

"Oh, but it will be, Father. Believe me, it's going to be a lot of trouble to you."

"Very well, dear." The door closed once more, with the Duck on the other side.

"It must be very strange, having a teenager for a father," said Emma.

"It's a nightmare," I said. "I keep hoping I'm going to wake up and find I imagined him, but every time I do, he's always there." I touched her hair. "You're real though, aren't you, Em?"

"I'm afraid so…" she smiled.

"Don't apologize, Em," I moved my hand round to brush her cheek. "I'm glad you're here…"

"Stephen, I—"

The door opened and the Duck interrupted:

"I'll bring you some extra candles—I know how scared you are of the dark," he said, grinning from ear to ear.

I could have murdered him.

"Thank you, Father," I said. "I know just where you can stick them."

"Don't mention it, Stephen—it's my pleasure."

"Yes, I can see it is," I said.

"See you later, Daddy's little soldier." He closed the door.

"He's just trying to wind me up," I said.

"Why does he do it? It's so childish."

"Exactly. He has to have his little joke," I said.

"Doesn't he realize how nervous you must be feeling about tomorrow?"

I was glad she'd brought that little matter up. I was up for a bit of self-dramatization and false modesty.

"Oh that," I said. "Drink?"

I sauntered over to the writing bureau where I had seen the Duck take out the decanter of fine Madeira and the two glasses. My back was to her, but I could feel her sorrowful eyes following me.

"No thanks. You don't sound too concerned, Steve. This is serious."

I lifted the lid of the bureau. "I know it's serious, Em, but what can I do? I just have to accept my fate." I opened the little letter drawer and slid my hand inside.

"You could apologize to Monsieur De Quipp—I'm sure he would accept your apology," said Emma.

I felt for the hidden catch, to open the secret compartment. "I hope you haven't been pleading for my life, Em," I smiled.

"Travis doesn't want to fight you," she said.

"Doesn't want to kill me, you mean," I laughed. I was still fumbling for the release mechanism.

"Don't say that."

I caught my finger on something sharp and spun away in pain.

"Shit!" I sucked my bleeding nail.

"What have you done?" she cried.

"It's nothing," I held up my hand. "Just ripped the nail off my trigger finger, that's all."

"Let me see." She came and took my hand and inspected it. "That looks nasty."

I pulled my hand away and let it fall to my side. "It's nothing," I said. "Wouldn't have made any difference anyway—I can't shoot a gun, Em. I don't know one end of a gun from the other. They say De Quipp's a crack shot. I don't stand a cat in hell's chance."

"You can't fight with a broken nail," she said. "Call it off, Steve. Please call it off."

My gaze fell upon her beautiful sea green eyes—those selfsame eyes I had fallen in love with—and I was overwhelmed with emotions. I didn't know whether to kiss her, scream at her, push her away, or plead with her. I smiled and reached up to stroke her cheek.

"Em, that's not the way these things work," I said. "Some things cannot be undone. And we must bear the consequences of things we did in haste. Like when David Beckham got sent off in that Argentinian game. I'm going to miss football."

"This is all my fault!" she cried, biting her lip.

I grabbed her hard by the shoulders and winced as the pain shot through my nail. "No it's not! Don't ever say that! This is all my own fault. I asked for this."

"No, Steve. If I hadn't—"

I quickly put my finger to her lips. Emma kissed it. "This isn't about you, Em. I don't own you. I had no right to treat you like a possession. You chose De Quipp. And I should have accepted your decision gracefully."

"Oh, Steve, I'm so sorry," she sighed.

I thought about kissing her, but turned away instead and held my forehead. "My only defence is—but it's too late for all that now. I won't burden you with my—with my—feelings."

Her arms threaded around my waist and I felt her cheek rest softly between my shoulder blades. "Tell me, Steve. You can tell me now," she breathed.

Her warmth against my back felt like love returning. I folded my arms and smoothed her hands with mine. "Em, although I know I have no right to ask, will you promise me one thing?"

"What?"

"Will you tell my child about me?"

I felt her gasp.

"Em? Will you tell our child—I'm sorry his father couldn't be around for her, or him? I've always wanted a baby. I wonder what it'll be. Don't suppose I'll ever know now."

She suddenly wrenched her arms away. "Stop it! Stop it!" she cried, and threw herself face down on my bed, her whole body shuddering with sobs.

"I've upset you," I said, coming to kneel down by the bed to stroke her hair.

She turned towards me and pulled a stray swatch of hair from her mouth. Her eyes were flooded and looked a little pink.

Suddenly, I felt stung. I hadn't meant to go so far. I hadn't meant to hurt her. I suppose I was just having some revenge. But this was too much. I felt such a rat. But I never let that stop me.

"Don't cry for me, I'm not worth it," I said. "I never could bear to see you cry. I—I've had a good life—I've lived and loved—but then again—too few to mention—but now the chips are down I'm going to see it through and do it my—do it with a bit of style. What I'm trying to say is, I want to go out with a bang, Em."

"Oh!" she sobbed, fresh tears overflowing from her beautiful eyes.

"Er, no, I didn't mean that—um—what I meant was: I'll probably just get wounded, knowing me," I said, trying to wipe a teardrop from the end of her nose, but another one formed and took its place. I wiped that one away, but another one formed and took its place.

"I told Travis you weren't worth it," she sniffed. "I told him you were from a lower class."

"Yeah. I know. Thanks for that," I said.

"I said you were beneath him."

"Yeah, all right, Em," I said. "You tried."

"He comes from such a high class family, you see," she said, with a big sniff.

"Well, I am a baronet," I said.

"Please apologize to Travis, Steve. And then he can call the whole thing off."

"He could withdraw if he wanted to," I said.

"No, he can't," said Emma, shaking her head. "That's just it. It's a matter of honour for him, don't you see?"

I stared at her. Dumbfounded. I wasn't pretending anymore. I felt insulted that she thought she could ask me to back down, but not her precious Frenchman.

"What about my honour?" I said.

She dabbed at her eyes with the corner of the pillowcase. "Your honour?" she said, the corners of her mouth betraying a faint smile.

I stood up and studied her for a few moments.

She sat up and made attempts to straighten her clothes and hair.

"I thought you really cared about me," I said.

She wiped her eyes. "I do," she sniffed.

"No you don't—you just can't bear the thought of my blood on his hands, because you love him, not me..."

She didn't deny it.

"You came here for him—not me! Didn't you?" I cried. "I think you'd better go now, Emma."

"I can't leave you like this," she said.

"Just walk away, Em," I said. "Just go. Please."

She slid her legs off the bed and stood up. And tried to embrace me. I dodged away from her.

"You shouldn't have come," I said.

"It wasn't my idea!"

"No, your snobby boyfriend sent you."

"It was your father's idea, if you must know!" she said. "I wish I hadn't listened to him now."

"Are you trying to tell me the Duck wanted me to back down? I don't believe you," I said.

"Well, why don't you ask him yourself?" she said, bustling to the door.

"He wouldn't have said that—you're lying!" I said.

"Oh, believe what you like!"

And with those words, she flew out the door and slammed it behind her.

I tried to understand why the Duck would want me to pull out of the duel. It didn't make any sense—he'd spent all his time talking me into it. What was he up to? Reverse psychology? I shuddered to think. What I needed was a stiff drink. That reminded me of my fingernail. That made me remember the Madeira. That reminded me of my fingernail. That made me dismiss the Madeira. That made me remember the Duck's offer of a cold beer. That made me think of the bowling alley.

I went out into the long candlelit hall and looked up and down. How did I get up there? I walked all the way to the west wing—about half a block away—before I found a flight of stone stairs, spiralling up into the darkness. A red rope attached to brass cleats fixed to the wall—like the ones in stately homes, across the places where they don't want the general public to go, cordoned them off. There was a little sign hanging off it, which read: NO ADMITTANCE. I removed a lit candle from the wall holder, stepped over the token barrier, and started to ascend.

As I reached the first corner, a sudden draught made my flame wave about precariously. I stalled, shielded it with my hand and carried on up. I rounded a second corner, and saw a faint light above me. I reached a small landing, where there was a round window, letting a little starlight in. I was standing before a big oak door, with a sign painted on it, saying: PRIVATE—KEEP OUT. It was locked. I gave it a couple of firm nudges with my shoulder, but it wouldn't budge, so I went all the way back down to my room, lay on the bed, and rang the service bell.

Presently, there was a light knock on the door.

"Come!" I called.

Bentley the butler, looking rather theatrical in his scarlet and gold livery and white, powdered wig, entered, took a few paces into the room, and halted. He started to open his mouth.

"Yes, I rang!" I said, before he could get the words out.

There wasn't a flicker from him.

"May I be of some assistance, sir?" he asked, not looking anywhere in particular.

"Do you have a key to the attic?"

"The attic door, sir?"

"Yes."

"No, sir. The attic is off limits to all staff, sir," he replied.

"But you do have a master key?"

"A master key, sir? Yes."

"May I see it?"

"Certainly, sir." He pulled on a long chain, attached to his belt, and fished a bunch of keys out of his trouser pocket, counted through them and held one up. "This is a master key, sir."

"Let me see that."

He came closer and brandished the key.

"Take it off the chain," I said.

"Off the chain, sir? Certainly, sir." He fiddled with the ring and finally got it off. He held it up.

"Give it to me," I said.

He advanced and handed it to me. I got off the bed.

"Will this open the attic door?"

"I have never tried, sir."

"Now, Bentley," I said. "I want you to take off your shoes, climb in this bed, and pretend to be me."

"Pretend to be you, sir? Certainly, sir," he said. And without a moment's hesitation, he slipped his shoes off and started to get on the bed.

"No. Under the covers, Bentley." I said.

"Under the covers, sir? Certainly, sir."

I tucked him in and headed for the door. "Goodnight, Bentley," I said, blowing out the candles on my way out.

"Goodnight, sir."

* * *

I made my way back up to the attic door, inserted the master key in the lock, and turned it. It opened.

All this for a cold beer, I was thinking, as I threw a row of light switches I felt on the wall, just inside the door. Fluorescent lights bonged and flickered on throughout the length and breadth of the enormous attic. I blinked as my eyes adjusted to the unaccustomed brightness. I was expecting to find a full-size bowling alley, but what I found turned my legs to jelly and made my jaw drop open.

I was staring at a huge glass tank of greenish-yellow water, an enormous aquarium with a strange light dappling through it from the surface.

I tried to say something back to Jemmons, who was immersed in the tank and chained to a sort of cage thing, resting on the bottom. There were two clear tubes fitted to a mask on his face and columns of bubbles were streaming from his nose, but he could see me and was trying to communicate. Unfortunately, my eyes were quickly distracted by another pair of eyes, also staring out at me from under the luminous green water. Every hair on my body was crawling. It was a giant squid. Two of its tentacles suddenly moved and their suckers attached to the glass, like horrible toothless mouths. I cringed. I moved just my eyes back to the terrified Jemmons and now noticed several round weals all over the exposed parts of his body. I shook my head slightly. Jemmons's eyes widened in horror as I began stepping backwards, away from the tank. I swivelled my eyeballs slowly back to the squid as I retreated and attempted a smile, but it must have looked more like a grimace, because I could hardly control my jaw. The creature's mouth flared open malevolently and it showed me its fearsome beak. That was too much for me. I screamed and turned tail and ran, straight into the arms of my father, who was just coming to the top of the steps.

"Squid thing!" I blurted. "It's got Jemmons!"

"Calm down, I can explain everything," said the Duck, calmly switching off all the lights and relocking the door.

"He's in there!" I cried. "You can't leave him in there with that thing!"

"That wasn't Roger," laughed the Duck, patting me on the back and guiding me back down the steps. "What do you take me for? That was a replicant—one of Roger's alternative time-flux clones—a fully developed one I keep for emergencies."

"This is an emergency—Roger's being eaten alive!"

"I told you—that wasn't the real Jemmons," said the Duck.

"Well, he looked real enough to me!" I said. "He was crying!"

"Don't be daft—how can you tell if someone's crying if they're underwater?"

"He was crying I tell you! His face was like this." I pulled a wailing baby face. "And his body was covered in wounds where that thing had been at him. It was horrible! A bowling alley you told me—that thing could stand all the pins up in one go! What the hell is it?"

"Don't upset yourself. Let's just get you back to bed, you've got a busy day tomorrow," said the Duck.

"Busy day? I could be dead by breakfast time!" I pulled up as we reached the first corner and turned back. "I'm going back up there to get Roger."

The Duck gripped my arm. "No you're not. How many times do I have to tell you? That was not Roger. Roger is being held prisoner in the Castle."

"Well, I want to talk to that one up there. Just to put my mind at rest."

"He's a replicant—replicants can't hold proper conversations, they just copy what you do and mimic what you say," said the Duck. "That's probably what it was doing—it saw you were upset, so it copied you."

"Upset? I was bloody petrified!"

"Well, there you go then."

I swallowed hard and stared up at the door. Believe me, I didn't need much persuading not to go back up into that attic, Roger or no Roger.

"All right. What's that squid doing up there anyway?" I said.

We carried on down the steps.

"It's a pet," smiled the Duck.

"A pet? You expect me to believe that thing is a pet? It's a monster!"

"Its Latin name is Architeuthis clarkei, and you're quite right, Stephen, it is a big squid," said the Duck. "But that's only a baby one. They—"

"—A baby one!" I exclaimed.

"An adult Architeuthis clarkei can grow up to two hundred feet long," said the Duck.

"Well, what the hell have you put it up there for? It should be swimming around in a bigger tank—like the North Atlantic!"

"Brunswick was born in captivity—he'd be lost out there in the ocean."

"Lost? He'd only have to stick out one of his tentacles and he could feel Canada!"

We stepped over the red rope.

"You've had a shock," the Duck said. "But it is only an aquarium. Lots of people keep exotic pets—boa constrictors, tarantulas, vampire bats—"

"—Yeah, but even Dr Frankenstein wouldn't give that thing house room!"

"Brunswick is not a monster!" he insisted. "You are just being squidist, Stephen, and I won't have it! Architeuthis clarkei is a very intelligent lifeform—I mean, animal."

"All right, but why did you lie to me about the bowling alley then?" I said. "Ah, you can't answer that one, can you?"

"The bowling alley is on the other side of the aquarium," blinked the Duck. "I thought the tank made a nice backdrop to the lanes."

"Backdrop? I wouldn't fancy turning my back on that thing—how far can those tentacles reach?"

"Brunswick is not a thing," said the Duck. "His feeding tentacles are about thirty feet long."

"Feeding tentacles? How many has he got?"

"Five pairs."

"Yeah, and a beak the size of a skip."

"Did you know that of all the living creatures on the planet the one with the biggest eyes is a fully grown Architeuthis clarkei?" said the Duck.

"All the better to see you with in the darkei," I said.

We came to my bedroom door.

"By the way," said the Duck, "I'll have that master key back."

I handed it over, with a shaking hand.

"See you in the morning," said the Duck. "Bright and early. You can get some shooting practice on the terrace."

"Better late than never," I said. "I hope you know what you're doing, because I don't."

"No worries." He tapped his big nose. "Leave everything to me. We'll show that flash French fop what the Duckworths are made of."

"Just the exterior parts I hope."

"I'll bid thee goodnight," said the Duck.

"And the same to you," I said. "Oh, I almost forgot—we'll have to call the duel off—I've damaged my trigger finger." I showed him my broken nail.

"Hm, nasty. I'll get you something for that in the morning. Sleep tight."

"You expect me to sleep?"

He looked back. "I left you a little nightcap on your nightstand."

"Does it come with a matching bullet-proof vest?"

"Not that sort of nightcap. Don't worry—everything's in hand. Just leave it all to me."

I watched him waddle off down the hall. He stopped and waved to me, and then turned right down the master staircase. I let myself in and lay on my bed, fully clothed. My heart was pounding so hard I could hear it in the dark. I drank my nightcap and closed my eyes.

"Goodnight, sir," said a voice.

"Goodnight, Bentley."

* * *

And I slept the sleep of the damned, knowing that just the other side of the scallop-patterned rococo ceiling there was another giant member of the mollusc family. I kept expecting a tentacle to crash through the plaster mouldings and grab me up into that tank. I promised never to eat shellfish again, if I survived the night. But then I remembered that if I did survive the night I might die in my duel with De Quipp. What, I got to thinking, if his pistol did backfire, as the Duck assured me it would, and then I fired and missed, and De Quipp, meanwhile, recovered and reloaded and got a shot in? He would only need one. I decided on a back-up plan. If the chain of events I just described did happen, I was going to run like hell.

Chapter 3

Something was tickling my nose. I tried to brush it away, but it came back. I swiped at it again. And then I remembered that tentacle.

"Aaaagh!" I screamed, jumping off the bed. I ended up on the floor, face to face with the Duck. He was clutching a large wooden box to his chest.

"Get off me," he said, clambering to his feet. He brushed himself down and opened the box to check the contents. "You could have damaged 'em, you idiot."

"Don't creep around," I warned him, jabbing my finger in his face.

He produced a long barrelled gun from the case.

I leapt away from him. "What the hell's that?"

"A genuine Wogdon duelling pistol. Here, stick this plaster over your nail and you can get a feel."

I wrapped the modern plaster round my finger, without taking my eyes off the beautiful long-barrelled pistol.

"There, what do you think?" he said, passing it to me, handle first. "Try that for weight."

I grabbed it and got the feel of it, pretended to shoot things around the room.

"Don't wave it about," said the Duck.

"Is it loaded?"

"Oh, yeah," said the Duck sarcastically.

I pulled the trigger and the big hammer thing sprang down on the other bit with a dull clunk.

"Watch it!" exclaimed the Duck, ducking out of the way. "Here, give me that!"

He tried to snatch it out of my hand. I hung on to it and we wrestled.

"Naff off!" I said.

"Give me that bloody gun!" he quacked.

We struggled some more and then I let him have it.

The Duck cleaned it off on the gold embroidered sleeve of his black silk frock coat and carefully replaced it in its box.

"That's an antique," he grumbled. "Worth a lot of money."

"Put a bullet in it for me then—you said I needed a bit of practice," I said, quite fancying a go.

"It's a muzzle-loader," he said. "You don't use bullets, you use a ball. You ignoramus."

"I just want to make sure it works," I said. "I don't trust you."

"It'll work. He's the one with the problem," nodded the Duck.

"So, what do I do when his blows up in his face then?" I said, sitting on the edge of the bed to pull my boots on.

"Let him have it," said the Duck, making his hand into a gun and miming what I should do. "Make my day."

"Seems a bit unfair," I said.

"Unfair? It's him or you, mate!" cried the Duck. "Blow that sucker away!"

"Yeah, I know, but, all the same, it's a bit one-sided," I said. "I mean, I might, you know, hurt him badly without really meaning to."

"You mean kill him," said the Duck.

"Well. We're not playing tiddlywinks."

"Don't worry—you won't hit him—you'll be fifty feet away. You couldn't hit the side of a bus with one of these things from that range," said the Duck.

"I might."

"No way," said the Duck. "No. All you do when he goes down is raise your pistol in the air, like this, say: no contest, Monsieur, and empty the barrel in the sky."

"So why are we bothering to practise?" I asked.

"That's what we'll be practising," said the Duck. "I want to make sure you don't hit anybody. Me, for example. Come on—the sun's nearly up."

I smiled. "I like the sound of this. I'm going to come across as a right hero when I discharge my pistol in the air." I put on a French accent. "No contest, Monsieur—blam!"

"And this sort of thing spreads through the Gloucestershire set like a dose of the clap. The Duckworth family name will be solid gold round here, mate. I wouldn't be surprised if we get invited to a few top drawer balls," said the Duck. "Never know—might get you married off."

"Behave. I'm spoken for. Will Emma be watching?"

"Sorry, no women allowed on a field of honour. It's bad luck."

"Well, it's always bad luck for one of 'em, isn't it?"

"You just want to show off—it's not allowed! But don't worry, I'll make sure she hears about what a hero you were."

I straightened my cravat. "Just make sure she never finds out what really occurred."

"No worries. Just go out there and enjoy yourself, my son. It's your day."

I slapped his shoulder. "Thanks, Duck," I said. "You know, I had my reservations about this, but now I see what you were up to."

"You do?"

"Yeah. All you're interested in is making a name for yourself with your new neighbours."

"Guilty," smiled the Duck. "You got it in one."

"Don't worry, it's cool," I said. "I know what you're like, but I do see you've worked this so we both get what we want for a change."

"You get your brains from your father," he grinned.

* * *

We walked down the main staircase, side by side, two resolute figures, determined to uphold the family honour—whatever the cost to Monsieur De Quipp! There's something ennobling about walking to a field of honour at the crack of dawn, with your second, even when you know the duel has been fixed and you can't lose.

We crossed the elegant black and white chequered hall and entered the long gallery, passing all the paintings and household antiques my father had acquired recently. I wondered who all the noble figures in the portraits were. Okay, they were not ancestors, I know, but I felt sure they would have been proud of what I was doing, as long as you left out the bit about the cheating.

"Who's the guy in the ermine robe?" I asked, as we walked under a huge oil painting of a curly wigged Restoration-type with rosy cheeks.

"Dunno," replied the Duck.

"What about her?" I said, pointing at the full-length portrait of an equine-nosed young lady in a blue silk ball gown, leaning against a Palladian pillar.

"I think she's German," replied the Duck.

"Don't we have any real ancestor paintings?" I said.

"I'm going to get a few done—you, me, Emily and Emma—the kids—might even make up a few," he said.

"You could get Turner to do them," I said.

"No. He's too expensive. I know this bloke in Soho. You just send him some Polaroids, slip him a few quid, and he'll knock off as many as you want, all in period costume."

"That's right," I said, "do it properly."

"When do I have time to sit? I'm a hunted man. Besides, there's no money in portraits—nobody buys 'em."

The English aristocracy say that if you have to buy your own furniture, you are not a true aristocrat. Well, my old man bought his as a job lot, but at least he knew the makers personally.

We reached the end that backed onto the east terrace. Bentley was waiting for us with two glasses of Dutch courage on a silver tray.

"Cheers, Benters," said the Duck. He passed me mine. "There you go, Son, get that down you. Jamaican rum, from my plantation. That'll put hairs on your vest."

"I hope you're not a slaver," I said.

"Do me a favour," said the Duck. "I only bought it as an investment. I've never even been out there."

"Well, I don't suppose it matters," I said. "They'll be banning slavery in 1807, anyway."

Bentley raised an eyebrow.

"Probably," I added.

Bentley took our empty glasses.

"Thanks, Bentley," I said.

"May one be permitted to wish you good luck, sir?" he inquired.

"You may," said the Duck.

"The very best of luck, sir," said Bentley. "I hope you win."

"Thanks, Bentley."

"He won't need any luck, Benters," said the Duck. "His opponent's only a Frenchman."

"To be sure, sir," said Bentley.

"And no match for a Duckworth," I added, getting into the swing of the thing.

"I hope not, sir. I'm offering very good odds for you," said Bentley. He set off on the long walk back up the gallery.

"Odds?" I called.

"Just a harmless flutter, sir."

"On my life? How long?"

"Two hundred to one, sir," replied Bentley.

"I'm not that confident, Bentley."

"Against, sir."

"Against?" I turned to the Duck. "Does he know about the you know what?" I whispered.

"Er…"

"You said you wouldn't tell anyone!"

"I only told Benters—he's just taking a few side bets for me. At odds of two-hundred to one against—the punters are ripping his arm off!"

"You're running a book on your son's life? Haven't you got any scruples?"

"I couldn't resist it. Anyway, we can't lose." He tapped his box of pistols. "We've got an edge."

"Edge? That's a bloody cliff! It's cheating."

"I prefer the term *creative certainty*."

"This is all a tissue of lies, isn't it?" I said. "This whole set-up—the house, the title. What are you doing back here in this snobby society? You'll never fit in round here. You've only got one principle—get in first and do unto others before they do unto you. You'd be better off hobnobbing with the mob in twentieth century Las Vegas."

"I've got a condo in Vegas," said the Duck.

"Well, why don't you go and live in it?"

He opened the tall terrace doors for me.

"I'm sick of all this pretence."

"I'm an antiques dealer. This is where all the best stuff is," said the Duck.

We both stepped outside into the chill March air. The morning mists were still hanging in the trees and there was a muffled stillness everywhere.

"Give me that gun," I said.

The Duck opened the case as we walked to the terrace parapet and handed me a pistol.

"Sure this is the right one?" I said. "That's a point—how am I going to know which one's mine? They both look the same."

"Not a problem," said the Duck.

"Not for you maybe. You'll be hiding behind a tree."

"As the challenged," he said, patiently, "it is your privilege to have first dibs. Now, I will hold the case open towards you like this." He demonstrated.

"Right."

"No, left," said the Duck. "You choose the pistol with its butt on the left—the one you're holding. Got that—the left?"

"The left? Right."

"No—the left!"

"Yeah, all right, I know which side's my left," I said. "Here, hang on—your left or my left?"

"We'd better make up something, so you don't forget," he said. "I know—left—that's 'L' for loaded. Got that?"

"And 'R' for reject—I reject the right one," I said.

"No, the right one is on the left," said the Duck.

"Oh, shut up. Just point to the bloody thing!"

I aimed down at bushes and statues in the formal garden below us, and pretended to blow them away, with sound effects. Blam! Blam-blam! Pow!

"Give me that!" said the Duck.

I held it out of his reach and made him jump for it, till he gave up trying to take it off me.

"All right," he said. "Show me how you're going to shoot into the air after De Quipp goes down."

I pointed directly up into the air and pulled the trigger. Nothing happened, of course, because it wasn't loaded, so I did the sound effect. Blam! And the echo. Bla-blam!

"No," said the Duck.

"Yeah, well, I'll just do it my way," I said, tired of all his fussing.

"If you fire it straight up like that, you could have your eye out!"

"How?" I said sceptically.

"Give it here, I'll show you."

I reluctantly handed over the gun.

He demonstrated. "If you hold it right up above your head, like you had it, you'll have bits of hot lead and powder sparks falling straight down in your eyes. Hold it out like this—he held his arm out and bent it at the elbow—and discharge it away from your body, but directly up in the air. Got it?"

"Yeah. Give it here then."

"No, it's going away now, till we get there."

"Call that a practice? I haven't even fired the bloody thing yet!"

"Ammunition costs money." He put the gun carefully back in its brown baize lined case and shut it. "Come on, this way."

He dashed off down some steps on the eastern side of the house, leading to the formal garden. I followed on his heels. And caught him up.

"How far is it?"

"Not far. See those beech trees?"

There was a line of beech trees running parallel, but far to the left of the main avenue of trees—which, I think, were limes—and the Duck had indicated these. They seemed to border a level path going to a small bridge over a stream. It being early spring, they were not yet in leaf, but there were rookeries in the high branches, and the residents were stirring and drying their feathers in the sun, which was just beginning to break through. They let out a few piercing cackles as we approached.

You know that feeling you get sometimes when something just doesn't feel right? Well, I was getting it in spades.

We had traversed the garden, with its topiary and symmetrical hedging, and were just going down the verdant slope to the stream. It should have been a walk in the park, but it felt more like a walk in the dark.

"Wait," I said.

The Duck stopped and turned about. "What is it now?"

"I don't see De Quipp," I said.

"He'll be here," said the Duck.

I looked back at the house. It seemed impossibly large, sitting there in the perfect green landscape, with its neo-classical arches and pillars, and sheer walls, streaked with grime—like an illusion.

"There's something wrong. I can feel it."

"Your senses are working overtime. The old adrenalin's pumping."

"Is that what it is?" I gazed around me. "Everything just feels different."

"It's just nerves," said the Duck. "Come on. We'll be late."

I took my time, looked back at the house again, around at the terraces and trees and gardens, and then up into the empty grey sky. I thought I heard something. And if I listened very hard, I could just make out a roaring sound coming from beyond the clouds.

"What's that?" I said.

"What?"

"That noise. It sounds like the red-eye from New York!"

"It's just the wind," said the Duck.

"And the house!" I said. "It's aged, the stone's got dark patches—you scheming little rat! This isn't 1803! We're back in the third millennium!"

"Calm down," said the Duck.

I grabbed his arm and started swinging his scrawny body around and round. Though he tried to clutch it to his pigeon chest, the pistol case flew out of his other arm and skittered across the grass.

"You've brought me back! Why? Where's Emma? Oh my God, what have you done?"

I was whirling him around faster and faster. Both his feet left the ground and he was screaming at me to stop.

"Let me go! Let me go! Steve! I-can-ex-plain-ev-er-y-thing!"

I let go and the centrifugal force slingshotted him at least ten feet through the air and sent him skidding on his backside down the grassy slope. I ran after him and grabbed him by his stupid hippie ponytail before he could scramble to his feet. I wrenched his head back and stuck my nose right up against his.

"Start at the beginning and tell me everything, you devious little bastard!"

"All right, all right! The truth!" he cried.

"I knew there was something fishy going on and I knew you were behind it. Tell me!"

"Let go of my hair first."

I gave his head one last yank and released him. He immediately scampered away to fetch the box. I ran after him. He picked clods of earth off it and rubbed it clean with his sleeve.

"You maniac! Have you any idea how much a boxed set of Wogdons is worth?"

I gave him a shove. "I don't care," I said. "What are we doing here?"

"It was a safety measure." He straightened his glasses. "I've got a helicopter standing by on the other side of the house, if any of the combatants sustain a serious wound, I could have him in Bristol A and E in five minutes."

"You'll have to do better than that, unless you want to go there," I smiled. "Now, the real reason."

"That's the truth. I swear," he said. "I didn't want to take any chances with… with my son's life."

He held the gun case close to his heart and gazed off across the immaculate parkland, with a wistfully tragic expression on his face.

"I don't know what I'd do if I lost you, Son. Honest I don't."

"Yeah, very moving," I said. "Now tell me the rest."

He looked round at me, aghast. "That's all there is!" he quacked. "Don't you believe I have feelings?"

"Let me see," I started counting on my fingers, "there's greed, lust, selfishness, pride—"

"—What a low opinion you have of your father," he said, sadly.

But I wasn't buying any of it. "So, Bentley's in on it. Who else?"

"Just Bentley."

"Well, that's a lie for a start," I said. "How did you get De Quipp here?"

"De Quipp doesn't know anything—he still thinks he's in 1803," said the Duck.

"Where is he then?" I said, looking round.

"He's out riding."

I leaned forward to make a point of peering through Duckworth's thick-lensed glasses. "On his own? What if he rides straight into a motorway?"

"My, er, brother-in-law's chaperoning him," replied the Duck. "Now, can we get on, they'll be back in a minute."

"Which brother-in-law?" I said. "You must have dozens—you've got a wife in every century!"

"Rufus."

"Rufus who?"

"It's Aleman," said the Duck.

"Aleman the Blacksmith—from the Middle Ages?" I exclaimed. "You brought Aleman here? He only has two brain cells—and they're both illiterate!"

"Stupidity has its uses," said the Duck.

"Yeah, he does everything you tell him."

"He speaks Norman French," said the Duck.

"Wait a minute—Aleman's playing Captain Walrus—De Quipp's second—I thought I recognized that moustache!" I once wrestled Aleman the Smithy for the hand of the Duck's sister-in-law, an Anglo-Saxon wench named Betha. I threw the fight, but that's another story.

Suddenly, two riders appeared on the horizon, one silhouette riding tall and elegant in the saddle, the other short and fat, bouncing along beside him.

"They're coming!" said the Duck, seizing my arm.

We watched them ride down the hill into the avenue of limes and then cut across towards the bridge.

"What a farce," I said. "Okay, let's do it."

The Duck stopped and waved to them. I walked past him and headed for the line of beeches.

We met on the path. I put my hands in my pockets and posed. De Quipp was still astride his horse at one end—his second holding it steady—the Duck joined me at the other. My opponent dismounted in one smooth movement and started striding purposefully towards me. I set off immediately to meet him before he got to the middle, because I thought it would be bad form to allow him to come to me. Our seconds hurried along behind us, Aleman leading the two horses and the Duck carrying his box of guns. We were now both roughly in the middle of the little avenue of beeches, with the stream gurgling away down the bank, on my left.

"Get those horses out of here," I said.

Aleman hesitated and then, after a jerk of the head from De Quipp, led them to the other side of the break of trees, on the far side from the stream.

"So, Baron Duckworth," said De Quipp, strutting around me, hands on hips, looking me up and down, "you dare to teurn up."

I stood my ground and looked bored while he circled me.

"Have you come to talk or to fight?" I said.

"I yam a chevalier, a Knight of France," he said. "You insult mee, Baron Duckworth. Now I geeve you the chaunce to take hit back."

"No," I yawned.

"Vary well!" he snapped. "Then you geeve mee no choice—I must keel you."

"Pick a gun and let's get on with it then," I said.

We both turned to the Duck, who was shaking his head vigorously at me. I had no idea what he meant. He flipped open the catches on the gun case and offered them to us.

De Quipp went to inspect the pistols more closely, but did not touch them. He nodded approvingly at the Duck. Then he turned to me.

"You ask mee to choose?"

It suddenly dawned on me why the Duck had been shaking his head. I was just panicking and wondering what to do next, when De Quipp said:

"You insult mee, Baron! It was I who challaunge you—you must choose!"

I smiled.

Aleman, who had wound the reins of the horses around a low-hanging branch, rejoined us. We exchanged glances, but neither of us gave away any sign that we knew each other.

"You would like me to choose," said De Quipp, pointing his finger at my nose, "because you sink I yam the loweur one, but hin France an English Baronet his not so high as a chevalier."

"Whatever," I said.

"Ahem, I think you'll find you're about the same rank socially, Monsieur De Quipp, according to Debrett's," said the Duck, smiling with his teeth.

De Quipp shrugged. "Vary well, hif you say so, Sir Julianne. I will not quipple." He turned to me again and gestured to the case with a flourish of his hand. "Choose your weapon, Baron Duckworth."

I peered into the case and pretended to be making up my mind, because I didn't want to make it look too obvious that I was only going to go for one particular pistol. I put my finger to my lips. The Duck's right index finger moved along the edge of the box, and was clearly indicating the left hand pistol, as he held it open. I picked it up and weighed it in my hand.

"Good balance," I nodded. I looked along the barrel, with one eye closed and curled my lip. "Sight's a bit out." I made an effort to bend it straight, although there was nothing really wrong with it, not that I would have known even if there were.

The Duck scowled at me.

De Quipp quickly took the remaining pistol and expertly turned it over in his hands, checking that every moving part was in working order and the barrel was clean. And then he helped himself to more things from the case—a small flask, a lead ball, some little cloth wads, flint. Then, holding the flask in his teeth, he removed a rod thing from his pistol, which was slotted in under the barrel, directly in line with it. Mine had one, too, so I pulled it out and showed it to the Duck. The Duck shook his head. I shrugged.

"Ahem, Monsieur De Quipp?" said the Duck.

"Oui?"

"In England it is considered proper etiquette to let the combatants' seconds load the guns."

"Not so hin France," said De Quipp, briskly pouring gunpowder down the muzzle of his pistol.

I was trying to watch and copy him at the same time, but dropped my flask and bent my ramrod thingy when I went to pick it up.

"Well, this isn't France, is it?" said the Duck. "I must insist you abide by English rules."

"I hallways load my own pistol," said De Quipp, rapidly plunging his ramrod in and out to pack his powder down firmly.

Aleman, moving clumsily in his ill-fitting French cavalry sergeant's uniform, which was at least two sizes too small for him, came to my aid and straightened my rod for me. Well, the guy was a blacksmith in his own time, so he knew a thing or two about working metal.

Meanwhile, De Quipp had put the flint in the pan under the hammer and was pouring a little black powder in from the flask. I copied him.

"I insist, sir!" cried the Duck, still trying to get his hands on De Quipp's pistol, presumably because he hadn't had a chance to nobble it yet.

"Thees his most irreguleur!" cried De Quipp. "No shootist hin hall France would permit thees!"

"This is not bloody France!" cried the Duck. "Give me back my pistol!" And he attempted to take it by force.

"Non!" exclaimed De Quipp, struggling with the Duck.

"It's my pistol—I say who loads it!"

"I load hit myself!"

"Let it go—or I won't let you borrow it!"

"Thees his outrageeus!"

"Votre manteau, chevalier?" inquired the not so stodgy-witted as I had thought Aleman.

This had the effect of stopping the quarrel between the Duck and De Quipp, because De Quipp made a point of handing his primed gun to his second, so that he could take off his jacket.

The Duck came to take mine. Remembering the rules stated I should be attired in similar fashion to my opponent, I started to take it off. But then it occurred to me that it might give me an unfair advantage, by providing a few extra layers of protection between my skin and any pistol balls that might come flying towards me, so I quickly pulled it back on again.

"I'm keeping mine on, mate," I said, elbowing him away from me.

The Duck's attention switched to Aleman, who still had De Quipp's pistol, and now his coat as well.

"Give me his coat," he ordered, and took it, but snatched De Quipp's gun out of Aleman's other hand at the same time. And ran off with it.

"Sir Julianne!" exclaimed De Quipp, who had been rolling up the right sleeve of his shirt. "Geeve hit back!"

De Quipp gave chase. The Duck pretended to bump into me—and now we had a frock coat and two pistols in our fumbling hands.

"Switch it, switch it!" hissed the Duck.

I tried to grab De Quipp's coat.

"Not the coat, you pratt—the gun!"

I got the message and took the one he was trying to force into my hands, while letting him grab mine from me. We managed to effect this exchange under cover of the coat, so the Frenchman was none the wiser when he caught up with the Duck and snatched back what he assumed to be his own pistol. But, of course, he had mine. And I wasn't sure whether I had loaded it properly or not, because I didn't have a clue what I was doing, and couldn't remember if I had put a ball down the muzzle.

The Duck sidled up to me and spoke to me out of the corner of his mouth, while De Quipp did some impressive stretching exercises.

"Did you load it?" he said.

"I don't know. I don't think I put one of those balls in," I said.

"Yes you did—I counted 'em and there's two missing—shit—you must have loaded it. What order did you put the powder, shot and wadding in in?"

"In in? Um?"

"Think!" quacked the Duck, speaking through his nose, in that irritating way he had.

"I don't remember," I said.

"I yam ready," said De Quipp, tossing his head back haughtily and looking down his nose at me.

"Fingers crossed," said the Duck. "Let's hope you cocked it up."

"Get that helicopter revved up," I said, and did some running on the spot to practise my back-up plan.

"Gentlemen!" cried the Duck. "To your positions!"

I headed for the nearest tree.

Aleman tugged my sleeve as I passed him and turned me round.

"Monsieur, Monsieur!" he said, in a voice so deep and bass-toned it sounded as if it was emanating from somewhere down in the bowels, the bowels of the Earth. "Hit is zat way, Monsieur," he growled.

"You'd make a great lead singer for a heavy metal band," I said, having a private joke.

De Quipp was standing in the middle of the path, with his back to me, his pistol held aloft, alongside his head, like that famous poster of James Bond. The Duck was just staring at me with a crooked grin on his face, and pointing.

"Out there?" I said. "I'll be a sitting duck—there's no cover!"

"You will stand back to back with Monsieur De Quipp, sir," commanded the Duck.

"Old friends, bookends..." I sang, as I passed him. "Get me out of this!"

"Take up your positions, gentlemen," said the blank-faced Duck

I reversed into place, shoulder blade to shoulder blade and backside to backside with my adversary, only my backside must have bumped a little too firmly against his, because he instantly responded by giving mine an even bigger bump right back. I, of course, being at the seat of the Duckworths, so to speak, and thinking of the family honour, responded doublefold. The bum bumping escalated from there really and soon we were smacking backsides with huge exaggerated thrusts, neither of us prepared to give an inch, although, I'm sure De Quipp would have insisted on using centimetres.

"Stop it! Stop that! Gentlemen! Gentlemen!" flapped the Duck.

But De Quipp and I were well out of control, taking run ups and locking bums—like two confused stags—and then De Quipp lost it and turned on me, sticking the barrel of his Wogdon right up my nose.

"You try my payshaunce, Monsieur!" he snarled.

Aleman grabbed me from behind and dragged me out of harm's way, while the Duck tried to placate the mega-passionate Frenchman.

The Duck quickly arranged a compromise and got us to stand back to back, one pace apart, like two naughty schoolboys.

"Now, gentlemen," he quacked, "on my command, you will take six paces, stop, turn and fire at will. Remember, if you should discharge your weapon and miss, you must remain where you are on the field of honour until your opponent has discharged his weapon."

I turned my head towards him and mouthed the words: "Do something."

He merely blinked complacently. "Are you ready, gentlemen?"

"Oui."

"Nope."

"I am going to count to three, on three, you will slowly commence walking to your firing positions," continued the Duck, in a monotone voice he had adopted, because he probably thought it made him sound important and dramatic. It just made him sound like a pompous ass.

"Get on with it," I said.

"One…two…three," said the Duck, thus making the only contribution to the whole sorry proceedings he hadn't messed up.

I set off along the path, swinging my gun down by my ankles and looking around me at the purling stream, and up into the beeches and the green hills and the house beyond, wondering if these scenes were really the last I would ever see. I totally forgot to count! So, I just turned. De Quipp was already facing me, some fifty feet away, his arm outstretched, aiming directly at me.

"Oh, shit!" I exclaimed, got my gun up as far as my hip and it went off.

I felt the dull percussion reverberate through my hand and all the way up my arm to my skull. There was a blinding flash, followed by a shower of sparks and a very loud resounding bang. I was immediately enveloped in a pall of thick grey, choking smoke. I tried to stagger out of it, clutching my throat and coughing, my ears ringing with the deafening explosion, which I was so sure I could still hear, I thought De Quipp must be firing at me. I tried to dodge imaginary bullets by stooping low and weaving my head from side to side, as though I were doing some funky new dance. And then my ears popped and I could hear the horses snorting and the rooks shrieking from the trees like a coven of witches.

"Stand your ground, sir!" cried my father, who had retreated behind a tree on the brook side of the path.

"I can't bloody breathe!" I spluttered. The smoke was slowly dispersing in the wind, but somehow the pungent gunpowder smell was still hanging in the air.

Suddenly, Aleman ran up to me and started slapping my arm.

"Monsieur, Monsieur!" he snorted.

"Did I win?" I said.

"Non—you are hon fireur!"

He was right! The whole of my right arm was alight. I leapt up and down and blew at the flames, which only made matters worse. The sparks had clearly sprayed over my sleeve and burnt through to the lining, and now the fire was spreading—inside the garment! Aleman was pummelling me so madly I had to push him off before he broke my arm.

"I'll take it off!" I shouted—pulling my left shoulder and arm out and letting Aleman wrench the whole coat off my back.

He ran with it down the bank, dragging it behind him like a wacky firework display, and flung it into the stream.

I rolled my billowy white shirtsleeve up and rubbed my scorched arm, and checked for any blood on the rest of me. I was okay. I looked over at the Duck, who was leaning against a tree, with his arms folded, shaking his head.

"You could have told me," I said.

The Duck pointed up the path.

I turned round to find De Quipp still standing, side-on to me, in the classic duellist pose, with his arm fully extended, aiming his pistol straight at my heart.

"When you planned all this," I said to the Duck, "tell me, was this the worst case scenario, or did you think of anything else that could go wrong?"

"Don't worry," said the Duck. "I'll have you in Bristol Frenchay Hospital in under five minutes."

"Can you make that five seconds?" I said, closing my eyes.

There was a loud report and something punched me in the left arm, just above the elbow, and spun me round in a complete circle, only my feet stayed put and I tripped over them and fell to my knees. I opened my eyes and saw De Quipp running towards me through a swirling cloud of grey smoke. But stronger arms reached and held me first, before I pitched forward and smacked my nose into the dirt.

"Oh, Monsieur, Monsieur!" snuffled a gruff voice.

"Mon Dieu!" cried another voice. "I neveur miss! Such braveury, Monsieur!"

"Is he dead?" said the Duck.

Aleman was sitting on the path with me, cradling me in his arms. De Quipp took one look at me, dropped to his knees, and hung his head, uttering a prayer under his breath. Next, the Duck's big red spectacled face loomed into close view.

"Oh, Christ!" he exclaimed.

"It's just my arm," I said, trying to point.

"Shh. Don't move, Monsieur," croaked Aleman.

"It's more than that!" quacked the Duck. He reached inside his frock coat and whipped out a tiny mobile phone. "Get that bloody helicopter down here quick!" he quacked. "Yeah, to Frenchay!"

"Vite! Vite!" urged Aleman.

I looked down at my shirt. Aleman's hands were clasped around my chest, soaked in blood. I passed out.

Chapter 4

I think I remember being in the helicopter and the thump-thump-thump of the rotor blades.

I also think I remember opening my eyes fleetingly when the crash team were charging me through the hospital corridors on a trolley.

The last thing I remember was some doctor standing over me with a pair of those electric shock paddles, and some guy saying: "Okay, we have a pulse." But I might be being over-dramatic there.

Anyway, these were just fragmented memories. I believe there was also a giant squid in there somewhere, so they may not be that reliable. The next thing I really knew for sure was waking up and seeing the Duck's ugly mug, grinning down at me.

"How you feeling?"

"Nearly got me killed," I said, softly.

"Sorry. You needed six pints of blood," he said.

"A six pack," I said.

"Yeah. You were lucky, mate. Travis just missed your heart."

"Thought it hit my arm."

"Yeah, it did, but that's just a scratch. It did all the damage when it hit your rib and sheared off, came out your side and lodged in your arm. I reckon you put that sight out of line when you were messing about with it," said the Duck. "That's how he missed."

"I owe me my life," I said, forcing a smile.

"You owe Aleman, too. He stuck his fingers in the holes and stopped you bleeding to death," said the Duck.

"Little boy and the dyke. Thank him for me."

"Yeah, I will."

"Is he here?"

"No, I took him home. His wife's got another nipper on the way. He sends you his best."

"Betha's pregnant?"

"Yeah. Here, it's not yours, is it?"

"Get stuffed. Aleman's a good man. What about Emma?" I said.

The Duck helped himself to a grape. "All you've got to do is concentrate on getting better, mate," he said.

"Where is she?" I said.

"She's, er, still at Duckworth Hall. What do you think of your suite? Nice, innit? Nothing but the best for a Duckworth—you've got everything in here—cable TV, movie channel, your own nurse, you can even go online, if you want. Er, when you can move again. This is the luxury deluxe package—none of your NHS rubbish."

"Why isn't she here?"

"Who?"

"Tooth Fairy—Emma!"

"If that chick don't wanna know, man—forget her," he said.

"Get her here, Duck."

"I can't." He lowered his voice and looked over his shoulder. "I can't. She's back in 1803. Anyway, she doesn't want to see you. She and Travis are—"

"—De Quipp's with her?"

"I had to take him back, didn't I? He thought it was 1803. I couldn't let him stay here, could I? He'd be chasing cars up the motorway on his horse and having duels with traffic wardens."

"Get me out of here," I said. "I have to go back."

"I can't. The doctors say you're going to need at least another ten days to recover," said the Duck.

"I have to see Emma. You could get me out if you wanted to."

"But I'm not going to," he said. "It's for your own good."

I turned my face away from him. "Thanks a lot."

"Give it up, mate. Emma said your relationship was past tense. She and Travis got engaged. I'm sorry. Here, these grapes are nice, try one."

"Tired. Go away."

"Yeah. You get some sleep now," he said. "Anything you need, just tell the nurse, she works for me." I heard him get up. "I'll come and see you again tomorrow, hey? We'll soon have you back on your feet. See you, mate."

I heard him go out.

I stared up at the ceiling. I didn't know what to think anymore. The whole business with Emma and De Quipp was beyond belief. I kept thinking it wasn't serious, that I could sort it out and get her back, but now it seemed I was too late. I was stuck in a hospital two hundred years away, by the time I got out she and De Quipp could be in Napoleonic France saying their wedding vows. Our relationship wasn't just past tense—it was future tense, too! How could a stupid argument in a restaurant over nothing have ended up like this? That's how it all began, an argument over a stupid holiday. I just said I fancied going to the Far East to do a bit of backpacking, before we were both past it, and she went crazy. Why didn't she tell me she was pregnant? Did she really think I would make such a lousy father? I kept coming back to two things. What had really made her storm out of that restaurant and end our relationship after nearly three semi-blissful years? And how could she have fallen so deeply in love with a pratt like Travis De Quipp in just three weeks? Lying there, analysing it all, I came to a startling conclusion, and the only one that made any sense to me. The Emma who left that restaurant had not terminated our relationship, we had merely had a row, like all couples who've been around the block do from time to time—it was just a tiff and she'd walked off in a huff, that's all. It should have been no big deal. But what, I hypothesized, if the Emma in the restaurant and the Emma I met at Duckworth Hall were not one and the same? I was excited—my mind was racing—it was all starting to fit together. How could the real Emma behave like the Emma who was running around after a guy like Travis De Quipp? I knew Emma better than anyone and De Quipp was definitely not her type. He was too—too corny, too—tall, dark and handsome—too bloody Latin-looking!

"Well, she had me fooled," I said aloud.

"Mr Duckworth? Are you awake?" said a husky voice.

I lifted my head and looked down my bed. A slim young nurse, wearing a pale blue and cream uniform, was sitting in an armchair on the other side of the room, her long legs elegantly crossed.

"Uh, hi," I said.

"Hello, Mr Duckworth—I'm Brie, your nurse. Can I get you anything?" She laid the paperback book she had been reading down on the floor.

"Yes, can you get me a platinum MasterCard and a hire car, please?" I said.

"Well, I don't know, Mr Duckworth, I'll have to check with the other Mr Duckworth," she said. "But, I mean, why would you need a hire car, Mr Duckworth?"

"I want to drive it," I said.

"Oh, no, Mr Duckworth—you can't drive, you're still on medication."

She was off her chair and at my bedside, feeling my pulse, in the twinkling of an eye. I looked her up and down as she bent over me and counted my beats. Twenty to twenty-five, medium height, natural blonde, cupid bow lips, hair raked back in a neat French knot, slate blue eyes, no wedding ring. I knew my beats would be up.

"Maybe you could drive me," I suggested, raising my eyebrows.

She gave me a flirty look. "You're not well enough to be sitting up, let alone going for drives, Mr Duckworth." She took out her thermometer and gave it a shake. "Open wide."

I opened my mouth and she inserted it under my tongue and began timing it with her nurse's watch, which was still clipped to her breast pocket. A strangely erotic act.

"Do you have any idea how rich I am?" I said, appealing to the only part of her I thought I could reach quickly.

"I know this place isn't cheap," she said. "Now, please keep your tongue still a moment."

I stopped talking. She timed it a little longer, took it out, gave it a quick check, then another shake, and put it away in her pocket.

"You're running a temperature, Mr Duckworth."

"Think of a lot of money," I said. "Now double it. No, treble it. Think of Bill Gates. Even he doesn't have our assets."

"Oh, Mr Duckworth, behave yourself," she smiled. "Look, why are you telling me all this? I'm just a nurse, your brother hired me to—"

"My brother? Is that what he told you?" I laughed.

"Well, yes, he said—"

"Brie, that is so funny, I just can't tell you how funny that is. If you only knew. But you wouldn't believe me if I told you, so let's just stick to money. I've gotta go to Gloucestershire and I might have to go to France. Help me to get out of here and be my driver and I'll give you any amount you want."

She smiled, all wide-eyed. "Are you a prisoner, Mr Duckworth? This is some cell!"

"No. I'm not a prisoner. I just need to be places and the Duck—I mean, my kid brother, Julian—won't let me leave this hospital. You understand?"

"No, Mr Duckworth, I don't think I do. But your brother warned me you might try something like this."

"I bet he did. The rat. Ignore him."

"But I may lose my job and, anyway, you're really not well enough to be discharged yet, Mr Duckworth."

"Okay, Brie. Let's play it your way," I said. "Do you know the nature of my injury? How I got it?"

"There was a shooting accident on the Duckworth family estate—an old sporting gun went off—and you were in the wrong place at the wrong time," she said.

"Yes. That's about what happened. I just want to go back there and recover in my own bed. That's all I'm asking. You can come and take care of me. How soon can we leave? I mean, if you want me to wait, say, while you hire the car, that's okay. But do you think you could get me there, to

Duckworth Hall, without my brother knowing? I want it to be a surprise."

"Are you trying to tell me something, Mr Duckworth?"

"Yes. I want to go home."

"Did your brother shoot you?" she asked.

"No, not exactly. I mean yes. Which answer do you want me to give?"

"You blame him for your accident?"

"Let's cut the amateur psychoanalysis, Brie—I just want to go home. My brother's a pain in the ass, but I don't hate him or want to shoot him because he tried to kill me, or anything that interesting. In fact, we're very close."

"You mentioned some money," she said.

"Oh, yes, lots of money. How much do you want?"

"I don't know," she said, shyly. "You say a figure, Mr Duckworth."

"No, you say one," I said.

"I don't know how much to say." She bit her bottom lip. "All I have to do is drive you to Duckworth Hall?"

"Well, maybe France. But no. Just Duckworth Hall, if you want."

"Nothing else?"

"No strings, Brie. I swear. Name your price," I said.

"Ten."

"Ten thousand?"

She nodded.

"I'll make it fifty if you don't drive over any bumps."

She threw her arms around my neck and kissed me on the cheek. "Fifty thousand pounds!" she cried. "Do you mean it?"

"Oh yes," I said. "Now, how soon can we leave? Now?"

"Maybe tomorrow," she said. "I'll take another look at your wound in the morning. But how are we going to get a platinum MasterCard in one day?"

"Leave that to me—in fact, I'll do it now. Do you have my brother's new mobile number?"

"Yes. It's in my bag somewhere," she said.

"Go and get it and push that phone over here," I said.

She bustled away and rummaged in her handbag, which she had left over by the chair. I felt around my rib. It was well padded but very sore. I thought I could stand up, if push came to shove, but a wheelchair would be a top idea.

Brie wheeled me over the cumbersome hospital phone and handed me her address book, pointing a nicely manicured finger at the number of Mr Julian Duckworth.

I punched it in and let it ring. Brie sat on the corner of the bed and began massaging my shoulder.

"Where did my brother find you?" I said.

"He just called the agency," she said, her tongue just protruding enough through her soft full lips.

"What sort of agency?"

She pinched me. "A nursing agency! This is just physio, Mr Duckworth."

I heard the Duck's unmistakable quack on the line.

"Duckworth—speak—I'm in a hurry!"

"Hi, bro," I said.

"Who is this?" he snapped.

"Big brother," I said.

"Stephen?"

"I'm feeling better," I said.

"Good, good," he said. "I thought you might."

"Where are you?"

"I'm, er, in the car—the hospital wouldn't let me land me helicopter."

"I thought I'd do some entertaining," I said.

The Duck quacked, in that annoying way he has. "So, you've met Nurse Parker? You dog."

"Yeah. I need some wherewithal, man."

"Wherewithal?"

"Yeah, you know—folding."

"Folding?"

"Dosh—readies—money!"

"Oh, you mean plastic!"

"Yeah, I need a card," I said.

"Okay, I'll order one," he said.

"How long will that take?"

"Seven working days," he replied.

"I can't wait that long—give me one of yours."

There was a long pause while my miserly father tried to bring himself to part with one of his many MasterCards.

"Think of it this way," I prompted. "If I had my own, you wouldn't have any control—but if I'm using yours, you can keep tabs on my spending and put a stop on it any time you like."

"No, it's not that," he said. "I was just wondering how to get it to you. We're on the motorway and I'm in a hurry, mate. Do you need it today?"

"Yes," I said. "Just send it over by courier—and don't forget the PIN number. Cheers." I hung up. I winked at Brie. "We're doing a MasterCard transplant and my brother's going to be the donor!"

Brie smoothed my cheek with the backs of her fingers. "Are you really as rich as you say?" she purred.

"Down, girl," I said. "This is strictly business. I mean, don't get me wrong—you're very attractive and under different circumstances, I would be more than interested, but right now I just need your help to—"

"—What's her name?" said Brie.

"Emma," I said. "It's Emma."

"She's a lucky girl. You're amusing, stinking rich, passably good-looking—did I say, stinking rich? A girl could do a lot worse."

"Yeah, well, she did, in my opinion—she's, uh, not herself right now, but I think I know how I can talk her round," I said. "Yes, I think I can do that," I added, more to convince myself than my nurse.

"What's the other guy's name?" she said.

"The other guy? Oh, you mean Travis—his name's Travis."

"Hm. Nice name. What's he like?"

"Oh, you know, tall—"

"—Dark, handsome, sexy voice?" she nodded. She reached behind her head with both hands to fiddle with her knot, which had the pleasant effect of making her breasts present themselves like two propositions, and since she was sitting up higher than me, I got the, um, points, which I think was the, um, ideas. Now, I'm getting confused.

"Er, that's right," I said. "You know the type. You know, you're very easy to talk to, Brie—you have a nice, uh, personality. I feel as if I've known you all my life and I could tell you anything—you're a journalist, right?"

"With these nails?" she said.

"Yes, I see what you mean, they are very long, and, uh, pink, it would be kind of hard to—but you could be working undercover."

"Undercover?" she smirked. "That could be fun." She pulled back the corner of my sheet.

"No—that wasn't code, Brie!" I said. "Just be a nurse for me—what other uniforms do they have at that agency of yours?"

"Mr Duckworth! I'm a fully qualified nurse!"

"Yeah, and I'm Squadron Leader Biggles," I said.

"Who?"

"Never mind. Look, why don't you bring that paperback I saw you reading over here and read to me?" I said. "I like books."

She slipped off the bed and sauntered over to her chair to pick up the book. Her nurse's uniform didn't look regulation, the skirt was half way up her thighs and the rest was skimpy enough to cause a cardiac arrest.

"Yes, I got a second in English Lit at Oxford," I said. Actually, I got a third, but second rate sounded better than third rate. Yes, I did go to Oxford, but I think I went under it, or it went over me.

She waved the lurid cover of her paperback at me, as she retouched her lips with her lipstick.

"This isn't exactly Jane Austen," she said.

"Jane Austen?" I said. "What made you say that?"

She came back and sat on her spot, but this time wrapped her free arm around my neck.

"I don't know. Didn't she write books?" she said. "Where would you like me to start?"

"Chapter one—yes, she did, but—it doesn't matter," I said.

"Are we sitting comfortably?" said Nurse Brie, languidly raising one of her legs onto the bed and crooking it up.

She was wearing suspenders! Yes, I knew the Duck was setting me up, but what for? Did he think I was going to fall in love with his nurse and forget about Emma? Why was he so keen to make me forget about Emma? Unless he was just being kind. Like I said—why was he so keen to make me forget about Emma? There had to be an ulterior motive.

Brie began reading, in a talented voice—the kind guys would have paid premium rate call charges for, just to listen to her tell them what she did at the gym. I nestled back in my pillows and closed my eyes.

"Chastity Adams was the kind of girl who had never made a habit of sleeping around," whispered Brie, huskily, "but she decided in her sophomore year at college to experiment with every sexual experience, at least once, before going on to do missionary work—"

"—What's this book called?" I smiled.

"*What Chastity Did* by Prudence Withers," said Brie.

"Prudence is a guy," I said.

"You think so?"

"I know so."

"Well, he knows a lot about multiple female orgasms," she said.

"Please, read on," I said.

Chapter 5

The courier arrived at six thirty p.m. Brie woke me up. I found myself so firmly tucked in that I couldn't move my arms to sign for the package. My nurse had to loosen the sheets to release me.

"Into a bit of bondage is he, luv?" grinned the motorcycle courier.

"Give me that thing!" I said, reaching for his electronic notebook. "Where do I sign?"

"Just sign at the bottom with this pen, mate," he said.

I scrawled my name with the light pen, started to write Sloane, scribbled it out, and wrote Duckworth. "Here."

"Thanks, mate—forget your own name?" he laughed. He gave me my package and loitered, looking round at the room. "What's this then—the penthouse ward?"

I tore open the wrapping and found my card and a note from the Duck inside a cardboard gift box. I looked up at the courier and tilted my head to one side. "Yes?"

"Any reply?" he said.

"No." I turned to Brie. "Tip him, Brie."

"Cheers, mate."

He followed Brie over to her handbag and I read the note, it said:

Dear Stephen,

Guard this triple platinum MasterCard with your life.

The PIN number is on the other sheet of paper.

The upper limit is 100K, but don't go mad, as I am

not made of money. Tell Miss Parker not to let

you let her out of your sight. Have fun.

See you soon.

Love,

Julian

I ripped it up while I memorized the four-number code on the other sheet and then tore that up and dropped all the pieces back in the box.

Brie finished seeing our courier out and came back to me.

"What was that thing with the bed?" I said. "I was trussed-up like a kipper."

"Just habit," she smiled. "You fell asleep. I didn't want you to pull your stitches out."

She sat on my bed and smoothed my hair back off my brow. "Did you get it?"

I held up the box.

"Will it be enough?"

"Plenty and some," I said.

She kissed my temple and was up for a full one on the lips, but I turned my head away. "We have an arrangement," I said. "Let's stick to it."

"Okay," she said. "I just thought we might fool around. You enjoyed the book."

"You were making most of that up," I said.

"No I wasn't," she said.

"Yes you were, you weren't even looking at the pages half the time," I said.

"Well, what if I did?"

"You should write one yourself, Miss Parker," I said.

"What happened to Brie?"

"I think I like Miss Parker better," I said.

"It makes me sound like a dominatrix," she said, in her huskiest voice.

"Hey, stop that! If you want that fifty K, you have to promise to stop trying to seduce me."

"Miss Gummer must be very special," she said.

"Miss Gummer? I never told you her second name. How did you know that?"

"Your brother must have mentioned it."

"He wouldn't have told you that," I said suspiciously. I was suddenly seeing Miss Parker in a whole new light.

"I want to know how you knew Emma's surname. I didn't tell you. So, how come you knew?"

"All right. Your brother did tell me," she said. "And that's the truth. I'm not a real nurse, well, I did some of the training, but the agency I work for is not a nursing agency, strictly speaking."

"So what is it—strictly speaking?" I said.

"You know—you already guessed—I'm from an escort agency. Your brother wanted me to show you a good time—to make you forget this Emma Gummer, but I'm obviously not good enough and don't come anywhere near the perfect Miss Gummer." She dabbed at her eyes.

"Brie, my brother means well, but he sticks his big nose into things that are none of his business," I said. "You had a deal with him, but now you have a deal with me, and I bet I know who's paying you more."

"You are, Mr Duckworth," she sniffed.

"Then consider your arrangement with my brother terminated. It's just good business, Brie," I said.

"Okay."

"Let's move on."

"Yes, Mr Duckworth."

"Good. Now, why did you stop playing with my hair? Playing with the hair is permitted," I said.

She ruffled my hair and looked at me in a special way, the way someone else used to look at me.

"But don't fall in love with me—it's forbidden," I said, only half-jokingly.

I flinched. I had detected something deep within her eyes, which I can only describe as an angry flaring of the pupils. Like a frustrated child who has promised to behave, but still resents the telling off. But I might have been imagining things, because it passed so quickly and then she was smiling indulgently at me again.

"Don't worry," she said. "There's no danger of that."

"If I get a good night's sleep," I said, "maybe we could discharge me in the morning. I'll need a wheelchair."

"We have one," she said, studying my face with that strange look again.

"What's up?" I said.

"Nothing. I'll give you a sedative to help you sleep," she said.

She walked stiffly over to her handbag, took something out, and returned.

"Do you know how to do this?" I said.

"Yes," she said, pulling a sick grin. "They taught us sedation between bondage and flagellation class."

I was taking a liking to Miss Parker. But there was still something about her that troubled me, well, not really troubled me, but sort of made me suspicious of her, well, not really suspicious, as such, but slightly cautious, well, not exactly cautious, but a bit wary, well, not even wary really—I just had a funny feeling about her. Do you know what I mean? No, of course, you don't. Neither do I.

She produced a hypodermic syringe and squirted some out of the needle to get rid of the air, and then she pulled back the sheet to expose my side.

"Can you turn your hip for me, please, Mr Duckworth?" she said.

I twisted my lower body round as far as I dared and felt her inject into my right buttock, and then wipe it with a cold antiseptic swab.

"Okay," she said, covering me up again.

"Don't tuck me—" I started to say.

* * *

I slept fitfully. I was still getting my big squid nightmares. I woke up in a cold sweat, having narrowly escaped from one's multiple clutches. It was really weird because the one that was trying to get me could talk and we weren't even underwater when it attacked me. Well, it didn't really attack me, it was sort of trying to guard me, I think. The thing was wrapped around my bed, with its tentacles going right under the mattress and interlocking, kind of like an embrace. It was just sitting there on the end of the bed, staring at me with its huge black eyes. I forget what it was saying, but it definitely called me by my name. And then when I struggled and cried out it slid off the bed, but I was still trapped because Nurse Parker had tucked me in too tightly again. I wonder what Freud would have made of that. Well, here, for what it's worth, is my interpretation—that squid in the attic had scared the shit out of me and damaged me for life.

"Shh-shh," soothed Miss Parker, making a lovely 'O' shape with her lips. She was right up close and her breath smelt of fresh strawberries. That beautiful face was quite a tonic after what I'd been looking at all night, I can tell you.

I swallowed hard. "Nightmare," I said. "Keep having the same one."

"Oh, poor thing," she frowned. "What would you like for breakfast?"

"A wheelchair," I said. "Get me out of here."

"You've got a one track mind, Mr Duckworth," she said.

"Push me down it in a wheelchair then," I said.

"All right, I'll get you your wheelchair, but you must promise to eat something and let me take a look at those stitches."

"Coffee and toast—I'll take it in my wheelchair," I said.

"Oh, Mr Duckworth," she sighed, "haven't you enjoyed your stay here the teensiest bit?"

"I'll enjoy the bit when I'm leaving," I said.

She stuck her tongue out at me and went off to get the wheelchair out of a cupboard behind her chair.

"It was here all the time!" I cried. "Why didn't you tell me?"

"Because I was afraid I'd wake up to find you halfway up the M6," she said.

"That's a point. Do you have any idea where Duckworth Hall is?"

"Don't you?" she said, unfolding the wheelchair.

"No."

"I thought you lived there."

"Yes, I do live there, but this is the first time I've ever left the old family pile," I said. "And I was unconscious when they brought me here, so I don't know my way home."

"Oh, how sad," she frowned. "What is it that your family do exactly?"

"We're travellers."

"But you just said you've never left Duckworth Hall," said Miss Parker. "I'm confused, Mr Duckworth."

"Not that sort of traveller, Miss Parker," I laughed. "Antique entrepreneurial peregrinational ones."

"Oh, that kind. I'll take my fifty thousand in advance, if you don't mind, Mr Duckworth."

She pushed the wheelchair to the side of my bed and put the brake on.

"Anyway, what do you care if I'm telling you a pack of lies?" I said. "As long as you—"

"—Get my money," she smiled. "As long as you pay me—up front—you can tell me you live on the bottom of the sea for all I care."

"Hmm. I've been thinking about that, Miss Parker."

"How reassuring."

"What do you intend to do with all your money?" I said.

"Is that any of your business, Mr Duckworth?"

"It's just that I thought if you were planning to buy a car we could kill two birds with one stone," I said.

"Oh, I see," she said, sitting on the corner of my bed, and fondling my hair, "so now I'm not only going to be your chauffeur, but also an owner-driver."

"Does that matter?"

"Well, if we had a crash, you could claim on my insurance, Mr Duckworth," she said.

"Hmm. I didn't think of that. Actually, you'd be my chauffeuse, Miss Parker," I said, stalling. "Ah, but what if I insured it for you?"

"Done," said Miss Parker, kissing my forehead. "Now, I'm going to go and prepare you a big breakfast. And if you're a good boy, I'll feed it to you."

"Hmm. That sounds sexy, Miss Parker," I said. "In a strictly business sense of the word."

"Is business sexy?" she said.

"Oh, Miss Parker—business is sex," I said.

If you think a sin, can it be just as good as doing it? Well, if it is, I was unfaithful to Emma while Miss Parker was feeding me my breakfast. She did that mummy thing of opening her mouth every time she wanted me to open my mouth and making yummy noises to encourage me to eat. And sometimes when bits dribbled out she—but we'd better not go into that here. Anyway, I suppose it must have been Oedipal. Oh, God—why do we have to have You and Freud?

Well, I did manage to persuade Miss Parker to buy a car, but I couldn't get her to buy an English car, because we couldn't find one, so we—I mean, she—bought a BMW. And then we bought a map and she located Duckworth Hall, which turned out to be not that far from Highgrove, but then I didn't know where that was either, until we looked it up on the map. They're both in Gloucestershire, which is where anybody who is anybody would like to live, if they could afford the property prices and a book of speeding season tickets for driving up and down to Town. Town is what the toffs call London, only it is usually pronounced "Tine" in Gloucestershire-speak.

Miss Parker's driving was exhilarating, because she was such a brilliant driver and she drove so fast. But I never once felt alarmed, sitting next to her, with Radio One blaring and Miss Parker singing along to all the complicated lyrics of the Hip Hop songs, and pointing things out to me as we whizzed along the bendy, high-hedged roads. She was telling me about the Romans, because a lot of them lived in Gloucestershire a very long time ago. Did you know that they invented germ warfare? Miss Parker did. They used to catapult infected bodies into the forts and cities they were besieging. They were bastards, Miss Parker said, although it was wrong to judge them by contemporary attitudes, she supposed.

And then we stopped at a country pub and she wheeled me in and got me a pint of real ale and a Ploughman's for lunch. She even played darts with some locals and beat them easily, with a nine-dart finish. I was beginning to think there wasn't anything Miss Parker couldn't do.

And then, when we were only a few miles from Duckworth Hall, she pulled into a lay-by and we started snogging. It all happened so naturally. I couldn't help myself. I think I was falling in love with her. And by the time we pulled into the long and winding driveway up to the Hall, I was besotted with her. It was hard to imagine how anyone could be more sotted in such a short space of time.

Bentley answered the door and seemed more surprised to see Miss Parker than me. I didn't even know he knew her.

"Miss Parker?" he said. He glanced down at me, in my wheelchair. "Sir Stephen?" And then back at Miss Parker. "But I thought Sir Julian said you were to remain in hospital for the rest of the week."

"There's been a change of plan," said Miss Parker. "Take Mr Duckworth up to his room. He needs rest. I must speak to Sir Julian. Where is he?"

"He is away, Miss Parker," said Bentley, taking over the handles of my wheelchair from her.

"Damn. When will he be back?" she said, going through to the hall ahead of us, leaving the old butler to push me in.

"Well, I could let him know you are here, Miss Parker. Perhaps, he will return," said Bentley.

"Then do so," said Miss Parker, carrying on up the hallway and turning left.

"Where are you going?" I called.

"I won't be far, darling—Bentley will see to you!" She disappeared round the corner.

"Where's she going?" I said.

"Going, sir?" said Bentley. "She didn't say, sir."

"I know she didn't say! But you must know where she went, Bentley."

"Oh no, sir, I couldn't possibly know that, I was here with you the whole time, sir."

He wheeled me to the foot of the stairs and helped me out.

"Don't we have an elevator?" I said. "Or one of those stair lift things?"

"I am afraid not, sir—Sir Julian likes to keep the Hall in its original condition. Oh, yes, Sir Julian is very particular. Bentley, he's very fond of saying, my home is an antique, if you look after it, it'll be worth a bomb some day."

He assisted me to the top of the master staircase and left me leaning against the balustrade, while he went back down, folded up the chair, and carried it up to me. I sat back in and he pushed me to my room.

"Bentley, how well do you know Miss Parker?" I asked, as he helped me onto the bed.

"I believe she works for Sir Julian, sir."

"Has she been here often?"

"Often, sir?"

"How many times has she been to Duckworth Hall?"

"How many times, sir?"

"For God's sake, Bentley—it's a simple enough question! How many times has Miss Parker been here—a dozen times? More?"

"Less, sir."

"Less than a dozen?"

"More or less, sir."

"Bentley—if you don't tell me—"

"I believe I heard the doorbell, sir." He drifted towards the door.

"Bentley! Come back here! Bentley!" I shouted. But I was wasting my breath, he was silently closing the door behind him.

* * *

There were always strange goings on at Duckworth Hall, of course, but that afternoon, strangely, nothing much happened. I was left—no, I was abandoned in my room—unable to raise myself off my bed. Not only that, no one was responding to my frequent tugs on the service bell sash. And then the room began to darken and I knew it must be after six in the evening, because around St Patrick's Day the days and nights are of equal length, it being near the vernal equinox. I tried to occupy myself by counting the shell mouldings on the ceiling, but, as I lay there, my thoughts kept returning to the lovely Miss Parker. I wondered why she hadn't been to see if I was all right, but I always expected her to come through the door at any moment. I hadn't given up on her. Up until then, all my thoughts and feelings had been a mixture of frustration—at being left helpless—and happiness, because I had met Miss Parker. But then when it grew dark I started to worry that something might have happened to her. I became desperate to see her and lapsed into listlessness and melancholy. None of this—my over-sensitive state of mind and growing dependence on Miss Parker, I mean—struck me as odd at the time. I didn't think I was sick or going mad, or anything like that, I just thought I was in love.

Not even when I discovered a remote control on my bedside table, realized it was for the TV across the room, switched it on, and saw pictures of a serious fire at a private clinic on the local evening news, did I think anything weird was going on. Even though I recognized the name of the hospital—Scrublands—as the very one Miss Parker and I had been staying in.

And then the Duck suddenly burst into the room and switched on the chandelier.

"Well, they've got her! It's all over! That's it!" he ranted, flinging his hands about in the air. "That's all my plans down the khazi!"

"Where's Miss Parker?" I said.

"It's Jemmons," said the Duck, wagging his finger in my face. "I said we should go and get him out, but, no, you were too busy chasing after Emma Gummer—now he's sold us all down the river. Well, we can't stay here—they'll be blowing this place up next. Come on, on your feet—we're out of here!"

"What about Miss Parker?" I said.

"Miss Parker? Miss Parker?" he said. "That's who I'm on about, you duffer! She's not Miss Parker—she's the Princess Mormagleea of Whatsit. I can never remember these foreign names."

"Miss Parker is a princess?"

"Yes—and she's taken quite a shine to you."

"Really? Miss Parker likes me?" I said.

"Likes you? She's in love, mate. She only asked me for your hand in marriage. But, like I said, all that's down the pan now. We've got to get out of here fast—tempus fugit, man!"

"But I can't move."

"Don't give me any excuses—come on—get off that bed!"

And the Duck grabbed my ankles and pulled me round, so that my toes were touching the floor. Then he put his arms around me like a dance partner and lifted me up.

"Come on—on your feet!" he quacked.

"You lead."

I was in no position to argue and, besides, I didn't want to, even though my side still felt too tender and painful for me to be walking around—let alone going dancing—but my compulsion to find Miss Parker was too strong.

"My wheelchair." I flung my hands out for it.

"No you don't," said the Duck, pulling me back. "If you put your arm around my neck, I'll walk you down to the machine."

"Machine?" I said, courageously setting one foot down in front of the other and wincing with the wave of pain this simple exercise sent down my left side. "Where are we—ah—going?"

"Are you on something? To get her back, of course—I've invested too much time and money in her to let them have her."

We continued to the door.

"Who?"

"Who?" He grabbed my chin and peered into my eyes. "Well, your pupils aren't dilated. Did she slip you something?"

"Who?"

"Who? Miss Park—Princess Mormagleea!"

He kicked the door open wider so there was enough room for us both to pass through.

"Um? I think she gave me a sedative," I said.

We shambled on down the corridor like a couple of drunks.

"That was no sedative, mate—that was love potion number nine! Can't get her out of your head, can you?"

"I'm very worried about her," I said. "Who did you say took her again?"

"Temporal Criminal Pursuit! Only it's a new lot. These mothers are into zero tolerance—if they can't catch you, they blow up your house. Property prices'll be going through the roof round here—literally, mate!"

"Miss Parker's in danger!" I cried.

"Well, of course, she's in bleeding danger—that's what I've been trying to tell you—we've got to go and get her out," said the Duck. "I hope whatever she put in your tea wears off soon—you're no use to me mooning over her. Mind the steps."

We came to the top of the stairs. I grabbed for the banister with both hands and the Duck steadied me down, one stair at a time.

"Where have they taken Miss Parker?" I said.

"Same place they send all category A felons—the Castle."

"Is it far?"

"Is it far? Nobody knows where it is! Don't you remember anything from last time?"

"I like Miss Parker," I said.

"Oh, shut up. What you need is a pot of hot black java. Sober you up."

We descended the stairs and he led me across the hall and down the same corridor Miss Parker had taken.

"This is the same way Miss Parker went," I said.

"Is it?" said the Duck. "We'll have to put up one of those blue heritage plaques—Princess Mormagleea passed this way, March the twenty-second, 2002."

I stopped dead in my tracks. "Twenty-second?" I said. "But it can't be!"

"What're you on about?"

"Did you say it was the twenty-second of March?"

"Did I? Well, I meant the nineteenth. I'm a time traveller—I never know what day it is—they're all the same to me, aren't they!"

"Oh," I said.

We carried on shuffling along.

"Wait!" I said, pulling him up again.

"What is it now? We've gotta split, man."

"There are no paintings on the walls and all the chairs in the corridors are gone. Also, there was no grandfather clock back there in the main hall, and I'm sure there used to be one. It stood on the eleventh and twelfth squares, if you count back from the front door," I said.

"Did it?" said the Duck, giving me a funny look. "What are you—the bloody Rain Man? Bentley removed it—everything worth taking has gone into storage in Bristol, in case this place goes up."

"Oh," I said.

"Come on—tempus fugit." He walked me a few more paces and leaned me against the wall, while he unlocked a door.

I looked back along the corridor.

"Hello," I said.

Two men in black leather suits and black motorcycle helmets, carrying what looked like oxygen tanks, or fire extinguishers on their backs, were standing in the main hall.

"Hey?" said the Duck, opening the door. He looked over his shoulder. "Crikey! Time plod!"

He grabbed me and slung me into the room. It was a library without any books.

"Where are all the books?" I said, looking up at the walls of empty shelves.

The Duck ignored me and hastily locked the door behind us.

"Give me a hand with the desk!" he cried, running past me to the bay window to put all his weight behind it.

"Quick—help me push it up against the door!"

I gazed out the window overlooking the rear of the house. I was looking at a helicopter standing in the darkening meadow on the far side of the terraced gardens. Suddenly, it blew up. It was like a cartoon explosion—it just jumped up in the air a few feet, flipped over and crashed back down on its rotors.

The Duck spun round. And we both watched in silence for a few seconds, as the wreckage belched out thick wreaths of orange flames and billowing black smoke.

"There was no bloody need for that," said the Duck.

"Was it insured?" I said.

"Of course it was insured—but not against attack from another dimension!"

We heard someone try the door handle and both looked round. There was some shuffling about and then hissing sounds, like gas escaping.

"There's someone trying to get in," I said.

"Plasma guns!" quacked the Duck.

He forgot about the desk and ran over to one of those sliding ladders librarians use for getting books down off high shelves. He clattered up the wooden rungs and fiddled with something in the back of the very top one. A whole section of the shelving, measuring about nine feet across, rotated round on a pivot, like a giant turnstile, revealing a hidden chamber.

"Well, don't just stand there, you idiot! Get in!"

At that moment, there was a loud whoosh and a huge tongue of flame licked under the door, scorching the parquet floor.

I walked through the gap in the wall.

"It's a garage," I said.

The Duck activated the secret switch again and rode on the ladder as the revolving shelf completed a one hundred and eighty degree turn.

There were power tools on hooks all around the walls, an inspection pit and hydraulic car lift, tool lockers, workbenches, oxy-acetylene gear— it was a fully equipped garage. An immaculately polished white Ford Cortina was perched on the platform, over the pit. I noticed a rubber button set into the floor and stepped on it.

"Are you doing it up?" I said.

"Doing it up? That's the machine. Don't you remember anything? Stone me—it's moving! You've pressed the door—" His voice tailed off.

I turned round to see why. The Duck was nowhere to be seen.

"Duck?" I called, looking round for him.

I was just wondering where he could have got to, when the whole section of the wall swung open again and a big whoosh of flame shot into the garage from the library.

"Give it up, Doctor Zee!" squawked a mocking voice, which sounded like it was being strained through an electric megaphone.

I looked up and saw the Duck swinging off the top of the ladder, narrowly avoiding the spout of flame by leaping over it. Stumbling to the car, I slid down into the inspection pit feet first—believe me, you don't feel the pain in these situations. I popped my head up and saw the Duck scampering towards me on all fours. He punched the rubber button. The whole wall was automatically set in motion again, but not before one of the time cops from the hall had charged in and given the place a sweeping burst with his flamethrower. He paused for a second or two to admire the scorch marks he had made and the burning plastic handles of the tools all around the walls. And then he turned his attention to the Duck, who was still lying on the floor, utterly helpless.

"Do not move, Doctor Zirconion! Or I will fry you alive!" his voice crackled, and now I could see he had a grilled box thing strapped across his mouth, through which he was speaking.

The Duck turned over on his back and put his hands behind his head in a submissive gesture, but I saw his heel move over the door button and cover it. I wanted to help him, but I couldn't think what to do.

"You got me," said the Duck.

I saw him spur the button with his heel and the door swung round and knocked the time cop off his feet. The Duck was up in a flash, putting the boot into his fallen enemy's groin. But there was another one at the top of the ladder.

"On the ladder!" I shouted.

The second time cop had raised his flamethrower, one-handed, and was preparing to fire. I could hear the gas being pumped into the nozzle. But the Duck kicked the button twice in quick succession and the cop was swung away, juggling with his flamethrower, which had been jerked from his grip and went off. We heard him screaming, on the other side, as the door slammed shut again.

"Well done, Duck!" I cheered, clapping my hands.

He stamped on the nozzle of the other time cop's flamethrower and gave him one last kick before dashing over to give me a hand up.

"You were a big bloody help," he said, a bit uncharitably, I thought.

"I'm injured," I said.

"Yeah, well, there were only two. And they were no match for me." He pressed a button on a hanging control box and lowered the car. "Get in, we haven't got much time—it won't be long before the rest suss out where we went."

I opened the passenger door and climbed in. The Duck ran round to the driver's side and jumped in next to me.

"I like the flash dashboard," I said.

"Flash? It's not flash—it's all functional." He twiddled some dials and switched on the ignition. The engine roared and row upon row of pulsing lights and electronic screens came up. "And complicated. Got to know what you're doing to drive one of these. She's slowed down your alpha waves, mate."

"It's him again," I said, pointing out the side window.

The guy the Duck had just beaten up was back on his feet and aiming his flamethrower at us. He fired and it burst into flames.

"Backfire!" quacked the Duck. "Very nasty."

Chapter 6

We surged forward and the room we were in seemed to wobble and become watery, then all the colours ran horizontally, just like different coloured wet paints running into one, and flowing away on either side of us, like a Damien Hirst painting. I watched it stream past the side window and turn into a muddy mess.

"That was really weird—" I started to say, turning back to the Duck. "What's that?" I said, pointing through the windscreen.

The Duck grinned. "That, mate, is the temporal vortex."

"It looks like we're going down a big red plughole," I said.

"We are now travelling down the Route 66 of history," said the Duck. "We're Easy Riders, man. I'm like that one Peter Fonda played—Captain America—and you're the other one."

"I'm the one with the cowboy hat," I said.

"No, not him—the other one—the one who got killed first by those rednecks," said the Duck.

"Can't I be the cowboy one?"

"No, you're like the other one—he wasn't right in the head," said the Duck.

And then he started singing "Born To Be Wild." I don't think he knew the proper words, but then neither do I, so I'm not sure.

"Is this the way Miss Parker went?" I said.

"No." He carried on singing.

"Which way did she go then?"

"Don't know." He sang on. Beating out what he thought was the backbeat on the steering wheel with his multi-ringed fingers.

"Where're we going?"

"To pick up Travis," he said. "He can be the cowboy."

"I don't like Travis," I said.

"Travis is cool," said the Duck.

"He stole my girlfriend and shot me," I said.

"Well, yeah, but don't make a big deal out of it, man—you've got Miss Parker now and you're getting better all the time. Look on the bright side."

"My side still hurts and Miss Parker's in prison," I said.

"Man, you are so negative. I think that aphrodisiac's wearing off— you're sounding like your old self."

We suddenly stopped and the same room, more or less, that we had just left a minute or two before materialized around us. One moment there was only red and black noise and then the walls and ceiling began to colour in. It looked just like some unseen artist was speed painting a perfectly detailed picture of the interior of the garage, starting and continuing in about a hundred places at once and completing the painting in a matter of seconds.

The next minute, we were out of the car and the Duck was performing the same trick with the rotating bookcase, and we were back in the library of Duckworth Hall, only it was March 1803, not March 2002. And there weren't any guys with flamethrowers charging about. The Duck patted his desk and gazed around the room.

"They'll trace all this back and destroy it on the day the builders finish building it," he said, "but at least I saved my books, preserved what really matters, these few realms of gold, safely stored, with the barbarians hammering at the gate."

"You never read them," I said.

"That's not the point—they cost me an arm and a leg—worth a lot of money at third millennium prices," he said.

"You could buy some more."

"Buy some more, buy some more—it took me weeks to buy this lot. What would you know about the art of collecting? You—whatsit."

"Philistine?"

"That's the word. Come on, let's get some grub and break the bad news to Travis," he sighed.

"What bad news?"

"He's Princess Mormagleea's personal bodyguard. I told him she'd be fine with me up in the third millennium—he'll go ape when he finds out she's been arrested by the TCP."

"He might challenge you to a duel," I said.

"Hey, that's a point. You tell him."

"Me?"

"Well, she's your fiancée," said the Duck. "It'll sound better coming from you. He respects you now. He says you're the bravest man he's ever had the honour to shoot."

"Fiancée?" I said.

"Yes, didn't I tell you? I said you'd marry her."

He headed out the door, I followed him, and we bumped straight into Bentley, who had just been about to knock.

"Bentley!" quacked the Duck. "Why are you always creeping around?"

"I'm sorry, Sir Julian, do excuse me, but I was just coming to see if you had returned, sir." He looked at me. "Good evening, Mr Duckworth."

"Hello, Bentley," I said. I tapped the Duck on the shoulder. "Hey, could we discuss what you just said?"

"No time right now, Stephen—Bentley will see to you." He hurried off down the corridor.

"Hang on!" I said.

"Don't worry, sir, I'll see you to your room," said the butler, taking my arm.

"Oh, no you don't," I said. "I'm not going back up there. Where's Miss Gummer?"

"Miss Gummer, sir?"

"Don't start all that," I said. "Listen, you just toddle off and do some butling, I'll find Miss Gummer myself. I'll be all right."

"Yes, of course, sir," said Bentley, letting go of my arm. "But you are bleeding rather, sir."

"Bleeding? Where?" I looked down at my chest—the bandage was blotted with blood. "Oh my God!" I immediately felt faint and fell back against the doorframe.

Bentley supported me at the elbow. "I think you should let me take a look at that, sir," he said.

* * *

I don't mind admitting, I was shocked when my gunshot wound started bleeding again. It must have happened when I was dodging flamethrowers. Bentley was great—he helped me back up to my room, had a look at it for me, and changed the dressing.

"I am not an expert in these matters, sir," he said. "But I think sir has been rather overdoing things. Such a serious wounding requires bed-rest, lots of bed-rest, sir."

"Are you sure you've plugged the holes, Bentley?" I checked my new bandage, to see if any more blood was blotting through. "I think I need a plumber."

"I believe we may safely say I have fixed the pipe, sir," he replied.

"Thanks, Bentley. How about something to eat and drink?"

"Certainly, sir."

"I'll just have a sandwich or something."

"Haven't been invented yet, I'm afraid, sir. I can bring you some bread and cold meat, but I can't put it between the bread."

"Thanks. I'll do that. And tell Miss Gummer I'd like to see her," I said.

"I am afraid that will not be possible, sir."

"Why not?"

He glided out.

"Why the hell not?" I called.

There was no answer.

* * *

There was no answer and he never returned. Nobody came. I waited. And waited. And wait—I felt like I was in that play by Samuel Beckett, with the laughs edited out. I think the love potion, or aphrodisiac, or Spanish fly, or whatever it was Nurse Parker injected me with in that private clinic, was wearing off, because I was thinking straighter. In fact, I was getting pretty damned annoyed and impatient with everybody, but since none of them were around, I took to thumping my pillow. The last thing I wanted to do was sleep. That blood loss had scared the hell out of me, but not enough to make me stay in bed. I got up slowly and painfully. There was something very odd going on. I was starting to remember things. Little anomalies. Like that thing with the dates—was it the nineteenth or the twenty-second? And if Nurse Parker was really a princess and De Quipp was her bodyguard—what country were they from—not France, that's for sure, because the Duck couldn't even remember the name of the place she was the princess of. And why were those Temporal Criminal Pursuit goons after her? She had to be a time fugitive. And then there was Travis himself, if he was supposed to be guarding Princess whatever-her-name-was's body, how come he was chasing round after Emma's? And hanging out with the Duck? Always dodgy company. And if the two of them were time travellers, why was the so-called Monsieur De Quipp masquerading as a Frenchman and playing out dangerous duels? And last, but definitely so not least, what was Julian Duckworth's part in it all? Past experience told me it would have to be a leading one—the starring role. It was time to look for some answers.

I decided to try the direct approach—I would go downstairs and confront everyone outright, since they all seemed to be in the same conspiracy. But I didn't even make the door, before I started getting stabbing pains in my chest. They doubled me up. I clutched at my bandage. To my horror, I felt something warm and sticky—my hand was plastered in blood! I staggered in reverse and fell back on the bed.

I was frantically pulling the service bell cord and shouting for help—I thought I was going to die—but still nobody came. And then I realized that by panicking I was making my heart pump faster and losing more blood, so I tried to remain calm and just lay there on my back, staring up at the ceiling. And it worked. I managed to slow up my breathing and get my heart-rate right down.

Now, two things happened. First I stopped bleeding, but also, and more improbably, the pain suddenly went away. I don't mean it eased off or dropped to a bearable level, I mean, it just stopped. Abruptly. It was odd. Odd enough to arouse my suspicion. You have to remember my brain was in full conspiracy alert mode. And have you ever noticed how easy it is to make any given set of facts or statistics fit your personal theory about something, no matter how outrageous or bizarre it all sounds? This is called market research. For example, people think of tulips because they feel guilty about not washing their cars on Sunday mornings, because tulips have waxy petals and people associate this and their scent with car wax. Therefore, stick a tulip on your tin of car wax and your sales will double. But, having said all that, I was dealing with a weird and convoluted thing—the Duck's mind—so logic didn't apply, even irrational advertising logic.

What if, I thought, the Duck was behind everything? If he were in league with Miss Parker and De Quipp, would he really have allowed De Quipp to fire a real bullet at me, his son? Yes, he would! But if he wanted me dead, all he had to do was invite me up onto the roof of Duckworth Hall and push me off. Besides, I didn't really buy that—the Duck was my father, after all is said and done, he would never let me be killed. Or why would he have bothered to make me immortal? Blood is thicker than water and all that. Therefore, I reasoned, he must have tried to control the duel, but failed when the pistols got mixed up. But what if that had been a double bluff, simply to fool me into thinking I had been shot? But why? It didn't make sense. But if my training in advertising had taught me anything it was that things did not have to make sense. If the public always acted sensibly big business would be small business. It was time for a little good old-fashioned, new and improved, authentic, just-like-mom-used-to-bake-it irrationality.

Tentatively at first, and then with feverish abandon, I unwound my blood-soaked dressings. Soon I had coils of soiled bandages all over my bed like a vampire's party streamers and I was down to the last fat gory wad, sticking to my chest. I peeled it off. And gasped.

Whatever I had, it wasn't a wound. Whatever I was looking at, it wasn't normal medical practice. It was more like malpractice. I was looking at a small plastic sachet, with a blood-matted nozzle attached to the end, connected to a plastic tube, taped to my side and running up under my armpit to my shoulder and disappearing under the adjoining bandage around my arm. I had definitely been duped. But, if I wasn't shot, what the hell was wrong with me? I started unwinding the bandage on my arm, wondering what I would find next. As the tail of the bandage slid from my arm, I gulped.

Something small, complicated, and electronic was not only taped to my arm, but actually embedded in the flesh! It looked like a mechanical leech. My instinct was to pull it off me, but I was too terrified to touch it. I could see blood inside the "back" of the thing and wiring connected to diodes, like little antennae. A hypodermic probe protruded from it, going into my artery, like a drip, but there was also a long golden filament running through it. I knew this was no ordinary drip, because drips feed plasma or drugs or saline or nice things into the body to do something good and this thing was clearly pumping blood out, as well as fulfilling some other devious function I could not yet fathom. Which is not good. Notice I never said fiendish. Alliteration was never my strong point.

I sat up and reached for my bedside candle to take a closer look. Sharp spasms of pain shot through the left side of my torso. Blood began dribbling from the nozzle in the end of the sachet. I placed the candlestick holder back on the bedside table and I lay back down. The pain stopped and the blood flow reduced to a drip. I sat up again—the pain came back and the blood spluttered out once more. I lay back down. Both stopped. I sat back up—they started again. I lay back down. They stopped. I was beginning to get it. I wrenched the thing off my arm and hurled it across the room. Alarming amounts of blood spurted from my puncture wound. I quickly wrapped the bandage back around it and pulled the knot tight with my right hand and teeth.

There was no other explanation for it, my father was repressing a subconscious desire to kill me by transferring his loathing for me into imaginary bullets and projecting them from a duelling pistol, which he had placed in the hands of the stigmata of a love rival from a joke, who was holed up in a bell tower in Westphalia, because he saw himself as a failure. I know there are a few flaws in this theory, but I'm still working on the metaphors with my analyst.

That was it for me. That moment was the end. The Duck and I were finished, as far as I was concerned. I was going to find Emma, get the book of twentieth century sporting achievements and records the Duck had promised me as a wedding present, find the Duck, make him take me to the 1920s, tell him to get lost and never have anything to do with him or time machines ever again. I couldn't begin to think what was going on or what all the lies and treachery meant. I didn't want to know—I just wanted out.

I found a clean shirt and frock coat in the closet, put them on, and went to look for Emma. I decided not to tell anyone I knew about my phoney wound, because it would give me the element of surprise. But, then again, maybe I was just in denial.

* * *

I scoured that house. It was eerie—they were all gone, vanished into the night. Candles were burning in most of the halls and rooms, there was evidence on the dining table that several people had eaten a meal that evening, the doors were all locked, the windows all closed, there were no signs of a struggle—just stillness and silence, upstairs and downstairs and in my lady's chamber. Well, I did find what I assumed to be Emma's chamber, because I recognized some of the clothes she had worn hanging in one of the wardrobes. I must have searched Duckworth Hall high and low for the best part of an hour. It was such a vast place I didn't get to every corner, every nook and cranny, but if there was anyone around, I never saw him. And, of course, I didn't go up into the attic—I already knew what was up there. I sat down on the master staircase, eating a piece of cheese and a carrot, and drinking champagne from the bottle, racking my brains to think where else I could look. There just wasn't anywhere left—except the—I threw down my carrot and descended the rest of the stairs two at a time, skidded on the black and white tiled hall floor, as I turned the right hander into the corridor, and sprinted up to the library door. It was locked. Why the hell didn't I think of it before? I didn't bother trying to force it, the thing was made of solid oak, so I dashed back along the passage to the hall, down the rear corridor, through the salon, and out through the back door to run round to the window.

The library was in darkness. I looked about me on the ground for something heavy, found a loose cobblestone and broke in. I was soon on the top of that ladder, feeling about in the back of the shelf for some sort of lever to operate the turnstile mechanism. It didn't take me long to find it. It felt like a trigger and when I pulled it the whole section of the shelving swung round and I was in the Duck's secret garage. But there was no sign of the Duck or the white Ford Cortina. I switched on the electric lights and looked around for any clues to his whereabouts. There weren't any, so I was naturally very disappointed and frustrated. And that is why I found a spray can and a hammer and trashed the place. I vandalized every single tool and surface in that workshop. I totalled it. Now, I know that was a bit juvenile of me, but it felt good—God, it felt good. And I thought I had just cause. And, anyway, it got my adrenalin pumped up—pumped enough to go and get a cutlass I'd seen hanging on a wall in the dining room and a set of master keys from the key cupboard in the cellar, and head for the attic.

You see, during those mad ten minutes in my father's garage, expressing my insecurities, it had occurred to me that if my dear schizophrenic father was lying to me through his teeth about everything else, why would he be telling me the truth about Jemmons and the squid? Ergo, that was the real Roger Jemmons up there!

And, boy, I so did not want to go back up there. You know in those horror movies when the victim goes into the one place in the haunted house nobody in their right mind would go, and you wish he would just run out the front door like any normal human being, well, it felt a bit like that. I kept telling myself to run away, run away, but something just compelled me to keep going up those dark, winding stairs, with my candle flame fluttering with every puff of draught, step after step, up and up. Actually, I think I wanted to sever the tentacles of that squid because they represented the various influences and holds my father had over my life. I hadn't yet learnt how to express my feelings for my father. I still needed to verbalize them.

Anyway, I eventually unlocked the door, switched on the lights and there was no squid in the tank—just poor old Jemmons. And was he glad to see me! If that's a replicant, I thought, I'd like to see how animated the real one could get. As soon as he'd blinked and got his eyes used to the light and saw me, he was rocking up and down, stamping his feet, opening and closing his eyes, nodding his head. I walked over to the glass—my spine squirming like an eel—and mouthed the words:

"Roger? Is that you?"

He nodded vigorously.

"But how can I be sure?" I said.

He twisted his wrist round and flicked two fingers in the shape of a "V" at me.

"Yeah, all right, mate—there's no need to be offensive, I am the rescuer here."

I looked for a way up to the top of the tank. It was just a pro-size aquarium filled with luminous green water. Like in one of those old freak shows, Jemmons was submerged and chained to the bars of a metal box, which he was sitting on. His ankles were shackled, too, and he was wearing a simple, but adapted, scuba mask, with two plastic pipes coming off the mouthpiece, trailing up to the top and out over the rear of the tank.

Roll up, roll up—come and see The Tentacled Man, I smiled to myself.

I walked round the back to see where they went and found them attached to an air pump—they looked like feed and return lines. But there was a third pipe coming off a large plastic drum, also with a pump fitted to it. I opened the lid and peered in. It was full of water with bits floating in it, but it smelt organic—some sort of foul-smelling soup, I guessed. I was just going to go back to the front of the tank, when I noticed the bowling alley stretching away into the unlit depths of the attic. So, the Duck hadn't been lying about everything, I thought. I wandered onto the lanes and looked around for a light switch. I could see bowling balls lined up on the auto-returns and four sets of pins in the distance, at the end of each lane—and then I spotted the fridge against the far wall. I went over and helped myself to a cold beer and took it back to the front of the tank with me. Jemmons saw the bottle in my hand and pulled a face.

"All right, I'm thinking," I mouthed.

The tank was about fifteen feet high and there was no obvious way up—no ladder or platform to climb, just the sheer four sides of the glass. I gave Jemmons a little wave and walked round it again, looking for an answer. It had me foxed. I took a swig of my beer. And then I had an idea. I sauntered back to Jemmons and tried to mime what I wanted him to do. I clamped my teeth together and pointed at him. He nodded but looked uncertain. Then I pointed at myself, put my bottle on the floor, and acted out me climbing up the side of the tank. He looked puzzled. I pointed at him and made a gesture to indicate his mask and how I wanted him to clamp it tightly in his teeth. He got the message. His eyes widened in alarm and he began shaking his head frantically. I waved my hands to calm him down.

"Don't worry," I mouthed. "I'll soon have you out of there."

I picked up my bottle and took a couple of gulps. Jemmons was still rocking on his box and shaking his head at me. I put my bottle down, took off my frock coat, and rolled up my sleeves, gazing up at the fifteen-foot glass wall and nodding to myself. No problem, I thought. Jemmons had somehow rocked himself closer to the glass and was kicking it. I waved. He shook his head and glared at me. I picked up my beer and pointed at it.

"I bet you could use one of these," I mouthed. I clamped my teeth at him. "Hold on tight," I said.

And then I strolled round to the back of the tank, spat on my hands, grabbed the breathing tubes, and tried to climb up the side of the glass. I got about four feet and fell back down on my ass. Just as I was about to get up and try again, both ends of the tubes wriggled over the top of the tank and fell on me, splashing me with water. I peered through the glass. Jemmons was sitting on his box with his back to me shaking his head and rocking about violently, a mega stream of bubbles flowing from his head.

"Oh shit!"

I looked around me—dashed onto the bowling lane, grabbed two balls and ran round to the front of the tank. Jemmons saw the bowling balls, realized what I was going to do, and tried to duck. I wound the first ball up and threw it with some force at the tank. It bounced off and hit me in the shin, skittling me over. I scrambled to my feet. Jemmons was swaying from side to side, his cheeks puffed out, trying to hold on to his last lungfuls of air. I ran at the tank and bashed it with the bowling ball. I wasn't making any impression on it. It wasn't even marked.

"It's toughened! They used toughened glass! What's the matter with these people—don't they know we may have to break these things in an emergency? Some people, they just go around making problems for the rest of us!"

Jemmons was dying. I snapped out of the terminal rant I was in and redoubled my efforts. I used both hands this time and swung the bowling ball from above my head. The shock waves shuddered up my arms, but the dumb glass didn't break. Jemmons was swaying more slowly and there were fewer bubbles coming from his mouth and his eyes were tightly shut. I was desperate. I started running a few more feet back each time and charging at the glass, banging on it with all my might with my bowling ball. I was shouting a lot. I think I was cursing the people who make aquaria again, but I might have moved on to glass blowers. I don't remember. I had hit my fatal panic alert button. I was probably just making noises like those weird little Michael Jackson cries he puts in his songs, near the end.

Suddenly, there was a sharp splitting sound. I stood back—my mouth wide open. A white tarantula of cracks had appeared in the glass right where I had been beating it. Jemmons's eyes opened and we looked at each other in expectation. There was another, louder, splitting noise—I backed away—a long lightning bolt of a crack shot out from the small spidery one and stopped abruptly a few feet from the top right corner of the tank. There was a slight pause. I instinctively scampered over by the sidewall. And then the whole front of the tank just exploded and spewed the fifteen by fifteen sheet across the room in a shower of water and glass. I closed my eyes and heard two thuds against the wall. When I opened my eyes, two "daggers" of glass were sticking in the wall either side of my head. I felt like a knife-thrower's assistant.

"And for my next trick," I mumbled.

The water emptied in a matter of seconds and was washing around my knees, and splashing up the walls, but most of it just frothed and flowed straight out the door and ran down the stone staircase in a torrent.

As soon as the water level began dropping, I waded across to the tank and lifted Jemmons's head up. Water came out of his mouth and he gulped in air.

"Are you okay, Rog?" I said.

"Kill the Duck," he gasped.

"Kill the Duck—kill the Duck," I sang, as I checked out the padlocks on his ankles and wrists. "I'll have to saw these off. Wait here while I go and get a hacksaw. Kill the Duck."

"Come back," he said. "Might come back."

"Who?" I said. "The Duck? He's long gone, mate."

"No," said Jemmons. "It."

"Oh, that," I said. "Yeah, right. I'll run. Kill the Duck."

I set off for the garage where I remembered seeing, and for some reason not destroying, a hacksaw. I was just on my way back up with it, when I noticed the bottle of Ruinart 1730 and the half-eaten carrot and cheese I'd left on the main staircase were gone.

"Kill the Duck—kill the Duck," I muttered to myself, and continued on up the stairs.

There was a lot of water still washing around the far end of the upper corridor of the west wing. I splashed through it and was just turning to go up the steps when I ran into Bentley, carrying a silver tray with my champagne and leftover supper balanced on it.

"Bentley!" I exclaimed. "You asshole!"

"Good evening, sir," he said. "We appear to have a leak, sir. There has been a seepage into the blue drawing room. I fear some paintings may have been damaged."

"You'll be damaged and leaking in a minute—get up those stairs—I've got a job for you!"

"Yes, sir," he replied. "Will sir be dining in this evening? The rest of Sir Julian's party have already eaten and—"

"—Oh, shut up," I said, giving him a shove up the steps.

The old butler walked ahead of me at a sedate pace, nose in the air, his tray rock steady.

"Look what I found creeping around!" I called to Jemmons, as we walked into the wrecked attic. "Good old Bentley!"

"Good grief, sir!" exclaimed Bentley.

"Hello, Bentley," said Jemmons.

"He's a snake," I said.

"Yes, you are a snake, Bentley?" said Jemmons.

"Mr Jemmons, sir—what in heaven's name has happened?" said Bentley.

"You should get an Oscar," I said, giving the treacherous butler an elbow in the rib. "Here, take this and make yourself useful."

"Yes, of course, sir," he said. He put down his tray and I handed him the hacksaw. He took it over to Jemmons, knelt down in a puddle, and began sawing at the ankle chain.

"Bentley here knows more than he's letting on," I said.

"Bentley," said Jemmons. "Do you know more than you're letting on?"

"If you say so, sir," said Bentley.

"Yeah, and I'd be careful what you say with him around—he's hand in glove with my father," I said. I went over and got the champagne and took it back to Jemmons to hold it to his lips while he swigged. "Listen to this," I winked to Jemmons. "Hey, Bentley," I said, "where's Miss Gummer?"

"Miss Gummer, sir?" said Bentley.

"You see," I nodded. "He knows, but he's not saying."

"She's on her way to Bath to stay with the Mason-Wrights. I believe Miss Emily and her father are taking the waters, sir," added Bentley.

"He's just saying that," I said to Jemmons. And then to Bentley, "How would you know?"

"Because I drove her to the local coaching house in the phaeton this morning, sir," replied Bentley, continuing to saw through the chain.

"You see," I said to Jemmons, "he's making it up."

Bentley's arm jerked as the saw severed the last half millimetre of link.

"I think you should be able to prise that open now, sir," he said. He set to work on the wrist chain.

Jemmons forced his ankles apart. I got down and grabbed the chain and pulled. The link bent open and Jemmons's legs were free. Jemmons twirled his feet around.

"Feel good?" I said.

He nodded. "Good."

"Hurry up with his wrists, Bentley," I said. "We're wasting time here."

"I'm going as fast as I can, Mr Duckworth," said the butler. "Are you taking Mr Jemmons somewhere, sir?"

"Like I'd tell you," I said. I smiled at Jemmons and shook my head. He grinned back.

"Mr Duckworth, sir—might I have a word?" said Bentley, carrying on with his hacksawing.

"What?" I said.

"In your ear, sir," said Bentley, looking at me over his shoulder and rolling his eyes towards Jemmons.

I crouched down next to him, so that our heads were level. "What is it?"

"You do know that this Mr Jemmons is a replicant, sir?" he whispered.

I laughed. "Nice try, Bentley," I said. "Oh, you're good."

Bentley shrugged and went on with his work. I looked up at Jemmons, who was staring off into space. True, Roger Jemmons was not the smartest man who ever drove a time machine down the temporal vortex, but I was going to need his help, if I was ever to find Emma again and get even with the Duck.

I stood up and walked around to Jemmons's other side, to have a quiet word in his ear.

"Don't trust Bentley. Is your machine here?" I said.

Roger kept looking straight ahead and nodded.

"Good. We're going to need it, mate—the Duck's away—and it's only a matter of time before Temporal Criminal Pursuit get here." I patted his shoulder. "How's that chain coming, Bentley?"

"Nearly through, sir," said Bentley.

Suddenly Jemmons let out a piercing peacock cry—it freaked the hell out of me. Bentley nearly jumped out of his skin and dropped the hacksaw.

"Good grief, sir," said Bentley. "What was that?"

I stooped down in front of Jemmons and looked into his staring eyes. "Don't worry, mate—your ordeal's nearly over," I said, patting him on the knee. I looked over at Bentley, who, without taking his eyes off Jemmons, was feeling around on the floor for the saw. "You see this man," I said to Bentley, "he's been through hell. My father put him in that tank with a bloody great giant squid—what you just heard was delayed shock. He's traumatized. Now, hurry up. I'm getting him out of here."

"Yes, sir," said Bentley, hurriedly finding his cut on the chain and sawing for all he was worth.

Jemmons was soon freed and stood up. I embraced him and patted his back. He embraced me back.

"We'll get through this together, mate," I said. "If anyone had put me in there with that thing I'd need counselling. Hang in there."

I let go and tried to step back, but Jemmons kept hold of me. I gave him another hug and tried to pull away again. He still wouldn't let me go.

"Yeah, all right, mate—don't overdo it," I said, shoving him off.

Jemmons belched and looked around him.

Bentley, I noticed out of the corner of my eye, was edging away from us.

"Where do you think you're going?" I said.

"The tray, sir." He picked up his tray and put the hacksaw on it.

"Don't go sneaking off," I said. I turned back to talk to Jemmons, but he was gone—he was looking around over by the wall, kicking at something with his foot. "We should split, Rog," I said. "Tempus fugit, mate."

Jemmons bent down and picked something up. He had found the cutlass.

"Yeah, bring that—we might need it," I said. I turned round and wagged a warning finger in Bentley's face. "And you are going to show us where we can find some guns," I said.

Bentley whipped the hacksaw off his tray and charged at me with it.

"Aunt bloody—!" I exclaimed, dodging to my left.

Bentley pushed me out of the way. I heard a loud CLANG, swiftly followed by an even louder KERRANG! I kept my head down and wheeled away, screwing my neck round at the same time to see what all the noise was about. Jemmons was hacking at Bentley with the cutlass and Bentley was fending him off with his tray and hacksaw like a gladiator.

"Hey, Rog?" I shouted. "What the hell are you doing?"

Jemmons whacked Bentley out of the way and lunged at me. I ran behind Bentley.

"It's not Mr Jemmons, sir," said Bentley. "It's a replicant—and it's unstable!"

"Unstable? He's bloody lethal!"

Bentley's trusty silver tray took another scything blow, and he parried two more vicious sword thrusts with his hacksaw.

"Try and hold him off," I said. "I'll find something."

"I'll do my best, sir. Please hurry, sir."

I patted Bentley's shoulder and ran off down the side of the aquarium to find something to stop the replicant with. I could still hear the CLANGS and cries of the combatants as I hunted about. I wanted something long and heavy, but I couldn't see anything that fitted the bill.

I didn't know how much longer Bentley's brave rearguard action would last, so I settled for two bowling pins. I dashed off down the lane and grabbed them and was just turning round to go back when I saw Bentley running along the other end of the lanes, chased by the sword waving Jemmons, in silhouette.

"Bentley! Down here!" I cried.

Bentley dropped his shoulder and swerved to his right to come down the far lane and cut back towards me. The replicant was slow to react, but then turned like a machine, looked round, saw us, and charged.

I lobbed one of my pins at him. It seemed to hit his shoulder and glance off, clunking, skidding and spinning up the wooden lane and smacking into the back of the tank. The replicant was momentarily halted but then let out another terrifying peacock scream and came on. I threw my second one at him and it struck him full in the chest, and bounced off. And then he was on me and somehow I got my arms out and we were hand to hand, only he still had the cutlass and was trying to wrench his hand away from mine to slash at me with it. The real Jemmons was a big man, a burly Plymothian matelot, and this thing possessed all his strength and some. I fell back on the lane under the weight of his onslaught, still desperately trying to hold him off. But I knew it was only a matter of seconds before he overpowered me and ran me through with that cutlass. I wanted to scream but I couldn't afford the energy. I just held him there with every ounce of strength I had left.

Suddenly, there was a loud hollow crack, like a batsman hitting a boundary—the force left Jemmons's arms, the cutlass clattered to the floor, his elbows buckled and he slumped onto my chest. I peered round his shoulder and saw Bentley standing over us, holding aloft a bowling pin with both hands, ready to deliver another blow.

"Are you all right, sir?"

"Kill the Duck," I gasped, and passed out.

Chapter 7

Okay, so I got it wrong. The Duck didn't always lie and Bentley was a pretty good guy after all. But that still left me plenty to bitch about.

Bentley helped me to my feet and we locked the thing in the attic.

"Why did the Duck lie to me about my duelling wound?" I said, as we made our way downstairs.

"He never said, sir," replied Bentley.

And I believed him. When a man who has just saved your life tells you something you tend to believe him. Unless, of course, he was the one who was trying to kill you. But, then, you might still, because he had the chance and he didn't, so you think maybe he might just be the one person you really can believe. Have you noticed how everything is true and everything is faintly ridiculous, when you think about it? When you really think about it.

"But you were in on the bit about my joke-shop wound," I said.

"Sir Julian did tell me about the arterial catheter, yes, sir."

"So that's what it was. I could have bled to death."

"It was my responsibility to see that you did not, sir," said Bentley.

"Thanks for that, Bentley. But I wish you'd told me."

"Yes, I'm sorry, sir. I was following your father's strict instructions."

"Bentley, you must never let my father make you do things you know to be wrong. It's no excuse to say: oh, he made me do it. Or, oh, I knew it was wrong, but he told me it would be all right. Those are the morals of the playground, Bentley."

"Yes, sir. Presumably, that is why you tried to switch the duelling pistols when your father asked you to cheat, sir?"

"Yes—that was different—my life was on the line! I had no choice!"

"Yes, I see the difference, sir."

"Good."

"You mean one may pick'n'mix one's morals, sir?"

"Yes, Bentley—that's exactly how it works. And don't get caught."

* * *

We reached the main hall. I looked over at the long case clock.

"Time's running out, Bentley. You know there isn't much point in lying anymore," I said. "So, why don't you tell me everything you know? And maybe if we pool it with what I know, we might be able to make some sense out of all this."

"What would you like to know, sir?" said Bentley.

"I would like to know who Travis De Quipp really is."

"Shall we go along to my private apartment, sir? I'll prepare some supper," he said.

"I'm not hungry, thanks, Bentley, but I could use some strong black coffee."

"This way, sir."

We walked down the rear corridor and up a flight of back stairs to a mezzanine landing, where Bentley unlocked a little door and ushered me in.

The butler's quarters were modest and comfortable, but contained an office with an impressive desk—underlining his importance in the day-to-day running of the house—as well as a sitting room, bedroom and kitchen-diner. Bentley showed me through and sat me down at his small dining table, while he put the kettle on the stove.

"De Quipp is not a Frenchman," he said, as he hand-ground the coffee. "I believe him to be travelling incognito, sir."

"He's a time traveller?"

"Yes," nodded Bentley. "Though I am not sure whether he is from the past or the future."

"Or maybe the present," I said.

"Well, yes. However, what I do know is that he never sleeps."

"Never sleeps?"

"He was allocated a room, but he has never used it, sir," said Bentley. "And there is something else that strikes me as very odd about him, sir—he never eats."

"He never eats? Are you sure, Bentley?"

"Quite sure, sir. At mealtimes he pretends to eat, but—and this is rather disgusting, sir—he spits it out onto the floor."

"That is odd. I mean, I used to do it all the time at prep school—especially on cabbage days—but it's definitely odd for a guy his age. What's his connection with my father? I mean, how did he get here?" I said.

"Ah, now that I do know, sir. He arrived here shortly before you in Mr Jemmons's time machine."

"In Jemmons's machine? So he was with Jemmons when Jemmons was arrested and imprisoned in the Castle. He must have escaped," I said, half-thinking aloud.

"Yes, sir, I think that's what happened, because he and Sir Julian have gone to pick up Monsieur De Quipp's vehicle, which I believe he was forced to abandon."

"So that's it!" I smiled. "The Duck's not bothered about rescuing Jemmons—all he's interested in is De Quipp's time machine. I bet you it's got advanced technology."

"I have no knowledge of that, sir." He mashed the coffee beans and poured boiling water over them.

"So where does the Princess fit in?" I said.

"The Princess, sir?" said Bentley, filtering the coffee. The fumes from which were so overpowering, I fancied I caught a whiff of the plantation owner's cigar in there.

"You've never met the Princess? You didn't know Miss Parker was really a princess?"

Bentley shrugged. "That is certainly news to me, sir." He poured a cup of the thick, black, steaming coffee and handed it to me.

"Does this stuff come with a Government Health Warning?" I said. "Parker must be an alias. De Quipp's her bodyguard."

"You must be mistaken, sir—Monsieur De Quipp arrived alone," said Bentley, joining me at the table.

"Are you absolutely sure about that?" I said.

"Absolutely, sir."

I looked at him through my steaming coffee. "Hm. Now that is interesting," I said. "Anyway, what about Jemmons's machine—know where that is?"

"I think so, sir," said Bentley. "But—"

"Good, I'll be needing it," I said briskly. "But first you are going to have to drive me to Bath—I want to see Miss Gummer and I have to speak to Mr Mason-Wright—he's the only one who knows where the Castle is. Can we drink this and get started?"

"Tonight, sir? I am afraid that will not be possible, sir."

"Why?"

"There is no moon—the horses would not be able to find their way. Which is why there are no overnight coaches, sir," he said.

"I was forgetting all that. Well, first thing then," I said. "How long will it take?"

"Only a day or two, sir."

"A day or two?" I exclaimed, spurting out a mouthful of coffee. "But it's only down the road!"

"What road would that be, sir?"

* * *

Actually it took us thirteen hours to travel just fifty miles, first by an open trap and horses to the nearest coaching station, then overland by mail coach to Bath. I say overland because that is what it felt like, despite the fact that we were—I was assured by Bentley—riding on the main highway to the Westcountry. The "road," which was little more than a ploughed track, took us into Bristol, by which time my ass felt as numb as a punch bag, and then out of town on the southern route to Bath itself. We arrived at the house the Mason-Wrights were renting in the famous Royal Crescent—which was only about thirty years old at that time—at around seven in the evening, having been dropped off in the aptly named Julian Road. Yes, I wondered that, too. And, no, it wasn't. I think it was named after Julius Caesar because it's all neo-classical in Bath.

A maid answered the door.

Her eyes flashed to me and then back to Bentley.

"Why, Mr Bentley, sir," she said. "You're unexpected."

"Just tell Mr Mason-Wright and his daughter Sir Stephen Duckworth is here," I said, before Bentley got a chance to explain. I was keen to get inside and find something soft and motionless to park my butt on.

She curtsied to me and opened the door wide. "Do come in, sir. I'll go and announce you to Mr Mason-Wright and Mistress Emily."

Bentley and I stepped in and waited, while the maid closed the door behind us and hurried off down a passage, branching off from the reception hall. We removed our hats and gloves.

"You did know I'm a baronet, Bentley?" I said.

"No, I did not, sir. Well done, sir."

"Thank you, Bentley. My father bought the title for me. Might as well use it now that we're here. These things impress people. Especially in Bath, if Jane Austen's anything to go by. Personally, I couldn't care less about such things," I said. "I'm not a snob, Bentley."

"No, sir."

I caught myself in the hall mirror and adjusted my cravat. I cut quite a dashing figure in my elegant Georgian clothing, consisting skin-tight cream breeches, riding boots, snug bottle green frock coat, white Byronic shirt, and fashionable matching neck scarf thingy.

"However, one has to keep up appearances," I said.

"Allow me, sir."

I allowed Bentley to straighten and tighten my cravat for me.

"That—that feels a little too tight, Bent-ley," I said, reaching up to loosen it.

"Really, sir," said Bentley, slapping my hand away and pulling the necktie even tighter.

"Bent-ley-let-go-of-me-you're-chok-ing—"

Bentley swung me around and smashed my back against the mirror—which cracked.

"I believe that's seven years' bad luck, sir," said Bentley, only now there was a look of repugnance in his eyes and a sneering tone in his usually subservient voice. He wrenched me off the wall with tremendous force and flung me down on my knees.

"You're-not-Bent-ley," I gasped.

I heard the sound of boots pounding into the hall behind me.

Bentley addressed them over my head, "This is his *son*," he said, pronouncing the word like an oath.

I felt two pairs of hands grip my arms from behind. I tried to twist my head round to see who they belonged to, but Bentley jerked my neck and made me face the front—though I did catch sight of two redcoated soldiers in the broken mirror.

Although Bentley was looking into my eyes, he wasn't talking to me, he was talking about me, "He knows nothing. Zirconion keeps him in the dark," he said. "Put him in the cellar with the others."

"What am I—a mushroom?" I said.

The two redcoats pulled me to my feet.

Bentley, or whoever he really was, held up a hand for them to wait, before they dragged me off. He looked away to the side to throw me off guard, and then slyly wound his arm back and punched me hard in the solar plexus. I was totally not expecting it. I doubled up. All the air rushed out of me and I was left gulping for breath.

"You," said Bentley, with great venom and hatred, "are an abomination before God!"

Now I knew who he really was—he was an agent for Corrective Measures, a tyrannical government agency operating out of the fourth millennium, responsible for overseeing the purity and godliness of the human race. Sort of like a cross between television evangelists and the CIA, only honest. Oh, and this lot didn't ask for money. Or give you any, as the case may be.

The redcoats marched me backwards up the hall.

"You cliché!" I yelled, craning my neck round to see where they were taking me.

And then something very peculiar happened—we passed through a time portal. The Duck had told me about these contraptions once, though I hadn't been paying much attention at the time. However, if my memory serves me well, the best way to describe them is: they're like short time corridors, sort of pathways bridging relatively brief periods of time. You walk into one end and it's like stepping through a vertical wall of flat calm water, and then you find yourself in a mini temporal vortex—you can actually see the other end—then you're through and out the other side, and into another time zone.

Apparently, Corrective Measures have thousands of the things spread around the world, in various towns and cities. Think of them as kind of police stations or holding tanks for time criminals. The one I was in was probably connected to several other locations they had under surveillance, and may even have been set up solely for the ongoing Zirconion case. My father, whose real name was Doctor Zebulon Zirconion, must have had a Department of Corrective Measures file on him the size of the Texas School Book Depository. I don't know why I thought of that. Kill the Duck.

But from a Corrective Measures point of view, sexual partners meant "damned offspring" and all the Duck's kids, I guess, had to be rounded up, sooner or later, because the demographics and purity of the future was being messed up by his philandering. Well, it was all very complicated. Actually, I was the finest fruit of his loins, ever, because he had made me in his own image, so to speak, and immortalized my gene string. As he was fond of telling me—I was going to live forever, just as long as nobody killed me in the meantime. I should add that sex in the fourth millennium had been reduced to gene matching and *in vitro* insemination, even within marriage there was no actual, er, physical fulfilment. As far as Corrective Measures were concerned, I was a vile mutant—and my father something worse. I, at least, agreed with them on that.

Anyway, I had walked straight into a typical Corrective Measures trap. And found myself being spun round and marched on the double down a wrought iron staircase to an ill-lit basement. Two black-uniformed guards were sitting at a table set against the wall outside a heavily padlocked door. They stood up as soon as they heard me being brought down.

"More genetic waste," said one of my redcoat escorts.

One of the modern-looking guards took out a set of keys and went to get the lock. I noticed a newspaper open at the racing page on the table. My heart skipped a beat when I caught the name "DETTORI" in a headline.

"Get in there, mutant!" he said, swinging the door open. The other guard grabbed my arm and threw me into the gloomy cell.

The door slammed behind me and I heard the key turn in the lock. I kicked it in that way new prisoners do.

"You'll be hearing from my mother's gynaecologist!" I shouted. "I'll have you know my foetus was passed A1 by the Royal College of Gynaecology!"

"I doubt that," said a familiar female voice.

"Emma?" I exclaimed, spinning round.

Her pale face appeared from the darkness and was joined on either side by two more friendly ones from my past—Sydney Mason-Wright and his delightful teenaged daughter, Emily. They looked like one of those chiaroscuro portraits by Rembrandt. There was just enough light coming from around the door to make out their pale faces.

"Tree! Emily!" I cried, rushing to embrace all three of them at once.

I kissed Emily on the cheek, then Emma on the cheek and then shook Tree's hand. We called Sydney "Tree" because of his height—he must have been nearly seven feet tall. I looked them up and down, hardly able to believe that they had put us all together. All three were still in Georgian period costume—the girls in big taffeta evening dresses and Tree in a tasteful frock coat and fancy floral waistcoat. They must have been on their way to the Assembly Rooms when they were nabbed.

"Stephen, dear Stephen," said Emily, still holding onto my hand. "How good it is to see you."

"If only it were under better circumstances," said Tree.

"Well, at least we're together," I said, looking at Emma as I said it. She rolled her eyes away.

Emily lowered her voice. "What news of Jools?"

"Um? Don't take this the wrong way, but I'd like to ask you all one question each before we go any further," I said.

"Is this some kind of test, Stephen?" asked Tree.

"Do you mind?" I said.

"Not at all," shrugged Tree. "We can't be too careful, and it works both ways—"

"Does it? Oh, yeah, I see what you mean. I didn't think of that. Okay, you first then, Tree," I said. "What were you doing when we first met?"

"Knitting," replied Tree, without hesitation.

"Oh, for God's sake," said Emma. "This is so Stephen Sloane."

"Now you, Emma," I said.

Emma folded her arms and assumed a bored posture by shifting all her weight onto one hip.

"What was the first present I ever bought you?" I said, hoping to stir some romance in her at the same time as checking that she really was Emma Gummer.

She itched the corner of her mouth. "A cheap watch," she replied.

"No—before that—the very first thing," I said. I rocked my head rakishly. "That day in Brighton—you know, that day."

She thought for a moment, remembered and gave me a sick smile. "A peppermint flavoured ice cream," she said.

I got eye contact with her and raised my eyebrows and smirked. "Remember what we did with it?"

"You said one question. It's Emily's turn." She looked to Emily.

I turned my attention to Emily. Emily looked worried. Her smooth brow puckered.

"Emily, what are you going to call your baby?"

Her face broke into a broad smile. "Stephen!" she cried.

"Oh, puh-leeze!" said Emma.

"Okay," I smiled. "You're all who you say you are."

"Now you," said Emma.

"Me?" I laughed. "Like Tree said, I must be who I say I am or I wouldn't know what to ask?"

"Are you refusing?" said Emma.

"No, no—of course not. Go on then—ask me. Ask me anything."

"What's the capital of Hungary?"

"Um? I know this. Oh, I know it. Um? Sophia? No—Danube! No, that's the river. Um? Don't tell me, I do know this. It's on the tip of my tongue—I definitely know this."

"He's Sloane," said Emma.

"Slovenia!"

A guard hammered on the door. "Keep the noise down in there!"

"Let's go over there where we can talk," said Tree.

Emily led me by the hand into the darker depths of the cellar, I could just make out some battered looking chairs and a ragged old sofa as my eyes adapted to the murk. There were two trays on the floor with the remains of a meal on each. Emma sat on a chair, Emily and I sat down on the sofa together, still holding hands. Tree leant against the wall and scraped at the mortar with something.

"Our only escape plan," he explained in a whisper, showing me a fork.

"How thick's the wall?" I said.

"Not as thick as you," said Emma.

"I don't know," replied Tree. "But if we can remove one brick, it should make it easier to pull the rest out."

"Go for it," I said. "The way I see it, we've only got one chance—we have to find out where the Duck's furniture is stored. It's in Bristol somewhere."

"Don't we have enough furniture?" said Emma.

"I think there's something hidden in the Duck's furniture that may be of great use to us. And if I'm right— "

"—But why has Jools put his furniture into storage?" interrupted Emily.

"It's a long story, Emily. Temporal Criminal Pursuit paid us a visit. The Duck knew they were coming and cleared the house. They've got a new policy now—if you're out when they call, they blow up your house."

"But that's so mean," said Emily.

"Yes, but with a good lawyer, I think they could sue the Duck for destroying their bomb with his house."

"Are you saying they've blown up Duckworth Hall?" said Tree.

"Not the old Duckworth Hall—but maybe the one in the third millennium," I said.

"Oh, Papa!" cried Emily.

"But I don't see how that can have any relevance to our present situation—this is 1803," said Tree.

"No," I said. "We've been moved forward. There's a time portal up in the hall, didn't you see it?"

"We were blindfolded," said Emma.

"Well, this is definitely the late nineteenth century or early third millennium," I said, "because I saw a newspaper outside and it mentioned Frankie Dettori."

"Who's Frankie Dettori?" said Tree, who was from the 1960s, originally.

"A jockey," said Emma.

"Not just any jockey," I said. "He once rode seven winners in seven consecutive races at the same meeting, on the same afternoon."

"Really?" said Tree. "Did you back him?"

"Well, no, but I was watching it live on TV—it was amazing—hey, that's a point! I could put some money on those horses—"

"—Will you get to the point," said Emma.

"The point is," I said, lowering my voice, "I believe Jemmons's time machine is hidden in that furniture, and without it we'll never get away from these people."

"Where's Julian?" asked Tree.

"Isn't he coming to save us?" said Emily.

"I don't know—I wouldn't bank on it, Emily, I think his Superman suit's at the dry cleaners—he's gone with De Quipp."

"With Travis?" said Emma, suddenly coming to life. "You must have that wrong."

I decided to give them the heroic version, neither would have thanked me for the real version. "They've gone to rescue Jemmons. Apparently, he's being held in a Corrective Measures prison," I said.

"Who's Jemmons?" said Emma.

"A fellow traveller and a friend," said Tree. "Where have they taken him?"

"You don't want to know," I said.

"The Castle?" said Tree.

"I think so."

"Oh my God!" Tree stopped digging and bit his knuckle. Emily left my side and rushed to comfort him.

"Papa, oh, dear Papa—come and sit down," she said, leading her father back to the sofa.

"Here, give me the fork," I said. Emily took it out of his hand and passed it to me. I got up and went to continue scraping away at the mortar.

Emma came and leaned against the wall next to me, to talk to me quietly.

"What's up with him?" she said.

"He spent seven years in the Castle—it traumatized him," I said.

"And are you telling me Travis has gone to this place?" she said.

"I don't know—I think so." I was struggling to dig in the same place as Tree, because he was so much taller than me. It was awkward to reach and work comfortably.

"He told me he had to return to his father's estate in Fontainebleau," she said.

"That was a porkie then, wasn't it?" I smiled. I started in another groove lower down.

"Sloane, I don't expect you to understand what Travis and I have, but I'd have more respect for you if you didn't try to rubbish it."

"I know what you think you have," I said.

"What's that supposed to mean?"

"You've been slipped a love potion to make you think the sun shines out of his—"

"Stephen," said Emily, "would you please pass me that bottle of water on the chair. Papa's mouth is dry."

Emma picked up the bottle before I could reach it and took it over to them.

I carried on scraping.

Presently, Emma returned—this time she kept her back to the Mason-Wrights and leaned in so close to me, that she was practically biting my ear off. I thought she was going to.

"You just can't accept it, can you?" she hissed. "Get used to it, Stephen—it's over. Travis and I are going to be married."

"Dream on," I said.

She jabbed me in the rib with her fingers. "You sad, pathetic loser!"

I turned to face her. Our lips were so close that we were sharing the same breath. "You've been drugged," I said. "And pretty soon it's going to wear off. Travis De Quipp is not French, he has not gone to seek his aristocratic old mother's permission to marry you—or whatever line he fed you—and he is not in love with you—but, what's more—you are not in love with him! So get used to that!"

She just glared at me—speechless for once.

I went back to my scraping. "I'm just sorry I had to be the one to tell you," I said.

"Lies," she said. "All lies."

I wiped my brow and ignored her, busying myself with the task in hand.

We worked the mortar in shifts, all night long. And eventually our hard work and patience was rewarded and Tree managed to dislodge the first brick. But, to our big disappointment, we discovered there was a small gap and then a second wall. But Tree was right, of course, the other bricks came away much more easily once we'd got the first one out, and soon we had a gaping hole big enough to start scratching and loosening a stone in the second wall. It took us ages to scrape round the joints. But when we eventually did, Tree and I found that if he held me up, I could simply kick it through. There was a loud rumble when it fell onto the neighbouring cellar floor, but the guards, who were quite far away and probably asleep, never came in. We were working in total darkness and so had no idea what was actually in the other cellar. We were just hoping it would lead us to a way out. I went first.

"What's in there?" whispered Emma.

My feet had hardly touched the floor. "Well, there's lots more black stuff and then there's some darker stuff—"

"Can you see a door?" said Tree.

"Not yet," I replied, bumping into some sort of tall, wide structure. I heard a telltale chink. "Sounds like a wine cellar in here," I whispered. I ran my hand over a few bottles and felt blindly along the shelf, for the end of the aisle. "Come through!" I called.

I heard one of the others clambering in. There was a thump and a rustle of skirts behind me. I looked round and strained to see who it was. I couldn't see a thing, but I could hear another one being helped through. I waited and listened.

"That's it," said Emma. "Now put your feet down—I've got you."

"This way," I said. "Hold onto my coat tails." I heard a few chinks and then someone bumped into me and patted my bum. "Watch it, Em," I smiled.

Her hands moved up to my shoulders and then smoothed down my spine to find my tails. It felt quite erotic.

"Sorry, Stephen," giggled Emily.

"Oh. It's you," I said. "Is everybody in line?"

"I'm in," said Tree, from the back.

"Emma?" I said.

"Let's all do the hokey-cokey," sang Emma. "Oh, hokey-cokey-cokey!"

The girls giggled.

"Shh! Right," I said. "If the layout's the same, the door should be to the right, just at the end of this shelving, then straight ahead, then left. No talking."

"Yes, sir," said Emma.

Emily giggled again.

I set off slowly. Took three paces and walked straight into a brick wall. The others piled into me and there was pandemonium in the ranks.

"Oh—sorry!" said Emily, falling into me and feeling me all over.

"The idiot—what's he stopped for?" cried Emma.

"Oops! I do apologise, Miss Emma."

"It's a dead end," I whispered, rubbing my knee. "Go back the other way. Turn round, Emily. Go back the other way, Tree. Emily—stop that—turn around!"

"I'm trying," protested Emily. "Don't be so nasty to me, Stephen."

"I'm sorry, Emily. Here, let me help you."

"Oh, Stephen…"

"Er, sorry…"

I heard the chinking of many bottles and felt the shelving swaying. I tried to hold it steady.

"Who's rocking this wine rack?" I called.

A cork popped.

"Oi! Put that back—is that you, Emily?"

"No, I didn't do anything—it just popped out," she said, suppressing a giggle.

"That's because someone's shaking it—we'll have the whole bloody lot exploding in a minute!"

"Bloody hell!" exclaimed Emma. "It's Bollie! Taste that, Emily."

"Taste?" I said. I reached for Emily's head and felt round her hair to her face. She was drinking from a bottle!

I tried to grab it from her lips, but it wasn't her hands holding the bottle, and it was quickly wrenched away from me. "Emma? Give me that champagne!"

"Sod off!" said Emma. "Get your own."

I heard the rustle of her skirts as she turned away from me, out of arm's length. There wasn't enough room to get past Emily, whose enormous dress was pressed up against the sides of the aisle so tightly that she was practically wedged in. I heard some glugs and then two or three big swallows. Emily thought I was coming on to her, as I tried to reach Emma, and responded by fondling my face.

"Oh, Stephen," she said.

"Emily! Will you get off—"

"Oh, you beast," whispered Emily, with a throaty laugh.

"Sloane, put that girl down!" laughed Emma.

"Stephen," said Tree, sternly, "I hardly think this is the time or place—we must get these young ladies out of here."

Emma let out a big belch. "Oops! Pardon me!"

"It's not me—tell her!" I said.

"That wasn't very gal-lant, was-it, Sloane?" hiccupped Emma. "You snitch!"

There were more giggles from Emily.

"For God's sake lead us down your way, Tree," I said.

We started moving again—this time in the opposite direction.

"Oh, do the hokey-cokey!" sang Emma.

"Be quiet!" I whispered.

"Why don't you be quiet, Sloane!" jeered Emma. "You're doing my head in."

"Can we all calm down, please," said Tree.

Emily reached her hand back to me and wanted to hold mine. I took it and let her lead me.

We must have zigzagged all around that bloody wine cellar, like four blind mice, but could we find a door?

No! Eventually, I called timeout to go over the game plan.

"This isn't getting us anywhere," I said.

"What shall we do?" said Emily.

"Oh, let's just get drunk," said Emma.

"Trouble is we've changed direction so many times I'm disorientated," I said.

"So what's new?" said Emma. I heard her take her umpteenth swig.

"You're drunk," I said.

"So what—you're stupid, but I'll sober up," said Emma.

"Don't be so nasty, Emma," said Emily.

"Why—do you fancy him?"

"Emma!" cried Emily. "Stephen's going to be my stepson when Jools and I are wed!"

"So what?" said Emma. "Never heard of Oedipus?"

"Ignore her, Emily," I said. "You're seventeen, I'm twenty-six, I refuse to even think of you as my mother—let alone my lover."

"Please, let's not go into all this now, everyone," said Emily's father.

"But I am attracted to you," whispered Emily, in my ear.

"And I love Emma," I whispered back.

"But she's horrible to you," whispered Emily.

"I know—it's an adult thing," I said.

"I am an adult," cried Emily.

"What are you two lovebirds whispering about now?" said Emma.

"If only we could find the damn door," I said.

"What does it feel like?" asked Emily.

"Well, it's a sort of warm, passionate feeling—you know what it feels like—you love the Duck, don't you?" I whispered.

"I meant the door," said Emily.

"Oh—Door?"

"I can feel something sticking in my back," said Emily.

I pulled her away from the wall and felt around, found a small doorknob and turned it.

"It's here!" I said.

"Let me see!" cried Emily.

"Oh, jolly good show!" said Emma. "Now I'll be able to see what vintage I'm boozing."

I opened the door. The darkness was not absolute. There was faint light coming from somewhere above us. My eyes slowly adapted and dim shadowy shapes began to solidify from the gloom. I could just make out, to my left, a flight of stairs, leading up from the passageway, and something attached to the wall, directly opposite me, on my right.

"What's out there?" said Tree.

"Looks like a hotel basement," I said. "Don't push, Emily."

"I want to look," squeaked Emily, squirming her head under my arm.

"And what makes you think that?" said Emma.

"Well, there's a fire extinguisher on the wall for one thing and a sign saying, TO HOTEL LAUNDRY ROOM," I said.

"Ha-ha," sneered Emma.

"Stay here—I'll take a look round," I said.

"I'll come with you," said Emily.

"No," I said. "There'll be a night porter somewhere and the place'll be alarmed."

"Oh, let her go," said Emma. "They won't be expecting anyone to be breaking out."

Emily grabbed my hand and we slipped outside.

"Let's try down here," I said, indicating the passage to our right.

We ventured into the semi-darkness and came to a metal mesh cage, with a cold storage room and boxes of fruit and vegetables stacked inside, presumably to keep out vermin.

"I think this is the rear of the hotel," I said, indicating the faint light ahead of us. "All these old Georgian houses have a garden—there must be a way up to it. Ah, yes, look—steps."

I was pointing through a glass door into a small courtyard with stone steps leading off it.

"Tell the others," I said. "I'll see if I can open the door."

Emily squeezed my hand and doubled back.

I knelt down at the door and inspected the catch and tried to see if it was wired. It seemed easy enough to open, but I was worried about setting off a burglar alarm.

I heard the sound of light footsteps and the rustling of dresses and then the others surrounded me.

"What are we waiting for?" whispered Emma.

"It's probably alarmed," I said.

Tree stepped forward and reached up to point at a wire leading out from the top of the doorframe. "There," he said. "D'you see that?"

"Anyone know how these things work?" I said.

"They cut them in movies," hiccupped Emma. "But you've got to pick the right one—like blokes, eh, Emily?"

"Just snap it, Tree," I said.

"No," he said. "That would only break the connection. There are two wires, they touch when the door is closed, but when the door is opened the circuit is broken and that's what makes the bell ring."

"Really?" I said. "So, any suggestions?"

Suddenly, we heard a door open, somewhere behind and above us—and then light footsteps descending rapidly. We all looked round—a block of light spilled into the corridor from the service stairs.

"The night porter!" I said. "He must have heard us."

"He might just be doing his rounds—they check for fires," said Tree. "Hide!"

We all fled to a recess, opposite a short passage, leading off at right angles from the back door, which just seemed to lead to the foot of some fire stairs.

"Did you close the cellar door?" I whispered, as we all stood with our backs pressed to the wall.

Tree nodded.

We heard the porter trying doors and then his footfalls receding to the other end of the basement. We all shook our heads and looked along at one another in relief, thinking we had got away with it, but Tree, very deliberately, put his bony finger to his lips. The footsteps came back and grew louder and louder. I held my breath. A man wearing a top hat and tails, who wouldn't have looked out of place in the Victorian period, came and stood just a few feet away from us and stared for a moment or two at the back door. In his fancy doorman's uniform, he might have been a ghost. He turned and looked across at the fire escape, completed the half turn, and headed back up the passageway. We listened to his footfalls receding, all the way back up the stairs. Emma whispered something and Tree whispered something back to her.

"Shh," I said.

We continued to hang on every sound the porter made, until we heard the door close. And then I stepped out of the shallow recess and looked up the hallway. All was silent and still.

"He's gone," I said.

Everybody stepped out. Tree and Emma went straight to the door. Tree had something in his hand and was trying to slide it into the slit along the top of the door. I noticed Emma was still holding her half-drunk bottle of champagne by the neck.

"What're you doing?" I asked.

"Emma had the idea of using the foil off the champagne bottle to make a connector—so that we can open the door without breaking the circuit," said Tree.

"Will that work?" I said.

"Yes—if the wires are close enough to the end." He felt around.

"Don't look so surprised," said Emma, taking another swig of champagne. She passed it to Emily, who took a mouthful and got bubbles up her nose.

I was beginning to feel redundant. I reached to take the bottle from Emily, for a celebratory drink. Emma snatched it out of my hand.

"Get your own," she said, and made a mocking cross-eyed face at me.

I went over to Tree. "It's getting light," I said.

"Try that," said Tree, holding a long loop of rolled up foil in the top of the door.

I turned the catch and eased the door open a little.

"Go on," said Tree, still holding the foil in place.

I inched it open farther and farther, until I thought the girls would fit through.

"A bit more," said Tree.

I opened it another half an inch.

"Stop!" said Tree.

"Okay, Emily—you try," I said, wedging the door firmly between my feet and hands, so that it could not move.

Emily blew me a kiss, wound in her skirts around her hips and legs and shuffled through the gap.

"Em," I said.

Emma gathered in her skirts and squeezed through.

"Now you," said Tree. He held the door still for me.

I slipped through the opening easily, not having such voluminous clothing on as the women, and found myself crowded into the little courtyard with them. Emma was supporting the heavy champagne bottle while Emily drank from it.

"You'll get her drunk," I said.

"She's all right," said Emma. "Aren't you, honey?"

"I can take my booze," said Emily.

"She sounds it," I said.

The girls headed up the steps.

Tree was carefully closing the door behind him.

"So far, so good," I said.

"The mutants are over here!" cried a voice, from somewhere up in the garden.

Emma and Emily were already halfway up the steps, their top halves silhouetted against the dark blue sky. And before either Tree or I could act, the girls had rushed up the remaining steps and were wrestling with someone. They bundled him down to us and we dragged him into the courtyard and laid into him. Now the poor guy had all four of us onto him. Emma had him by the hair and Tree started stuffing something into his mouth—I think it was his lace neck scarf. We soon had him down and I sat on him with Emma. He went quiet and limp.

"What're we going to do with him?" I said.

"Emily, see if there are any others," said Tree, crouching down to unbuckle our prisoner's belt. "We'll have to tie him up and leave him here."

I watched Emily go and pop her head above the steps, scope the garden and then come back down.

"There's no one there," she reported.

"Sit him up," said Tree.

Emma and I got off him, but kept a hold on him, while Tree fastened his hands behind his back with the belt.

"He'll just run off and tell the others as soon as we go," I said. "We need something to tie his ankles up with."

Emma suddenly bashed him over the head with her champagne bottle. He slumped forward into my arms.

"He won't now," she smiled.

"There was no need for that," I said.

"Kidnapping, unlawful imprisonment, messing my hair up," said Emma. "I'd say he got off lightly."

Chapter 8

Twenty minutes later we were walking arm-in-arm down Julian Road, on the lookout for taxis. Tree had several gold sovereigns on him, he told us, concealed in a belt wallet, and Emma, amazingly, still had her plastic and was looking for a cashpoint. I just wanted to know what the date was. It was so early in the morning the streets were deserted, though a few cars and vans went by and lights were coming on in windows as we walked. And then we turned a corner at the bottom of the hill and saw a coach parked outside a hotel, with a queue of people boarding. As soon as they saw us, of course, they began clapping and laughing. The girls curtsied and Tree and I bowed.

"We can't stop," I said, "we're late."

"Just one picture," shouted an older guy with a camera, in an American accent.

"Oh, come on," said his wife. "Look at their dresses, Frank—they're beautiful. What are you shooting—a movie?"

"It's a play," I said.

"But it's going to be made into a movie," said Emma. "And I'm going to be the star."

By now we were surrounded by thirty or so American tourists, happily clicking away with their cameras or getting the whole thing down on video.

"Really? What's it called, dear?"

"Could you just move over there, young feller—sir, would you stand next to this beautiful young lady."

We were being posed against the backdrop of the elegant Bath street, while pairs of them shuffled to and fro to take turns standing alongside us. The coach driver switched his engine off and took out a newspaper. I broke away from the frame and shouted up the steps of the coach to him.

"What date is it, mate?"

"Twenty-third."

"Yeah, but what month and year?"

He raised one eyebrow. "How much have you had?" he said.

I pulled myself up into the coach and nicked the paper off him.

"Just checking a horse I backed!" I said.

It was Saturday, the twenty-third of March, 2002.

"Cheers." I threw the paper back at him and darted off the coach.

The tourists were still happily snapping and recording away on the pavement, I barged my way through the throng to the others and grabbed Emma and Emily's hands.

"Come on," I said. "We're in luck—if we hurry."

"Oh, don't go!" cried our fans.

"Yeah—sing us a song from the show!"

"Hey, Darcy—one more!"

"Sorry," I said. "We're late for rehearsals!"

Tree was still caught in the melee, but obviously enjoying himself, grinning from ear to ear.

"Which part do you play, handsome?" I heard one of his lady admirers ask.

"I am the father," beamed Tree.

"Are you famous?"

"Well, I have walked the boards in some illustrious company in my time, madam," admitted Tree, still holding his nose in the air for more pictures.

"Like with who?" said his admirer's husband.

"Surely you mean, with *whom*, dear boy," said Tree. "Oh, Sir Larry, Raff—the usual suspects, you know."

"Come on, Sir John!" I called. "We have to be in make-up in five!"

"Oh my God—he's a Sir!" cried another lady fan.

I left the girls and waded through the crowd to seize the "star" by the sleeve.

"If that guy's a knight—I'm Hilary Clinton!" said a male voice.

"We really do have to go now," I said.

I pulled Tree clear and we ran after the girls, who were already lifting their skirts and rushing away.

"Hey—you never told us the name of the play!" cried one of the women.

"Tempus Fugit!" I shouted back. "And so must we!"

* * *

We hurried on along the street, still keeping an eye out for a cab. I spotted a telephone box but no one had any change to put in it, so that was out. We eventually found ourselves in the famous Circus, one of Bath's most spectacular buildings, set imposingly in the middle of a roundabout.

"Let's wait here," I said. "There's bound to be one along in a minute."

"You can wait if you like," said Emma, "I'm going to find myself an expensive hotel and take a nice long bath."

"Oo, that sounds lovely," said Emily.

"Hold on—you're not going anywhere," I said.

"I beg your pardon," said Emma, wrinkling her nose and narrowing her eyes at me—I recognised that look, and backed off.

"What I mean is—we should stick together—these guys who are after us are not playing Scrabble, Em. You're on their list—remember?"

"Don't worry, I haven't forgotten," she nodded, "I'll be reporting them and you to the police."

"Me?"

"You got me into all this, Sloane," she said.

"Well, believe what you want, but the police won't do anything—they'll just think you're crazy," I said.

"We'll see," she said.

"Well," I said. "You'll never see De Quipp again, if you don't come with us."

She thought about that for a few seconds. "Oh, yes, Travis," she said, hazily. She rubbed her brow.

"Are you all right, Miss Emma?" said Tree.

"Emma!" cried Emily, as Emma swooned.

Both of us caught her just as her knees gave way from under her.

"It's the drug they gave her," I said. "All this excitement and fresh air—she must be coming down."

I held her in my arms, supported now by both Emily and Tree. Her lashes fluttered and her eyelids flickered opened. She looked at me as though through a mist.

"Steve?" she said. "What happened? Where am I?"

"Don't worry, love, I've got you," I said. "You lost your way inside, Em, but now you've come back to me." I kissed her hair softly. "Oh, Em, you're back again…"

"Where—where's Travis?" she muttered. "I want Travis."

"Oh, not him again!" I said. I handed her over to Tree. "Here, you take her—I'll see if I can get us a cab."

My mind was swirling with anguished thoughts—what if she hadn't been drugged? What if she really did love him? How could I ever get her back? I tried to banish them from my mind and concentrate on the task in hand—getting to Bristol and finding that warehouse. A black cab swung into the roundabout, I stepped out into the road and flagged it down. It skidded to a halt only a few feet away from me. The driver stuck his head out the window.

"Have you got a death wish?" he shouted.

"Actually, I'm planning to live forever," I smiled.

"Where to?"

"Four for Bristol," I said, opening the rear door. The others were already making their way over.

"The airport?" he said.

Tree and Emily helped the still-woozy Emma onto the back seat. I climbed in next to the driver.

"No—we're looking for a furniture storage warehouse," I said. "What I need is a Yellow Pages or a business directory—you wouldn't happen to have one, would you?"

"This is a taxi not a phone box," he said. "So, you don't know where you're going—where are you from—the Costume Museum?"

I laughed. "Oh, that's very good," I said. "Just drop us off at any industrial estate in Bristol and we'll take it from there."

He set his meter running and pulled away.

"So, what are you people doing?" he asked, taking the road out of Bath towards Bristol, which was only ten miles or so away.

"We're making a film—it's low-budget," I said, "so that's why we're chasing round after props."

"What's up with her?" He nodded at his rear view mirror. He meant Emma.

"No breakfast," I said. "Stomach cramps—you know these actresses—always trying to lose weight."

"She looks in pretty good shape to me," he said.

"Yeah, well—no pain, no gain," I said. "Anyway, enough of us—what about you—do you do anything special at all? I mean, apart from driving this."

He shrugged. "What do you mean?"

"I don't know—ballroom dancing—stand-up—impressions of famous people—drag art-iste…"

He had taken his eyes off the road and was staring at me. I looked dead ahead.

A minute later we were all standing at the roadside—miles from anywhere—and I was trying to thumb a lift.

"You must have said something to him," said Tree.

"No—we were just talking about his hobbies and the next thing he's telling me to get out of his cab," I said.

"He said you were weird," said Emily. "Well, I think he had weird eyes. I didn't want to ride in his smelly cab anyway."

"I feel sick," said Emma.

A coach appeared in the distance. And I noticed its right indicator was flashing.

"I think that coach is stopping," I said.

"It's the Americans," said Tree.

"Look, Emma—they're stopping for us!" cried Emily.

Emma turned away and threw up in the hedge.

* * *

It was true, our American friends were on their way to Glastonbury for the day, but had persuaded their driver to stop and pick us up. Fortunately, there were plenty of empty seats, so he didn't complain, but he wasn't too keen on making any detours to industrial estates, though he was heading for Bristol to pick up the motorway west, so he wasn't going out of his way. And, anyway, during the ride I got a gold sovereign off Tree and went forward to have a word with him. I just gave him the same story I gave the taxi driver, but I said it was a play. And then I gave him the antique gold piece and he agreed to drop us off at an industrial park he knew, just on the outskirts of Bristol, where he said there were several furniture storage depots. He knew because he used to drive for a removal firm. He cheered me up when he added that the one he had worked for was a high quality one and all the toffs used it.

* * *

However, two hours later we were on our way by taxi to another industrial estate, having bribed our way round the first one, and drawn a blank. I should have guessed—the Duck would never use a classy, expensive removal firm—he would go for the cheapest! I asked one of the storage warehouse managers which one was the cheapest. He gave me the name of the one with the most competitive rates—he would not use the word "cheap." It was a firm called Scorpion Shipping and Storage. I just knew it had to be the one.

But when we got there, I started to have my doubts, the roads weren't made up and the whole place looked rundown and abandoned, but we found a shabbily dressed old guy drinking tea and listening to the radio in a hut. I told the others to wait in the cab while I spoke to him.

"Hi. Good morning."

"Who're you?" He turned down his radio.

"I work for Duckworth Hall Estates, I'm the, er, restorations manager. I need to check a few items in the, um—the inventory."

"Got a chit?"

"No. I—"

"Can't go in then," he said. He turned the volume knob back up on his radio.

I leaned over and turned it down again. "But it is all here?" I said.

"Hey!" he said. "Who do you think you are?"

"Renovation and repair," I said. "Duckworth Estates. I need to check our property."

"You can't go in that storage unit without proper authorization," he said. "Gotta have a chit. Now, clear off, before I call security."

"What security?" I laughed.

"We've got dogs—big brutes they are—they'll have you," he said.

"Now, look here," I said. "I only want to go into the warehouse, check one or two items and I'll be on my way. I'll make it worth your while."

He licked his lips. "No, I can't," he said.

I produced three gold sovereigns. "Know what these are?" I said.

"Let me see," he said, he took them greedily and tried to bite one. Then he inspected the dates. "These are nice," he said. "Not nicked are they?"

"Of course not. They're sweeteners—we give them away to our special clients and service people—anyone who does us a favour." I tapped my nose.

He liked that and grunted. "How much they worth?"

"About a hundred each," I said. "Probably a lot more to a collector."

"You just wanna look?" he said, pocketing the gold coins.

"We'll be about an hour—that's all," I said.

"We?" he said, raising his backside off the chair to see through the window.

"Me and my three assistants—they're just restorers—two young ladies and good old Mr Tree, my chief, er, restorer," I said.

"Why you dressed funny?" he said, as though he'd only just noticed the fact.

"When the visitors come to the Hall they like to see a bit of history," I said.

He nodded. "Oh, yeah, that's right, I've seen that on the telly," he said. But then he screwed up his face and began shaking his head. "For all I know though, you could be thieves."

I laughed. "No way!" I said. "Look. All you've got to do is lock us in there—how can we rob anything if we're locked in? Then when we've finished you can search us all before you let us out."

He pouted his lips and nodded, felt in his pocket and produced a set of keys. "It's only repros and fakes, anyway, innit?" he said.

"Yeah—it's just tat really," I said.

He stood up. "So why you restoring it then?" he said, as he led me out of the hut.

"Well, that's just a technical term," I said. "What we're really doing is making it look older."

"I'm with you—I've seen that on the telly, too—they call it distressing," he nodded.

"Well, yes, it can be," I said.

"Here, these coins better not be repros," he said, suddenly having the thought and pulling up sharply.

"They're genuine antiques, mate—just look at the dates on 'em," I said.

He checked. "You're right."

"Er, Mr Tree?" I opened the passenger door of the taxi. "Bring the girls this way, we're going to do the restoration work *in situ*."

"Yes, Mr Sloane," said Tree.

The watchman walked me over to the door of the warehouse and had a sudden thought. "Ah! But how do I know the dates aren't faked?" he said.

"Well, while we're locked in here, why don't you phone a friend and have them valued. I think you'll find they're worth a lot more than three hundred quid," I said.

He nodded. "I could," he said, half-convincing himself.

"And while you're at it—have this one valued, too." I slipped him a fourth gold sovereign and patted his shoulder. "Never know when I might need a man of your integrity again," I said, tapping my nose.

"I'm always here," he said, unlocking the door.

I stood aside to let my three "assistants" go in ahead.

"What's your name?" I said.

"Dennis," he said. "But my mates call me Den."

"As in, den of iniquity?" I said.

"Who? In the nick with he? Who was?"

"I'll be in touch, Den—might have some more jobs I can put your way," I said, going in.

He started to close the door. "I'm always on hand. One hour you said?"

I stopped in mid-step. I had decided to check him out with one of my questions. "Oh, by the way, do you know anything about football?"

"Rovers supporter—man and boy," he said.

"I was having an argument with a colleague of mine about Yeovil Town's old ground—he reckoned it gave them an unfair advantage," I said. "What do you think?"

"Well, there wasn't much of a slope there," he said.

"That's what I said," I smiled. He was clear. Yeovil's old ground had a marked slope—anyone who lived in the Westcountry all their life would know that. "See you in sixty minutes." I waved goodbye.

He locked us in and I put my ear to the door and heard him whistling a happy tune as he walked back across the gravel to his hut.

The others had switched on all the lights and were draped over various pieces of furniture. Emma was reclining on a chaise longue, Emily was sitting on a Chippendale, with her feet up on another, and Tree was perched on a chest of drawers, with his feet still flat on the concrete floor. I looked around the packed windowless warehouse at all the antiques, piled on top of each other, higgledy-piggledy—four-poster beds like weird sailboats, wardrobes and tables galore, ornate mirrors and clocks, gleaming porcelain and silverware, Manhattans of books, acres of oil paintings, enough chairs to seat a dozen orchestras, marble statues, trunks and boxes—it went on and on. I had no idea where to start.

"There must be hundreds of millions of quids' worth here," I said.

"Why don't we sell it then and move to the South of France?" said Emma languidly.

"I wish," I said. "Right, let's get cracking."

"It would help if we knew what we were looking for," said Emma.

"You just lie there, love," I said. "And keep an eye out. That watchman might come snooping round. Tree, Emily. I want you to have a wander round and see if you can spot anything that looks out of place—something you don't recall seeing at Duckworth Hall. It has to be something fairly large, say, bigger than a suitcase."

Tree scratched his head. "But I haven't seen half this stuff before—the Duck's always buying new things."

"I don't remember all those Gainsboroughs," said Emily.

"Is that what they are?" I said.

"Well, that big one's a Watteau—and those little ones over there are mostly Fragonards and Constables," she said.

"You know a lot," I said.

"Emily's studying art," said her father. "The Duck takes her round to meet the masters when he has time."

"That Leonardo da Vinci's a scream," laughed Emily. "He only said he wanted to paint me—in the nude!"

"You sure that wasn't Leonardo DiCaprio you met?" I said. I forgot she wouldn't have seen Titanic and so wouldn't get my lame attempt at a joke.

"Who?"

"We'd better get on. Tree, you take that side, mate, and I'll have a look down here. Emily, can you just wander down the middle—you seem to have a good memory."

"Can't I go with you? I don't want to be on my own—it's spooky," said Emily.

"Don't worry, Emily," said Emma. "Auntie Emma will be here. She'll keep an eye on you."

"Thanks a lot," said Emily, sticking her tongue out at her.

We each set off on our allotted pathways through the muddled up museum of the Duck's acquisitions. It was a bit shocking to kick something while you were reaching to look in a cupboard or a drawer, or behind something, and then look down to find it was a Titian or a Rubens. And then there was all the ticking and chiming that was going on—from all the clocks—a constant reminder to me that our time was running out.

What we were looking for was a time machine, but since time machines could be disguised in a hard holographic shell, they could look like anything, even something animate, like a horse, for example. They could also be set to a default matrix—the Duck's was a white Ford Cortina—Jemmons preferred a late eighteenth century sailboat. To make matters worse, the dimensions of the holographic shell were variable—it could be any size, although it had to be something large enough to climb into, so it couldn't be a vase or a candelabra, or anything silly like that.

I spotted one of the Duck's prize possessions—a Harrison long case clock, which always stood in the main hall at Duckworth. It was just wide enough to squeeze into. In fact, I almost climbed into it once by mistake. I opened the door and felt around inside. What I was feeling for was a rather cold and squishy invisible tear in the fabric of the matrix—the way in. But it wasn't there.

"Stephen—come quickly!" cried Emily, from the other side of the high ridge of antiques.

I hurried down to the end of my path and rounded the corner— Emily was about halfway along her aisle, pointing excitedly up at something. Tree arrived from his aisle and we both jogged down to her.

"See that battered old sea trunk up there," she said. "Well, I've never seen it before. And I'm sure Jools would never buy anything like that!"

"Yes," I said. "A sea trunk—it's perfect—Jemmons loves all things nautical."

"I know," said Emily, gleefully.

I stood on a card table and tried to get it down, but it was just out of my reach.

"Papa, you try," said Emily.

I jumped down and helped him up onto the table. Tree, of course, reached it easily and was even able to undo the catches and open the lid. He peered inside.

"Well?" I said.

"Just silverware and bric-a-brac," said Tree, holding up a handful of spoons, wrapped in greaseproof paper.

"Feel around for the slit in the matrix," I said.

He felt around. Cutlery chinked. He shook his head.

"Nothing."

"Oh, I'm disappointed now," pouted Emily. "I was so sure I'd found it."

"Never mind—keep looking," I said.

I gave Tree a hand down from the wobbly table and decided to go and see how Emma was doing. I could just see her head sticking up above the end of the chaise longue at the far end of Emily's aisle. I was convinced the time machine was somewhere in the warehouse, but if I was wrong, we would have to start thinking of a backup plan.

"Hi, Em," I said. "What you reading?"

She looked at the title page. "*The History of Tom Jones, A Foundling.*"

"Ah, good old Henry Fielding.".

"I suppose you've read it."

"Uh, yes, well, I know it."

"Did you ever actually read any books at university?"

"I've read bits of that one!" I said. "Wrote an essay on it—well, on Fielding. And, um, uh, the other one—Richardson!"

"Have you found anything?"

"No. That's why I wanted to see you."

"Well—you're seeing me."

"Yes, I'm seeing you. Did I ever tell you you've got a great neckline—no, I mean, the way it curves and sort of joins up with your, um, your shoulder, it's all smooth the way it sweeps down like that."

"What do you want?"

"Plan B," I said. "When Dennis the watchman comes back, keep him talking—if we can't find the time machine, we'll have to take some of this stuff to sell—getaway money."

"You want me to beat him up?"

"Yes—no! Just distract him," I said. "Of course I don't want you to beat him up. Beat him up."

"Well, we'll have to tie him up or he'll phone the police," she said, batting her eyelids at me—I think she was being ironic.

But I thought I'd better just check to make sure I wasn't getting the come on. I perched on the edge of the chaise longue.

"How about a quick snog for old time's sake?" I said.

"Get lost."

I got up and held my hands together, as though in prayer. "All right, all right—forget I asked—it was a moment of weakness—I'll never ask again!"

"Promise? Because frankly, Stephen, I find it rather embarrassing the way you simper around me."

"I don't simper!" I exclaimed. "Simper around you. I'm just still wearing the vestigial grin of your former lover. We were going out for nearly three years!"

"Two and a half."

"Well, anyway, keep an eye out—and keep an eye on the time."

She held up her hands and shook them to show me her bare wrists. "No watch. The one you bought me broke, remember?"

"Oh. That's a point. Nor have I. I left it at Duckworth Hall when I put this lot on. I wonder how long we've been in here."

"About fifteen minutes because I've read thirteen pages and it takes me just over a minute per page," she said.

"Does it? It only takes you a minute to read a whole page? That's fast—do you actually read the words?"

"Yes, but I don't have to move my lips at the same time like you, so that's why I'm faster," she said.

"Well, women read quicker than men, it's a well known fact," I said.

"They also read more—that's a well known fact, too. That's why they know more."

"If you say so, dear," I simpered. "Anyway, if it takes a woman fifteen minutes to read thirteen pages—how many pages will she read in—?"

"—Fifty-two an hour," said Emma, batting her eyelids again at me.

Yes, she was definitely taking the mick.

"Well, there's a clock over there anyway," I said.

"Where?" She craned her neck round. She really did have a beautiful neck. Funny but I went out with her for nearly three years and never really noticed just how long and perfect it was till then. "Oh, there. Is it working?"

"The others are so I don't see why that one—" I stared long and hard at the elegant grandfather clock. It was just standing there against the wall, in the corner. On its own. Wheels and cogs were turning in my head.

"What is it?" said Emma.

"That's a Harrison long case," I said slowly.

"So it is—what's a Harrison long case?"

"It's worth a fortune," I said. "There can't be two."

"We can't take that," said Emma, "we'd never get it in the taxi—I assume we are escaping by taxi again. Hello?"

"That's it!" I laughed. "That's the one. In the hall—when the Duck was taking me to the library, I said the clock's been moved. It was on the wrong tile."

"Could you translate that?"

"That's it! That's the time machine!"

Chapter 9

For once I was right. I called Tree and Emily and showed them the portal in the holographic shell of the clock; it was inside the pendulum casing. Although Emma had been in time machines before, she hadn't really known much about it—the first time she was kidnapped in one, the next time she jumped out of one and the last time she had been brought back by the TCP in one, and had understood very little of what was happening. So, when she found herself standing on the deck of Jemmons's sloop, fully conscious of what she was seeing, she was amazed.

"But where are we?" she said, looking round at the crackling red and black "sky" of the time continuum.

"In the vortex," I said. "It's like a tunnel—when you travel up or down it, you travel through time."

"The warehouse is still all around us, Miss Emma," said Tree, "we have simply crossed into another dimension. When we set the machine in motion, we will not move from this spot, although it will appear so. We will remain at these same co-ordinates, in Bristol. This is a time machine, but it is not a time and space machine. That means if we wish to return to Georgian Bath we will have to transport the clock there."

"I was going to say that," I said.

"Papa!" called Emily, who had gone below. "Mr Jemmons has tea and there are muffins and butter!"

"That's another good thing about time machines," smiled Tree. "Food can never go off in them because it never gets old."

"So if I stayed in here I'd remain forever young?" said Emma.

"Theoretically," said Tree.

"Think I'll take up sailing," said Emma.

* * *

Getting to a safe house proved to be a complex exercise. Tree owned a houseboat—a converted barge—which he kept on the Avon in Bristol, during the late 1950s. This was back in his arty days, when he had aspirations of becoming a serious painter. Then two things happened that destroyed his career. First Peter Blake, Hockney, and Pop Art exploded on the scene, here and in America, and Tree thought it was just a flash in the pan, and carried on doing his landscapes. And then he got called up to do his National Service. He served eighteen months in Aldershot, Hong Kong, and Malaya with the Army Catering Corps.

When he was demobbed in 1962, the kind of traditional art he'd wanted to do had been sidelined.

The upshot of all this was the houseboat he had been living on had remained empty for most of the two years he was away. Tree proposed that they go there to hide out. So, we had to travel back a few hundred years to a time when the industrial estate was just pasture, get out of the machine, carry it up to the top of a nearby hill—which had never been built on—and then go forward in time to late September, 1960.

This is complicated, I know, but all we had to do then was transport the clock to Clifton, where the houseboat was moored. We managed to persuade a local garage owner to drive us there in his van, for two of Tree's gold sovereigns.

So by lunchtime we were all safely aboard the Mason-Wright houseboat, "The King of Prussia," eagerly trying on his old beatnik clothes. I chose a pair of baggy black trousers, a black roll-neck sweater, and short black leather jacket. It was all miles too big for me, but I could have passed for a cool late fifties, jazz-loving student type. Tree struggled into an old pair of blue jeans, a black roll-neck sweater like mine, and a duffle coat. Our host, interestingly, had a wardrobe full of young women's clothes on the boat, too, so the girls were not left out. He explained to us, rather unconvincingly, I thought, that they belonged to a girlfriend. She must have been a very tall one.

So, there we were sitting up on deck in the sun, all wearing shades, enjoying a post-lunch spliff and planning our next move. We must have looked like a jazz combo taking five.

"Maybe I'll grow one of those goatee beards," I said, rubbing my chin.

"Well, it would get on mine," said Emma.

"Maybe a 'tache like Monsewer De Crapp then!"

"You couldn't! You haven't got anything there!"

"Children, please!" said Tree.

"I really dig these clothes," said Emily.

I noticed with Emily how effortlessly she adopted the attitudes and language associated with whatever costume she was wearing. And she looked good in her fishnets, pink plastic skirt, tight black top and biker jacket—and had even tied her hair back in a fashionable ponytail.

Emma, who was similarly dressed, but had opted for a white woollen jacket, instead of the leather, took the joint from Emily.

"It's just good to get out of those stupid big dresses," she said.

"Tree, I know you don't like talking about it, mate," I said, "but we have got to start thinking about finding the Castle."

Tree nodded and gazed across the river.

Emily patted his knee. "It's okay, Daddy."

"I don't know where it is," said Tree. "It was always freezing there, I know that. It's on a small rocky island in the middle of an ice sheet. That's all I know."

"Sounds like the Arctic," said Emma, passing me the joint.

"No, I don't think it was," said Tree. "Some of the inmates made lenses out of ice and tried to take sightings. On clear days, we could make out people moving about and a coastline."

"Did you make a map?" I said.

"There was a map," said Tree, "but I was never shown it. I was not in the inner circle, you see. I—I was afraid to escape. I refused."

"That's nothing to be ashamed of, Daddy," said his daughter. "You were thinking of me and Mummy."

"Yes, I just wanted to serve my time and live to see my family again." He patted Emily's hand.

I handed him over the joint. He took a deep toke, held it in his lungs, and exhaled.

"I made some sketches while I was there. There wasn't much to see, I just needed to keep drawing, you understand."

"Have you still got them?" I asked.

He nodded.

"Can I have a look?"

"They're just rough drawings I did with some homemade charcoal."

"Are they here?"

"They're in Somerset."

"Could you get them?"

"Yes, but I don't think they would tell you much," said Tree.

"I'd still like to see them."

"I keep a Morris Minor in a lock-up round the corner. I'll drive down there this afternoon and get them."

"I'll go with you, Daddy," said Emily.

"We'll stay the night down there and drive back first thing," added Tree. "Emily needs sleep."

"Well, I'm staying here and getting some sleep right now," yawned Emma.

"I'll keep you company."

She gave me a sick look.

"I meant on the boat—not in your bunk."

* * *

It was hard. I mean knowing Emma was asleep in a cabin not more than a few feet away from me. Once or twice I went and opened the door quietly and looked in on her, as she slept. I wondered what she was dreaming about. Probably De Quipp. Well, whatever it was, it was a long one—she slept right round the clock.

* * *

Late that evening, when she still hadn't woken up, I decided to go for a stroll along the quayside to collect my thoughts, and put the day to bed. Nowadays, that stretch of the River Avon—the old Bristol Docks—is practically a Heritage site, with re-conditioned cobblestones, gift shops and eateries, but back then it was a pretty rough area. A red light district. And I was soon propositioned by a young lady of the night.

"Looking for business, love?" she said, stepping out of the shadows.

"No, actually, I'm just having a dark night of the soul and I was wondering if Sartre might have been right and I really did choose this life for myself, or whether, as the great medieval thinkers say, everything is predestined. What do you think?" I said.

"I think you need a good—"

Suddenly, we were both distracted by a piercing scream.

It seemed to come from the houseboat.

"Good answer!" I said, as I set off sprinting along the quayside, then broke into a trot and then, by the time I reached the barge, I was walking and gasping for breath.

"Emma! Emma!" I panted.

She came rushing up from the cabin, straight into my arms.

"Steve—Steve! Oh, thank God! There's someone down there! He—he was touching me!" she cried.

I looked around the deck for something to negotiate with and picked up a marlinspike.

"Maybe it's Tree," I said, hopefully.

"It was definitely not Tree," she said. "He was all sweaty and horrible—his hands were filthy! And he was stinking of beer and fags!"

"It's just some old tramp," I said. "Wait up there."

"No, he was young," she said, going up the gangplank to the quayside.

"All right, a young tramp then."

I took a few steps down into the cabin. "Come out of there!" I shouted. No one answered. "I'll call the police! I'm going to count to three. One-two-"

"All right, all right—keep your hair on," said someone with a Liverpudlian accent. "I was only lookin' for somewhere to kip, man—and now there's all this."

An unkempt young man, wearing tight-fitting black trousers, a white open-neck shirt and a black leather jacket similar to mine emerged from the galley area, holding up a bottle of milk and a packet of biscuits.

My mouth fell open. God—I recognised him! A tingle wriggled around in the back of my neck.

"Okay," I said. "Right, well, help yourself to the, um, milk—I'll find you somewhere to, uh, kip—you scared my girlfriend."

"Sorry about that like," he said. "Cheers."

I stumbled back up the stairs and waved Emma down from the quay.

"What? *What?*"

"Do you know who that is?" I whispered.

"I don't care if it's Prince Charles—get him out of there—now!"

"I think it's John Lennon," I nodded, grinning all over my face. "That's only John Lennon!" I bit my bottom lip. "It is, Em—I swear it is. It's John Lennon."

She shook her head. "It can't be. What would John Lennon be doing in Bristol? The Beatles lived in Liverpool, didn't they?"

"Yes, and they played in Hamburg," I said. "But they must have played all over Britain before they were famous. This is 1960—they haven't made it yet. That guy down there changed the world, Em! That's the twenty-year-old genius in embryo. And he's on our boat."

"Tree's boat," she corrected.

"Don't say anything," I said. "Let me do the talking."

"Don't you always?"

We went back below. Emma smiled at our guest and scuttled through to her cabin to put some more clothes on. I sat down at the small dining table opposite him, to watch John Lennon drinking milk.

"Mind if I smoke?" he said.

"Go ahead, man," I grinned. "Yeah, yeah, yeah."

He gave me a funny look and offered me an untipped Woodbine. I carefully took it out of the packet and studied it, thinking I'd keep it and maybe get him to sign it later.

He lit up. "Are you going to smoke that or eat it?" he said, offering me the lit match.

"I'll save it," I grinned, putting it behind my ear.

"Please yourself," he shrugged.

"Yeah, I'll *please, please me*," I smirked. "What's your name?"

He thought for a moment. "Er, Johnny, Johnny Silver—what's yours?"

"No, what is it really?" I said. "Go on—you can tell me."

"What is this—twenty questions?" he said.

"My name's Steve Sloane—now, tell me your real name—you're from Liverpool, aren't you, *Johnny*?"

Just then, Emma returned.

"Well, is it *him*?" she said.

"Who?" said our incredible guest. "Who d'you think I am—the King of Siam or something? Do I look like Yul Brynner with this mop?"

I laughed and shook my head. "It's him," I said.

Just in that split second I caught a red flash in the back of his eyes—faster than a lizard's blink. A chill ran up my spine. I had seen that telltale sign before. That was no Beatle—that wasn't even human! I tried to conceal it and kept smiling.

"Look, we think you look like a singer in a, er, fab band we saw at the Cavern Club in Liverpool. Are you John Lennon?" I said calmly.

He grinned. "I didn't want to give me real name—Johnny Silver's me stage name like, but, yeah, since you're fans—it's true—I am he," he said.

"Really?" said Emma, sitting down next to him. "Have you written any good songs lately?"

"Well, as a matter of fact, I have, love—so you really dig our music?"

"Yeah, we do," said Emma. "Is Paul—?"

I kicked her foot under the table. She shot me an annoyed look. I attempted to signal to her that he wasn't the real John Lennon, by making a slight shake of my head and pointing at him with the hand I was resting my chin on. But our visitor was now looking directly at me.

"What?" she said.

"What's up, man?" he said, through lips now as cruel as Caligula's.

Suddenly he stuck an arm out and grabbed Emma by the throat, and then gripped her forehead with his other hand, without even looking at her.

"Don't move, Sloane!" he yelped, losing the Scouse accent. "You know I could crush her skull with one squeeze!"

"Please!" I said. "Don't hurt her! I'll do anything you say."

"She is with child," he said. "Your child—mutant!"

I heard light footsteps coming down the stairs. I looked round. It was the prostitute I had met on the quayside a few minutes earlier. Now I could see who she reminded me of—Jody Foster! They had clearly delved into my mind on a previous encounter and fished out a few likes and dislikes. They knew the type of people I was likely to trust, the personal favourites I wouldn't question.

"Where are the others?" she barked.

"They were not here," said the male Corrective Measures agent. "We will wait."

She slapped me across the back of the head. "Where are they, Sloane? Tell us!" She hit me again.

I don't want to brag here, but I should point out these agents were not humanoid—they were androids from the fourth millennium—and when they hit you, it bloody well hurt. I slumped forward and laid my head on the table, to try and stay out of range.

"I don't know," I said.

"You are a liar!" screeched the female, pinning my head with her hand and applying pressure. "If you do not tell us I will squash your head into paste."

"For God's sake tell them, Stephen!" cried Emma.

"Don't worry love—they won't kill us, they need us for research."

"We do not need you in full working order," said the female android. "Your ears, nose—these fingers—they are expendable."

"All right, all right," I said. "I'll tell you. But first tell him to let Emma's head go—and let me sit up."

She nodded to the John Lennon look-alike and he released Emma's skull. She let me up.

I rubbed the back of my head. I knew I was in a no-win situation. I had no plan, so I decided to play for time, until I could think of one, or an opportunity presented itself, so I suppose you could call that a sort of plan. It depends what you mean by plan really, doesn't it?

"There are two others," I began. "One is very, very tall. The other is young, a young female. She is not so tall really, she's sort of average height, well, maybe a little below average height. She has hair the colour of gold or some might say it's more the colour of ripe corn in sunshine. And it kind of moves like a cornfield—you know that way corn moves when the summer breeze passes over it? It's like an ocean, rolling waves and ripples from end to end of the field. Of course, the individual strands are not as thick as a stalk of corn..."

Emma looked at me incredulously and then at each of the engrossed androids in turn. And shook her head.

I continued in this vein for nearly an hour. You have to remember our captors were androids—half-machines—they were not going to refuse any information I was prepared to reel off. They would be storing it all in their memory chips, collating and processing it, adding little bits here and little bits there to their files, reviewing and revising—cross-referencing—the whole time I was talking. They had never met me before and probably thought it was the way I always talked. Besides, they wouldn't think it was a waste of time to let me carry on spinning out my tale, like Scheherazade. They would just think they were extracting an excellent statement from me—very detailed and full. Just the way Corrective Measures liked them.

"Coffee?" said Emma.

"Yes, please, Em," I smiled, breaking off briefly from my discourse. I checked with the droids. They both nodded. "Make that three, love."

"...so why, you might ask, did we compare him to a tree—we might just as well have compared him to a lamppost or a flagpole. Metaphors are all a matter of personal taste, don't you think? That was a rhetorical question—you don't have to answer it if you don't want to. I know you're not here to answer questions—that's what you want me to do—right? Er, that was a rhetorical question, too—when I said 'right.' Um, I think. Anyway, where was I? Oh yes—Shakespeare's use of metaphor and simile in the sonnet sequence..."

* * *

Two hours later I was still going strong.

"...you see, what the neo-classicists were attempting to do was eradicate all ambiguity and—and wishy-washy woolly thinking and imagery from their writing—"

"But not Pope," interrupted John.

"Well, true, um, he was into extended metaphor," I said.

"The whole Rape of the Lock," nodded Jody, helping herself to another one of John's cigarettes.

"The whole of 'The Rape of the Lock,'" I agreed, not too sure about that one. "You see, Romanticism, as exemplified by Keats, Byron et al, at this particular period in the Age of Enlightenment would have been almost incomprehensible to Dryden. He could only see the classical model."

"The baroque was dead," said Jody.

"As a doornail," I nodded, patting her hand, where it lay on the table, next to mine.

"The rococo rules!" exclaimed John, punching the air with his fist.

I smiled and waved my arms about like a conductor. "Light, airy—ephemeral—with the delicacy and grace of a butterfly's flight, the perfection and symmetry of a shell."

"Hmm," sighed Jody gazing off into space. "Like Watteau's swinger."

"Well, the word swinger has other connotations these days, but, yes, grace personified," I smiled. We linked arms and swayed together to the imaginary music we were hearing.

"What's a swinger?" said John.

"Er, love," I said to Emma, "do you think you could make some more coffee?"

Jody put her hand over her cup. "Not for me, thanks, Stephen."

I looked to John.

"Oh, go on then," he grinned.

"Make that two, love," I said.

Emma came and snatched our cups off the table, chinked them together, and said to John, "A swinger is disgrace personified, love." And then she stamped out to the galley and slammed them down on the draining board.

"Er, and so to Lord Byron," I said. "Byron was a Romantic from the quiff of his mullet to the polish on the toes of his riding boots…um, did you know he had a club foot?"

* * *

In the wee small hours, long after we had progressed to the wine, we retired to the cushioned lounge area and were lying about listening to Tree's collection of jazz records, and rolling joints. I had totally corrupted the two androids from Corrective Measures. The power of free expression of the self is staggering. In '60s America, psychologists introduced the concept of the freeing the inner self to the initiates of a convent, within six months over half the sisters had broken their vows and left the institution, and the rest were practising a sort of lesbian version of free worship. It's true!

"…I like the Parker—it's freer—don't you agree, Stevie?"

"Jody, you don't know what you're talking about—how can you sit there and say that?" argued John.

"All I'm saying," said Jody, "is that Bix's syncopation is more accessible and the Bird's technique is a natural extension of that. Stephen, tell this creep what I mean for pity's sake!"

"The Bird flies, man," I said. I jumped up, stuck my thumb in my mouth, and played the imaginary sax stops up and down my chest with my other hand. "He floats, he flits!" I skipped around the cabin. "He blow that horn like he's grown a new tongue, cats—it don't just sing—it makes *lurve*!"

Jody laughed and clapped her hands. John shook his head and poured himself another glass of red wine.

"You the man!" he said.

"Sit down, you buffoon!" hollered Jody, finally.

"Who you calling a buffoon, girl?" I laughed, throwing myself back down on the bench seat with her.

"I'm going to bed," said Emma, who had been sitting at the dining table. She padded past us in her bare feet. We heard her slam her cabin door and all fell about laughing.

"So," said Jody, playing with my hair, "the French existentialists, led by Sartre, were not only saying we had free will, but that we have too much?"

"Too much choice," I nodded, topping up my glass and Jody's with more wine. "We don't know what to do with it all. We walk into a supermarket, we don't even know what breakfast cereal we want to snap, crackle or pop. That post-industrialism-consumerism complex—that whole Freud-Bernhays thing—has spawned a new religion—shopping! The will has been set free! We can be and do and buy whatever we want! We're all so free it's like being in a cage of freedom!"

"I like that image," said John. "Cage of freedom. Oxymoron. Bravo, mon ami."

"But we still have Rome," sighed Jody. "We still have original sin and we still have guilt. We are still repressed by that medieval rack inside our heads—those old philosophers, like Aquinas, still tell us it's all preordained. The bastards!"

"Well, not Aquinas—he, er, sort of believed in free choice," I corrected.

"Sorry. I meant that whole Spanish Inquisition—Reformation-Counter-Reformation chain thing—it's still pulling us, spinning our souls on the wheel of St Catherine! Whipping us to the Cross!" cried Jody, with scary passion. "We'll never be free! God isn't dead in our heads, man!" She burst into tears and threw herself against me and pounded me with her fists. "I just want to be who I want to be—I just want to be me! I have to be free! Oh, Steve—set me free!"

I held her head in my arms and stroked her hair. "Shh, shh—I've got you, babe..."

* * *

At dawn my students and I were sitting cross-legged up on deck, meditating and composing freeform poems.

"...rain drops Venn diagrams on the still lake," offered John.

"...the peeled lips of their swastikas speak of rage rage rage!" hissed Jody.

I was worried about Jody.

"...but they also spoke of love love love," I added, "uh, because love is all you need."

John opened his eyes and nodded at me. "Cool, man," he said dreamily.

"...there is nothing you can do that cannot be done," I went on, "nowhere you can be where you are not supposed to be—it's easy..."

It seemed to be working.

Jody said, "...all you need is someone else to live in hell with..."

"...there is no one you cannot be if you really want to be somebody—it's easy..." said John, getting the hang of it.

"All you need is love—la-la-*la-la-la*! Keep it up!" I sang, conducting them with one hand, while I lifted myself up with my other.

"All you need is love—la-la-*la-la-la*!" we all chorused.

"Now," I said, backing away, towards the hatchway, "keep adding verses and don't stop, till I get back."

I swung down the last few wooden rungs of the hatch stairs into the main cabin, pleased with myself, and found Emma lounging full length on the sofa bench, reading a paperback and sipping coffee.

"Hallelujah! Give me black coffee!" I cried, clapping my hands and rubbing them together.

We could just hear John and Jody singing their improvised version of "All You Need is Love" right over our heads.

"In the pot," said Emma, without taking her nose out of her book.

I poured myself a coffee and went over to join her on the bench. She was forced to move her feet slightly to make room for me, and tutted.

"Well, aren't you going to say anything?" I said.

"Morning, Sloane."

"No, I meant about that," I said, pointing my finger up at the ceiling.

"You mean, The Temple of the Seventh Day Sloanites? Yeah—tell them not to chant so loud, I'm trying to become one with this book."

"Emma, last night they were going to crack open our heads like eggs—now they're singing hippie anthems and making up avant garde poetry. I've converted them!"

"Yes, but into what?" she said. "I think I liked them better when they were psychopaths."

"Well, I think I did a pretty good job," I said, a bit miffed. "What you reading?"

She flashed the cover in my face and carried on reading.

"Hm, *Lucky Jim*," I said. "Isn't that supposed to be funny?"

"It's hilarious," she said, without lifting her eyes off the page.

"Then why aren't you laughing?" I said.

"I'm laughing in my mind. Now, leave me alone—go and sacrifice a goat or something."

I was not put off—I had just converted two aggressive automata into peace-loving poets—I was on a roll.

"What first attracted you to me, Em?"

"Your silence."

Undeterred, I said, "I wonder what love is." I clutched my coffee cup to my heart. "They say love grows and it can die, but it can't be organic, can it? 'Cos the lover still lives on. Is it merely a bio-chemical reaction? I ask myself. Or just an instinctive animal urge, over which we have no control, no say in the matter? Can this be all there is to love? I think not. I think love is like a faith, a faith in the one you love."

Emma heaved a huge sigh and turned the page.

"I have faith in you, Em. A faith that cannot be shaken or broken. I will never give up my faith in you. Because I love you."

"The baby is not yours, Stephen—it's Matt's," she said, without interrupting her reading.

I drank the rest of my coffee in one, got up, walked stiffly out to the galley, and smashed the mug in the sink. I charged back in.

"Matthew bloody Turner! How could you sleep with that shithead— that bird-brained, fish-faced, ass-licking, little shite of a pratt? How could you?"

"I thought he was your mate," she said, finally looking up from her bloody book and smiling sweetly at me.

"Mate? Mate? I hate the little tosser! I hate him! I hate everything about the slimy, two-faced bastard! You slept with Matthew Turner? I hope you showered all the slime off afterwards! Do you realise you're carrying the seed of Matthew Turner? Men like Matthew Turner shouldn't be allowed to breed—they should be castrated at birth! That's a point—when's the little shit's birthday? I could fast forward to the day he was spawned and go round to the maternity unit and do it myself!"

"But you told me you wanted good old Matt to be your best man," said Emma. "Oh, my mate, Matt will do it—Matt's so cool—Matt this, Matt that. Do you really want him making his speech in a squeaky voice?"

"This is all one big joke to you, isn't it?" I yelled.

"Do you still love me now?" she smiled.

"No—I do-bloody-well-not! You two-timing, little tart! I hate you! I hate you—I hate women!"

"Well," said Emma, "so much for your unshakable, unbreakable faith. That was short and sweet. He's declared a fatwa on me and all my kind." She returned to her paperback and calmly read on.

"You should have told me all this before—I've made a right dickhead of myself chasing round after you. The Duck was right, there's plenty more where you came from, Gummer!"

Emma turned another page.

"And another thing—I never trusted you—oh no, I knew there was something going on between you and that slimy creep Turner. I knew it. I knew you two were at it!"

"Well, you were wrong then, because I made it all up."

"Hey?"

"The baby is yours and I have never had an affair with Matthew Turner," said Emma, looking up at me with her head tilted to one side, eyebrows arched.

"What? You expect me to fall for a line like that?" I laughed.

"No, I couldn't care less what you think," she shrugged. And went back to her book.

"You made it up?"

"If you say so, Stephen." She read on.

"Why?"

"I wanted to test that unshakable, unbreakable faith you had in me. I have to admit it was much stronger than I imagined—it lasted all of three seconds longer than I thought it would," she said. "I'm flattered—not."

"That's not fair. Come on, Em—you—you said the worst thing you could possibly say to a guy," I said. "All right, you put me to the test and I took the bait and—"

"You failed miserably."

"I admit I fell for it. If it had been anyone other than Matt Turner—"

"What difference would it have made who I'd shagged?"

"Well, Matt's my best mate."

"Your best mate? A minute ago you were going to jump in your time machine and de-bollock him at birth!"

"Yeah, but that was just a normal male reaction."

"Sloane, there is nothing normal about you."

"Emma, it's in our genes, love—we're programmed to react that way—haven't you heard of the harem-castration syndrome? It's been around since the dawn of time. Guys want to mate with as many females as possible and try to stop the rest of the lads in the tribe getting a look-in. It's all perfectly normal and healthy," I said. "That's why I was behaving a bit off with you. I didn't mean it. I didn't mean it, darling. Love? You didn't think I meant it, did you? All that stuff…"

"Don't simper, Stephen."

A voice called down from the hatch. "Hey, man, like, is everything okay down there?" It was John. "We thought we heard someone screaming."

"The coffee was a bit hot!" I shouted up. "Go back to your meditation!"

"Uh, cool. Uh, actually, Steve, Jody, and I thought we'd go and find ourselves now, if that's all right with you."

"Find yourselves?" I said. "Where?"

"Wherever it's at, man," said John.

"It could be within us or without us," said Jody.

"Yeah, like far out or all in the mind," said John.

"What do you think, Steve?" said Jody. "Can we make it?"

"Well, I don't know, it's a wild and wacky world out there, you guys."

"Yeah, but, um, you know, er, if we can kinda like tune in, man," said John. "We just might stand a chance, don't you agree?"

"Go for it, man."

"Hey, wow—like love and peace, man!" cried John.

"We knew you'd understand, man," said Jody. "So long, Steve, love and peace, man. You, too, Emma."

"Yeah, love and peace," I said.

"Just do it," said Emma.

We heard them tramping up the gangplank and chattering excitedly as they left on the voyage of self-discovery we call life. Yeah, it was kind of funny hearing them express themselves like that, but kind of touching, too.

"You know, in my own way, I think I really helped those kids," I said.

"Steve, don't kid yourself," said Emma. "You turned them into Sloane clones—their lives are going to be hell."

I thought about that. "You may just have a point there. I'll go and call them back."

"Oh, leave them alone!"

"Yeah, you're right. Em, can't we stop all this fussing and fighting now? Can't we be friends again?"

"I am your friend, Stephen," she smiled. "But I love Travis."

"But you can't mean that, love," I said. "It's so—so irrational—we're expecting a baby together. We still have issues here."

"I love Travis De Quipp. End of story."

"Look, will you please just try something for me a minute?" I looked round for a pen and paper. I found a desk diary and a biro on a shelf. I tore out a note page from the back and handed it to her. "Here, take this pen and paper and try to focus in on your subconscious feelings for Travis."

"My subconscious feelings for Travis?" she said, pulling a pained expression. "What do you mean?"

"It can mean anything you want it to mean—I just want to prove to you how irrational our emotions can be. This is classic market research, trust me," I said.

"Anything?"

"Whatever comes into your head when you think of Travis," I nodded. "Don't think about it—just let your pen flow over the paper."

She drew a long cigar-shape and passed it to me.

"What's that supposed to be?" I said.

"You tell me," she said, sucking the pen.

"Well, let me see, it could be a, um, it looks like a, um, what the hell is it?" I said. "It looks a bit phallic." I ripped it up. "You did that on bloody purpose!" I said.

"Got a bigger piece of paper?" she smirked, and went back to her book.

I stormed off up the stairs. Just as I got to the hatchway, a big black Norton motorbike, with two people astride it, zipped up in leathers, wearing goggles and black helmets—one big, one small—drove onto the quayside, mounted the end of the gangplank, and bounced down onto the deck. The tall driver switched the roaring engine off and the little one jumped off the back and lifted her goggles up.

"Steve!" she cried, running to throw her arms around my neck and kiss me. "Oh, I missed you."

"Emily, Emily," I smiled. "How did it go?"

Tree dismounted. "Don't ask," he said.

"They blew up Daddy's farm!" cried Emily excitedly.

"Oh, no. What happened?" I said. "Come below—I'll put the kettle on."

"They blew up everything—even the wood shed!" said Emily. "They even blew up the car! They would have blown us up if Daddy hadn't remembered his old Norton—they locked us up in the barn with it, and Daddy got it going and we smashed through the door like James Bond! Then we rode over to Taunton and bought all this biker gear—isn't it just the coolest?"

"Yes, yes—you must tell us all about it," I said. I turned her round and faced her down the steps. "Later."

I stood aside to let Tree go next and patted him on the back.

By the time I got down to the cabin, Tree and Emily had removed their helmets, unzipped their leathers and were lounging on the bench seats. Emma was already putting the coffee on, so I sat down at the dining table. Then Emily stood up and gave me a little fashion show on the pretence of following Emma out into the galley. I heard her chattering away, telling Emma all about their narrow escape in Somerset.

"So what happened?" I asked Tree.

"They were waiting for us," he sighed. "Either they got very lucky or someone tipped them off."

"Tipped them off? How? I mean—who?"

"Wish I knew."

"We've had a couple of visitors here, too," I said.

"Here?" He looked around. "Where?"

"Don't worry—they've gone—I got rid of them," I said.

"When was this? You didn't tell them where we were, I hope?" said Tree.

I shook my head. "No way, man. I just persuaded them to get a life. And they left."

"Just like that?"

"Just like that," I said. "Mind you, it took me all night to talk them round."

"I think I need to ask you a question," said Tree sternly.

"Yeah, I understand. Go ahead," I said.

"What did you borrow off me at Knebworth?"

"A Tibetan hat," I said.

Tree smiled and reached out his hand. I stretched over mine and gave him five.

"They must be tracking us somehow," said Tree. "The net's closing. You might have seen two off, but they'll be back as sure as eggs is eggs. We'd best leave as soon as we can."

"Yeah, tempus fugit. Did you manage to save the drawings?" I said.

He put his hand inside his leathers and pulled out a bundle of papers, and tossed them on the coffee table.

"Nice one!" I said.

I slid off my seat and picked them up, and began leafing through them. They were mostly interiors—sketchily drawn scenes of men and women sitting around in what looked like an ancient dungeon—there were a few others of inmates exercising, but they were all enclosed by walls. I was disappointed. And then I found two, right down the bottom, that were exactly what I had been hoping to find—they showed the view from a cell window—one looking towards a distant coastline, which seemed to curve around like a horseshoe, and the other from a completely different viewpoint.

I held it up.

"Where were you when you drew this?" I asked him.

He took it from me and looked at it for a moment or two. "That's looking east," he said. "I was recovering from frostbite—that's the view from the infirmary window."

I sat down next to him and pointed. "What are these outlines, here and this flat-topped one here?"

"Islands," he said.

"I was hoping you were going to say that," I smiled.

"Why—how does that help us?" he said.

I fetched the diary from the shelf and took the biro out of my jacket pocket and showed him. "Because it means we can do this," I said. I drew a crude aerial idea of the Castle, set on an ice sheet, with a wavy line for the coast and the two islands in their relative positions. "It's rough, I know, but we can get it much better by really studying these two drawings, and any more I may have missed. We can make a map."

Emma and Emily brought the coffees in.

Tree shook his head. "I still don't see how a bad map is going to help us to find the Castle," he said.

Emily gave her father his coffee and sat down next to him. Emma put mine on the coffee table and then sat down on the coffee table next to it, picked up my scribble, quickly discarded it, and began turning over Tree's drawings, one by one.

"We are agreed the Castle is somewhere in the British Isles?" I said.

Tree nodded, wearily.

"But we don't know where and we don't know when?" I said.

Tree nodded and rubbed his eye. I could see that the memories were almost too painful for him to even think about. I turned my attention to Emily.

"Emily, do you remember you once told me your father believed the Castle to be in our distant past—in an Ice Age?" I said.

"Yes, Stephen, I do." She looked to her father. "That's what you said, isn't it, Daddy?"

Tree nodded and sighed. "It is in the past," he said.

"You mean the Castle is in the past?" I said.

"Yes," sighed Tree.

"How do you know?" I said.

"Steve, stop pressing," said Emma. "Can't you see Tree's upset?"

"No, it's all right, Emma," said Tree. "Stephen's right—we must try to find that evil place and get poor Roger out."

"And Jools," said Emily.

"The Duck is quite capable of taking care of himself," said Tree. "It's Roger Jemmons I'm worried about. He has been a good friend."

"There's been no sign of the Duck," I said. "I think we can assume the worst, Tree. I'm afraid I haven't told you everything."

Everybody's attention immediately focussed on me. I told them the whole story, more or less, though leaving out the bit about my, uh, brief emotional attachment to Miss Parker or the Princess Mormagleea, or whatever her name was.

"Are you sure that wasn't the real Jemmons in that attic?" said Tree. "The way you tell it, it sounds to me as if he could have been attacking Bentley not you. He might have known Bentley was a traitor."

"Oh, he meant me all right," I said. "Damn near had my head off."

"Do you believe all this stuff about a princess? It sounds far-fetched to me," said Emma, to the others.

"And why would she dress up in a nurse's uniform and nurse you? It sounds a bit kinky to me," said Emily, pulling a face. "Did she wear thigh boots?"

"Emily!" said Tree.

"Look, what am I—an unreliable witness? I'm only telling you what I saw and heard," I said.

"Travis is in danger," said Emma, thinking aloud. "We have to find this place."

"That's what I've been trying to tell everybody—it's the key to this whole mess. Something is going down and the Duck's at the bottom of it as usual," I said.

"Well, I think Julian and Travis have been very brave," said Emma. "You're the one who's been completely useless in all this."

"*What*? Well, you would say that, wouldn't you—if loverboy's involved it can't be dodgy, can it?"

"Travis has more honour in his little finger than you'll ever have," said Emma.

"Weren't you listening to a thing I said? They set me up—they're as thick as thieves!"

"They probably just wanted you out of the way, while they rescued this princess, because they knew you'd be absolutely useless!" she said.

"Emma-Stephen-please," said Tree. "We must not allow personal rivalries to cloud our judgement. It's plain what must be done. We must go to the Castle and—and rescue whoever needs rescuing, if anyone does need rescuing—I mean, if we can find the place, which I very much doubt. Stephen and I will purchase some more suitable clothing and leave as soon as we work out where it is we're going."

"Hang about!" said Emma. "You're not leaving me here—I'm going with you."

"And me," said Emily, taking Emma's hand, in an act of sisterhood.

"Don't be daft," I said. "You're both pregnant!"

"Oh shut up!" said Emma. "We're only a few months gone—we're not invalids!"

"Yeah!" said Emily.

Tree and I looked at each other in dismay.

"Well," said Tree. "It's probably all academic anyway—it's highly unlikely we'll ever find the place. It'll be like looking for a needle in every haystack in England."

"Then let's get started," said Emma.

I folded my arms, leaned back, and smiled at her. "Go on then—what's your plan?" I said.

Emma turned to Tree. "Tree, you said the Castle is in the Ice Age—do you have any idea which one?"

"Which one?" said Tree. "Well, I don't know."

"Then what made you think it was in an Ice Age?" she asked.

"There were woolly mammoths—"

"Mammoths?" I said.

"Big hairy elephants, dear," said Emma. She turned her attention back to Tree. "That does sound like the last Ice Age. The woolly mammoth is believed to have died out some eight thousand years ago, though the last Arctic incursion had receded by about twenty thousand years ago and lasted around ten thousand years. So that means the Castle is almost certainly situated in a time window somewhere between 30,000 and 20,000 years ago. The Late Pleistocene."

"How do you know all this?" I said.

"Saw a Discovery Channel programme about it," said Emma. She turned back to Tree. "Do you think, with your artistic training, that you and Emily could look at the drawings Stephen picked out—and this one I found of what looks like another view of the ice sheet—and visualize a map?"

"Let me see that," I said.

Emma ignored me and passed the sheet to Emily.

"We can try, can't we, Daddy?" said Emily, taking the drawing from Emma. "I know how to transcribe perspective drawings into plans—Mr Wren showed me."

"Sir Christopher Wren?" I said.

"Who else, silly?" said Emily.

* * *

Emma had taken charge and I knew from that moment on I would be taking a backseat. It was my own fault. I'd been trying to be sarcastic when I asked her if she had a plan, not relinquish any control I might have had! She had us all organised within minutes. She quickly sussed that Emily had more idea about technical drawing than her father and got her to work alone on the rough map. Meanwhile, she had Tree drawing her a plan from memory of the Castle, on which she herself worked intensively and sensitively with him. I was detailed to make coffee, but once I'd done that, I was just standing around with my hands in my pockets. I watched Emma as she talked to Tree or checked on Emily's progress, encouraging them with a word of praise here, a smile there.

It started off innocently—I was admiring her—but it developed into something a bit more voyeuristic, when I fixated on the way her calf muscle curved into the neat scroll of her heel, or the way her sweater tautened each time she twisted round to speak to Emily, or the way her hair fell across her face and she let it stay there for a few moments before lazily pushing it aside with her hand, which, to me, was, uh, very attractive. And then, of course, there was her mouth—I loved Emma's mouth—and her eyes, but especially her mouth. She had perfect, smooth, full lips—in fact, she had actually modelled an entire range of lipsticks, from red through to blue—I still had the magazines with the adverts hidden behind my wardrobe—believe me, I have spent hours poring over those close-ups. I find it extremely erotic the way her lower lip pouts, while the upper lip sort of juts up proudly and you just get this glimpse of her teeth through the very suggestive gap between her—

"—Sloane!"

"What? Oh—Em."

"Stop leching," she said. "Can't you find something useful to do?"

"I wasn't leching. Leching."

"Why don't you go and clean the time machine or something?" she suggested.

"Clean the time machine?" I said. "It's not a car—no one sees it, it's in another dimension."

"I know—" she said, suddenly having another idea, "why don't you go and buy up as many Ordinance Survey maps as you can find?"

"We just need the coasts, Emma," said Tree.

"Only the ones with coastlines," added Emma.

"Uh, and what do I use for money?" I said.

"Here, take my credit card." She dug in her jacket pocket and passed it to me. "Give me your hand." I gave her my hand and she wrote her PIN number on my palm. "This is the number. Oh, and get some more cigarettes—you know my brand. Anyone else need anything?"

"I'd like some pistachio ice cream please," said Emily.

"Tree?" prompted Emma.

"We need tobacco and papers, Stephen," he said.

"Wait a minute," I said. "There aren't any cash machines yet—this is 1960. You haven't got a bank account!"

"Oh. Well, can't you use the time machine?"

"You want me to use the time machine to go shopping?"

"Is that a problem?"

"Of course it's a problem," I said. "I can't just jump in and—"

"Oh, please don't make a fuss, darling," she sighed.

The word "darling" shut me up instantly. I smiled sweetly at her.

"All right, I'll go." I stooped down and kissed her cheek. "I'm doing this for you, *darling*," I said.

She inclined her head towards me and we exchanged one of those intimate looks only those who have had something going would understand.

"We have got to have a long chat," I mouthed.

"Not now," she mouthed back, and turned away.

Chapter 10

It wasn't such a big deal using the time machine to go forward to the third millennium to use Emma's cash card. I deliberately arrived at night with Jemmons's machine in default mode and found myself floating on the river aboard an old sloop. She was called *La Belle* and she was Jemmons's pride and joy.

* * *

I had to wait around till morning for the shops to open, but I used some of the time up by walking into the city centre and withdrawing two hundred pounds from Emma's bank account. I was walking on air. I had that nice warm feeling inside me again. Things were looking up. All because—well, I don't want to talk about it... Then I found an early morning café and had a full, greasy, English breakfast. I started wondering how much Ordinance Survey maps cost and how many I'd need, and decided I might need more than the amount I'd taken out, so I went back to the cashpoint and withdrew another hundred. I was just walking up the High Street, to see if there were any stationery or bookshops opening early, when a police car screeched out of a side street and skidded up to the kerb, quite close to me. As I was looking round to see who they were after, I saw a second police car coming up the other way, and suddenly twigged—they were after me! It was the damn credit card—I'd forgotten the police were still looking for me in the third millennium—they wanted to question me about Emma's disappearance. Now, here I was using her plastic. No way was I going to stick around and try to explain the truth to them—they'd put me in an asylum!

I legged it past the first police car and made it to the corner—I could hear them reversing at high speed behind me. I kept running, desperately looking for somewhere to run to—and then I spotted a big department store just opening its doors across the street. It was my only chance. If I could get inside I might just be able to hide or lose them. I didn't hesitate. I put everything into reaching the entrance—pumping my arms and legs like pistons. And then I was pushing open the heavy glass door and running on carpet past hundreds of hanging handbags and glass counters full of cosmetics, past the elevators, rails of shirts and sweaters, socks and ties—someone shouted at me—I just kept running—and then I saw double glass doors. I had run straight through the ground floor of the store and was exiting it. It wasn't my original idea, but I never stopped to look around or think about what I was doing. And then I was in another street and running across that into a pedestrian walkway. On and on I ran, until I was in the next street over. I still didn't stop or look round. I was straight across the road and looking for another cut-through to the next street. I found the first one and darted down it.

Then I saw a multi-storey car park and the back of a restaurant with three wheelie-bins outside and an alleyway leading off somewhere else. I got behind the bins and threw my back against one. My chest was heaving and wheezing. My breath sounded like one of those old steam engines—thumping out a powerful panting noise. The sweat was pouring off me. I knew that I only had to get back down to the river and I'd be safe, so I didn't think my situation was hopeless. I just thought that for a twenty-six year old I was really out of condition. I vowed never to eat another breakfast like that again. It was bran and juice for me in future.

* * *

I realized the police had been just waiting for someone to use Emma's credit card, and when I took that money out in the middle of the night I must have alerted them. And when I used it again later that morning, they probably couldn't believe their luck. They simply got a mugshot of me from the ATM and the rest was down to the CCTV cameras Big Brother has in every city centre up and down the land. Well, I didn't take any chances after that scare, I worked my way back down to the quays using backstreets only and took the sloop back a few days, then I returned to the city centre to do my shopping. But I couldn't resist going up to a police car I saw parked in the high street and asking the driver if he knew where I could buy an Ordinance Survey map. He directed me to W H Smith's.

* * *

For the return trip I was careful to switch the holographic matrix over to the clock again, and also made sure I didn't arrive too soon and meet myself. Meeting yourself is dangerous—it's like standing between two mirrors and seeing infinite images of yourself, only the images are real and multiply, and some can even evolve into clones like that one of Jemmons in the attic—so I set the time control for the middle of the afternoon. We had stored the machine in an empty forward cabin, so the co-ordinates were already locked in. I arrived back on board precisely where I had departed from and headed excitedly along the central passageway to the living quarters, in the stern of the barge.

I had all the maps covering the coastlines of England, Scotland, and Wales—and I had also bought detailed maps of Ireland, just in case. And, of course, I hadn't forgotten everybody's goodies, so I was feeling pretty pleased with myself as I burst through the door.

"I'm back!" I shouted. "Emma? What's wrong with her?"

Emma was lying on the cushioned bench seat in the lounge half naked and Tree and Emily were holding her down. I threw down the shopping bags and rushed to her side, skidding along the floor on my knees to bring my face in line with hers.

"Emma? What's the matter? What the hell's happened?"

"Steve—there's something in my back," she sobbed.

"Where? What?" I knelt up straight and looked down her body. "Where?"

"It's on her other side," said Tree.

I leaned over and saw to my horror a pulsing green light about the size of a shirt button, under her skin. There was no visible scar—but it had actually got inside her somehow.

"Emily noticed it when I was in the shower," said Emma.

"Stay calm, Em," I said.

"Can't you take it out?"

"How? No, we have to leave it there—I think I know what it is."

"What?" said Emma.

"I don't think it's anything to worry about."

"That's easy for you to say! How did it get in there?"

"I don't know."

"Then how do you know what the damn thing is?" said Emma. "Tree, take me to a hospital—I want it removed right now!"

"We can't go to a hospital, Em, they'll just ask a lot of awkward questions and call the police or, even worse, the military," I said. "Remember I told you about that gadget on my arm? Well, I think this is something similar."

"It's nothing like that thing you described!" cried Emma. "Yours was just a bloody catheter! This is inside my body!"

"Em, I left something out," I sighed. I looked at Tree and Emily and then back at Emma. "I was also drugged. They slipped me something in that private clinic—I lost about three days and—and I thought I was in love with Miss Parker."

"So you screwed the nurse—what's that got to do with this?" said Emma.

I could see she was becoming highly stressed. And kept my voice calm.

"I didn't screw the nurse. What I said was I became infatuated with her—just like you have become obsessed with Travis De Quipp—"

"Oh, for God's sake!" exclaimed Emma. "Not that again—you're the one who's obsessed! Tree, Emily, please call me an ambulance."

"You're an ambulance," blurted Emily, and quickly covered her mouth with her hand. "Sorry—it just slipped out."

Tree looked to me. I shook my head.

"Stephen's right, Emma," said Tree. "This looks like another implant—it's too much of a co-incidence."

"Oh, not you as well!" she cried.

She tried to raise herself up but we all held her down.

"Let go of me! I'm going to Casualty—I want this thing removed! Get off me!"

"Emma—listen to me—is it hurting you?" I said.

"No."

"Then just leave it. It's just one more reason for us to find the Duck as soon as possible. He knows about these things. He'll know what to do," I said. And then under my breath I added, "He probably put it there."

"All right!" she snapped. "Now let me up!"

"You won't go to hospital?" I said.

"No. Now get off me—all of you!"

We let her go. She jumped up, pushed me out of the way and rushed to her cabin, crying. Emily hurried after her, closing the door quietly behind her.

I went over and got the bags and brought them back to the coffee table.

"I got all the OS maps—how did Emily get on?"

Tree shuffled through some papers on the floor and handed me a neatly drawn map, depicting the Castle island, the two islands in the bay, and the horseshoe-shaped coastline. A simple arrow indicated north. She had even drawn a cute cartoon of a family of mammoths crossing the bottom of the page.

"This is the best she could do," he said. "She's made four copies. I estimate the distance from the Castle to the coast to be no more than fifteen miles east—the islands are a little less again—though the one on the right is the farthest away. This is taking the curvature of the earth and a rough idea of the Castle's height into account."

"That narrows it down a bit. You see, this layout—the land shape—this pattern of three islands can't be that common, can it?" I said. "It's just going to take a shedload of patience to find somewhere that looks like it on one of these maps."

"Then we'd best get started," said Tree.

We took a map each and I went over to work on the dining table, while Tree laid his out on the coffee table. Later Emily came out to make Emma a coffee and get her cigarettes. I gave her the two remaining copies of the map she had made and a bundle of the ones I'd bought. She took them back with her, saying that she thought Emma would prefer to work in her cabin.

We worked all the rest of that afternoon and into the early evening. I went to see how the girls were doing a couple of times, but they had only turned up a couple of possibles, though neither of them quite fitted in with the direction of north on Emily's map, so they were dismissed. The map-checking continued into the night. Every time one of us found somewhere we thought might be the place, the others pointed out something that excluded it—either the distances were out—the compass bearing off—the presence of other prominent landmarks that would have been visible—something was always wrong. Eventually, we ran out of maps. Everyone wanted to go to bed, but I produced my less detailed Irish maps and we carried on for another hour or so. We drew another blank. Finally, disappointed and beaten, we all turned in.

But I couldn't sleep. As I lay there I suddenly thought about the Somerset Levels. Somerset was once encroached by the sea. I didn't really know how, but I knew the landscape and coastline must have looked very different back in the Ice Age. What if Glastonbury were one of the islands in the bay? And the other was flat-topped Cadbury! The idea excited me—I leapt from my bed and rushed back into the lounge to get out the map of Somerset. That would mean that the Castle was Brent Knoll! It had to be—everything was spot on. The coastline was the Mendips to the north, the Quantocks and Blackdown Hills to the west, and the Dorset Downs to the south.

I woke Tree, dragged him out of bed, and showed him.

"Somerset? It can't be," he said.

"Compare Emily's map," I said. "See, there—and there—the islands—one pointed and one flattish. It all fits."

"It seems to fit," he yawned. "But how come we couldn't see the coast of Wales to the north? There was just an ice sheet. We, we were looking at it for seven years—you're hardly likely to forget a thing like that."

"You haven't," I said. "What you were looking at was the edge of the Great Ice Sheet itself, beyond the frozen Bristol Channel. It's an optical illusion—because you were looking at white on white, you couldn't tell where one ended and the other began."

"It's possible I suppose," he said. "Show Emma and Emily in the morning. Now can I get back to sleep?"

I could hardly wait till morning, got impatient and went into Emma's cabin to wake her up at seven a.m. Emily had crashed out in there with her. They were both only half awake as I launched into my brilliant theory.

Halfway in, Emily muttered, "I thought Cadbury was a man-made hill. It was flattened off much later."

"It wasn't, was it?" I said. "Are you sure?"

"Yes, I think so," said Emily. "Would you be a dear and make us a cup of coffee?"

"Yeah, sure. But let's just think about this first—how certain are you about Cadbury?"

Emma butted in, "The sea-level would have been about four hundred feet below what it is today, anyway."

"You're kidding!" I said. "There was tons of water about—it was the bloody Ice Age!"

"Yes, but it was all locked up inside the ice sheet—it was thousands of feet thick," she yawned. "The sea-level sank—you could walk to France, Stephen. Now, about that coffee."

* * *

I walked back to the galley, where Tree, who had heard me moving about, was already up and making a pot of coffee.

"The theory's blown," I said, slumping down on a stool.

"Yes," he nodded. "Cadbury's an ancient earthwork—but not as old as the late Pleistocene. I remembered when I got back to bed."

"Well, I wish you'd come and told me," I said. "I've just made myself look a right pillock in there. Also, the water-level would have been—"

"—Yes, way too low," nodded Tree. "So, I got to thinking—your landscape fits so well—why couldn't it be in the future—a New Ice Age, though not as severe—a thinner ice sheet—higher water levels?"

"Is that possible?"

"I don't see why not—what with global warming—maybe the thing was just getting started," said Tree, pouring four coffees.

"Ah, but what about the mammoths? You said there were woolly mammoths."

"Genetically cloned from the DNA of those frozen Siberian ones and the Indian Elephant, its closest relative," said Tree. "A new species for a new climate. A lot of that malarkey went on in the third millennium. They were cloning everything from carrots to humans—till the Clone Wars. Then it was banned."

"You mean human clones will one day fight real humans?"

"No I mean carrots will fight humans," he said. He picked up two of the cups and set off for the sleeping quarters.

"You are joking!" I said.

"No—some smart alec developed a self-picking variety—they formed an underground alliance with the turnips and potatoes and revolted in East Anglia and the American Garden States!"

* * *

A new plan was made over breakfast. It was decided that Tree would take the time machine forward to the end of the third millennium and find out when the woolly mammoth was genetically brought back from extinction, and what date the mini Ice Age occurred. He would then go to that time period and look up the maps for the Somerset Levels. If a prison or a castle was ever built on Brent Knoll there would be some record of it somewhere. There was no risk, he assured us—he would just look it all up in a Personal Leisure Education And Simulated Ultra Restful Environment-Dome. These things were the twenty-ninth century equivalent of a phone box, the internet and an amusement arcade all rolled into one, but they had a teleportation service and access to much more information, as well as *realview* links to the rest of the world and all the new space colonies. You could receive food and drink inside them, sleep in them, obtain a divorce, or, if you were really bored with life, pay to enter a virtual reality world in which your wildest dreams could be realized. By the last century of the third millennium the old expression, *get a life* had evolved into, *have you got change for a life?* The smart answer to which was, *yes, but do you really want this change?* If there was a danger, Tree informed us, it was that some people found PLEASURE-Domes so seductive that they never came out of them again, even though they were no bigger than a seaside changing-hut. They just signed all their money and possessions over to the company that sponsored or owned the particular one they had taken a fancy to and retired in them. The late twenty-ninth century landscape was apparently littered with these strange cylindrical booths, topped with their characteristic onion domes, which Tree told me were matter transceivers. They sounded to me like the end of civilisation.

* * *

Six hours later I was blaming myself:

"I should have gone with him," I said.

Emily was sitting on the lounge bench—crying her eyes out—being comforted by Emma.

"The best laid plans of trees and men," I said. "We're right up the creek now. Literally. Stuck on a barge in Bristol in nineteen-bloody-sixty. Black and white telly, two lousy channels, and the worst food in Europe. Oh well, at least we've got England's 1966 World Cup win to look forward to. I checked the last time I was in the third millennium—thirty years of hurt? England won't win it again for at least a thousand years!"

"Oh, shut up, Stephen," said Emma. "Can't you see Emily's upset?"

"I'm sorry, but this is just typical of the sort of luck I have," I said.

"This isn't just about you, you know—we're all in this together," said Emma. "Emily, do you want to go for a walk? We can get away from his moaning."

Emily sniffed a nod.

I watched them climb the wooden staircase and listened to them walk across the deck and go up the gangplank. And then I went and got the big tub of pistachio ice cream from the fridge and scoffed the lot. I did start to feel a bit guilty, not just about eating Emily's ice cream, but also about not seeming to care about old Tree. Anything could have happened to him. He could have been dead for all I knew.

* * *

It was starting to get dark. I lay on the lounge bench and closed my eyes. No sooner had I shut them than I began to have the strangest, most vivid dream—a floating dream. I know I was floating on a barge, but the river was so calm and the barge so heavy that there was hardly any sensation of movement. No, this was a gentle rocking motion, accompanied by a peculiar pulsing vibration. And then I got the impression that I could hear water dripping—thousands of tiny droplets of water. It was quite a restful feeling, even though the dream was so lucid. I opened my eyes and smiled—the whole of the barge's interior, fixtures and fittings, superstructure—even the cups on the table and the little curtains at the windows—were imbued with blue, green and red light. What I mean is, certain straight lines were turning a neon red, while anything with curvy lines—like the light bulbs, empty ice cream tub, my clothes, were blue, and even green in patches, but not ordinary green, because all the backgrounds to the solids were black, so the colours looked brighter. It was as though someone had sketched the cabin on black paper with crayons made of light. I noticed the pulsing sound was getting louder and changing pitch. It sounded like someone repeatedly opening and closing a squeaky door, only the tone of the squeak was low-pitched and evenly modulated.

I sat up and looked around me. All the colours were pulsing. I reached over and drew aside the curtain and peered out. The quay was slowly sinking. Two pairs of women's legs ran by. I heard someone shouting my name. But I was unconcerned. It was just a dream. I lay back down and closed my eyes, a smug smile on my lips. And then I heard a banging on the window and sprang upright, tore back the curtain and saw Emma and Emily's horrified faces.

"It's sinking up!" I said.

I rolled off the bench and launched myself towards the stairs. The noise had become much louder now and the colours were pulsing quicker to keep up. I could hear myself clattering up the stairs, but my legs and arms felt heavy and I realized my feet were sliding off the same rung and my hands were pulling on the same parts of the handrails. I wasn't getting anywhere! Then I really panicked. The noise was now deafening—the coloured light a rapid flicker.

"I can't get up! Can't get up!" I yelled.

The barge was like a coloured X-ray all around me. Although I couldn't see the outside, I could see through the interior of it to the forward cabins and down into the bilge. I could even see through the wooden rungs I was trying to climb up. It was as if the whole molecular structure of the barge was breaking down. I was terrified. I kept trying to pull myself up but I was only able to scale a few rungs. I heard a voice above me.

"Steve! Steve! Take my hand!"

I looked up and saw Emma reaching down to me. I let go of the rail with my right hand and tried to stretch it up to her.

"I can't," I said. "Get off! Go!"

"No!" she shouted. "You can reach! Try—come on!"

I made one last effort with what little strength I had left and blindly threw myself up, hoping she could grab my hand. I felt her hand snap around mine and hold me. And then her other hand locked onto my wrist and she was practically dragging my whole body weight up the ladder, though I was helping as much as I could by pulling on the rail and trying to kick off the rungs.

And then we were in each other's arms rolling on the deck, desperately trying to keep hold and yet stand up at the same time. I could see the gangplank was gone and we were level with the streetlights on the quay.

"It's going up," I gasped. "We'll have to jump!"

We staggered up and were thrown against the gunwale—our bodies naturally bent over the side, like we were both being sick. Suddenly, I really did feel sick—in a few seconds we rose a hundred feet at least, but no one told my stomach. Emily's face was a pink speck on the quayside. We were rising higher and higher above the rooftops of Clifton and could soon see all the lights of Bristol laid out below us. There was no way either of us could have jumped—the river was already just a thin black ribbon we might easily miss. But then suddenly I was amazed to see Emma trying to climb up on the rail. I pulled her back.

"Are you mad?" I shouted. "You'll kill yourself!"

"We've got to try!" she cried.

But, in the next instant, there could be no second thoughts, no more arguments—the decision was taken out of our hands. The barge suddenly stopped rising and shot off to the west at lightning speed, and it was all we could do to hang on for dear life.

Chapter 11

We must have looked like a UFO to the casual observer, out walking the dog, or spending a romantic evening up some lonely country lane. The old barge was lit up like Las Vegas and we were hurtling high up in the night sky over some of the most sparsely populated countryside in England. We headed straight west above the Mendip Hills and angled down into the Somerset Levels—a distance of some thirty miles, covered in a matter of moments. Emma and I watched the whole journey, spellbound, clinging to the safety rail—too terrified to move, in case the wind snatched us away.

"What's happening?" cried Emma, as our descent speed slowed.

The landscape had assumed a sort of monochrome glow—all ghostly pale and streaked with shadows.

"I can see Glastonbury—and, look—there—is that Brent Knoll?" I said.

"The light!" said Emma. "It's getting lighter."

She was right. The night was draining away, fading from the zenith point, and leaching back to the horizon.

"It's another day—" I started to say.

"Ice!" screamed Emma, throwing herself on me like a rugby player and bringing us both down on the decking with a double thud.

There was a huge jolt, followed by a crunching sound and then a prolonged scraping and bumping. We didn't dare look up to see what was happening, but it was pretty obvious to us both that the barge had landed and was skidding on ice.

By now the evening had peeled away and we were squinting up into a glaring grey sky. On and on the heavy boat rumbled like someone bowing a very large violin. We could feel it shudder on every uneven patch and skewing round and round as it raced along, but it was gradually slowing down. Once it had slowed to a safe speed, we both clambered to our feet. We looked around us and then at each other.

"You know where this is, don't you?" said Emma, her breath smoking in the cold air.

"Well, it's not the Ally Pally Ice Rink, that's for sure," I said.

The barge was back to normal again—all the strange lights had vanished and whatever force had been holding us was gone.

"No sign of life," said Emma. She shivered and wrapped her arms around herself. "Brrr—it's freezing. I'm going down to find something to put on." She went below.

I blew into my hands and climbed up onto the roof. I walked forward. Though the barge was still skidding, it was now a gentle slide, and I could easily keep my balance. I was so confident I even put my hands in my trouser pockets. When I reached the end I rested one foot up on the bow, something in the manner of a figurehead. We were barely moving by now and the ice was making a pleasant groaning sound, rather like a long, comfortable fart. Finally, we ground to a halt. And everything fell silent.

"We've stopped, Em!" I shouted.

"Steve?" said Emma.

"I'm up here!" I called.

I looked back and saw her head and shoulders pop up above the flat roof.

"I brought you this." She held up a dark brown coat. It was probably Tree's old army trench coat.

"It'll be miles too long for me," I said.

"Who cares what you look like out here?" she said.

I walked back and jumped down to join her on the aft deck. She held the coat open for me to slip on. "There you go," she smiled.

"Thank you," I said, staring at her. She stared back at me for a moment or two, as though remembering something, and then looked away.

I was just enjoying being with her, without us niggling at each other. It felt just like old times—except for the very unEmma-like clothing. She was wearing a green anorak with a hood, a bit like an old-fashioned parka. It looked at least three sizes too big for her, but she had rolled up the sleeves and somehow managed to make it look quite stylish.

"Where did you find that?" I said.

"It's Tree's. Doesn't it feel funny to be here?" she said, gazing around. "I mean, after looking at all those maps."

"It's not like I imagined," I said. "Everything's so white—I can hardly pick anything out."

"I'll get the shades," she said, making her way back down the stairs.

"Good idea. And put the kettle on!"

"Watch it, Sloane."

I turned around and leaned against the wheel, looking back out over the stern. I wish I hadn't. I wish I could have spent just a few more blissful minutes with her, undisturbed, without worrying about where we were exactly, or how much trouble we were in. Now I knew. Something very large and very fast was approaching us from what I took to be— going by the orientation of our landing and the track we had left across the ice—north, because although we had come from the east our stern had clearly slewed round to point in that direction. I was tempted to shout down to her something tough like, *we've got company*, but settled for:

"There's a big white thing coming!"

"A what?" she shouted up.

"We've got company!" I yelled.

"God—where?" she cried. I heard her clattering up the stairs.

By the time she reached me, the huge hovercraft-like vessel was alongside, towering over us like an enormous wedding cake. We were straining our necks to look up at the rail to see if we could see anybody— it must have been some fifty feet up. The next thing, there was a loud hiss and a portal opened in the hull—a metal gangplank shot out—half a dozen fur clad military types, wearing goggles and waving batons, charged out and boarded us. Four of them grabbed us by our arms; the other two started sticking slabs of what looked like plastic explosive everywhere.

I was going to say, *where are you taking us?* But, instead, I said to one of them, "I bet you listen to Neil Diamond records when you're off duty."

They never said a word back, but made us run into their mothership with them, because if we didn't our feet would have dragged. We found ourselves in a large hangar. I noticed dozens of snazzy snowmobiles parked in bays and quaint slogans painted on the walls, saying things like, *Security is Power*, *Purity is Order*, and *Unity is a Lovely Girl*. Actually, I made that last one up, but you get the gist.

A bad-tempered looking guy with an electronic clipboard and lots of gold braid and colourful insignia on his uniform—an officer—marched up to us, looked me up and down, and snapped:

"You are Sloane!"

"Yeah," I said. "What if I am? I'm allowed to be if I am."

One of his men prodded me with his baton and about forty thousand volts shot up my arm and rang the bell in the fairground test of strength contraption up in my brain.

The officer stretched his neck to loosen his collar and stepped to his left to address Emma.

"And you are the pregnant female," he sneered.

"No, that's me," I said.

Another forty thousand volts shot up my elbow and stir-fried a few million more of my brain cells.

Emma pointed sideways at me. "He made me do it, officer," she said.

I smirked to myself. Yeah, I remember that evening, I thought. I was like a wild animal that night. A beast.

Suddenly, we heard a series of loud explosions coming from outside on the ice.

The officer flinched each time one went off and then permitted himself a curt smile. "That was your boat," he said. "We blew it up. No more picnics on the river for you."

"I have a confession to make," I said.

"Speak!" he yelped.

"It wasn't our boat."

Our interrogator nodded and another forty thousand volts sizzled my wok. And then he began pacing up and down, talking to us, but not bothering to look at us, in a mechanical voice.

"You are mutants and time fugitives—there will be a trial, but the verdict will be guilty as charged, and you will both be taken to the Castle, from which no convict has ever escaped and lived to sell the film rights."

I raised my hand. "I have a question," I said. "Can you give us a ballpark figure on the length of sentence we can expect to receive?"

"Life!" he cried shrilly. "Life! You will each receive life sentences!" He calmed his voice right down. "But this may be commuted to fifty years for good behaviour and if, of course, you plead guilty."

"And is there a rehabilitation program in place?" I asked.

"Rehabilitation? What is this?"

"Re-training, help with housing, counselling—that sort of thing," I said.

"He means when we get out," said Emma.

"Oh, you mean when you go to the labour camp? Yes, you will get a hut," said our interrogator. "Now, I will conduct the trial." He checked his clipboard. "Let me see, ah, yes—*if the prisoner pleads guilty, go directly to question five.* Do you both plead guilty?"

I looked to Emma. "Guilty, love—yeah?"

"Yes, please," she nodded.

"So—both prisoners plead guilty—we go to question five—*Will you ever do it again?*" He looked up. "It's multiple choice. Is it: *a) Never, b) Unlikely, c) Maybe, or d) Definitely*?"

I looked to Emma to confer. "What do you think, love—*unlikely*?"

"I would have said *a) Never*," said Emma.

"Yeah—we won't do it again, will we? Put us down for *a) Never*," I said. "And what was it we were pleading guilty to again?"

I got the cattle prod again for that one.

The officer keyed another tick in the box and marked other places with crosses, and then handed me the clipboard and his electronic pen.

"Here, sign there, there and there—and then the female has to sign here, here and here," he said.

I signed and talked at the same time, "I was wondering—is the captain of this old bucket licensed to conduct marriages?"

I heard a loud buzz and smelt the faint odour of burnt pork...

* * *

I came round in a metal box cell. There were no windows and little air. Emma was sitting next to me with her chin resting on her knees and her back against the wall, looking cheesed off. We were both wearing shackles on our ankles. I rattled mine.

"Hey—wow! So they married us!" I cried.

Emma elbowed me in the ribs.

"A girl's entitled to expect a nicer honeymoon than this," she said. "Not to mention groom."

"Oh, darling, don't go all picky on me—we haven't seen our room at the Castle yet," I said. "It sounds kind of swish—I wonder if they have medieval banqueting nights. I hope we get the Guinevere Suite."

"Really, Steve," said Emma, "I'm feeling pretty uneasy about this."

"Uneasy?" I said. "I'm bloody petrified! But we mustn't let these people see we're frightened—they like frightening people. It turns them on." I rattled my shackles again. "All this S and M."

"Don't get any ideas, Sloane."

"Hey, Em. You remember in Orwell's *1984* when they've got old Winston in room 101 and they're threatening him with his worst nightmare—having his face eaten alive by rats?"

"Oh shut up!"

"No—listen—and then they say we'll stop if you say, don't do it to me, do it to Julia! You know, Julia, his girlfriend? Me Julie."

"Yes," sighed Emma. "Do we have to talk about this now?"

"What if they said to you, you can choose one of you to go free—who would you choose?" I said.

"Me, of course," she said.

"Yeah?"

"Isn't it obvious?"

"It is?"

"Yes—there's two of me, isn't there? Me and our unborn child," she said. "You'd choose us, wouldn't you?"

"Oh, yeah—absolutely! If you put it like that. Of course—no question, Em," I said.

The door swung open and two fur-coated guards looked in.

"Right—who's first?" one of them said.

"Him!"-"Her!" we both blurted, pointing to each other.

They pulled me roughly to my feet. "I love you, Em!" I called back, as I shuffled out with them.

"Yes, I know you do!" called Emma. "If you see Travis—tell him I love *him*!"

They led me along the wide passageway, which I noticed had sets of coloured lines painted along its sides. Like in a big hospital. I noted that we were following the white one mostly. The design of the ship was very plain, big and plain: big staircases, big walkways, big rivets, big doors—big bolts and knobs on the doors—every little thing was big! I think it was what you would call neo-Brutalism.

"Why have you split us up?" I said, desperately trying to keep up, but it was difficult with the leg-irons on.

"She goes to the women's cells," said one of my guards, giving me a helpful push along.

"But I thought we would be together?" I said, remembering Tree's drawings of male and female prisoners enjoying free association in their open-plan dungeons.

"You might breed," he sniggered.

The other one—a surly looking guy—said something to him in another language—I think it was a future language, called Worldese—and they both laughed at me.

We came to a big lift and they shoved me in ahead of them.

"What is so wrong with breeding?" I said. "Where I come from it's all we ever think about. What did they do to you guys—remove ninety-eight percent of your brain cells?"

"Breeding is for filthy animals of the field," said the talkative one.

"Come on, guys—why should they have all the fun? In my time, we have magazines filled with great pictures of girls who look fit for good breeding—we even have demonstration videos showing all the best breeding techniques and variations—breeding's an art form—in fact, I have a black suspender belt in breeding—I'm a breeding master—"

"Silence! You disgust me, you degenerate!" said the other one.

"Ah, so—you've seen my video!" I said.

He poked me with his cattle prod thing and sent me crashing against the big white elevator wall.

"You know that stick's just a substitute for the one you should be using to breed with," I said.

He wanted to hit-me-baby-one-more-time with his shock stick, but his mate blocked his way and said something to him in their lingo to calm him down.

The door hissed open and we stepped out on deck into highly reflected sunshine. I shielded my eyes. My guards pulled down their goggles. The walkway we were on curved around the vessel's central superstructure, with a continuous rail on the outside and identical doors and portholes on the inside. There were big white pom-pom guns mounted at regular intervals around the rail, making it look even more like an iced cake. I knew there was no means of escape. If I jumped, there was a fifty-foot drop onto hard ice, and if I threw myself through a door I wouldn't have got far in my shackles. So I bowed my head to avoid the dazzle and settled into a steady shambling gait between my captors.

We were moored alongside what looked like an enormous iceberg, but then I realized it was the side of a hill—a hill of glaring snow. I looked up, expecting to see the Castle at last, but the summit of the knoll, which rose steeply from the flat landscape of the Somerset Levels, was obscured by mist.

I could already see a strange bridge or jetty spanning the chasm between the vessel and the hillside. It was unusual because I couldn't see any visible means of support or, more alarmingly, any handrails.

"You expect me to walk across that?" I said.

My guards said nothing, but when we came to the stepping off point, they shoved me on and it was too dangerous to resist. Once I was standing on the structure, which was no more than four feet wide, I found to my surprise that I did not have to move—the path simply carried us through mid air towards the hill, like a people mover at an airport. I couldn't bear to look down but I did move my eyes to the left and right repeatedly—though there wasn't much to see. I could make out a platform at the end of the moving jetty and miles and miles of ice sheet, stretching away to every horizon.

"There used to be a motorway through here," I said. "Which way is Weston-Super-Mare? We used to call it Weston-Super-Mud." I chatted away. "Jeffrey Archer was born there—you must have heard of Jeffrey Archer—the literary genius? Dickens, Tolstoy, Joyce, Archer—don't tell me you don't read these guys any more? Guys?"

I knew my guards were right behind me, but I wasn't going to risk turning round to look at them. I was just hoping they were going to say something—anything—anything that might tell me where we were and what the date was. Though I didn't really expect them to answer me—it would probably have been a breach of security. On the other hand, they might quite genuinely not have known what the hell I was on about. I mean—I wasn't that sure myself.

I stepped onto the metal staging and stamped my feet on terra firma—though it was only the size of an opera box with a three-foot high handrail around it.

"That's better," I said, turning round. My guards were gone and so was the bridge!

But the piece of neo-Brutalist confectionery was still moored there and I could see a few tiny figures walking about on it, just following orders. I waved to two who looked like they might be the same ones who put me on the jetty thing, and shouted, but they were probably too far away to hear me.

"What am I supposed to do now?" I called.

Suddenly, there was a great roaring noise and the huge hovercraft rose several feet in the air and shot off across the ice sheet. I watched it until it reached vanishing point.

* * *

There was no way off the metal staging I was perched on—just sheer drops on all sides and no door. I was there so long, I thought it might be some sort of slow execution—instead of shooting people or hanging them, you just leave them on a lofty metal platform in sub-zero temperatures and let them freeze to death. The other thing that worried me while I was waiting there was I didn't see Emma being brought off, so I had to assume she was still aboard and was being taken somewhere else. It was all very sinister. Naturally, I did what all Brits do when the chips are down and the situation looks hopeless, I stiffened my upper lip— which wasn't difficult because it was frozen to my bottom one.

* * *

Help came from a most unexpected quarter when it arrived—a bosun's chair bumped me on the head. These things must be the precursors of ski lifts—although they are nowhere near as lethal as a ski lift. They consist of a wooden board slung on a rope. Now normally they are used to hang off the side of ships so that the occupant can do repairs or paint the hull, but this one was suspended from somewhere far above me, so far above me that I couldn't see where it was coming from or who had sent it down, because the other end of the rope disappeared into the mist. Actually, I ignored it at first because there was no way I was going to go anywhere on anything that flimsy—especially not a hundred feet or so up into the clouds.

I cupped my hands and shouted up.

"You must be joking!"

The chair gave a little jiggle.

I cupped my hands again.

"I would rather freeze to death!" I yelled.

The chair started swinging about, slowly at first, but then more and more wildly. I had to duck and dodge out of the way. Eventually I caught hold of it and gave it a firm yank.

It yanked back fiercely—almost lifting my feet off the ground. I let go and it flew up in the air and bounced around uncontrollably. Finally, it settled down into a benign swing. A metallic sounding voice crackled down from the mist:

"Get into the chair! You will be perfectly safe."

"Safe? You call that safe?" I shouted up. "It's a bloody death-trap!"

"Get in!"

"No!"

"This is your last chance, mutant."

I folded my arms and looked out at the blank landscape.

"I am going to count to three," continued the metallic moron. "One…"

I ignored him.

"…Two…"

I leant against the rail and stared at it.

"…Three!"

The chair began to rise slowly. I watched it get to about twenty feet before I broke.

"All right!" I shouted. "I'll sit in your stupid chair!"

The chair carried on going up.

"Are you deaf?" I cried. "Send it back down, you bastard!"

The chair stopped. But it was way out of reach.

"What did you call me?" crackled the voice.

"Nothing," I said.

"Yes you did—you called me an illegal product of a bestial coupling," said the controller of the chair.

"Well, I'm sorry!" I said. "I lost my rag! Now lower the bloody chair—I'm freezing my bollocks off down here!"

"That's too good for your kind!"

The chair started to descend. Very slowly.

"Come on, you moron," I said.

The chair abruptly halted.

"I heard that!" said the voice.

This time the chair was just within reach—if I had been prepared to climb up on the rail and leap for it, I probably could have got it. I thought about it, because I didn't want to have to snivel to whoever it was up there again, but then I took a look over the side and saw how I high up I was and changed my mind.

"Sorry," I said.

There was a long pause.

"How sorry?" came the metallic response.

"Very," I said.

"What did you say?"

"I said 'very.'"

"You don't sound *very* sorry."

I climbed up on the handrail, jumped off, and caught the chair. The chair and I—plus about eight feet of rope—landed on the floor of the platform with a resounding thumpety-thump. I quickly untangled the board and sat on it, making sure my legs were securely through the loop.

"All right, I'm on—you can pull it up now," I said, without a trace of smugness in my voice. I just wanted to come in from the cold. I wasn't looking to score any points.

Nothing happened.

"Haul away!" I yelled up, hopefully.

Still nothing moved.

"I'm waiting," I called.

Slowly, the dope on a rope started feeding it down, until I had spirals of it around my feet. I folded my arms.

"That is very funny," I shouted up. "Now, can we stop assing about— I demand that you imprison me!"

"Tell me how sorry you are again," said the smug, moronic control freak on the other end of the line—I know what rope I'd have liked to see him dangling on!

"I," I said. "Am very." I paused. "Sorry!"

"Well, why didn't you say so in the first place?" said my tormentor.

The rope started to go up until all the rope that had been paid out was gone and the line tensed. At last I started to ascend.

The chair felt very springy going up, bouncing up and down and slowly turning round and round, but I just kept opening and shutting my eyes, holding on tight and gripping that board with my buttocks. Soon the staging I had spent so many happy times on looked no bigger than a matchbox, and I entered the mist.

"Most cons have to walk up here," crackled my metallic voiced friend. "You must have friends in high places to get a ride up in the chair."

Now, I must admit I thought the whole episode on the platform was a bit bizarre. And I do admit I was not amused and, therefore, may not have been in full command of my mental faculties, and maybe that's why I never caught on. There was just something about that idiot up there that didn't ring true. It wasn't so much the voice—that was obviously disguised and strained through a megaphone—no, it was the sheer petty, juvenile, bloody-mindedness of him.

"Duckworth—you bastard!"

I heard a metallic quack.

Chapter 12

"You should have heard yourself," laughed the Duck, from somewhere in the mist. "It was bloody priceless!"

I had got to the point where my ascent was halted and could now see above me that I had been riding on a chair suspended from nothing more than a bendy wooden boom, with a simple eyelet and pulley on the end. It was nothing more than a giant fishing rod.

"Where the hell are you?" I shouted.

"Over here."

I looked round and could just make out the grey stones of a battlement. And then I saw a hook thing coming towards me. I followed the pole it was on and saw the unmistakable red specs on the big nose of the Duck's intent face. He was standing on what looked like a large stone windowsill, directing operations. I noticed there was a bullhorn hanging around his neck on a piece of string. There was also a bald-headed guy with him, holding the pole, which they were operating like a gaffe. They snagged the hook on the line and tugged. I began to rock violently and edge towards the sill. When I was near enough the Duck reached out and pulled me in.

Before I had a chance to hit him, he was embracing and kissing me.

"Get off!" I said, pushing him back. I snapped the loudhailer off him and threw it on the floor. "I'd like to shove that thing right down your throat—I could have frozen to death!"

The Duck's little helper picked up the bullhorn and handed it back to him. I blew into my freezing hands and stamped my feet on the sill. It felt hollow.

"What is this stuff?" I said.

"A fibrous-plastic compound," said the Duck. He put his arm around his helper, a plump, florid-faced little man, dressed like the Duck in a black boiler suit, with huge cargo pockets sewn all over it. "And this is a hydrocarbon one—meet, Reggie."

"Thanks, Reggie," I said, offering him a handshake.

Reggie wiped his hands on the seat of his pants and shook my hand, nodding and grinning all over his moony face. "It's an honour, Mr Duckworth, sir."

"Actually, the name's Sloane," I said. "But you can call me Steve."

"Reg is my right hand man," said the Duck, slapping him fondly on the head. "Aren't you, Reggie? You can say anything in front of Reggie. So, what kept you?"

"What kept me?" I shivered. "You kept me—!"

"It was just a little wind up," smirked the Duck.

Reggie ran over to a huge wooden capstan to show me what they had used to reel me in.

"Wind up," he said.

"Yes, very droll, Reg," I said, through chattering teeth.

The Duck helped me down off the sill. I knocked on the wall and got the same hollow sound. "Is this whole place made of plastic?" I said.

"Yeah, everything you see is phoney," said the Duck.

"You're in your element here then," I said.

"Very funny. Every time we dig a bloody tunnel we fall straight down the sewer. And that's not fake nor funny. It was built as a theme park around the turn of the twenty-second century. The post-Disney period. It's a right little box of tricks."

I looked around the tacky winch room, with its joke-shop cobwebs, toy rats and rubber bats, touching and poking things. "I couldn't even get banged up in a real dungeon. I have to end up in a bouncy castle," I said.

I picked up a stuffed rat and gave it a squeeze—it squeaked.

"Er, I wouldn't do that if I were you, mate," said the Duck.

"Why not? Its only a—" The rat suddenly sank its fangs into my thumb. "Aaagh!" I shook my hand and it flew across the room and shot through a crack in the wall.

"Aunt bloody Nora! It bit me!"

"I told you this place was full of surprises," said the Duck. "That reminds me—we'd better be getting back to the dorm before they start moving the walls around. Come on, Reg—chop, chop—track us back!"

Reggie ran out the door. The Duck grabbed me by my trench coat and dragged me out after him.

"Moving walls around?" I said.

"It's like a maze in here—they keep changing it all around, so we never know where we are," he said. "But don't worry, Reggie has the best nose in the business—he'll sniff out the way home. Come on—it's nearly curfew."

"Wait!" I said.

"What?"

"I want to ask you a question," I said.

"There'll be time for all that later—"

"Now!" I pulled him back. "Um? Um?"

"Well go on then! We haven't got all day!"

"Shh! I can't think—no, wait—I know—there's a painting in the long gallery at Duckworth Hall—a woman leaning against a marble column— what nationality did you tell me she was?"

"Hey? How do you expect me to remember a bleeding thing like that? Australian?"

"No."

"Dutch?"

"No."

"She was French then!"

"No. German. Close enough. All right, you're the real Duckworth—anyone impersonating you would have got it right first time," I said.

"Now can we get on? Reggie's waving at us."

"Lead on, Horatio."

We hurried on along the straw-strewn passageway after our tracker, who darted around a corner as soon as he saw we were following him again.

We pounded along and turned right into a plastic brick wall, which knocked us both back flat on our backsides.

"Oh, no!" cried the Duck, leaping to his feet. "They've started playing silly beggars!" He hammered on the wall. "Reggie! Reggie? Can you hear me, mate?"

There was a faint reply.

"He's miles away," said the Duck, looking around desperately for inspiration. "Damn it. We're lost."

"What's the worst case scenario?" I said. "We sleep here the night and miss supper?"

"We are supper if we sleep here, mate," said the Duck, chin in hand.

"What?" I exclaimed. "Tell me you are jesting!"

"Do I look like I'm bloody jesting?" snapped the Duck, his eyes flaring like two jellyfish behind his big specs. "Now, shut up and let me think a minute."

I rubbed the back of my creeping neck and looked round anxiously.

"Don't tell me what it is," I said. "I don't want to know what it is—just get us out of here."

"All right—I'm thinking. Got it!"

"What?"

"Get all the straw you can find and pile it against this wall—well, go on then!" he said.

"What're you going to do?" I said, scampering away a few feet to gather up handfuls of straw off the floor.

The Duck removed his megaphone and started smashing the electrical part open.

"Arson," he quacked.

I carried on bringing the straw and making a big heap, while he sat cross-legged on the floor and tinkered about with wires he had ripped out of the bullhorn.

"That's enough," he said. "Find me some little dry bits—for kindling," he said, getting up on his knees and shuffling into position with his broken megaphone.

I made him a tiny pile of tinder and he shorted two bare wires together, trying to get the sparks to drop onto it.

"So, er, what's the big hurry?" I said.

"Thought you didn't want to know," he said, continuing to try and catch light to the straw.

"Yeah, well, I don't—what is it?"

"Bugs," replied the Duck. He thought he might have a spark and started gently blowing the tinder.

"Bugs?" I said, looking around on the floor.

He started shorting his wires again. "Not real bugs," he said.

"Good. I hate creepy-crawlies."

"They're electronic clones—the bugs recycle—er, human protoplasm into a kind of cellulose and use it to repair the Castle—it's a very efficient ecosystem actually."

"That's all right then." I thought for a moment. "Wait a minute! Are you saying these things eat you alive and turn you into walls!"

"Don't worry," said the Duck. "When you've been stung a couple of hundred times, you'll be paralysed and won't feel a thing."

"So it just hurts the first one hundred and ninety-nine times?" I said. "And then you get to lie there and watch yourself being turned into wallpaper?"

"Cup your hands round that kindling," he said. "There's a draught."

I draught-proofed the tinder with my hands. "Come on, Duck—light the bloody fire!"

"Stop breathing on it then!" he quacked.

He sparked the wires and managed to get the tiniest red sequin of fire going. He was at it in a shot, gently blowing and coaxing the orange glow into life. Once it flamed the whole lot went up in a whoosh.

"Straw!" he quacked. "More straw!"

I scuttled off to forage. But then, remembering the flesh-recycling bugs, I dashed back with just a couple of quick handfuls.

"More than that!" cried the Duck. "Hurry up!"

I ran off around the corner, because I'd used up all the closest stuff. As I was bending down snatching it all up, I could hear the Duck calling to me.

"Come on—it's going out! Quick!"

I hared back round the corner with a huge armful, threw it on the blaze we had going and rushed off to fetch more, without being asked. This time I had to go even farther afield to find the stuff—almost all the way back to the winch room. It was then that I heard them. It sounded like a high-pitched chattering noise at first. But then it grew louder and louder till it became a mechanical din—like rows and rows of those old Burroughs adding machines all working at once! And then I saw them. Thousands of them! Scuttling out of every crack and orifice for as far as the eye could see. My flesh crawled with them. My limbs stiffened and seized up. Some inborn animal instinct wouldn't dare let me turn my back on the shellac army.

"Duckworth!" I screamed, my eyes bulging out of their sockets as I tried to take them all in.

"What?"

"B-B-Bugs!"

I heard the sound of running feet.

"Flippin' heck!" quacked the Duck.

I tore my eyes away from the heaving mass of twitching antennae, quivering claws, and segmented legs and looked round at him.

"Can't we turn them off or something?" I said.

The Duck was standing some twenty feet away, holding a handful of burning straw.

"Yeah—you take all the spiders and centipedes and I'll do the beetles and cockroaches—how the hell can we turn all that lot off? Anyway, we'd need screwdrivers."

"Screwdrivers? I'll need toilet paper in a minute!"

"Smell that?"

A curious pungent odour filled the air.

"What is it?"

"That's the formic acid they're giving off," said the Duck. "It's digestive juices. Better move back."

I kept my eyes on the black tide, pouring along the passage towards me, and walked backwards.

"Throw it down!" cried the Duck.

I dropped my bundle. The Duck threw his straw torch on it and it burst into flames, barring the way of the bug invasion. The column halted and started edging back.

"They don't like that!" he quacked.

"Now what?" I said, seeing that wasn't going to stop them for long. Some were already demonstrating their rage and climbing up the wall to bypass the traffic jam.

"Leg it!"

I didn't need telling twice. I was around that corner before the Duck and running headlong towards the burning plastic wall, which had caught and was belching out sooty billows of thick toxic smoke. I just did a running jump at it, hoping to smash through, but I rebounded off it and only succeeded in catching my shoe alight into the bargain. A dollop of molten plastic had attached itself to the sole. I danced around, stamping it out.

Meanwhile, the Duck picked up the remains of his bullhorn and started bashing at the melting wall with it.

By this time our eyes were smarting and we were both choking on the poisonous fumes. And the clattering noise was all around us.

I noticed the first few spiders and cockroaches scampering nimbly round the bend, high on the wall.

"They're here!" I cried.

"Don't worry, Son," shouted the Duck. "We'll suffocate to death before they get to us."

"You're a comfort in a crisis," I yelled back.

I had an idea. Taking off both my shoes and using them as gloves, I scraped them on the melting plastic and started smearing it across the floor a couple of yards away from us, to make another barrier. The Duck, now on his knees to try and avoid taking in lungfuls of the airborne toxins, carried on bashing the hole bigger, kicking me over any burning bits of plastic he managed to dislodge. We worked feverishly like this for what seemed like five minutes at least, but it was probably more like thirty seconds.

"Give me your coat!" yelled the Duck.

I lay down on the floor, wriggled out of it and threw it to him. A huge spider came within inches of my face. I crushed it with my shoe. It crackled and buzzed and a small wisp of smoke came out of it. I looked round to see what the Duck was doing, because I could hear him beating something. It was the fire—he was beating it out with my coat and then trying to grab the sides of the hole with it to put the melting plastic out.

"Okay!" he said. "You first."

I galloped over on my hands and knees and, using the coat as a fire-blanket, climbed through the hole. I felt something firm.

"There's a floor," I said. "Feels soliddddddddd!"

I had given it a thump to make sure it was safe and promptly toppled off the edge—to find myself falling headfirst down what seemed like a bottomless shaft. I kept my hands out in front of me as I fell, but there was nothing to grab onto to break my fall. I was, of course, screaming at the top of my voice the whole time I was falling, anticipating that final crunch and certain death. And then I hit the water, the thick, slightly warm, putrid-smelling, scummy water. I think I must have just got a whiff of it before I plunged into it. It smelt like a sewage treatment works I used to cycle past when I was a kid—kind of gassy and sour. And it tasted even worse!

I tried to clamp my eyes and mouth shut, but it was too late. I'd already taken in nosefuls of the stuff. And when I choked and attempted to spit it out, I only let in more. I opened my eyes and saw a dim sepia-tinted light. I swam towards it. This all took a matter of seconds. As I ascended, I heard an almighty plunge nearby and saw a vague shadowy figure out of the corner of my eye, floundering—the Duck. I broke surface and dog-paddled around, bumping my nose on the sides of the shaft, until I found an outlet. Then I heard a splash and lots of gasps.

"Deep!" spluttered the Duck. "Can't—"

"Swim? Yeah, I know," I said. I breaststroked over to him and grabbed him by the collar of his slimy boiler suit. "Typhoid, diphtheria, dysentery, trench-foot—I shudder to think what we're going to catch in this muck."

"Don't worry," panted the Duck. "Way out—that way."

He pointed to the outlet I had already discovered. I swam us towards it. It led to a channel with a big grille blocking the end.

"What next?" I said.

"Ladder," said the Duck.

"Where?"

"Up—up there," he gulped. He spat something out and it plopped into the water and swam away.

I craned my neck round and saw a rusty, slime-festooned ladder bolted to the wall.

* * *

A few minutes later we had managed to climb up it and were hauling ourselves into an enormous drainage pipe. I could stand up in it and stretch my arms out—just like the guy in that famous Leonardo da Vinci drawing. The Duck, on the other hand, was still on his knees, spluttering and coughing—a bit like the flea in that crap drawing by Blake.

"It's just down there," he said. "It leads to the dorm."

"Ah, a warm shower, something hot to drink, clean sheets," I said, helping him up.

"You'll be flippin' lucky," he said.

"I was afraid you were going to say that."

We slopped and slapped along the tunnel till we came to a hole. The Duck clambered down it. I followed him and found myself on a landing overlooking an enormous boiler room or laundry—it may even have been a kitchen, for all I knew. It turned out to be all three and more, but we didn't go down into it that night, we went up a flight of steps instead, and through a door, which brought us out into a warm corridor. I could hear and smell human beings close by.

"We can get cleaned up in here," said the Duck. "They were originally built for the public."

He directed me into a long empty washroom with dozens of toilet cubicles down one side and dozens of white porcelain hand basins down the other.

"Reminds me of my old prep school," I said. "No showers?"

"There's *a* shower, but it's not hot," said the Duck.

"Don't care," I said. "When you've survived two years at St Winifrid's Preparatory School for Boys, you can endure anything. Take me to it."

* * *

We showered in our clothes and then took them off, put them all back on again inside out and showered in them again—that was the Duck's idea—and, finally, we showered with them off. And then put them back on wet. Memories of St Winnie's came flooding back.

I had lost my trench coat and my shoes—the Duck, amazingly, seemed to be completely intact. But from what he told me, he had fallen in the Castle bilge loads of times and showed me the tidemark around his neck to prove it.

"So, how long have you been here?" I asked, as we walked along a warm passageway towards the din.

"Six months," he replied.

"Six months? Who else is here? Has Emma turned up yet?"

"All in good time, mate," he said, as we came to an impressive looking dungeon door. "Welcome to H Wing!"

He threw open the door and all I could see was row upon row of bunks and a mass of identically dressed inmates milling about. They were all wearing the regulation black boiler suits—though all variously adapted and customized by their owners—and all, as far as I could make out, male.

"Isn't Emma here?" I said, attempting to look around farther on tiptoes. I could make out a far wall, but all I could see on the right, in the distance, were bars and bright lights beyond.

"No—it's men only in this dorm. Come on, let's change out of these wet clothes," said the Duck, shoving a couple of the guys out of his way and dragging me through the throng. Everyone we barged past looked round aggressively, or in annoyance, at first, but, seeing it was the Duck, immediately grinned and apologized—and I noticed they all called him "Doc" or "Doctor."

"What's with the 'Doctor' thing?" I said.

"They make us use our real names and titles in here," he said. "Everyone of these men that you see is a time traveller—and not just any old time traveller—we're all re-offenders—men who have escaped many times before. Corrective Measures hasn't found a prison that can hold us yet. So it sends us here—no man or woman has ever escaped from the Castle." He lowered his voice. "I intend to be the first."

"Yeah-yeah. You mentioned women—where are the women?" I said.

"They're in a separate dorm—and that's off limits," said the Duck. "This way."

I hurried after him. "Off limits? Well, when am I going to get to see Emma?"

"It's a prison, Son—not a blinking knocking shop," said the Duck. "You'll see her soon enough. Now, button it—they don't like us talking about birds. We're supposed to be getting re-educated."

"What—not to think about women? That's a bit dangerous in an all-male dorm, innit?"

The Duck gave me a lopsided grin. "Come on—you'll be all right—you're with me."

I patted him on the head. "That's very reassuring."

He knocked my hand away. "Hey! Don't touch the barnet—in this place that's considered dating!"

I whipped my hand away and wiped it on my backside, then quickly switched to my trouser leg, looking round to see if anyone had noticed.

We turned sharp left and headed down a walkway between two rows of bunk beds. All the bunks in these rows had canopies over the top bunk and black curtains around the upper and lower for privacy—like puppet theatres. The Duck stopped at one and drew back the curtain to reveal a comfortable enough looking berth, but without any personal touches or possessions, not even a shaving mirror.

"This one's mine—I reserved you the top bunk," he said.

"It's all a bit Spartan," I said. "How did you know I was coming?"

"I heard it on the grapevine," he said. "Go up and get out of those damp things, I'll find you something dry to put on."

There was a small ladder. I climbed up it and rolled into my bunk to begin stripping off. I heard the Duck rummaging around beneath me for a few minutes.

"Give me the wet ones," he called up. "And don't leave anything in the pockets or your bunk—from now on you carry everything you own in your biggles."

"What's a biggles?" I said.

"One of these things I'm wearing," he said. I noticed he was now wearing a dry one. "Someone nicknamed 'em after the Biggles flying suit and it stuck."

I passed him down my bundle of wet clothes. And he handed me up a neatly folded boiler suit like his.

"It sounds a bit Boys' Own to me," I said, pulling my new dungeonwear on. "Just tell me what your escape plan is and let's get the hell out of here."

"Don't mention that word!" hissed the Duck, through clenched teeth.

Two curtains opened across the aisle and two heads popped out. One of the guys, who had one of those handlebar moustaches British pilots used to wear in the Second World War, said, "What plan, old boy?"

"Nothing—he's new!" snapped the Duck. "There is no bloody plan. Now, go back to bed, Archie!" He reached up and swished the guy's curtain shut.

The other one, who looked foreign—perhaps from the Eastern Mediterranean—winked and gestured the Duck over.

"I am useful," he whispered. And he drew his forefinger across his throat.

"I'm sure you are, Ali—but there is no plan," said the Duck. "It was just my friend over there getting the wrong end of the stick as usual."

Ali nodded across at me. "I will fight him—you will take the stronger," he said.

"Oh, go back to sleep!" said the Duck, swishing his curtains across.

The Duck climbed up my ladder and eyeballed me.

"What?" I said.

"Rule number one," he quacked, "—keep it shut! Careless talk costs plans."

"What's the big deal anyway?" I said. I lowered my voice. "Why can't they think up their own plans?"

The Duck gave me another of his lopsided grins. "There's only two men in this prison who command any respect—and you're looking at one of them," he said.

I looked around him. "Where?" I said. "I can't see anyone."

"Me," he said, blinking his eyes patiently.

"Oh, you meant you. And who's the other one—The Birdman of Brent Knoll?"

"The Colonel," said the Duck.

"Who's he when he's at home?"

"You'll meet him soon enough—now stay in your bunk and keep shtum—I'll be back in ten minutes." He swished the curtain in my face.

I swished the curtain open and called after him. "The Colonel and the Doctor? You're having a laugh!"

* * *

It was a long ten minutes—more like forty—before I heard the ladder creaking. I must have been half-asleep, because the first I knew about it the whole frame of the bunk was shaking. The curtains parted and a familiar face grinned in at me like an enormous Mr Punch.

"Ahoy there, matey!"

"Rog!"

"Gangway!"

I moved back and drew my legs up. Jemmons hoisted himself in and shuffled up alongside me on what was my pillow, but he was so big and burly that his head pushed the canopy up. Next came De Quipp, looking just as dapper and handsome as ever in his drab biggles, which he had customized with dozens of cargo pockets, all of which seemed to bulge with something. He tried to sit near me, but I gave him a wide berth—pardon the pun—and virtually kicked him down to the foot of the bunk, from where he had the nerve to smile at me. I glared at him. Finally, the Duck climbed in, drew the curtains closed behind him and sat right in the middle, with his back resting against the rail separating my bunk from the vacant neighbouring one—the one in the next row over.

"Right," he said, slapping his thigh. "I've made some inquiries and a prisoner fitting Emma's description was brought in early this evening."

"Thank God for that!" I exclaimed. "I never saw them take her off."

"No," said the Duck, "they brought her round the other side of the island by snowmobile. You came in the tradesman's entrance."

Jemmons patted my shoulder and gave me a smile of encouragement. De Quipp scowled at me.

I threatened him with my finger. "If you even say her name, I'm going to break your neck, Mon Sewer," I said. "I know all about that little love charm you implanted in her—I'm onto you."

He said nothing but looked a little uncomfortable. He and the Duck exchanged a glance and then the Duck turned on me.

"That's enough of that, Stephen!" he said. "We're all comrades now."

"I'm not his comrade!" I said.

"You don't know the full story, Son," said the Duck. He glanced at De Quipp again. "I'm sure that when you do, you will look upon Monsieur De Quipp with fresh, er, insight."

"I don't think so," I said, pulling a face at De Quipp.

"That's enough! We have got to work together!" snapped the Duck. "Without Monsieur De Quipp's help we'll never get out of here. We need him."

"You may need him," I said. "I just want to see him rot in hell."

The Duck opened his mouth to have another go at me, but De Quipp merely raised his hand and the Duck closed it again.

"Is he working you with a pedal?" I said.

"Forgive me, Stephen," said De Quipp, dropping the fake French accent he had used up till then. "Help me and I will help you."

"That's better—you used your real voice. I knew that other one was phoney," I said. "I don't forgive you, but I will help you to free the Princess. In return you will get Emma and me out of here. Have you got that?"

The Duck looked to De Quipp. De Quipp looked deeply saddened, but replied, "It's a deal, Stephen."

He held out his hand. I looked at it for a moment or two and then reached out and shook it. His hand felt cold and clammy, as though he had poor circulation. I studied him more closely—his face looked pale and drawn. I put it down to the six months he had done in the Castle.

The Duck put his hands over our hands and grinned at us. We both withdrew our hands.

"Now that we've got that settled," he said, "let's get down to business. We go tomorrow night."

"Tomorrow?" said Jemmons. "Ah, there's no moon."

"Precisely, Roger—everything's in place—there's no need to delay it any longer," said the Duck.

"Wow, that soon," I said.

"You have a problem with that, Stephen?" he said.

"No. No," I said. "It's just that I've only just got here. I haven't had a chance to be a prisoner yet—you know, bait a few guards, play cards with the lads, dig a tunnel—the sooner the better, Duck."

"Er, could you call me 'Doctor' while we're in here, Stephen?"

"Okay," I said, "Doctor Duck it is."

Roger nudged me with his elbow and I heard him stifle a laugh. The Duck gave me his sick grin. I noticed De Quipp was smiling at me, too, but, dare I say it, admiringly.

"I have befriended the trustee, Reggie Goldenhair—" continued the Duck.

"—That pipsqueak!" exclaimed Jemmons. "I wouldn't trust that little runt any farther than I could throw him!"

"And neither would I," said the Duck. "Under normal circumstances—but needs must when the devil drives, as they say."

"He'll betray us," insisted Roger, folding his arms tightly across his barrel chest.

"I hope so," said the Duck. "I'm counting on it. 'Cos I've told him the wrong plan—and he thinks he's coming with us."

"Are we talking about the same little bald-headed bloke who helped you to winch me up?" I said.

"The very same," confirmed the Duck.

"Your right-hand man?"

"I only told him that to gain his trust," said the Duck. "Everybody in here knows he's a grass, but I'm going to set him up to distract the guards from our real escape route."

"Which is?" I said. "We're not going down in that bloody chair, are we?"

"That's the diversionary plan," said the Duck. "By tomorrow night every guard on the Knoll will be watching that winch room on their security cameras. Reggie will turn up and someone who looks like me will turn up. But we will be elsewhere, my friends."

"Where?" I said.

The Duck tapped his big nose mysteriously. "That is for my mind only at this stage," he said.

"How do we know it's not a daft plan?" I asked.

"Daft?" quacked the Duck. "Do you really think a place like this could hold a man like me? I've worked it all out, mate. Don't you worry about that."

"I just think we should all know what we're getting into," I said. "I mean, everyone knows you're insane."

"Steve's right," said Jemmons. "We have a right to know."

"Don't you start as well!" cried the Duck.

"The plan will work," said De Quipp suddenly.

Jemmons and I turned our attention from the animated Duck to the calm-faced aristocrat—if he was one.

"I see, Duck," I said, staring at De Quipp. "You and the Count of Monte Cristo here cooked this up together—right?"

"You have my personal guarantee the plan will work," said De Quipp.

"All right," I said. "Let's say I believe you, just answer me one thing— where do we go when we get down onto the ice? Anybody thought about that?"

"Of course, we've bloody thought about that," said the Duck. "It's all in hand."

"I'm asking him," I said, nodding at De Quipp.

"I have a ship," said De Quipp.

"A ship?" I said. "What sort of ship? And where is it? There's nothing out there but miles and miles of ice."

"A time ship," replied De Quipp.

"Where?"

"He's not going to tell you where it is, is he?" said the Duck.

"Why not?" I said. "I thought we were all comrades now."

De Quipp pursed his lips and studied me for a second or two. "If I told you where it is hidden, you would not need me. Is this not true?" he said.

"If you mean—would I leave you out there on the ice and take off in your ship if I got the chance? The answer is yes," I said.

"I appreciate your honesty," said De Quipp. "And what about the Princess—would you abandon her, too?"

I shook my head. "No, just you, mate."

"That is all I needed to know," smiled De Quipp. "My ship is in string stasis—I have a device to activate its dimensional drive. Once we are aboard we can transflux to any time or place. In other words—we would be uncatchable."

"What's string stasis?" I said.

"He means it's in a sort of time envelope," said Jemmons. "It's out there but not in the same dimension at any one time."

De Quipp gave Jemmons a nod of approval. "A simplistic way of putting it, but essentially the fact."

"This machine can cross temporal space, mate," quacked the Duck. "It's bloody interplanetary!"

"Now I know why we're all in this mess," I said.

"Are you saying this is all my fault? I was helping the Princess—" cried the Duck, looking mortified.

"Oh, forget it," I said. "All right, suppose I buy all this—where's the device?"

De Quipp unbuttoned the collar of his biggles and pulled out a cranberry-coloured glass rod, which he was wearing around his neck on a length of cord. It was about the size of a throwaway cigarette lighter but tapered at one end. It could have been a temporal space machine key—on the other hand, it might just as well have been a Christmas tree decoration for all I knew.

"Satisfied?" said my father.

I looked at him. "If he's lying, I'm going to hold you personally irresponsible," I said. "How do we get Emma and the Princess out?"

"Leave that to me," said De Quipp.

My mouth fell open. I turned to the Duck. He smiled and nodded. I looked back at De Quipp.

"If that thing's not out of her back by the next time I see her," I warned him, "I am going to take that key around your neck and shove it up your—"

"—Stephen!" said the Duck.

"And snap it off," I added.

"I will remove the device," said De Quipp.

"Would you mind telling me why you put it there in the first place?" I said.

De Quipp shrugged. "I found her attractive."

I smiled. "It might be fun to beat the real reason out of you some day, De Quipp," I said.

"You won't be beating anyone up, if you keep this up," said my father. "Because we'll leave you behind."

"Oh, shut up, Dad," I said. "You oldies always stick together."

"So, how in tarnation *are* we getting off this rock, Doc?" asked Jemmons, changing the subject.

"We are going over the wall," said the Duck.

"Over the wall?" I said. "How original—now, why didn't everybody else think of that? Oh, I get it—you mean, we're committing suicide— well, that's one way out."

"On snowboards," said the Duck, raising one eyebrow.

Jemmons and I looked at each other in horror.

"Snowboards?" we exclaimed.

Chapter 13

It was the dumbest escape plan I had ever heard in my life. The Duck only expected us to strap our feet to some homemade snowboards and ski off the top of the battlements. The Road Runner could have come up with a more sensible plan. I estimated the walls to be at least fifty feet high. But that didn't matter, I pointed out, because even if we did survive the jump and landed in the snowdrifts that gathered around the foot of the walls on the windward side, as the Duck assured us they did, we would probably be killed attempting to ski down the rest of the Knoll's four hundred odd feet slope. The Duck was adamant that it could be done and once he had an idea in his head there was no shifting it. The meeting ended with me stating that I intended to remain in the Castle and serve out my sentence, Jemmons saying he was going to jump off the wall and walk down the slope, and the Duck promising De Quipp, who seemed to be silently running the show, that we would all do as we were told on the night. And then De Quipp and the Duck left together—the Duck in a huff—and Jemmons hung round for a chat. I wanted to tell him about the replicant of him I'd found in the Duck's attic. He wasn't as surprised to hear about it as I expected him to be. I didn't even get a chance to tell him about the squid, or the tank, or how the thing had tried to kill me before he said:

"Aye. They were using it to try and communicate with my head."

"Your head? Who?" I said.

"De Quipp and the Duck. Sometimes there can be a link between replicants and their originals," he told me. "They wanted me to tell it where the Castle was."

"And you actually knew about all this?" I said.

"I was getting some very strange dreams," said Jemmons, scratching his ear. "I thought I was going stir crazy."

"I see, you mean a psychic link. Did you get through?"

"Not in a manner of speaking, but the Duck must have wheedled what he wanted out of us," said Jemmons. "And then the voice in my head just stopped. Funny that."

"Yes," I said. "That is strange. Anyway—"

"—It stopped dead."

"Very odd," I said. Call me sentimental, but I had serious reservations about telling him that I had assisted in braining his other self to death.

"It was almost like it died," said Jemmons.

"Really?" I said. "In its sleep most like."

"Oh no," said Jemmons. "I was picking up a strong signal that it died a very cruel and violent death. I was getting attached to that voice. What sort of a human being could murder a poor defenceless replicant like that? Replicants have feelings, too, don't you think, Stevie?"

"It's an interesting moral issue," I said. I stretched and did a little yawn.

"I'd better let you get some kip—we've got a busy day tomorrow," he said, climbing over me and out onto the ladder.

"Yeah, it's all downhill from here. Goodnight, Rog," I said.

He suddenly stopped and his lip curled in hate. "If I ever find out who done him in—I'll make him pay," he said. He looked around to make sure no one was listening and whispered, "You don't think it was the Duck who did for him, do you, Steve?"

I was tempted, but said: "I wouldn't have thought so, Rog. No."

"Only it kept repeating the same message over and over again near the end," said Jemmons.

"What message?"

"Kill the Duck, Kill the Duck."

* * *

After I got rid of Jemmons, I tried to sleep, but it wasn't long before the Duck returned and swished my curtains open.

"What the hell did you think you were playing at?" he quacked. "You showed me up, you little toss—"

"—Not now," I groaned, trying to turn over and face the other way.

He poked me in the back.

"You will do as you're told, young man—if you want to see that bird of yours again!"

I rolled back and grabbed him by the scruff of the neck. He gripped my wrists and we wrestled.

"If you harm one hair on her head—I swear I'll harm all yours!" I said, through gritted teeth.

"Let go, you mad pratt—you'll have me off the ladder!"

I jerked him violently to the left and let go. He disappeared. There was a thump, followed by two or three sympathy-seeking groans and then I heard him climb into his bunk, muttering to himself. I drew my curtains and closed my eyes again. A few seconds later, I felt a kick in my back through the mattress.

I ignored it. There was a pause and then another kick.

"Don't be childish, Father," I said loudly.

Two more kicks followed. I swished open my curtains and dangled my head down. I was looking at him upside down—he was lying on his back with his foot raised in mid-kick about to boot my mattress again.

"Caught you!" I said.

He rolled over on his side and rested his chin on his hand. "You're bloody coming," he said. He sat up and pleaded with me in an urgent whisper, "How can I leave here without you? We go together or not at all—that's what I meant when I said you wouldn't see Emma again—she'll be stuck in the women's dorm. And you'll be in here."

"How exactly do you intend to get her out?" I said.

"That's all in hand," he said. "But it's not going to happen if you don't come, because, like I said, if you don't go, I don't go, and the whole thing's off, so—"

"—All right, all right! I'll do it," I said. "Now let me get some sleep."

He tried to kiss me but I pulled my head back up, had a quick look round to make sure no one saw, and quickly closed my curtains. I lay there for what seemed like hours, listening to the sounds all around me slowly dying down, until the whole dorm fell into a hush, disturbed only by the occasional raised voice somewhere far off on the other side. There was still a bit of light coming through the threadbare curtains, but then all the lights went off at once, apart from a few low emergency lights. I felt cocooned and snug in my bunk. I must have dozed off.

* * *

The next thing I knew there was a red translucence in one of my eyes. I opened the lid and saw a dazzling light surrounded by darkness. It made me start, but then someone's hand covered my mouth. It felt cool, soft—female!

"Memma?" I mumbled.

"It's me—Brie," whispered a husky voice. She directed the beam of a small torch up onto her face.

I jumped upright. "Princess!" I blurted, too loudly. I lowered my voice to a half-whisper. "Princess Mormagleea. What—what are you—how did you get in here? Where's Emma? Is she here?"

There was a click and everything went black.

"One question at a time—move over, I'm coming in," she said.

"No—you can't—I mean, what if—?"

She had obviously climbed up into the neighbouring bunk and was now squeezing through the bars and pulling herself into mine. I had no option but to budge over and let her in.

"How did you get in here?" I said, as I felt her hair brush my face and the pillow move. I knew then her head must be right next to mine, because I could feel her breathing all over me. It was a rather pleasant soapy smell, as though she had just showered.

"I bribed a guard," she said.

"You bribed a guard—why?"

"I wanted to see you." She giggled. "I can't see much though. Wait." She fumbled about. I heard the click again and the torchlight came back on. "That's better—now, where did we leave off? Oh yes, I remember—"

I caught a brief glimpse of her eyes, staring deeply into mine, before they closed and she kissed me full on the lips. I knew it would be useless to resist, but I didn't respond to her. Lucky, I thought, I still had my biggles on and had decided to sleep on top of the itchy woollen blanket rather then under it. She broke from the kiss.

"What is it with this bunk?" I said. "It's been like Piccadilly Circus in here all night."

"Well," she said, playfully touching my nose, "you must be a very popular boy. From where I'm looking you are anyway—" She closed in for another snog.

This time I held her off.

"Which one are you tonight—the Princess or Nurse Parker?" I said.

"Does it matter?"

"Well, yes it does, you see, because I'm in love with Emma—and you know that," I said.

"That's not the impression you gave me at the clinic and when I drove you back to Duckworth Hall," she smiled. "You couldn't keep your hands off me then, could you? You naughty boy. Remember, darling?"

"Yes, I, er, remember," I said. "And want to know what I think?"

She ran her fingernail down my cheek, while her eyes wandered all over my face. "Tell me."

"I think you drugged me—slipped me a Mickey, as they say—to make me believe I was in love with you."

"You mean like a pheromone added to your drip? Now would a princess do a thing like that?" she purred.

"What do you want?" I said.

"I thought that was obvious—I want you," she said wide-eyed. "And I always get what I want."

"Stop that. Get off. You know I'm not in love with you—wait! No! I'm in love with someone else." I pushed her off.

"You can't be in love with Emma," she said.

"Oh, but I am."

"She can't love you like I love you—she can't give you all the things I can give you—"

"—I don't want things. I just want Emma," I said. "So, be a good girl and go. You're wasting your time."

"Time. Now there's something I can give you that your precious Emma hasn't got. You and I are not like Emma, Stephen, are we? Emma will die in the mere blink of an eye, but aeons will come and go before we are dust," she said.

I turned over on my back and stared up at the darkness. The Princess stroked my hair.

"When Emma is sludge and bones in the dirt—you will not even have lived your first day in the sun," she said. "Think, my love, could you bear to watch her age, her beauty fade, while you thrive and remain forever young?" She took my hand and held it to her smooth cheek. "Feel my smoothness—I am in perpetual bloom for you, my love. You are mine." She plunged her lips down on my mouth and kissed me hungrily.

I pushed her off roughly.

"I might want a different one every generation," I said. "And I can always wear a bit of make-up to make myself look older. Me and Em could have years together."

"You're mine!" she hissed. "Your father has betrothed you to me."

"Well, he can just unbetroth me then because I'm marrying Emma," I said.

"The dowry has been arranged and accepted! You cannot withdraw now!" she cried.

"What dowry?"

Suddenly, the curtains swished apart and the Duck's face loomed in.

"What's all the bloody—oh, hello, Your Highness. Well, isn't this nice and cosy—"

I seized him by the throat and pulled his nose up close to mine. "What's all this about a bloody dowry?"

"Um? Princess, I wonder if you wouldn't mind giving me a few minutes alone with my son—I haven't had a chance to go over the final details with him yet. There's still one or two wrinkles to iron out," he said.

"A deal is a deal, Zirconion," said the Princess. "Do not disappoint me!"

She climbed back into the next-door bunk and we heard her rattling down the ladder into the other aisle. The Duck pulled my hand off his throat and climbed into my bunk.

"What's the matter with you? You could have ruined everything," he said. "Haven't you got any bleeding sense up there?"

"What's the dowry?" I said.

"There're delicate negotiations going on—I'm trying to secure our future and you're charging about like a bull in a bleeding china shop."

"What's the dowry?"

"Why can't you marry the Princess and keep the other one for back-up? I mean—you don't only have to have one," said the Duck.

"Why don't you marry her—that's a point—why don't you marry her?" I said. I thought aloud, "Why doesn't he marry her himself? There must be a reason."

"I can't marry her—she wants you," he said. "She's all over you. She doesn't want me. You're better looking."

"Don't give me that, you creep—if you wanted her—I wouldn't get a look in. So, there has to be another reason. What could it be?" I said, still half-talking to myself. "There must be something in it for him—it must be the dowry—something to do with the dowry—"

"I am here, you know," he said.

"What's the deal?" I said.

"Nothing. It's just tradition, innit? A token gesture of esteem for the family of the groom," he said.

"Yeah. I bet," I said. "What can it be? What can it—?"

As with all questions, the answer always seems obvious when you see it. I laughed.

"What?" he said.

"The ship," I said.

"What ship?" he said.

I put on a sing-songy voice. "The time and space machine—the interplanetary craft."

"Oh that," he said.

"Yeah—oh, that—that's the dowry—that's what you've been after from the start—that's the reason for all this—why Emma and I split up—the duel—that thing with Jemmons and the squid—it all happened because you wanted to get your grubby little hands on that machine!"

"That's right—blame me for everything as usual!" he blustered. "Atlantis sank—blame the Duck! Oh dear, London burnt down—blame the Duck! God died—it must have been Duckworth! I'm sick of carrying the can for everything that happens on this bloody planet!"

"And that's why you want to get off it."

"Yes—I mean, no—who said I wanted to get off it?"

"The Princess' time-space machine—or one like it—is the dowry, isn't it?" I said. "Isn't it!"

"Right—I'm going to give you the full S.P. on this one—she twisted my arm."

"Don't give me that—you're in league with her."

"In league with her? She's way out of my league, mate." He leaned closer and whispered, "She's had hundreds of husbands but she wanted to try a human one for a change…"

At this point in his narrative, my hair started to stand on end.

"…I suggested Jemmons, because, well, just because. Anyway, Roger wasn't around, was he—he was off travelling. So, I showed her that old replicant I had of him and she likes what she sees—so, anyway, to cut a long story short, she goes after him. I was only trying to help her out. The next thing I know, all hell breaks loose and she's back at Duckworth Hall saying she's lost her machine and I have to help her get it back. Well, it wasn't anything to do with me, was it? I mean, if she lost her machine that's her—"

"Wait—wait a minute," I said. "Let me get this straight—the Princess is from another planet and wanted to marry Roger?"

"Yes. But she couldn't because they ran into Temporal Criminal Pursuit and got arrested. And then the Princess escaped in Roger's machine, leaving hers behind."

"I think I'm with you. But why would she want to marry Rog? He's old."

"Mature," said the Duck. "Some women go for the more mature man."

"Yes, but she had millions to choose from—why did she have to pick him?"

"She's only interested in her own kind," said the Duck. "She wanted a traveller—got something in common then, haven't they?"

"So why didn't you marry her?" I asked again.

"Well, I, er, thought about it—but then when she came back, she saw you and you were perfect—what with you being immortal. You see, Roger would only have been able to serve her for another twenty or thirty years."

"Serve her?" I said.

"Keep your voice down! I meant that in the Shakespearean sense of the word—you know, service—give her one!"

"Yeah, all right, I know what it means. So, you're just acting as her pimp then?" I said.

"Yeah-no! I'm not her blinkin' pimp!" he quacked. "I've been giving her advice, showing her round—"

"Trying to work out how you can fleece her more like—"

"Doctor? Are you there?"

He grabbed my sleeve and put his hand over my mouth. "Shh! She's coming back—if we don't do as she says we'll never get off this rock. You've got to go along with this engagement or she won't help us to escape," he whispered. He called through to her, "All done, Your Highness. We've had our little heart-to-heart." The Princess poked her head back into the bunk. "It was all a misunderstanding. I've brought Stephen up to speed with the arrangements now, haven't I, Stephen?"

"Yes, I think I get the picture," I said.

The Princess crawled through and cosied up to me again.

"I would like a small wedding, darling—no more than fifty—" she started to say.

The Duck bailed out and slid down the ladder, so that just his head was sticking up.

"Fifty like you?" he quacked. "Er, the ideal number."

"Thousand," added the Princess. "Just my immediate family."

The Duck's head disappeared and we heard a thud.

My bride-to-be tickled my nose with her manicured finger and stretched across me to draw the curtain.

"And now to bed," she cooed languidly.

I snatched the curtain open again and sat bolt upright. "Now, just a minute!" I said. "This is out of order!"

"But what is wrong, my little pumpernickel? I thought all the crinkles had been flattened out."

"Well, I've still got one sticking up," I said. And could have kicked myself.

"Oh, Stephen," she giggled. "You naughty-naughty boy!"

"No—I mean, this is most improper, Your Highness," I said, trying to stall her.

"Improper? But why? I thought you Earthmen were always ready for a bit of the other."

"Ah, yes, but no—not now we are officially engaged, Your Highness," I said. "It's, um, forbidden before the marriage ceremony."

"But I can't wait that long—the wedding could take hours to arrange once we are out of here!" she cried.

"Hours?"

"Surely a few dozen practice ones won't do any harm."

"A few dozen? What—in one night?"

"It's not enough?"

"Enough? What planet are you off—Libido?"

* * *

It was a struggle but I eventually got her down from heavy petting to light petting, and then all the way down through kissing, flirting and writing each other's names out repeatedly, to the correct way to lay out the paper doilies at a wedding reception. I fobbed her off with every excuse and caveat in the manual of courtship etiquette—the one I was making up as I went along. It was like trying to stop the tide coming in, but I did a Canute and managed to persuade her to return to the women's dorm to start putting her trousseau together. I also told her she had to wear something old, something new, something borrowed and something blue, to which I added—just to try and delay the quickie marriage she had in mind—and something you can't find. That last one really stumped her.

Chapter 14

I awoke to find myself face to face with the Duck, who had white froth all around his mouth and a toothbrush sticking out of the side. He removed it.

"Late night, mate?" he smirked.

"That is the weirdest woman I have ever met in my life," I said. "What planet did you say she was from?"

"Dunno. Did you—you know?"

"What time is it?" I yawned.

"Time to go and meet the Colonel."

"What do I want to go and meet him for?" I said. "Don't we eat in this place?"

"You'll be lucky. Breakfast finished an hour ago."

I sat up and pushed him. "Well, why didn't you wake me? I'm bloody starving!"

"I thought I better let you sleep in," he grinned. "After your night of unbridled passion. What was she like? Bit of a goer, is she?"

"Oh, shut up."

I shoved him off the ladder and climbed down. I stood in the aisle and had a good scratch. The Duck dug in the breast pocket of his biggles and handed me a lump of bread.

"Here, I saved you this."

I looked at it, thought about throwing it at him, and started trying to gnaw into it. It was rock hard.

At that moment Jemmons swung round the corner, with a towel slung over his shoulder.

"Morning, shipmates!" he waved jauntily.

I waved back tiredly and leaned against the frame of our bunk. The Duck ferreted in another one of his cargo pockets and produced a battered looking toothbrush with half the bristles missing. He rubbed some of the froth off his brush onto the bent stubs and handed it to me.

"Here, you can have a go with my old one. Give it back when you've finished," he said. "Hiya, Jemmers—been for your run, mate?"

"Aye. I like to keep in shape," said Jemmons.

"Yeah, well," said the Duck, looking him up and down. "You should." He turned back to me and looked down at my bare feet. "We've got to find you some shoes. What size do you take?"

"Mime," I said. I had the toothbrush and the lump of stale bread stuck in my mouth at the same time. I was having one of my private jokes.

"Grow up," said the Duck. He looked round and spotted a pair of boots under the opposite bunk. "We'll borrow Archie's—he won't mind—you can give 'em back after our interview with the Colonel." He bent down and swiped them. "Damn—he's taken the laces out—some people just don't trust anybody, do they? Here, you'll have to grip with your toes."

I stepped into the well worn out, army-style boots.

"There you go," smiled the Duck. "Slip-ons."

I attempted to walk and left both boots behind me. They were at least two sizes too big for me. I walked back patiently and stepped into them again and adapted my gait to a shuffle, rather like one of those cross-country Nordic skiers, and they stayed on.

The Duck nodded. "Perfect." He nudged Jemmons. "Hey, Rog, guess who Stephen slept with last night."

"Who?"

"Only the Princess."

"The Princess?" exclaimed Jemmons. "You slept with the Princess?"

"Nothing happened," I said. "And nothing ever will happen—I'm only keeping her sweet till we get out of this mess. And guess who dropped me in it."

Jemmons's eyes switched to the Duck. "Aye, that sounds about right—he tried to fix me up with the little monster, but I wasn't having any of—"

I wondered why Jemmons had suddenly stopped and looked at the Duck. The Duck pretended to be stroking his hair, but I could tell he'd been signalling like mad to Jemmons.

"What?" I said.

"I just don't want him to put you off," said the Duck. He pointed a finger of admonishment up at Jemmons. "And I'll thank you not to call my son's intended a little monster."

"I wouldn't call her a monster," I said. "But she is very peculiar. She's got cold hands, I know that."

"Naaah!" quacked the Duck. "I thought you said nothing happened."

"Can we get off this subject? What about the Colonel?" I said. "Let's get him over with."

I shuffled up the aisle and Jemmons fell in with me.

"Hey!" called the Duck. "Aren't we forgetting something?"

Jemmons and I both looked round. The Duck indicated me.

I shrugged. He walked up to me and snatched his toothbrush out of my breast pocket.

"Mine, I think!"

We went via the washroom, so I was at least able to rinse my hands and face. Jemmons let me use his towel. The Duck kept hurrying us. We descended into the long oblong well of the basement I had looked down into the day before. A great hum of humanity emanated from it—interspersed with tuneless whistles, cackles, and shouts. Now it was full of black suited convicts going about their daily routines. Some were pushing trolleys piled high with dishes and cutlery, others were washing up, or emptying slops into tureens or down drains, and still more were hanging about in groups, sitting at tables or standing in the aisles, just talking. The warm, clammy air smelt of bread ovens and laundry, and the body odour of sweaty human beings. I was glad I hadn't eaten breakfast.

"Where are we going?" I asked.

"To G Wing," said the Duck. "The Colonel runs things over there, so behave yourself."

"I don't do saluting," I said.

Jemmons and I were walking alongside each other. The Duck, who was leading us, nodded to just about everyone we passed, and they in turn nodded respectfully back. Though I hated to admit it—he did seem to have some authority in the Castle. We strolled on and on through the massive underground hall, flanked on both sides by a tangled network of pipes and boilers, past rows and rows of dining tables with their regiments of chairs, through flexible plastic doors into a laundry section, busy with workers loading and unloading enormous washing drums and driers. The noise and steamy stench was suffocating. Finally, we came to the end and a screen of bars blocked our way.

The Duck went straight to the gate in the middle and pressed a buzzer. Two leather-clad guards—a bit like bikers—emerged from a side room inside the reception area and came over. I noticed one of them was carrying a Bible, with his finger stuck in it, saving a page.

"Doctor?" smiled the one with the holy book. "How can we help you?"

"Three to see the Colonel," said the Duck, indicating himself, Jemmons, and then me.

The guard's eyes strayed over to me. I gasped and quickly stared down at my feet. It was John—the android—the one I'd met and befriended on Tree's barge.

"Is he expecting you?" he asked.

"We've got an appointment."

"Wait here."

He nodded to the other one, who whipped out a phone and punched in some numbers, turning away from us, so that we couldn't read his lips or hear what he was saying. He wasn't on it more than a few seconds, before he turned and nodded to John the android, who unlocked the iron gate and let us through. He showed no signs that he recognised me. I decided to do the same. They frisked us and sent us on our way, which lay down a dingy walkway no wider than a train carriage, which seemed to go on for miles.

"How much farther is it?" I said, struggling to keep my shuffle up to pace.

"Stop whinging—it's only down the end," said the Duck, who was striding ahead.

"G Wing's on the other side of the Castle—the lay-out's the same," said Jemmons.

"You mean I've got to walk through another basement?" I groaned.

* * *

Yes I did, and another checkpoint, and up another flight of stairs, and through the maze of bunks that was G Wing. Unlike H Wing, the prisoners in G Wing had arranged their bunks in the form of a giant maze, so that when you entered at one end you had to walk twice as far to get to the centre, which was very annoying, for a man in my footwear, but it was where the Colonel liked to hold court. I, of course, whinged, so Jemmons offered to give me a piggyback through the maze part. But I was too proud to accept, so I just took off my boots and carried them. And that's why I was barefoot when I entered the Colonel's inner sanctum—a corral of bunks with only one way in and out.

The moustachioed Colonel was easy to spot—he was dressed in an immaculate British Army officer's uniform with three pips on the epaulets, and was sitting at an impressive looking plastic desk, flanked by two guys in smart black boiler suits, without the usual customized cargo pockets. Several of the Colonel's other ranks were there, leaning against bunks, lying on bunks—there was even one sitting on top of a bunk, keeping a look-out.

"Ah, Zirconion—sit down," said the Colonel, in that rather absentminded, upper-crust tone British Army officers used to adopt in the good old days before Dunkirk. He spotted my feet and pointed his baton at them. "Why isn't that man wearing his boots?"

"Yes, I'm ever so sorry about that, Colonel," said the Duck. "Some blighter swiped his laces. You can't trust anyone in this place, can you—excepting yourself, of course." He rounded on me. "Put your boots on!

Presenting yourself to the Colonel without your boots on—whatever next!"

I dropped my boots on the floor and stepped into them, with the wrong feet.

"Get a grip, Zirconion!" cried the Colonel. "Find the culprit and make an example of him. We run a tight ship on G Wing. A damn good flogging—that's what the men need."

"Yeah, and I bet you'd volunteer to let them give you one," I said.

"What? What did he say?"

"Nothing, Colonel. Now, about our little agree—" said the Duck.

"Sergeant-Major Willis!" barked the Colonel.

"Sah!" screamed a guy a few feet to my left—right in my ear—clicking his heels together and jumping to attention.

"Get that man a set of laces—boots for the use of—from stores at once!"

"Sah!" screeched Sgt-Major Willis, marching away on the double.

"Cheers, mate," I smiled.

The Colonel fixed me with his double-dash eyes, his military moustache quivering with rage. "You will address me as 'Sah'!" he bellowed.

"He's new, Colonel," said the Duck. "He doesn't know the drill—I'll soon lick him into shape." He turned on me again. "Stand up straight when you're talking to a superior officer!" he quacked.

"I'm not in the army," I said. "If he wants to play soldiers—that's up to him—but I'm not signing up."

"Give that man a damn good flogging!" yelped the beetroot-faced Colonel, springing from his chair like a jack-in-the-box. "Chalmers—Bauhaus! Lash him to the wheel!"

Two men moved towards me from my left, but the Duck got to me first and punched me in the stomach. I doubled up and dropped to my knees—the Duck got me in a Jap stranglehold and forced my face down on the floor.

"Eat dirt—you insolent scum!" he quacked.

"You're-you're-stran-gl-ing-me," I stammered.

But the Duck kept squeezing.

"For pity's sake let him up, Doctor," I heard Jemmons pleading. "You'll throttle him!"

"Do you submit?" said the Duck.

"Naff-off!" I croaked.

The Duck squeezed even tighter.

"Submit?"

I shook my head.

He jerked my neck back.

I nodded and slapped the floor.

"Say it!" he quacked.

"Sub-mit!" I gasped.

He let go and shoved me aside.

"Most impressive, Doctor," said the Colonel.

"Not so tough now, is he? I get a lot of his sort—they think they're hard—but they think again when I get through with 'em."

"An admirable display of discipline," nodded the Colonel.

"Well, I have done the SAS unarmed combat cour—agh!"

I pulled both the Duck's ankles from under him, leapt to my feet and put the boot into him twice, before my boot flew off and I was dragged away by Chalmers and Bauhaus. I remember seeing my other boot drop off and some of the Colonel's men kicking it around like a football for a lark—until the Colonel bellowed at them.

* * *

I was taken down into the basement and tied by my wrists to the pressure control wheel of a boiler. It was so high up the pipe that my feet barely touched the ground. I remembered seeing a film about some guy who was hung up like this and seemed to recall he died because something happens to the heart, so I was a bit concerned. I was also worried that the Colonel himself might come down and whip me. I mean, I know there are some people who would pay good money for that sort of thing, but I'm not like that. In the event, I was only hanging around for about half an hour before the Duck and Jemmons came to my rescue and quickly cut me down.

"You pratt!" quacked the Duck. "You could have got us flogged—I had to do some pretty nifty footwork up there to get you off. Colonel Tippet was all for making an example of you to his men."

Jemmons held my head steady in his arms and poured some water over my lips from a small saucepan.

"Boots," I panted. "Archie's boots."

"Don't worry about the bloody boots—I've got 'em," said the Duck. "And the laces. They're the least of your worries. The Colonel's only refused to help with the escape—if you go!"

"He's a bas-bas-bastion of old school discipline," I said.

"He also controls half the bleeding nick—the half we have to escape from," said the Duck. "The Colonel's agreed to create a diversion while we're up on the west wall. And that happens to be right above us. With any luck every guard on G Wing will have his hands full."

"Just wish we had a better plan," I said, as Jemmons helped me up.

"Yeah," said the Duck. "—Hey? It's my plan!"

"Exactly."

"Listen, mate, it's all about descent time," he said, helping Jemmons to walk me away. "I've done all me sums—we'll be off that wall before they even know we're away. I'll have us down quicker than a tart's knickers. As long as you watch what you're doing, there's no risk."

"Duck!" I said.

"What?"

He walked into a pipe.

"Mind that pipe," I said.

* * *

We returned to H Wing. John the android was no longer on duty on the gate. I climbed back in my bunk for a doze while I waited for the lunch bell. The Duck and Jemmons went off to see a man about some snowboards. I could only have been asleep an hour when I had an unexpected visitor. It was Travis De Quipp.

"What do you want?" I said. "No—don't come up—I'll come down."

I tumbled down the ladder.

"I feel I must put the record straight," he said.

"Have you removed that thing from Emma's back?" I said.

"Thing? Oh, yes—it has been de-activated—it will now dissolve and cause her no further problem," he said.

"That better not be a lie," I said.

"Shall we walk?" he invited.

"Where?"

"It is almost time for the pig swill they call food in this place to be served, perhaps if we take a slow walk—the scenic route, as you English say."

"Okay," I nodded.

We walked down the aisle.

"I always liked you, Stephen," he said.

"I always hated you, Travis."

"Yes, of course, but now I hope that we may lay old rivalries aside and work together," he said.

"Just like that?" I smiled. "Not a chance."

"All that matters is the successful conclusion of our business."

I took that to be code for the escape. "During which," I said, "I will be keeping a very close eye on you, De Quipp, or whatever your name is."

"That will be a little difficult I am afraid." He stopped and looked down at his highly polished boots.

"Why?"

"Because I will not be going with you," he said gravely.

"Why?"

"I am to play a small role in the diversion."

"How?" I said, walking on.

"I will be pretending to be the Doctor—or Sir Julian, as I still prefer to call him—in the winch room."

I glanced across at his noble profile. I still didn't trust him, but there was something vaguely heroic about his demeanour—the way he clasped his hands behind his back, the slight stoop, the thoughtful look ahead of him—that rang true.

"With Reggie the nark?" I said.

"Nark?"

"Snitch—informer."

"Ah, yes. With the traitor Reggie Goldenhair," he said.

"You're doing this for the Princess?"

"It is my duty," he said. "I am sure she will attend to my rescue later. She is a fine woman."

"I'll remind her," I said.

"Thank you, Stephen." He paused and bowed.

"If I remember," I added.

We continued.

"You are to be married to Her Royal Highness, I hear."

"Er, yes," I said. "When all this is over."

"Congratulations. You will make her very happy, I think."

"Well, I'll try. I, um, just hope I can live up to her high expectations." I was referring to her sexual demands, but De Quipp thought I meant something else.

"You already have, Stephen," he said. "That is what our duel was about."

"I thought that was about Emma."

"No. That was merely to provoke you into a fight," he said.

"You never loved her?"

"Never. It was a test—a test of your manhood," he said. "To see if you were made of the right stuff. You passed with flying colours I am pleased to say."

"Funny, I seem to remember I lost that little charade," I said.

"Yes, but you did not back down. The man who marries the Princess must show no fear," said De Quipp. He patted my shoulder. "You were very brave."

I thought about telling him the truth, but since he was in the mood for confession, I decided to press him for more information.

"What was that blood thing about then?"

"Oh, just a device to keep you out of harm's way—there was so much going on—Corrective Measures were closing in, we were all planning our mission to the Castle—the Princess did not want you involved. She wanted to keep you safe."

"She was looking out for me?"

"She is always looking out for you," he said. "And now I think I have said too much."

"One more question," I said. "Have you told Emma any of this?"

"Emma? Does she matter anymore?" he said—rather heartlessly, I thought.

I stalled. Something didn't sound right—how could this apparently honourable man, a man who seemed so sensitive and selfless when it came to the Princess, speak so callously about Emma? I was picking up some mixed messages and it was making me feel uneasy.

"Does she still mean something to you?" he questioned.

"Not in that way," I said. "But she is a human being and I still care about her safety and her state of mind."

"And that is all?"

"Well, she *is* still expecting my child," I shrugged. I was confused, watching my words—it was like I was playing a game, without knowing the rules, or even the name of the game—or the point, for that matter.

"You will have many offspring with the Princess," said De Quipp.

"Number isn't really an issue is it though?" I said. "I mean one child is as important as a thousand."

"What a strange species you are," said De Quipp. "In my world one must be prepared to die for the good of the many."

That explained why he was risking his life, or, at the very least, his freedom, for the rest of us.

"Where exactly is your world?" I asked.

"Oh, you wouldn't know it," he said.

"Well, I might."

"Do you know where the Dropsyplevlapachord Sentaxia is?"

"Um?"

"It's appluvial to the Gannexquadadraxl Cyclopse Ring."

"Is it?"

"Beyond the Mormagleean Spydra."

"Oh—that appluvial! Why didn't you say?"

* * *

De Quipp and I strolled around H Wing—not that there was much to see but bunks and bars—and had ourselves a fascinating conversation. He wouldn't tell me much about his world, but I did draw him out on one or two other interesting details. For example, he had not slept with Emma, they had not been to bed, or spent the night together and their entire courtship had not progressed beyond a kiss. They hadn't done anything. Anything at all. I was relieved to hear this because it would have been immoral to seduce Emma by foul means. And I was sure Emma would also have been relieved that she had not been taken advantage of when she heard the bitter truth about her precious Travis. I must admit though, I allowed myself a secret portion of smugness in the knowledge that I had been right all along.

* * *

We met up with the Duck and Jemmons for lunch—Reggie joined us, too, but the Duck discouraged any other inmates from sitting at our table, which was set a little distance apart from the others. Our own personal Judas tried to pump us in his own crude way for more information about the escape. The Duck handled him like a shark angler toying with a minnow.

"So, what happens when we hit the ice, Doctor?" asked Reggie.

"We hit the ice running, Reggie baby," drawled the Duck. "The rest is going to be legendary."

"But where do we run to?"

"Our friends on the outside will take care of that end," said the Duck.

"The Resistance?" whispered Reggie.

The Duck looked both ways and leaned in. "Otherwise known as The Levellers, Reggie—they are going to smash this Government one day—there'll be anarchy and then the big boys will step in and take over."

"The big boys?" said Reggie.

"The Desperate Men."

"I thought they were called The Levellers," said Reggie, scratching his bald head.

"They're just a front—it's all political—The Angry Old Men have had enough," said the Duck.

"But I thought you just called them The Desperate Men," said Reggie.

"They're just being used—it's the Angry Old Men who run the show—they come from the highest levels of society," the Duck told him.

"Toffs?" said Reggie. "Like who?"

"The brother-in-law of the Over-Controller's cousin for one," said the Duck. "Now, that's enough, 'cos the more you know the longer they'll torture you for if you get caught."

"They won't break me," said Reggie.

"Reggie," said De Quipp.

"Yes, Monsieur De Quipp?"

"Take my plate back."

"Yes, Monsieur De Quipp." He scurried away with his own and De Quipp's plates.

"You take unnecessary risks, Sir Julian. What if the Over-Controller does not have a cousin with a brother-in-law?" said De Quipp sharply.

"Oh, but he does," said the Duck, wobbling his head as he trumped De Quipp. "When these fascists blew up Duckworth Hall back in 2002, a new family took over my land and rebuilt on it—they were called Neuville—they're still around somewhere—only now I've found out they're related to the Over-Controller. That was just a little historical pay-back."

"You should not make our business personal," said De Quipp, clearly irritated at being wrong.

The Duck quacked, "Everything's personal De Quipp. That's what makes it fun."

* * *

Our lunch party broke up. The Duck said he had to see someone about foot-straps for his boards. I didn't want to get stuck with De Quipp, so I made some excuse about wanting to find my clothes in the laundry, because I'd left something in the pocket of my leather jacket. So, poor Jemmons found himself left with De Quipp. I didn't wait around to see where they went. I had suddenly remembered John the android and wanted to see if he was on guard duty. I had no idea what I was going to say to him if he was, I just had a compulsion to see him, maybe ask him if he remembered me. I had decided it couldn't do any harm—he could hardly turn me in.

It was a long walk, but Archie had allowed me to go on borrowing his boots and since they now had laces in them, I made good, comfortable progress to the gate.

The guards were in their guardroom. I pressed the buzzer. Both guards came out. One was carrying a Bible.

"What can we do for you?" asked John the android, still showing no indication that he knew me.

"Could I just have a word with you—over here?" I pointed along the bars and started walking.

He shrugged to the other guard and followed me. The other guard watched us for a moment or two and then went back inside.

"What's all this about, convict?"

"Er, remember me, John?" I smiled.

His head tilted slightly to one side. "No. And my name is not John. You must have me mixed up with someone else, convict."

I looked anxiously towards the guardroom and then back at John. "Don't you recognise me at all?" I said.

"Why should I? I have never seen you in my life before."

"You can drop the religious robot routine now, mate," I smiled. "You remember—me, you, Jody and Emma—that night on the boat. What a party that was! Drinking, dancing—you and Jody getting it on—"

"Stop! These are serious accusations, convict!"

"They're not accusations, John—I'm just saying we had a great time, man—we philosophized about life, art, and love—chilled to the Bird playing his axe—"

"—Silence! You are impure—and a thief! It is in the good book! You are all damned! It is forbidden to speak to you of such things! Move away from the bars!" he barked, waving his Bible in my face. "Back—thou art the foot soldier of Satan!"

I stepped back a couple of paces. "What happened to you, John? Did they get Jody, too? You must remember Jody. You were going to do the Kerouac thing with her—you know, go on the road—find yourself."

He felt his temple and stared at me, almost as though he was beginning to remember.

"Love and peace, man," I said. "Do your own thing, yeah?"

He swallowed hard and looked down at the book he was clutching so tightly in his hands, and then back at me. His eyes were switching from side to side.

"I love you, man," I said.

"Fornicator!" he screeched. "Blasphemer! Liar! Devil worshipper! False prophet! Sperm of Satan!"

He put the fear of God into me. I backed away and turned tail and ran. I looked back a couple of times—thinking maybe I'd turn into a pillar of salt—and he was still standing there, bent and rocking forwards and backwards on the same spot, screaming at the top of his voice. And then he dropped to his knees and his partner came to his aid. I carried on running.

Finally, I ran out of gas and hid behind some laundry trolleys. I squatted down with my back to one and then I sat right down and closed my eyes, with my feet pushing against another one. I don't know what I'd expected John to say, or how I expected him to react, but it saddened me to think that all my good work had been in vain. I know he was only an android, but I was sort of proud of my two conversions, and I really wanted to know what happened to Jody. I would most likely never know.

My mind switched off. I opened my eyes and let them stray over the laundry on the other trolley. It was probably safe to come out, but something kept me sitting there—a kind of lazy boredom. For a while, there didn't seem much point in doing anything. And then I had an idea that snapped me out of it—completely unconnected with John and Jody—it was about the wheels on the laundry trolleys. They were fixed on the underside of the trolleys like those caster wheel things you find on furniture. Only these were made of clear plastic and reminded me of my old skateboard wheels. I hope you can see the way my mind was working. Why not grab myself four to take along—just for a little extra insurance? If I had four holes drilled in my snowboard, I could just slot them in and be lightning when I got down on that ice.

* * *

In the middle of the afternoon, I was lying on my bed, wondering where everybody was, when a bell rang. There was a commotion below. I swished my curtain open. The guys were climbing out of their bunks and filing down the aisle like Pavlov's dogs.

"Hey!" I shouted. "Where's everybody going?"

"ReEd!" grinned Archie, the flyer-type, who had loaned me his boots. "To the Hall!"

I scrambled out of my bunk. "Can you eat it?"

"ReEducation classes, you chump—come on, it's *How to Resist Sex* today—we'll be late."

"Think I'll give it a miss," I said, turning back.

He caught my sleeve. "House rules, old bean."

I went along with him—curious to meet the guy who was *gonna* deconstruct *my* sex drive.

We filtered into the flow of the main queue and found ourselves jostled and swept out of the dorm and along to what looked to me like a cinema. The Duck was already there, with De Quipp, Jemmons, and the ubiquitous Reggie Goldenhair. This was pointed out to me as soon as I came through the door by one of the guards directing the human traffic. The Duck was waving like mad from the back row. I smiled and waved back.

"I'll sit with Archie," I said, out of the corner of my mouth.

The guard grabbed my arm and practically threw me up the steps.

"Doc says sit with him!"

Archie tried to follow me, but was pushed away.

I trudged up the steps. The Duck was cleaning his specs. He flapped a hand.

"Pull up a pew, man—the show's about to begin."

I slumped down in the end seat.

The house lights dimmed. The screen lit up.

An orchestral soundtrack rose. Lots of swirly violins and bassy adagio—reminded me of one of those hilarious Hollywood B movies from the forties, which, of course, were always in black and white and not meant to be funny. A family of puritans were leaving a white picket-fence church. Could have been New England in the snow. A caption popped up: How to Resist Sex, Part 69.

I sniggered and looked around at the others to share the joke. But they were all deadly serious—their eyes fixed on the flickering screen. All except Jemmons, who was nodding off.

A monotone voice-over droned. The guy sounded like a mix of Walter Cronkite and Virginia Wade. I didn't know about Celebrity Voice Synth back then.

* * *

"These are the Whatmores, an ordinary God-fearing family, living in an ordinary God-fearing town. Father is a respectable undertaker and lay preacher. His good wife, a school ma'am. Their daughters, Prudence, seventeen, and Mercy, eighteen, were their pride and joy."

* * *

We got close-ups of them all as they were named. The Abraham Lincoln pa, clutching the good book. The dough-faced ma, shepherding her little women. First, Prudence, a poker-faced bespectacled critter with a slit mouth as taut as a rubber band, and then her sister—Mercy! I did a double take. The pouting madonna stepped out onto the apron of the little church and flashed her doll eyes at the camera. She stretched her neck languidly in the sun and drew her black hood up over her platinum blonde bun.

* * *

"Till temptation came calling…"

* * *

The music built and struck a succession of tragic chords.

I chuckled and took another look along the row. Rog was snoring. The Duck had sunk right down in his seat—and was eating what looked like popcorn! A sort of darkly satisfied leer spreading across his face, his head wobbling, as he absently shovelled in the sticky mess. De Quipp stroked his 'tache and looked faintly amused. Reggie blinked nonstop and gazed in awe at the twenty-foot vision of temptation up on the screen.

The Whatmores filed through the braille of grave mounds to their hearse. Pop folded his lanky grasshopper body in behind the wheel. Ma and the girls climbed in alongside him and the music and the cameras and the lighting followed them down a painted board mainstreet. The mainstreet of Hell—lurid and loud, flashing lights and lowlife on every street corner. And there was some strange symbolism going on—milk churns outside a grocer's store looked like shiny silver artillery shells. Icicles looked similar, only, of course, pointed down. And as the hearse passed, the icicles steamed and melted away—and—weirdest of all—a rotating barber's pole turned into a solid red tube as it turned, becoming the only colour in the monochrome film. And it was all intercut with close-ups of miserable Mr Whatmore and his expressionless family. The whole thing was so bizarre and disturbing, I thought I was watching a car advert.

* * *

"The Devil finds work for innocent hands…"

* * *

Fade to Prudence reading her bible while mom stitches another quilt and pop measures up another stiff. Cut to Mercy, upstairs on the window seat, reading her bible. But she looks bored, distracted, her blank eyes drift from the text and latch onto a drawer in her dresser. She lays aside her bible, rises slowly, and goes to open it…

"Snap their bones and blind them! Clip their wings and bind them!"

* * *

We see Mercy reach in and take out a shiny little cylinder. She twists it and the room is suddenly filled with a bright vermillion glow, emanating from the point of a lipstick.

* * *

A jazzy saxophone and tom-toms explode from the everywhere-sound system, as crazy Mercy leaps and capers around the room, waving her lipstick about like a kid with a sparkler. And then she's ogling herself in multiple mirrors and applying it thickly to her lips and doing what looks—to me anyway—like simulated sex. She rips off her bonnet and lets her hair fly! And then she's flinging herself on the bed and tearing off the rest of her clothes.

I sank down in my seat, my eyes glued to the screen, reached across Jemmons, and dipped my hand into the Duck's bag of popcorn.

That director had a ball—each time Mercy tossed her hair, a whip cracked. And we were bombarded by a succession subliminal messages, full-screen:

HARLOT. WHORE. BITCH. JEZEBEL. WANTON. WAR. RED. BUY EMPSON'S WHEETIES.

And when the action moved outside, we were treated to even more bizarre images: Mercy's blue breath; slushy steaming streets; exploding icicles; lipstick graffiti scrawled on shiny surfaces and human flesh. The naked—except for her lipstick—Mercy danced through a snowscape of tombstones and wandered wantonly into town. The actress who played her must have got frostbite in places frost could seldom have bitten. To cut the fifty-minute epic short, Mercy got hooked on evil lipstick, fell in with bad company and got herself arrested. Whatever they were trying to cure us of or convert us to, it wasn't working. What we were watching was nothing short of an art house porn movie!

Finally, the music swelled to a crescendo of emotion, as Mercy fell to her knees, her face scrubbed and blank. She raised her eyes to the light pouring in through the cell window and spoke those unforgettable, breathless words:

"Forgive me, Father…for I want to do it again…"

The End. Roll the credits. House lights up…

* * *

I looked along the line. The Duck was blowing his nose in a handkerchief. Reggie was still spellbound, following all the lines of words as they slid up the screen. De Quipp, rather disconcertingly, was staring directly at me. I looked away and nudged Jemmons.

"Hey, Rog—wake up—you missed that, mate."

"When you've been in every bawdy house from Union Street to Calcutta, laddie—that stuff's tame," he sniffed.

The Duck stepped past us, with De Quipp and Reggie in tow.

"Come on, Rog—we've got business," he said.

"Where're we going?" I said.

"You're not coming—I can't take you anywhere," said the Duck. "This is special business." He strutted off down the steps.

"Oh, please let me be in your gang!" I jeered.

* * *

Later, hanging out in my bunk, alone again, scratching my initials on the bedpost, bored out of my box, I saw the Duck walk by.

"Hey—have you got those boards yet?" I said.

"Will you keep your voice down!" he quacked.

"Where're you going?" I said.

"Never you mind."

I scrambled down the ladder and pursued him along the aisle.

"I need to do some work on my board," I said, keeping my voice down.

"What work?" he scoffed.

"Four holes—quarter inch in diameter," I said. "Two in each end."

"Hey? Don't be daft. What d'you want to do that for?"

"That's my business," I said.

"Well, you can't—'cos they're not here."

"Where are they then?"

He stopped. We were at the end of the aisle. He pulled me round the corner.

"What's all this about holes?" he quacked. "I haven't got time for holes."

"I want four, quarter inch round holes drilled through my board, one in each corner," I said. "About two inches in from the side and six in from either end."

"What for?"

"Just make sure it gets done," I said. I set off back up the aisle.

"Yeah, well, just you remember, mate—I give the orders around here!"

* * *

Pleased with myself, I returned to my bunk and had another look at the trolley wheels I'd nicked. I spun each of them in turn to make sure they were all nice and fast and didn't stick anywhere. When I'd satisfied myself they were perfect, I put them back under my pillow and just lay there staring off into space.

A moth fluttered past my bunk. I didn't take too much notice. And then it fluttered back again and hovered in front of my face. It was a small white thing with a handful of orange spots on each wing. I tried to swat it away with the flat of my hand, but it rose sharply and dodged the blow. I sat up and attempted to squat it between my hands, but again it evaded me and zoomed off down the end of my bunk, where it settled on the edge of the curtain, facing me.

Just then, Archie came back carrying three books. He climbed up into his bunk and gave me the Churchillian victory salute. I raised two fingers in what has come to be the peace sign in my time, and lay back down on my pillow, looking up at the canopy.

A minute or two later, I felt someone coming up the ladder and Archie's jovial face appeared—all handlebar moustache and teeth.

"What—ho, old chap—brought you that book you wanted," he beamed.

"What book?"

He thrust a copy of *Famous British Aircraft of the Second World War* into my hands.

"I've marked that page on spitfires I was telling you about—damn fine aircraft, the old spit," he said.

"Oh, that book," I said. "Thanks, Archie."

He rattled back down the ladder and returned to his bunk, whistling the theme from *The Dam Busters*.

I opened it to the page Archie had marked with a strip of paper, but couldn't see anything special about the old black and white photographs of spitfires or the captions around them. And then I noticed that he'd written something on the bookmark. It read, *Don't look now, but you're under surveillance—the moth at six o'clock.*

It had never occurred to me—but, yes, it made sense—there were mechanical beetles and spiders—why not mechanical moths? Its eyes would be microscopic cameras. I was under observation in my own bunk! I was just thinking what a violation of privacy that was, when I heard a THWANG!

Something fast and small had been fired from the direction of Archie's bunk and whatever it was had hit the moth and knocked it off the curtain. It all happened so quickly, I didn't see where the moth went.

"Got the little blighter!" cried Archie. He waved a small homemade catapult in a victory salute.

"Where did it go?" I said.

I looked around in my bunk for the moth. Archie hurried down his ladder and back up mine.

"There it is!" he said, grinning from handlebar to handlebar. "A direct hit. What?"

I followed his pointing finger and spotted the moth on its back in a fold of the blanket, its tiny legs still pedalling the air. Archie reached in and grabbed it in his fist and squeezed. There was a crunch. He opened his hand. The debris of the little electronic moth gave up a wispy plume of smoke.

"They must be very interested in you," said Archie.

"I can't think why," I said. "I'm just an ordinary time traveller like the rest of you."

He switched his eyes from left to right and leaned in. "I know there's something going down, old man—you can trust Flight Lieutenant Archibald St John-Jones to keep mum," he whispered.

"I have no idea what you're on about," I said.

"Walls have ears—what?"

"What?" I said.

"Careless talk cost lives and all that," he said. "Know the value of playing one's cards close to one's chest, old man—you don't need to tell me—I was there in forty guarding the skies over the Home Counties, giving Jerry a good roasting. What?"

"What?" I said.

"Good luck with the escape, old chap—that's all I'm saying—mum's the word," he said.

"Yeah. Right. Give my regards to Douglas Bader, mate," I said.

"What's that, old man—code?"

"Code?" I said. "You must know old tin legs."

"Only flew spits and hurricanes, old man," he said.

"No, Douglas Bader had tin legs," I said.

"Yes, spot on—old tin legs. Must dash—evidence to dispose of—tootle-pip, old chap!"

He slid down the ladder and hurried off along the aisle with his kill.

I remember I did a lot of chin rubbing after that rather bizarre incident and conversation. And when the Duck returned and disappeared into his bunk I went straight down and swished his curtain open to tell him about my concerns. I found him sitting cross-legged on his bunk, rolling a joint.

"Shut that bloody light out!" he quacked.

I climbed in next to him and watched him light up and take his first contented draw.

"How well do you know Archie?" I said.

He expelled a sweet-smelling cloud of marijuana smoke. "Archie? Why—what's he done?"

"It's more what he hasn't done," I said.

"What are you on about?"

"He was never a spitfire pilot for a start," I said.

"People in here get a bit carried away with their own importance," said the Duck. "They make a lot of it up."

"Yeah. I had noticed," I said. "But this guy's getting carried away with his own identity."

"Yeah, well, they exaggerate—most of them just stumbled into a time machine, thought it was from outer space, and pressed a few buttons," said the Duck.

"I'm not talking about all that," I said. "I think he's Corrective Measures."

"You what!" spluttered the Duck. He coughed uncontrollably. I patted his back. "What d'you mean he's Corrective Measures? How would you know?"

"He's supposed to be an ex-Battle of Britain spitfire pilot, right? But he didn't even know who Douglas Bader was."

"Why—who is he?"

"Well—I wouldn't expect you to know, but every English schoolboy who ever glued a model airplane together would know who Douglas Bader was. He was a flyer who lost both legs and still flew combat missions—he's a national hero. A legend. It's just not possible that old handlebars Archie wouldn't know who he was."

"Bit flimsy, innit?"

"The guy knocks out a surveillance moth with a catapult, comes over here, and starts pumping me about escape plans," I said. "I don't trust him."

The Duck considered the glowing tip of his spliff for a few seconds and then began nodding at me very exaggeratedly.

"No—no, you're wrong, man—Archie's as straight as a die," he said. "Besides, we haven't got an escape plan, because we're not planning to escape, so why worry?"

"Are you headbanging again?" I said. "Good stuff is it?"

The Duck gave me a lopsided grin and whispered, "Agree with me, you pratt—the bloody bed bugs are probably microphones!"

"Oh, yeah, well, I guess you're right, mate," I said. "I'm probably just being stupid, dumb, and silly. And he did lend me his boots so he must be a good guy." But I whispered, "And they're army boots—not air force boots."

The Duck took a tobacco tin out of one of the breast pockets in his biggles, stubbed his spliff out in it, and pressed the lid shut.

"Come on," he said, "let's stretch our legs."

We bailed out of the bunk and headed up the aisle. As soon as we were out of earshot of the bed bugs, I voiced another of my concerns.

"And another thing," I said, "there's something odd about De Quipp."

"Now De Quipp's kosher," said the Duck, sticking his finger in my face.

"He's a cold fish," I said.

"Hey? Who told you that?"

"What d'you mean—who told me that? Nobody—I worked it out for myself. He told me what he's going to do," I said.

"Did he? What's that then?"

"Don't start," I said. "You know what I'm talking about."

"You mean the diversion with Reggie?"

"What did you think I meant?"

"De Quipp knows what he's doing."

"I hope he gets caught and they hang him or something," I said.

"You're still holding a grudge," said the Duck.

"Holding a grudge? The grudge I've got is too bloody big to hold—I can't even lift it!"

"Keep your voice down."

"And don't think I've forgotten your part in all this either," I said. "When we get out of here, I'll be settling a few scores."

"Don't rush to judgement, mate—I've been looking out for you, if you did but know it."

"This is about you and a new machine," I said. "Anyway, I don't want to talk about it now—it'll keep. Did you get those holes drilled in my board?"

"Four quarter inch diameter holes—two each end," said the Duck. "Sorted."

"Good. By the way, any news of Tree?"

"Tree? What's he got to do with the price of fish?"

"He went looking for this place. But he never returned," I said.

"Hey?" He seemed genuinely surprised. "Well, where's Emily?"

"Well, she's fine, I think."

"You think? Where the hell did you leave her?"

"It's a long story. She's still in Bristol," I said. "We didn't exactly leave her there—we were kidnapped on a barge—they sort of time-ported us here."

I told him what happened and why we were in Bristol in the first place, and how the whole barge suddenly took off.

"Crikey! I heard about that new gadget TCP developed—they find out your dimensional co-ordinates and then sling a sort of temporal mesh over you. It's a bit like a fishing net, only you have to imagine the water is time and you're the bleeding fish," he said. "It's scary if they've got that working."

"If?" I said. "They did it!"

"All the more reason for us to lay our hands on the new technology," he said. "Like a machine that can dodge about through time and space."

"All of a sudden it's 'us,'" I said. "I don't want anything to do with time machines after this little lot—you can drop me and Emma off in 1920s New York with a copy of that sports' results book you promised me for a wedding present. I'm retiring."

"Fair enough. Meanwhile, I would appreciate a bit of help—we're not out of the wood yet, mate."

We found ourselves in the washroom. A couple of guys were swamping down the floors with mops. The Duck walked straight over to a shower and turned it on full, to drown out our voices.

"I think I know where Tree went—it's Emily I'm worried about," he said, looking genuinely concerned.

"So am I, but where the hell's Tree?"

"Tree is an addict," said the Duck, doing one of his lopsided grins.

"You mean booze? What? Drugs?"

He straightened his glasses. "No. Ever heard of PLEASURE-Domes?"

"Yeah. Tree talked about them just before he—"

"He spent seven years in one last time," said the Duck. "He likes to tell people, including Emily, that he spent them in this place, but he's never even seen the inside of a prison."

"I thought his drawings were a bit inaccurate—they don't look anything like this place—he had men and women in the same dungeon—dorm, I mean—he made it look like something out of Dungeons and Dragons."

"Just drawings. He made it all up," said the Duck.

"He got the islands right though—and a few other details," I said.

"Yeah. He's heard me talking about it, that's why. Anyway, never mind him—he'll be doing the Kublai Khan-can in some PLEASURE-

Dome somewhere in the middle of the late third millennium—we'll worry about him later. Now, do you know the exact date you were in Bristol?"

"Um?" I thought hard. "September! But I don't remember what day it was. No—wait a minute—it was late! Or, was it early?"

"Close enough," said the Duck. "Emily knows what to do—she'll rent somewhere under an alias we use and put an ad in the local paper for a flat mate. We'll pick her up later."

"I hope you're right—the place was crawling with Corrective Measures agents," I said. "So what are we going to do about Archie?"

"Leave Archie to me—I'll send him with De Quipp and Reggie to the winch room."

"Sounds good to me," I said.

* * *

We made our way down the steps to the basement and had a cup of tea. Some of the lads had pushed back the tables on the other side and were having a kick about.

"Look at 'em," said the Duck. "They'll spend the rest of their perishing lives in this place."

"They seem happy enough," I said, fancying joining in the game. "But I must admit, I never expected to find so many in here—there must be well over a thousand."

"Nearer two thousand," said the Duck.

"I wonder where they all came from," I said, just thinking aloud.

"Hey—that's a point. I shall return some day," said the Duck. "I shall return and set them free."

"Spartacus the Duck," I said.

He set his chin firm and stared at them, nodding to himself. He was off on one. "It is an offence to the Duckworth spirit to see so many brave lads banged up in here like this. The waste—the waste. Never have the many owed so much to the few. I never thought I'd see this—not on this sceptred isle—not in my—"

"—Teatime?"

"This is a concentration camp, mate—that's what it is!" cried the Duck. "These brave boys deserve their comforts—a home fit for heroes!"

"They're thieves," I said.

"Thieves. Where's the harm in going for a joyride up time's motorway? Answer me that."

"Think of the damage they've done."

"What damage? All right—make the punishment fit the crime then—give 'em community service—don't lock 'em up for life like common criminals. Can we not call that justice! What shall it profit a man if he gives himself and he's still out of pocket?" he reasoned, in Duck logic. "All they need is resettlement somewhere nice and quiet and a chance to pay back some of the overheads."

"Oh, I get it," I said. "I get it now—pay you, you mean? They'd be in your debt!"

"Yeah, you're probably right—I bet half of 'em wouldn't cough up. The thieving rats. Come on, we'd better find Jemmons and De Quipp and run through the final details for tonight," he said, rising from the table and waddling off briskly towards the stairs.

"What time are we going?" I said, catching up.

"Straight after supper—it's roast beef and spotted dick tonight—I'm not missing that."

Chapter 15

And so, cometh the hour, cometh the men. Six of us sat down at that last supper. I looked around at them all as they tucked into their roasts. There was Archie, a traitor and possible Corrective Measures agent; Reginald Goldenhair, nark; De Quipp, my arch-enemy and a man—well, alien—I did not trust; Roger Jemmons, whose clone had tried to kill me with a cutlass—how much did this Jemmons really know about that—more than he was letting on? And then there was the Duck, my nineteen year old father, who took part in a conspiracy to have me shot and left me to bleed to death in our family home, which he knew was about to be blown up by a Corrective Measures snatch squad—

"Hey! Where d'you think you're going?" said the Duck, as I hurriedly left the table.

"Er, I was just, um—"

"Siddown! Nobody leaves without the others," he said. "We haven't had our spotted dick and custard yet."

"I've lost my appetite," I said, slumping back down. "I was just going to go up and lie in my bunk."

"Yeah, well, mooning around up there won't help, just you stay there—and when they come round with the desserts—tell 'em you want a double helping of spotted dick and custard and give it to me," said the Duck.

"Are you going to eat those spuds, Stephen?" said Jemmons.

"Help yourself," I said.

"Here—scrape his Yorkshires onto my plate, Jemmsey—I'll have them," said the Duck. "Go on—give me his swede and carrot as well then."

"You should eat," said De Quipp, slicing off a small piece of his beef and placing it delicately onto his tongue.

I folded my arms and ignored him.

"Can't you-know-what on an empty stomach—what?" said our phoney pilot friend.

"Well, I don't know where you put it all, Archie—you must have hollow legs," I said. "You're eating like Douglas Bader."

The Duck gave me a kick under the table.

"Got to keep one's strength up, old man."

"Just mind you don't go through the ice, Archie—eating all that," I said.

The Duck whispered in my ear, "We've got a problem with him."

"What's that?" I whispered back, like a ventriloquist.

The Duck leaned in again. "He insists on staying close to you."

"Lucky me," I said, again without moving my lips.

"They must have told him and Reggie not to let you or me out of their sight," whispered the Duck.

I coughed into my hand and then spoke through it in the Duck's ear. "I've got an idea."

The Duck dropped his fork and bent down to pick it up. I dropped my napkin and bent down to join him, below the level of the table.

"What idea?" he said.

"Tell Ali we can only take one—him or Archie—the strongest gets the ticket," I smiled.

The Duck stifled a laugh. "Nice one, my son!"

We both sat up again.

I removed a biro from the breast pocket of the Duck's biggles and wrote this note on my napkin: *I'll go tell Ali.*

The Duck took his pen out of my hand, held it up to the light to check how much ink I'd used, and put it back in his pocket.

I got up. "Excuse me, gentlemen, but I have to go upstairs," I announced. "Be back in two pulls of a chain."

"Yeah, yeah—just do it—don't write us a bloody sonnet about it," said the Duck, waving his fork at me and pulling a pained expression.

I strolled through the dining hall on the lookout for Ali. I spotted him five tables away and tapped him on the shoulder as I walked past. By the time I reached the staircase up to the dorm, he was right behind me.

"The washroom," I said, without looking round.

He let me walk ahead a little way. I got to the top corridor and turned into the washroom. He followed me in.

I turned round and he tried to embrace and kiss me.

"What're you doing?" I cried. "Get off me!"

"Just Ali's little joke," he grinned.

"Yeah, well—you were a little bit too convincing, mate."

He walked over to one of the plastic mirrors and inspected himself fondly. "What you want?" he said.

"There's one place—it's either you or Archie. You'll have to cut cards or something," I said.

He turned round and pulled out a huge curved dagger from somewhere inside his biggles—all in one smooth movement.

"Aunt bloody Nora!"

"I think Archie won't make the cut," he said, curling lip like an Elvis impersonator.

"No killing, Ali," I said, sounding uncannily like one of my old school teachers.

* * *

I rejoined the others and smiled across at Archie as I sat down.

"What-ho, old man—touch of Delhi-belly?" he said.

I grimaced. "It feels just like someone's sticking a knife in me—d'you know what I mean, Arch?" I said.

The Duck kicked me under the table.

"I hope you're going to be fit enough to go over the wall, mate," he said. "We don't want any little accidents on the way down."

"Don't say that word," I said.

"What—'accidents'?" he smirked.

"No—'go,'" I said.

* * *

Half an hour later we were all ready to go. Now here's where it all got a bit strange. I stayed close to the Duck, but as soon as we got up on the landing both he and De Quipp darted into the toilet, telling me, Jemmons, Archie, and Reggie to wait outside. And then when the two of them didn't come back out, Archie started to get a bit jittery and went in to find out what was keeping them. We couldn't stop him. He never came out again. I still to this day don't know what happened to him in that washroom, but I've got a pretty good idea. Now, here's the thing of it—Ali then came out with the Duck and they both grabbed Reggie and dragged him off towards the dorm.

"Wait there!" the Duck shouted back.

"Hey? What about us?" I called after him.

I looked at Jemmons and we both shrugged. At this stage I didn't know where De Quipp and Archie were, so I said to Jemmons we should go in to the washroom and have a look for them. No sooner had we got through the door than the Duck barged into us and pushed us outside again.

"What the—? I thought you just went up there," I said.

"That was De Quipp," he said.

"But he looked exactly like you," I said. "Didn't he, Rog?"

"The spitting image," said Jemmons.

"It was make-up—we made a mask—hid it in the washroom—now no more questions," said the Duck. "Come on—I've had a new hole cut in the overflow pipe, the bugs sealed the last one up—our boards should already be in there."

He herded us towards the landing.

"Down here."

The great pipe ran along the back of the landing and right out over the basement.

"There's something very fishy going on," I said, as the Duck was removing a small section of the pipe, which had been pre-cut and carefully put back in place.

"Aye, and there's nothing new in that," said Jemmons.

"Just keep a lookout," said the Duck. He shone a torch around inside. "Right, Roger—you're the biggest—you first."

I had stepped over by the rail along the landing and was keeping an eye out for anyone coming up the stairs or around the corner from the wing. I looked round and saw the rear of Jemmons disappearing into the hole.

"Right, now you," said the Duck.

I hurried over and climbed up into the pipe, and then turned round and offered my hand to the Duck. He gripped my wrist and I hoisted him in. He brought the panel with him and now gently replaced it from the inside, using strips of, er, duck tape he got from one of his many pockets, while Jemmons held the torch light on it for him. Meanwhile, I had spotted the snowboards and immediately started looking through them for the one with the holes. There were five boards in all and I found two with holes in right at the bottom of the pile. The Duck had obviously copied me. I pulled one clear and took a laundry trolley wheel out of my thigh cargo pocket to try it in one of the holes. It fitted perfectly. If anything it was a little loose, but it was good enough for my purposes.

Jemmons was watching me.

"That's a good idea," he said.

"Just in case," I said.

The Duck came over, took the torch back off Jemmons, and picked up a board. "Bring the rest," he said, and set off along the tunnel. We took two boards each and followed him. I went second.

The tunnel was so big that even Jemmons only had to bow his head slightly to walk upright in it. It was the same tunnel the Duck and I came in through, but this time we were going the other way, though there was still a strong smell of biogas. It was strange to think that we were walking out over the dining hall, which was probably some twenty feet below us. The pool of light from the Duck's torch wobbled about ahead of us up the dark tunnel like a giant amoeba on a microscope slide, picking out swatches of green slime and casting eerie shadows.

"This is the storm drain," said the Duck. "There's a shaft all the way up somewhere."

"Like that one we fell down?" I said.

"No—nothing like that one—this one's got a ladder, according to the plans," said the Duck.

"Good," I said. "What about Emma and the Princess—how are they getting up?"

"We're meeting them—there should be a riot starting about now on G Wing—courtesy of the Colonel. The women's dorm is right above it, under the infirmary."

"Why don't we follow this drain all the way out of here?" said Jemmons. "Be a lot easier."

The Duck stopped and turned round. I bumped into him. He pushed me aside and shone his torch up into Jemmons's squinting eyes.

"Because, Roger," he said patiently, "we've already sussed that one—it doesn't go outside—it goes straight down into an underground lake—and then out into the sea. Which is under about thirty feet of bleeding pack ice—does that answer your question?"

"I'm sorry I spoke," said Jemmons, shielding his eyes with his hands.

The Duck turned on his heels and soldiered on, swiping a dangle of slimy stuff out of his face.

"Livingstone Duck," I sniggered.

"Shut up."

We continued in silence until we came to a thirty-degree downturn. Well, it looked pretty steep to me.

"I thought we were supposed to be going up," I said.

"It must be down here," said the Duck, slipping and sliding onward. "Come on—"

At that moment he lost his balance and splatted down on his backside. Jemmons and I sensibly held back.

"Looks dangerous," I said. "You sure that's the right way?"

"Course it's the right way!"

Jemmons pointed upwards. "What's that hole?" he said.

I could hardly make it out. "Throw me the torch, Duck," I said.

"Help me up then!" he quacked.

Jemmons held my hand and I ventured a little way down the slippery slope and grabbed the Duck's outstretched hand to pull him back up. He pushed us both out of his way and went straight over to shine the torch up the hole himself.

"No," he said. "That's not it. It's too narrow. That can't be it. Can it?"

"Lift me up on your shoulders, Rog—I'll have a closer look," I said.

Jemmons knelt down on one knee and I sat on his back with my legs around his neck. He kept stooped and bore me over to the hole. The Duck passed me up his torch. I got my head in line with the hole.

"All right, Rog."

Jemmons straightened up slowly and my head and shoulders rose straight up through the hole.

"What can you see?" called the Duck.

"Yeah—it's a shaft. This looks like a drainage hole—there's a grille—hang on, I'll try to move it."

I pushed up with the flat of my hand and dislodged the cover easily. Then I reached both my hands up and hauled myself through. When I stood up, I found myself in a shaft some four feet square.

The Duck's hands and then head appeared by my feet and I helped him in. Then we both reached back down to pull Jemmons and the boards up. Once we were all in the shaft, I kicked the grille cover back in place. We were now standing in a tight circle, staring each other in the face.

"Where's the bloody ladder then?" quacked the Duck.

"Um?"

"I told you it wasn't the right way!" he said, giving me a push.

I pushed him back.

The Duck snatched his torch off me and shone it up the shaft.

"I think I can get up there," said Jemmons. He handed us the boards and spat on the palms of his hands. "Give me some room, boys."

The Duck and I squeezed ourselves up into a corner. Jemmons braced his heels against one wall and fell forwards, stopping himself hitting the opposite wall with his hands. Then, drawing first his right foot up the wall and then the left, he began walking up the shaft, hand over hand. The Duck nudged me and I saw he had taken an orange fishing line out of his biggles and was tying the boards together. I passed him my two and went back to watching Jemmons.

"Sod that!" I said. "How far up does it go?"

"It's no height at all," laughed Jemmons. "Have you never been out on the yardarm of one of His Majesty's ships of the line in a force nine gale, crossing the Bay of Biscay, sonny?"

"Not recently, Rog," I said.

Jemmons disappeared up into the darkness. We looked at each other. The Duck, who was by far the shortest, stuck the torch in his mouth, paid out all of the nylon line, tied the end around his waist, walked out into the middle of the shaft, swung his arms about, looked up, clapped his hands, shuffled backwards, braced his heels against the foot of the wall, fell forwards, and knocked himself out cold on the opposite wall.

"What was that?" called Jemmons.

"Midshipman Duck just fell off the floor," I said.

Jemmons cackled and started whistling a hornpipe.

I picked up the torch and shone it in one of the Duck's eyes. The eyeball moved about. I did the same to the other one. I dropped the torch and jumped back with a yelp. To my horror—the Duck's eye was still and staring, but worse than that I could see the telltale red light of a camera lens in the retina.

"What's up?" called Jemmons, sounding farther away than I wanted him to be at that moment.

"The-the Duck's a-cl-clone!" I stammered. I started to shake uncontrollably.

"He's a clown all right!" laughed Jemmons, and carried on whistling.

The Duck was still slumped against the wall opposite me. Not moving. I reached out slowly for the torch, without taking my eyes off the shadowy figure. My hand touched the torch. Suddenly, another hand grabbed mine and I dropped it again with a loud gasp. Instinctively my arms and legs recoiled from the thing I had thought was the Duck.

"Give me that!"

"Duck?" I said.

"What?" He shone the torch in my face. I winced and averted my eyes. "What the hell's the matter with you?" he said. "You look like you've just seen a Benetton ad."

"You're a—you're a clone," I said.

"Clone. I'm not a clone. How am I a bleeding clone?"

"Your eye—your left eye—it's a camera," I said.

"Yeah, it's false. I had a digital one fitted years ago. Come on—to rest is not to conquer!" He stood up.

"So you're not one of them?" I said.

"Not the last time I looked. Here, hold that," he said, handing me the torch. He shuffled backwards to wedge his heels. This time he remembered to throw his hands out to stop himself. And then he was away, jiggling up the shaft like a mechanical monkey.

"Who is Matthew Turner? And how did you first hear about him?" I said, shining the torch on his face, as he ascended into the darkness.

"Your so-called mate," he laughed.

"They could know that," I shouted up. "What did you show me about him?"

"Newspaper clipping!" called the Duck. "He sold his story to the Sunday papers—made you look a right pratt! I still read it when I want a good laugh!"

That was definitely the Duck up there. I braced my heels, put the torch in my mouth, and fell forwards. And then I was shuffling my hands and feet up the sides of the shaft to join him. It was easier than it looked. The walls were, of course, made of a plastic resin and were uneven, so they gave plenty of grip. However, after several meters of this crab-like wall-walking, my arms and legs began to tire—but what was worse, I could hear the Duck panting and gasping somewhere above me. Now, if he fell it would be—

"Aa-aghhhh!"

I felt an almighty jolt on my back and instinctively dug in with my toes and fingers. Arms and legs were all over me. The torch beam was flashing about on the wall as I tried to flick off the tangle of fishing line that had fallen around my face and hair. Someone was panting very heavily in my ear like a nuisance caller in a hurry. And then I felt myself slipping.

"Carn't rold oo—gerroff!" I said, through a mouthful of torch.

I felt an elbow in my back and then a knee—some of the weight lifted off me. I could hear fingernails scrabbling on the wall overhead.

"Hang about," gasped the Duck. "Nearly there."

"Gerroff—hine going!" I mumbled.

At last the load came off my back—my fingers and feet flexed. My spine almost sprang back into position with the release of tension. It was lucky the Duck was five feet nothing much and as light as a feather. Now, if Jemmons had fallen—but let's not go there!

I snatched the torch out of my mouth and held it on the wall under my hand. "You bloody idiot!" I screamed. I craned my neck round and saw the Duck's red and puffy face grinning down at me. "You nearly had me off."

"I lost my grip," he said.

"You'll lose more than that when I get hold of you!"

"Ahoy down there!" called Jemmons.

"Ahoy, Rog!" quacked the Duck.

"Everything all right?"

"Yeah—Stephen slipped and I had to help him!" smirked the Duck, and sped away from me.

I grabbed the fishing line and yanked it.

"Hey—no! Pack it in!" he panicked.

I laughed ghoulishly and yanked it again.

"If I go—you go!" he sneered.

I let go and carried on climbing.

"Pipe down," whispered Jemmons. "Someone's coming."

"Hey?" said the Duck. "He's there."

I put all my effort into my climbing and got back into my rhythm. I found that if I exaggerated the movement in my shoulders I could climb better—just a little tip if you're ever in a similar fix. The best way I can describe it is you have to be like your own cox in a rowing team—egging yourself on in a set series of strokes. One, two, three—one, two, three, I was counting in my head. It really works.

"Wait—you pratt!" cried the Duck.

I felt my back crash into something bony. I rested my "oars" and held firm on the wall.

There was some scuffing and some groaning sounds above me. I closed my eyes and waited. I was burning up. The sweat was pouring off me. I tasted the salt in my mouth and felt its sting in my eyes. I shook my head to get rid of it. I felt tough. Like I could punch a hole in a wall with my bare knuckles. I made a few snorting noises—to psyche myself up.

"Cun on, arssholes!" I snarled.

"Right—up a bit more," said the Duck.

I twisted my neck round to try and see where I was going, but I couldn't make anything out. I twisted it round the other way and saw the Duck's face sticking out rather surreally from the wall.

"We're in another drain," said the Duck, sensing my disorientation.

I jiggled up the last few feet and he gripped my arms, to help me in, but I shrugged him off and hoisted myself in on my elbows. I spat out the torch and flopped down.

"Are you all right, mate?" said the Duck.

"Loose as a goose," I panted, my face still pressed to the cold floor.

"Well, give us a hand up with these boards then?" said the Duck, flashing his torch in my face.

"Put that light out!" hissed Jemmons.

The light clicked off. I raised my head and looked along the square-shaped drain. It was about four feet high and maybe only eight or nine feet long. Jemmons was kneeling at the end, holding something up and peeking out. Outside light was pouring in. Jemmons lowered the drain cover and hunched down in the foetal position, the shadows from the bars cast higgledy-piggledy stripes across his face and body.

I shivered. My body temperature was coming down and there was an icy draught from the opening. The pounding of several pairs of running feet passed over our heads.

"Four," whispered Jemmons.

"The riot's started," said the Duck. "Quick—help me with these!"

I got up on my knees and turned round. The Duck had produced a pair of gloves from somewhere in his biggles and was pulling them on. I pulled my sleeves down and got my hands inside them. We both dragged on the thin line and I felt it bite. And then it was hand over hand in a synchronized routine. I got my shoulders moving.

"What you doing?" said the Duck.

"Uh?"

"That thing with your shoulders—you brute!"

"Arg!" I said. "Arg-arg!"

"Arg-arg!" grinned the Duck.

We slung the boards in and sat down to get our breath back. The Duck gave me five and I slapped his palm and gripped it tightly.

"You-me-escape!" I grimaced.

"Not if you break my bloody fingers—get off!"

I threw his hand aside roughly.

"I think prison life's hardened you up," he said. "The sooner we get you back to civilisation the better—you're turning native."

"Arrrg."

"All clear, boys!" called Jemmons.

Jemmons was kneeling up and looking out again. We crawled along on our hands and knees to join him.

"Let me see," said the Duck, pulling Jemmons down and sticking his own head up. "We've come up in the courtyard. That's the infirmary over there." He swivelled his head round like a periscope. "No sign of any life. We'll chance it."

I grabbed the seat of his biggles and dragged him back.

"What you playing at? Get off!" he said.

"What about Emma?" I said.

"She'll meet us on the wall with the Princess," he said.

"Yeah, I've heard that one before," I said. "I won't be leaving here without her—and neither will you!"

"She'll be here," said the Duck, shrugging me off and climbing back up through the hole.

"After you," I said to Jemmons.

He didn't need any second invitation. I was just about to follow him, when there were dozens of chings and the whole courtyard suddenly lit up with blinding floodlights.

Chapter 16

"Stay right where you are, Doctor Zirconion!" crackled a severe voice.

"Crikey—we've been done up!" I heard the Duck cry.

I was paralysed. My mouth and tongue felt as dry as wrapping paper.

"Lie down on the ground!" ordered the echoing voice.

"It's ice flippin' cold!" complained the Duck.

"Get down, mutants!" boomed the voice.

I heard the grate of boots on the frozen ground and saw the Duck and Jemmons in my mind's eye being forced down on their bellies.

"Hands behind your heads!" came the next chilling command.

I flinched and shivered. There was a tramp of boots, running across the courtyard, coming closer and closer. The sweat was pouring off me again. I felt trapped. Frozen with fear. Somehow I unlocked my limbs and started to slither backwards along the drain, inching my way towards the ledge. My feet bumped against the snowboards. I stopped. The slightest noise might bring them down into the drain, but they would surely search it anyway, I thought, so what difference did it make? I kicked the boards back and back—right over the edge! They fell down the shaft with a terrible clatter and crash. The whole tunnel reverberated with the din. And then there was silence.

But something must have happened above ground, while I was deafened by the tumbling boards, because the lights had cut out and I could hear scuffling and strained groans and thuds—fighting! I alligatored my body back along the drain and clambered out. The cold air hit me in the nose and made it smart. I could see half a dozen shadowy figures silently kicking and shoving each other around, like a dumb show, just a few yards away from me. The Duck and Jemmons were in there somewhere. But before I could run over and help them someone barged into me and we both fell in a heap. I realized it was one of the guards and gripped his wrist—just as he was about to level his tranquilizer pistol at my face and pull the trigger. And as I turned on him and looked up I saw the Princess charging towards us. She grabbed him by his fur collar and threw him aside like a brat discarding a cuddly toy, and then pulled me to my feet with a single jerk of her arm. She gave me two air kisses.

"You're safe now, darling!" she smiled. "Stay close to me!"

And with that, she charged headlong into the others and began throwing them around as though they were no more than glove puppets. I stayed with her and pushed and thumped any guard who came near me or was slung past me in her wake. The Duck jumped dramatically on a guard who had been tossed aside by our superhero Princess and started showboating. Jemmons actually had the audacity to pull the Princess off one stricken guard and almost got slung to the ground himself for his trouble.

"Not him!" I yelled.

The Princess released her grip on Jemmons and made a point of dusting off the shoulders of his biggles.

"Sorry, Roger," she smiled.

"You don't need a bodyguard," I said.

"And there's no need to kill 'em," said Jemmons.

The Duck now had his victim in a Jap stranglehold and was shouting at the poor guy to submit. I think he must have already been unconscious when the Duck jumped him, because he wasn't responding.

"Leave him!" I said.

"He asked for it," panted the Duck. "He's gonna get it."

"Yeah, yeah. Get off him," I said.

The Duck dropped his head with a clunk on the hard ice and stood up. "Yeah, where were you when it kicked off? Hiding down the bleeding drain."

"Look!" I said, grabbing him by the front of his biggles. "Behave yourself—or I'll send you to your room!"

He slapped my arm away.

"This way, Stephen," said the Princess, patting my head.

We all ran down the quad after her to some steps in the western end, leading up to a square tower the Duck had earlier identified as the infirmary. All around us the high walls rose, crowned with towers and battlements. The courtyard was roughly the size of an ice hockey rink, with buildings in the form of towers flanking the middle of each side. To our left, on one of the long sides of the rectangle, was a large towered structure, with a faded old mock medieval sign across its façade, saying CASTLE AMUSEMENTS CO. It was decorated with laughing gargoyles and hieroglyphic gibberish. On the right was a matching building, only the sign wasn't in good enough condition to read, also it was covered in aerials and satellite dishes, which were obviously later additions. I don't know what was up the other end, but it looked like another square tower, matching the infirmary. A light snow began to fall.

I caught up and fell in next to the Princess.

"Where's Emma?" I said.

"She is waiting for us in the infirmary," she replied, without breaking stride.

"You're a pretty tough girl," I said. "I liked the way you handled yourself back there."

"I work out."

"You'd, uh, never—what I'm trying to say is: if we ever fall out after we're married, I want us to get counselling."

We crunched up the snowswept steps and passed a smashed searchlight, with a guard slumped over the mounting.

"Your handiwork?" I said.

She smiled modestly. "He wouldn't turn it off."

"He went out like a light," I grinned.

"We've left the boards behind!" exclaimed Jemmons.

"You and Rog go back and get 'em, dad," I said. "I'll stay with the Princess."

"Who's giving the orders round here?" said the Duck.

"I am," said the Princess. "Do as he says."

The Duck muttered something under his breath and he and Jemmons doubled back down the steps.

"You've got a way with him," I said.

"Through here." She ushered me in under the porch.

I was just going to open the door.

"Wait!" she said.

"What?"

She grabbed me and planted a sweet tasting kiss full on my mouth. We broke. I licked the greasy lipstick off my lips.

"Have you told Emma about us?" I said.

"She is of no consequence," said the Princess.

I remembered what the Duck said about us not getting out of jail without the Princess' help—he was damn right for once. I decided to play along.

"She's just a mortal," I said.

She leaned in to sink another one on me. I placed my finger against her puckered lips.

"But let's not keep her waiting—after all, she doesn't have as much time as we do."

I opened the door. A trapezium of light fell across the porch. I don't know why, but to my amazement, Emma was sitting on the first one in a row of six empty hospital beds, combing her hair. She was wearing a biggles just like mine. Only she looked good in hers.

"Emma!" I rushed to her.

"Hi, Steve," she said quietly.

She stood up and we embraced.

"I never believed you were really here," I whispered, holding onto her tightly. "I thought I'd lost you."

"The Princess—" she whispered. She stopped herself.

"What about her?" I said.

"Travis is—he's dead," she said.

I looked round to get the Princess' confirmation. She was applying some fresh pink lip-gloss. She closed her eyes and nodded. I turned back to Emma. I expected to see tears, but there were none.

"I'm sorry," I said. "I admit I never liked him, but I'm sorry he's dead."

"Yes, well," she said. She lowered her eyes.

"Did you love him?"

She shook her head.

"You do know about that other thing?"

"Yes," she said. "I know everything now."

"I'm really sorry," I said, rubbing her shoulder.

"It's not your fault."

"We must leave now," said the Princess.

"Yeah. Tempus fugit," I said.

I took Emma's hand and we headed for the door. The Princess opened it for us and I saw her look down at our hands. A corner of her upper lip curled a little. I hadn't noticed how glamorously she had made herself up when we were outside in the dark, but now in the light I could see the gleamer applied under her brows and on her high cheekbones and the dusky pink eye shadow and mascara. She looked like she was going on a Prada fashion shoot—not escaping from prison.

We stepped outside and the Princess grabbed my other hand and led us round the corner to the parapet and along the battlement walkway. By now the wind had picked up a little and the snow was swirling. But apart from that all was quiet and deserted. There was no sign of the Duck and Jemmons down in the quad, or any guards around the walls.

"Is this the west side?" I went to the wall and looked over.

"Yes," said the Princess. "This is where we go off."

Emma joined me and looked down.

"Down there? You are joking?" she said.

There was a fifty-foot drop and then what looked like quite a gentle slope, a bank of snow falling away to a slightly steeper one, and then beyond that the hillside gradually evened out until it reached the bottom. There was nothing then but the flat expanse of ice as far as the eye could see.

I squeezed Emma's hand. "Don't worry, love—I'll be right behind you," I said.

"I'd rather you were down there with a circus net."

The Princess caught my eye behind Emma's back. She did not look happy.

"Er, Princess," I said. "Have you ever done anything like this before?"

She peered over the battlement and then back at me. "Like what?" she said.

"Well, you know, it's a long way to jump," I said.

"That's not a jump, Sloane—that's a fall," said Emma.

"My people are trained in all-terrain survival techniques—we can endure any hardship," said the Princess. "We always get where we want to go and we always get what we want."

"Sounds like a marching song." I sang it, "Oh, we always get where we want to go and we always get what we want."

"Stephen—it's not funny," said Emma.

"Sorry—just trying to boost morale."

"Here they come," said the Princess, staring down into the courtyard.

I looked round. I could hear the Duck's voice even before I saw him. He was out of the drain hole and Jemmons was handing the boards up to him.

He looked over his shoulder and quickly spotted us.

"Well, come and give us a bloody hand then!" he quacked. His voice echoed eerily round the quad.

"I'd better go and help him," I said. "Before he bursts a blood vessel."

"Be careful, darling," said the Princess.

I shot Emma a glance. She raised one eyebrow and turned her face away from me, into the buffeting west wind.

I ran around the side of the tower and back down the steps. I was just getting to the bottom when I heard a commotion above and directly behind me. I wheeled round and saw a horde of men pouring out of the infirmary door, led by the unmistakable figure of the Colonel. I counted about twenty of them.

"Em—!" I started to shout, to warn Emma and the Princess, but then cut my voice off, because I thought it would be better not to draw attention to them.

"There he is!" cried the Colonel, pointing his baton down at me.

I turned and legged it. The Duck had already seen them and was just standing around watching. Someone fired a tranquillizer dart at me and it pinged off the ice near my feet. And then two more zinged past my head and almost hit the Duck. He skipped up in the air.

"What the hell is he playing at?" he quacked.

"Who me?" I gasped.

"No—that old fart up there!" cried the Duck.

I skidded to a stop and hid behind Jemmons.

"Hand that man over to me, Zirconion!" bellowed the Colonel. "He is not coming on this escape. I'm taking charge and I'm taking his place."

"Let's do a deal, Colonel," said the Duck.

"No deals, Zirconion!" said the Colonel sternly.

"Oh, no!" said the Duck, out of the corner of his mouth.

"Is he coming?" I said.

"No—the Princess is getting involved—why doesn't she stay where she is?" he whispered.

I peeped out around Jemmons and saw the Princess sneaking around the corner of the infirmary tower, towards the porch. There was no sign of Emma on the wall. I guessed she must have been told to stay around the corner, out of sight.

"I'm going to count to three, Doctor!" shouted the Colonel. All the Colonel's men raised their tasers and tranquillizer dart guns as one and aimed them at us. "One…"

"I better hand you over," said the Duck. "But don't worry, I'll come back for you some day."

"Two…" said the Colonel.

"Don't bother," I said. "I'm giving myself up."

"There's no need for that—we can take this lot, mateys," said Jemmons.

"Three!"

I patted Jemmons on the back and stepped out into the open.

"I'm coming in, Colonel!" I shouted. And I began walking back across the courtyard towards the steps, with my hands in my pockets and my head down. There didn't seem any point in holding up the escape on my account—if De Quipp could make the grand gesture then so could I. Anyway, I was fairly sure the Duck would be back for me—one day!

Suddenly, a piercing screech rang out—so loud that it gave me a sort of shock between my shoulder blades. I immediately looked up at the tower. Mayhem had broken out. The Princess was among them, flinging guys every which way and shrieking at the top of her voice. Grown men were screaming and scattering for their lives on that wall. They were firing their tasers and tranquillizer bolts at her, but nothing was having any effect. Some brave types were even leaping on her back, but they couldn't bring her down. I started running. I was near to the foot of the steps, when one of the Colonel's men came flying down at me. I dodged out of the way and he crunched into the ice, chin first. And then someone came charging past me from the other direction and bounded up the steps ahead of me, in a blur—Jemmons!

"Roger—no!" I cried, chasing him up.

I saw him wade in throwing punches, but he was heavily outnumbered and soon dragged down and kicked. Just as I got to him, I felt a terrific belt of electricity go through my leg, knocking me off my feet. An army boot swung towards my nose—I rolled out of the way and tried to fend the next kick off with my hands. The next thing, some guy was on top of me trying to hit me in the face with something. I heard the Duck's voice raised nearby. There was so much shouting and screaming going on and so many legs milling about, that I couldn't make out how close he was or what he was on about. I just concentrated on holding my attacker off. Somehow, I managed to twist his wrist back and make him drop whatever he had in his hand.

And then, suddenly, it all went quiet and everybody stopped in mid-fight. I pushed my guy off me and looked round. The Princess was lying lifeless in the porchway and standing over her was the Colonel, holding a two-foot long blade, dripping blood onto the snow.

"You bastard!" cried Jemmons, rushing at him.

One of the Colonel's lieutenants—Bauhaus, I think—stepped in his way and fired a tranquillizer dart into his stomach, sending him sprawling to the ground.

"Stone the crows," quacked a familiar voice.

I got up on my knees and looked to my left, where the Duck was still clinging to some guy's back, shaking his head in dismay. His spectacles were at a silly angle on his nose, where they had been half-knocked off in the fight.

"Take her inside," said the Colonel, sheathing the dagger back in his baton.

"Wait!" cried the Duck. "She's the only one who knows where the machine is! Let me see if she's still alive." The Colonel nodded and the Duck scampered over to her and knelt down by the body. He felt for a pulse in her neck and then put his ear to her breast. He tried a little heart massage. He shook his head and stood up.

Two men picked the Princess' limp body up and carried her through to the infirmary. I could see them laying her out on the very same bed Emma had been sitting on only a few minutes earlier. Jemmons was just a few feet away, so I crawled over to him on my hands and knees and lifted his head off the icy floor to cradle it in my lap.

"What are those things?" said the Colonel, pointing his baton at the snowboards, which were lying next to the drain where the Duck and Jemmons had left them.

"Skis," said the Duck. He came over and crouched down next to me to take a look at Jemmons.

The Colonel ordered four of his men to go down and fetch the snowboards.

"How is he?" said the Duck.

"Still breathing," I said. "But I'd like to get him inside." I lowered my voice to a whisper, "Emma's hiding round the corner somewhere."

"Don't worry," the Duck whispered back. He opened his hand and I saw a glint of blue-violet light. He clamped it shut again.

"The key?" I gasped.

"Shh!" He slipped it back into his hip pocket. "I got it off her when I went to have a look."

"You should be a pickpocket," I said. "I never saw you."

"The quickness of the hand deceives the eye, mate," he said. "I've got lots of skills like that."

"Yeah, all right. Is she really dead?" I said.

"I dunno. She looked brown bread to me."

The Colonel marched over and tapped the Duck on the shoulder with his notorious baton.

"Now, look here, Zirconion—what's the plan with these board thingies? How's a chap supposed to ski on that?"

His men had just returned with the boards and one was being held up for his inspection.

"It's like a surfboard," said the Duck. "You stand on it and steer it with your body."

"What the devil's a surfboard?" bristled the Colonel, giving the specimen a rap with his baton. "Is one expected to ride this thing off the hill? You must be mad—I said you must be mad."

The Duck stood up and folded his arms. "Well, that's the only plan in town," he said. "What happened to our deal? You said you were going to start a riot, not organise a bleeding breakout."

"I don't trust you, Zirconion," said the Colonel. "I don't trust you and I never did. And I don't like you either. So when you promised to return and free me and my men, I accepted merely because I thought a jolly good riot would be good for morale. But the riot went rather well—better than we anticipated—we have taken the whole of G Wing and secured the connecting tunnel. My men still hold it. So I said to myself—why the devil wait around for a man I don't trust and I don't like? I decided to take matters into my own hands. Now I find there's no plan to speak of and no means of escape even if we did manage to get down onto the Levels. You're a blithering idiot, Zirconion! You've wasted my time.

Give me one good reason why I shouldn't have you all flogged and thrown off the wall."

A bank of floodlights chinged on across the courtyard and the whole porchway and wall was lit up with dazzling light.

"Stand right where you are, you genetic waste!" boomed a stern voice, from a loudspeaker situated somewhere in the building that had all the communications equipment sticking out of it.

"Oh, great!" I said. "That's all we need. The master race is here."

"I thought you said your men were holding the connecting tunnel," said the Duck. "How come the bleeding guards are in the old Casino then?"

"Into the infirmary, men!" ordered the Colonel, leading the way.

His men fell in behind him and there was a sort of orderly stampede as they all filed in, leaving the Duck and me outside, with the unconscious Jemmons.

Tranquillizer darts started pinging and zipping off the steps and walls. We grabbed an arm each and dragged our fallen comrade gamely towards the infirmary door, but it slammed in our faces before we even got under the porch. Another hail of darts rained in and smashed and tinkled all around us. They had found their range.

"Now what?" I shouted.

The Duck dropped the arm he was holding and ran off around the corner of the tower.

"Bloody typical!" I yelled.

Jemmons stirred and attempted to sit up.

"Get up, Rog—get up! Come on, mate!"

I tried to pull him to his feet. But just as his backside lifted off the ground another tranquillizer dart struck him in the left buttock and he went out like a light again. I dropped his arm and ran off after the Duck.

As I careered round the slippery corner, desperately seeking Emma, a hand shot out and pulled me in. I found myself huddled up against a side door, face-to-face with Emma and the Duck.

"Do you come here often?" grinned the Duck.

"Where's the Princess?" said Emma.

"Um?"

"She's in the infirmary," said the Duck, while I was still trying to think of a less frightening answer than the truth.

"What's she doing in the infirmary?" said Emma.

"Er?"

"Um?"

Before the Duck or I could answer, three fur-clad guards, wearing dark goggles and wielding the obligatory cattle prods galloped round the corner. The Duck didn't hesitate—he was into them before they even spotted us. Give him his due—when his back's to the wall, the Duck will fight. I dashed out after him. The Duck had snatched a prod and whacked one guard down and was parrying shock sticks with the other, but mine was swishing his stick in my face and keeping me at bay.

"Run, Emma!" I shouted.

"Where, Stephen?" she shouted back.

"Anywhere!"

Emma ran off along the battlement walkway. The guard, who was fencing with the Duck, dipped his shoulder, sold the Duck a dummy—and sprinted after her. The Duck ran after him. I still couldn't get away, because my guy had me cornered and, what's more, was closing in for the kill. I felt the wall behind me and knew I was out of options, so I propelled myself off it with my foot and smacked into him. He was so surprised by my sudden counter-attack that I got my hands on him. We wrestled about. To be honest, he was winning this crude trial of strength. I imagine he did lots of bench-presses and stuff like that in his spare time, back at the barracks, so I was no match. The most strenuous task I ever performed in my job as an advertising copywriter was unjamming the Xerox machine. But I had a stroke of luck—he tripped over the guy the Duck had flattened and, losing his balance, fell backwards off the wall into the courtyard. I found the spare shock stick and hared after the others.

They had run all the way along the battlement and were fighting on the raised area inside a corner turret. I could just make out the Duck's head above the wall and his goggled foe swiping at him with his stick. I couldn't see Emma, but I could hear her voice. As I ran, a searchlight from the communications building picked me out like a bashful cabaret act, avoiding the limelight. I tried to lose its blinding beam, but it stayed with me and fixed on me all the way to the corner. Those who were operating it would have had a laugh when they saw me charge up the two steps to the tower, waving my stick, and promptly fall on my ass. As my elbow hit the icy ground, the shock stick jolted out of my hand and sailed harmlessly over the wall. Emma was cowering under the parapet. Now I could see that the Duck had been trying to defend her. I felt useless without a weapon. But even worse, my leg felt dead and I couldn't get up. The Duck, though, seemed to be giving as good as he got—though I think the loud quacking noises he was making must have been off-putting to his opponent. Rather like playing tennis against Monica Seles, I imagine.

Suddenly, his adversary—no doubt much more experienced in baton-fighting than a temporal engineering graduate—managed to flick the Duck's stick out of his grasp. And it, too, flew up into the night and out over the parapet. The Duck was at his mercy. Emma was at his mercy. I don't think he'd even noticed me, or, if he had, wasn't too bothered about the threat I posed on my current form.

The Duck leapt up on the battlement and, showing surprising agility, hopped over the gaps. I could see that he was teasing the guard, to draw him away from Emma. Emma edged towards me around the circular turret on her haunches. I kept one eye on the antics of the Duck and, as soon as Emma was out of the way, decided to crawl to his aid. But just as I got close, the guard whacked him in the groin. The Duck flew up in the air, let out a shrill cry and vanished off the wall.

Chapter 17

I gulped. Emma screamed. I was terrified that the guard was going to turn round. But this guard was so cocky he just had to take a look over the battlement at his handiwork. I speeded up my crawl grabbed his ankles and tried to topple him over, but he gripped the wall with both hands and pushed back. Fortunately, he lost his shock stick over the side as we struggled.

"Emma!" I shouted at the top of my voice.

She ran to my assistance and attempted to help me lift his legs up. But he was too strong—even for both of us.

"Get his hands!"

Emma stood up and tried to dislodge his fingers from the edge of the parapet, by pulling at them, but he resisted all her efforts—until she had the idea of biting them—that did the trick. He lost his grip with one hand and made the error of trying to grab her hair with his other. That was my chance. I flipped him over. He let out the most blood-curdling cry as he went—his arms and legs paddling madly through the air like a swimmer. I twisted round fitfully and slumped against the foot of the wall, shivering. Emma crouched down and patted my shoulder.

"Is the Duck—?" I couldn't bear to finish the question.

She nodded.

"God—are you sure?" I said.

"He's not moving," she replied and bit her bottom lip.

We stared at each other and both started to cry at the same time. We hugged.

"He tried to save me," she sobbed.

"I should have done something," I sniffed. "If only I hadn't slipped over—he'd still be alive."

I suddenly had a thought and got up quickly—pain shot through my shinbone. I ignored it and stamped my foot. Emma supported me around the waist.

"Are you okay?" she said.

"Yeah—I just gave myself a dead leg, I think—nothing feels broken." I turned round and looked over the parapet. "I've got to get down there— he might still be alive."

"Steve." Emma tugged my sleeve. "Look."

I looked over my shoulder. A platoon of white-furred and begoggled guards were streaming towards us from the direction of the CASTLE AMUSEMENTS CO building. More were running along the walkway from the infirmary.

"We could jump," I said.

"No thanks," said Emma. "You can if you like."

"No, I'll stay with you," I said, giving her a funny look.

"Hands up!" ordered the nearest guard, brandishing a huge rapid-loading tranquillizer rifle, with what looked like electronic imaging and guidance systems incorporated in it. It looked like a gun enthusiast's wet dream.

We stuck our hands up.

"There're two guys down there—" I tried to explain.

"—Shut up!" he screamed.

"One of them's yours—the other one's Doctor Zirconion—he's very important—send a rescue party down—"

He lurched forward and jabbed me in the stomach with the nose of his gun. "Stop talking! Lie down on the floor!"

"No," I said. I dropped my hands down by my sides.

He aimed his gun at me. Others flanked round us to back him up.

"Get down!" he barked.

I put my hands on my head. Emma did the same.

"Just cut the crap and take us back," I said. "I want to speak to an officer."

"Over there—quickly—move it!" he yapped, swinging the barrel of his big gun in the direction of the CASTLE AMUSEMENTS CO building.

Emma and I held hands and started walking, keeping one hand on our head. But one of the other guards took offence and ordered us not to touch each other and put our hands back up. The only other place I can remember ever being told not to hold hands with another human being was at school. But I was weary and I was cold, and getting inside seemed like a good idea, so I didn't argue with him.

The next thing I knew—guards were running and shouting behind us. I looked back and saw dozens of them retreating down the steps of the infirmary. Our guards ordered us to get down and took up defensive positions along the wall. Most dropped to one knee, but some, in advanced positions, actually lay down in the snow and took aim. A fluorescent greenish-yellow light was pulsing from the infirmary door.

"What the hell is it?" I said, thinking aloud.

"A rave?" said Emma.

Suddenly, two thirty-foot-long tentacles shot out of the porchway and whipped their way down the steps, scattering a few courageous guards, who had stood their ground. Those still in the courtyard turned tail and ran for their lives.

"Hold your positions! Hold your position!" crackled a voice from the PA system in the communications building.

Two more tentacles snaked out of the infirmary door, only these had rows of suckers on them and were much thicker. We all watched in awe. Speechless. And then the porchway exploded and the enormous domed head of a giant squid emerged—glowing with green light, its huge black eyes, staring and malevolent.

"Brunswick?" I murmured.

"What?" said Emma.

Some of our guards broke ranks and ran away along the battlement towards the CASTLE AMUSEMENTS CO block.

"It's a giant squid," I said. "The Duck had one just like it in a tank at Duckworth Hall, only he said it was just a baby one. Do you believe in co-incidences?"

"No way," said Emma. "Maybe it escaped."

"Yeah, and then it grew up, jumped in a time machine and came looking for its owner," I said, not taking my eyes off it. It seemed to have stalled in the porchway for a moment or two, though one of its tentacles was slowly feeling its way up the infirmary wall towards the top of the tower.

The loudspeaker burst into life again:

"On the count of three—you will all fire!" announced a somewhat shaky voice. "One...two—"

He didn't reach three. The giant squid's mouth flap had peeled back, revealing its massive beak, and shocked everyone into silence. Judging by the man's body lying on the ground at the top of the steps, it was about the size of a small aviary.

"Jemmons!" I exclaimed. "That's Jemmons! Wait here, Em."

I dashed off along the battlement, hopping, skipping, and jumping over the soldiers lying about, waiting to fire their weapons. I think they were so amazed to see me actually running towards the creature that they let me pass—they probably wanted to see what the beast would do to me. All I could think about was dragging Jemmons out of harm's way. I heard echoing footfalls behind me and looked round. It was Emma.

"Three!" boomed the loudspeaker.

A shower of missiles rained over onto the infirmary from the communications block. Emma and I hit the deck. More electric darts and tranquillizer tracers whined and zinged over our heads, homing in on the big target. I pressed my face into the snow and shut my eyes.

An almighty squawk reverberated around the walls, followed by several piercing screams, a strange slopping sound and multiple crashes and scrapes. I raised my eyes. The squid was gone. I heard firing behind me and looked round. The depleted squad of guards, who had remained with us on the wall, had turned to their right and were firing across court at the communications block. Only there wasn't much left of it—it was enveloped by the largest animal I had ever seen in my life—the giant squid. It was clinging to it like a gigantic hand and ripping it apart in several places at once, its undulating sets of tentacles working in tandem. Like the Duck said, the thing had five pairs—two extra long feeder tentacles and four pairs of suckered ones. It was trashing that building and nothing could stop it—the shooting from our side was merely a minor annoyance to it, which it dealt with in a vaguely flippant manner. It simply lifted its backside—if I may call it that—and squirted a pungent brown jet of ink at the guards, who all fell about screaming and holding their eyes.

"On your marks," I said, getting up into a sprint start position and turning round to make sure Emma had heard me. "Set?"

"Just go!" snapped Emma.

We set off at pace and both skidded and fell over when we tried to take the first corner too fast. We ended up rolling in a heap up against the side door of the infirmary. Incredibly, when we both sat up we were both laughing. I stopped laughing and leaned over and kissed her on the lips. She kissed me back. And then we had a proper one. You know, an adult one—tongues, loving moans, ruffling of hair—oh, I could dwell, I could dwell...

"Wait here," I said, looking lovingly into her eyes.

She thumped me in the arm. "Will you stop telling me to 'wait here' all the time—I'm coming with you," she said.

"Please, Em," I said. "I'm just going to check Jemmons, he might be in a bit of a mess—then I'm going to get the boards—if there's anything left of them—and then we're getting out of here. I think I know how to find the Princess' time machine."

She heaved a big sigh. "Don't be long."

"I won't."

I glanced across at the giant squid, which was still noisily tearing the communications block to pieces. Only now all the shooting had stopped and it was—I fancied—going about its work in a more leisurely manner, sort of enjoying itself, rather like a dog gnawing contentedly at a nice big juicy bone.

"Keep an eye on that thing," I nodded.

I snuck round the corner and to my surprise found Jemmons sitting up with his back resting against a pillar, watching our friend vandalising the Castle.

"Rog!" I called.

"Stevie!" he grinned.

I crouched down next to him. "You all right?"

"I've felt better," he said, reaching under and rubbing his backside. "Mind you, that warms the cockles of my heart." He nodded over at the giant squid.

"Can you walk?"

"I reckon so."

I helped him up. He rubbed his ribs and leaned against the pillar again.

Just then we heard a noise from inside the infirmary—like someone stepping on broken glass.

"What was that?" I said.

Jemmons raised a finger to his lips and craned his neck round the pillar.

"Steve?" called Emma.

"Emma?" I stepped out into the open.

Emma appeared in the smashed doorway.

"How did you get in there?"

"The side door was open." She picked her way through the debris and came to join us.

"Anyone else in there?" I said suspiciously.

She shook her head. "No. They've all gone." She smiled at Jemmons. "You must be Roger."

"And you must be the Emma he's always talking about—now I can see why," beamed Jemmons.

"Wait a minute," I said, looking past her into the wrecked hospital ward. "Where's the Princess?"

Emma looked back. "She's not in there. They must have taken her with them."

"I think it's time we got the hell out of here," I said. "Help me with these boards."

We all picked up an armful of boards and headed round to the west wall.

"I've got bad news about the Duck, Rog."

I told Jemmons what had happened on the way. I could see the news deeply saddened him. The snow was scarce now, flying about like bits and bobs of lace against the black sky. Jemmons and I looked over the wall. Emma refused to look and hung back.

"That's the turret where the Duck fell." I pointed.

"I can't see him," said Jemmons, screwing up his eyes and straining his neck to look along the foot of the wall.

"The snow must have buried him," I said.

"We'd better get down there," said Jemmons.

"Let go of me! Get off!" shrieked Emma.

We spun round—a begoggled guard had grabbed Emma from behind and was holding the tip of his shock stick to her temple. Jemmons lurched forward—I grabbed his sleeve and pulled him back.

"One more step and I'll fry her brain!" snapped the guard.

"What's the problem, mate?" I smiled.

"You will all come with me."

"Where?" I said.

He hesitated. He didn't seem to know. Maybe all the carnage had confused him, I thought—he's indecisive. I seized the moment.

"What's the point?" I said. "This place is history—that thing is going to total it before it's through."

He glanced across at the colossal squid, which was still contentedly gnawing away at the communications block. I noticed that two of its tentacles were reaching inside and groping about, like a kid playing with a doll's house.

"The fleet is coming—it will be destroyed," he said.

"You think?" I said. "Maybe you should think about getting out of here yourself."

"I-I must remain at my station."

"Listen," I said. "Why don't you forget all that rules and regulations mumbo jumbo and go and see if you can find your mates—they might be hurt and need your help. Let us go."

"No! Forbidden! Mutants! Seed of Satan—must eradicate the sperm of the devil—" he ranted.

"—John?" I said. "Is that you?"

His head tilted. I could see my own reflection in the black perspex of his goggles.

"Is that you, man?" I said, making myself look all smiley and pleased to see him.

"You know this droid?" said Jemmons.

"We go way back, don't we, John?" I opened my arms to step forward and embrace him.

"Stay back!" he cried. He depressed the button on his shock stick, it crackled and emitted tiny blue lightning bolts from the tip.

"Steve!" exclaimed Emma, in alarm.

"Hey, love and peace, man," I grinned. "The meaning of life is to live a meaningful life—remember, Johnny?"

"Don't move—I'll burn her!"

"Come on, man—that's Emma—you remember Emma, don't you, Johnny?"

I was convinced my amateur psychology was working and I could win him over with charm, just like I did before. But he wasn't having any of it. He suddenly took a swipe at me with his stick. Jemmons had seen enough—he lunged and grabbed my former devotee's wrist and slung him around. I abandoned the counselling and joined in. I got hold of his other arm—still locked around Emma's neck—before he squeezed the life out of her. His goggles got knocked off in the struggle and we faced each other momentarily, eyeball-to-eyeball.

"Don't do this, man," I said.

He tried to fling me off. Jemmons and I both held onto him. But he was way too strong. Jemmons, however, had been a former arm-wrestling champion on board His Majesty's Ships and was more of a match for him. He managed to twist the shock stick from his grip and make him drop it. And then I was on my own for a few terrifying seconds, clinging to the droid's back, while Jemmons bent down to pick up the stick. He was turning Emma and me around and around and we were in danger of spinning off the wall and down into the courtyard with him. And then I heard a loud whack followed by electrical crackles and spits. Smoke started to billow from the guard's sparking head.

It was whirling round and round, out of control, but it still wouldn't release Emma. I did the only thing I could think of to make it stop—I rugby tackled it. The android and Emma and I crunched to the ground. Jemmons fell on it and wrenched its arm from Emma's throat and I pulled her clear. We all stepped back. The android climbed to its feet and continued to turn round and round in circles. And then its head exploded and the headless body staggered off along the walkway towards the CASTLE AMUSEMENTS CO building, bumping into things and tripping over, but never quite managing to fall off the wall.

"You blew his mind," I said.

Suddenly, there was a loud WHEEEE noise and we all looked up to see that a bright red firework had exploded high up in the night sky above the Castle.

"Fireworks?" I said.

"That's a naval maroon," said Jemmons. "The squadron must be on its way. Come on—we'd better get out of here before they start shelling."

"Shelling?" I exclaimed. "The Castle?"

"Aye," said Jemmons. "With incendiaries—to do for that thing."

"But what about all the prisoners—the guards?"

"There're bunkers in the basement. They'll close the fire doors."

"Well, what are we waiting for?" said Emma, hands on hips.

We all hurried along the battlement walkway to the corner turret.

"Right," said Jemmons. "I've got an idea—Emma first."

"No!" cried Emma. "I'm not going first."

We heard the characteristic Doppler effect of a whistling incoming missile. Followed by a massive explosion—but it was outside the wall on the eastern side. A ball of fiery smoke rolled up. A foul smell wafted over.

"What is that smell?" I complained.

"Sulphur dioxide," said Jemmons. "They use brimstone in the incendiaries."

"How Old Testament. It smells like rotten eggs."

"That was a range finder," said Jemmons. "Come on—there's not much time. Emma, hold onto Stephen's ankles and I'll lower you both over the wall. You shouldn't have far to drop."

"No way," said Emma.

There were two more incoming whistles and the whole battlement rocked, huge explosions of flame burst over the courtyard. The giant squid reared two rows of tentacles and let out a defiant squawk. More fire bombs rained in wobbling our turret, making it feel flimsy, one of them scored a direct hit on the infirmary, which was immediately enveloped in flames. The heat on the battlement was now so intense it felt like someone had opened a kiln door.

"How do we do this?" shouted Emma, above the racket of whistling bombs, crackling flames and the shrieking squid.

"Stephen, you get up on the wall and take my hands," said Jemmons. I duly climbed up and took his hands. "Now, you, Emma, climb onto Stephen's back and slowly slide down until you feel your feet kick the side of the wall. Then you feel about and find his ankles and hold on as tightly as you can. Got that?"

"I think so," said Emma.

Emma got up on the wall and gingerly lowered herself onto my back.

"I had no idea this was going to be so nice," I said.

"Don't make me laugh," said Emma.

"Sorry."

"Right, now push yourself down him, Emma," said Jemmons. "That's it."

She stalled. "I can't—I can't!" she cried.

"Keep going, Em," I said. "This place is going to be barbecued any minute."

The well of the courtyard was a raging wall of flame, virtually obscuring the communications block from view—the giant squid appeared to be gone.

I felt her start to move again, very slowly.

"Oh, my God!" I cried.

"What?" said Emma. "I didn't do anything!"

"Look!"

They followed my stunned gaze—the Princess was running towards us along the burning battlement, leaping through flames.

"Stephen!" she waved.

She bounded up onto the turret.

"But you were dead," I said.

She swivelled her hip round and showed us a rip in the back of her biggles. "Look," she said. "The knife went in here, but it missed every vital organ and now the wound has sort of sealed up—it did not even bleed very much."

We all stared at the tear she was holding open for us. There was a small red gash where the blade had gone in, but nothing else. Her biggles, however, was split and torn all over and she was showing plenty of flesh. But she was so glamorous that she reminded me of an exotic dancer rather than a woman who had just been in a war zone.

"That is remarkable," I said.

Suddenly, the CASTLE AMUSEMENTS CO building exploded and burst into a ball of flame—we all flinched. Shards of burning plastic cascaded into the air and drifted down over the hillside like tickertape.

"Where is Doctor Zirconion?" she said.

"He's already down there," said Jemmons. "Give me a hand here, Your Highness."

Emma was holding me tightly around the waist and resting her cheek against my back. She felt snug and warm on me. I think that was as far down my body as she was prepared to go. Jemmons settled for that and he and the Princess began lowering us down the outside of the wall. Emma let out a few quiet squeals of unease, but held on bravely. I kept my eyes on Jemmons's face, watching the signs of extreme exertion increase as he bore the weight of us both. I couldn't see the Princess and assumed she must be anchoring him. And then, to my alarm, Jemmons himself started to come over the battlement—headfirst—and even he looked surprised. He was now holding my hands like a trapeze artiste— while the Princess stood up on the tower and held him by the ankles!

"Let go, Em!" I gasped. "You're not far."

She unclamped her hands and I felt her weight leave me immediately. I heard Jemmons let out a sigh of relief—and then the thud of Emma in the snow.

"Okay, Em?" I called, unable to see her, with my face turned to the wall. She was directly behind me somewhere.

"Okay!" she called up.

"Look out," I said. I let go and dropped onto the bank of powdery snow, landed both feet, fell backwards and pitched into a drift. Emma's hands were quickly on me, helping me up. Then we both stood aside and watched Jemmons push himself off the wall with his hands and fly out. He must have dived about ten or twelve feet, but rolled harmlessly down the slope, buffered by the deep snow. Not bad for an old guy. Emma and I waded through the drifts and pulled him to his feet. Then we all looked up at the tower. The Princess was gone! We looked to one another in puzzlement. Her head suddenly appeared again. She held up two snowboards.

"Coming down!" she yelled.

We cleared the area fast. The two boards sailed out and plummeted into the snow. Two more quickly followed. And then the last. We continued to look up. She just stepped off the parapet of the turret and tombstoned down the whole fifty or so feet, without any hesitation. None of us could believe it when she sank into a drift, got up, brushed the snow off herself, and calmly waded towards us.

"So," she said. "Where is the Doctor? He has something of mine, I think."

"You mean the key?" I said.

I felt Emma poke me in the back.

She smoothed my shoulder with her hand. A smile broke across her lips. "Exactly, my darling."

"He's over here," said Jemmons, standing over a mound.

We all trudged over to where Jemmons was now digging in the snow. I picked up a board and began digging.

"Careful," said Jemmons. "There's his head."

He fell on his knees and reached down into the pit and brushed the compacted snow from the pale tenant's face.

"He's still got his glasses on," I said.

The Princess wriggled in and nudged Jemmons aside with her hip and placed her ear on the Duck's chest. "Stand back," she commanded.

I felt Emma's hand fill mine as we stood and watched the Princess administering CPR. Jemmons watched her, too, for a moment or two and then continued to excavate the rest of the Duck's body. Emma and I fell to our knees and helped him. As I dug, my fingers struck something smooth and hard. I knew instantly what it was—I glanced across at the Princess to make sure she wasn't looking and then at Emma, who was busy clearing snow. I slipped it into my pocket and carried on digging. The Princess worked feverishly on her patient, only pausing from her alternate heart massage and mouth-to-mouth to put her ear again to the Duck's chest to listen.

"He's still breathing!" she said. "We need something to warm him up."

"The guard's coat!" I said. "He must be around here somewhere. Come on, Em—let's find him."

Emma and I set off to find the guard, who had fallen nearby. We both spotted a foot sticking up out of the snow and went about our macabre business—like Burke and Hare. I felt particularly squeamish about this spot of grave robbing, because I held myself directly responsible for his death. We sank our hands into the snow and dug down to his lifeless body.

"I can't look," I said. "Is he dead?"

"Well, his cameras are off," said Emma.

"Cameras? What cameras? My God—he's an android!"

"Come on—help me get his coat off," said Emma, undoing the first toggle.

"I'm really glad he's not human," I said. "That would make it murder. I wonder what you call it when you kill an android."

"Self-defence," said Emma.

We got one sleeve off and turned him over.

"Technically speaking, there was intent," I said. "I mean, in a court of law, I wouldn't have a leg to stand on."

"Neither would he, look—it's come off," said Emma.

"Oh don't—don't pull it, Em—for God's sake show some respect."

"Look, it's got all wires and bits inside," she said.

"Stop poking about in there!"

"I'm only looking. Ugh! What's that?"

I peered in. "It looks like a fried egg."

"Do androids eat fried eggs?"

I resisted the temptation to say "and chips," for a few seconds. "And chips," I said.

"What? I don't get it."

"You know: chips."

"No, it's no good," said Emma. "I can't ketchup."

I scooped a handful of snow in her face. "Oh, shut up!"

She grabbed up two handfuls and slapped them into my ears. And we fell about laughing and pulling each other around. It was just like the old days. When we used to have pillow-fights on Sunday morn—

"Hurry up with that coat, you pair!" yelled Jemmons.

Emma gave me one last push and bounded back with the fur. I chased after her, throwing snow at her back.

Jemmons directed me to take the Duck's legs and we lifted him out and laid him on the coat, which Emma and the Princess had spread out on the snow.

Another ground-shaking explosion erupted in the Castle and we all threw ourselves down and covered our heads with our hands.

"That was close," I said.

"Look!" said Emma, pointing to the turret we had been standing on just a few minutes earlier. It had grown into a pillar of flames and thick black toxic smoke.

"It's time we shoved off—tempus fugit," said Jemmons, offering me a hand up. He pulled me up a little too strongly and I barged into him. He stood me up straight and brushed me down. "Sorry, matey," he beamed.

"You don't know your own strength," I said. "What about the Duck?"

The Princess had put his arms in the coat and was just doing it up. The Duck looked like a big baby having his nappy changed, lying there on the snow, especially when the Princess sat him up and gave him a cuddle against her breast. She was just trying to warm him up I guess.

"How are we going to get him down?" I said.

"I can use the straps from his board to strap him to my back, Stephen."

"Can you manage that?"

"Oh, I think so," she said. "Do you still have the key?" she added, in a whisper.

"Yeah, it's in my—very clever, Princess," I smiled.

"The old one's are the best," she grinned. "Give it to me."

"I think I'll just hang onto it till we reach the bottom," I said.

"You do not trust me, my love?"

"You can trust me this time," I said, patting her on the head.

I moved away from her and looked down the hillside—it seemed steeper now that we were actually on it, than it had looked from the top of the wall. I trudged over and picked up my board and Emma's.

"I don't think I can do this," said Emma.

"Of course you can—it's easy," I said. "All you have to do is strap your feet on the board and—"

"—I'm just going to sit on and hold onto the straps like a rein," said Jemmons.

"Yes," said Emma. "I think that's what I'm going to do."

"Please yourselves," I said.

I started strapping my feet on my board. I'd done a bit of skateboarding and package holiday skiing in my time, so I was fairly confident I could make it. Once I had mine on securely I slid down to the Princess to see if she needed a hand. But she had it sussed. Emma and Jemmons were still trying to figure out a comfortable way of sitting on theirs.

"Need any help?" I said.

She hoisted the Duck onto her shoulders in a fireman's lift. "Just give me that strap—I will tie him to me so that he doesn't slip," she said.

I passed her one of the straps that she had already stripped from the Duck's board and she wound it round the Duck's wrists. As I was standing there, waiting to go, I felt in my left pocket for the glass key. It wasn't there. I thought I'd just forgotten which pocket I'd put it in. I dug into my right pocket—the key was gone!

"Are we all set?" said the Princess.

Jemmons and Emma both waved.

"Wait a minute," I said to her, out of the corner of my mouth.

"What's the matter?"

"Nothing."

"Have you lost something?" she said.

I looked at her sharply. "Did you take it?"

She shook her head. "You placed it in your right pocket, Stephen."

"You saw me do that?"

"I see everything you do, Stephen—I can't take my eyes off you, darling."

"I must have dropped it—I'll retrace my steps—"

"—No—don't worry, Jemmons has it," she said.

"Roger? But?" I looked across at Jemmons. He was sitting next to Emma, talking to her, and steadying her board for her. Butter wouldn't melt. "Are you sure?"

"When he helped you up—he brushed you down—that's when he took it," she nodded.

"But why? Why would he do that?"

"I don't know," said the Princess. "We'd better keep an eye on him—he might be working for Corrective Measures."

"Are you playing mind games with me, Princess?"

"I only lie when I have to," she said.

"That's all right then," I laughed.

"Are we going down this bloody mountain or what?" shouted Emma.

"After you, Ms Gummer," said the Princess.

"Come on, Roger—let's show them," said Emma.

Emma and Jemmons set off together at a sedate speed, slowing themselves down with their feet as they went.

"Be careful, Em!" I said.

I turned the nose of my board downhill and took off. The Princess was right alongside me in a flash. We shot past Emma and Jemmons and I had to begin zigzagging to slow myself down a bit. But the Princess kept up her speed, whizzed straight past me, and was soon a tiny blob in the blankness. I traversed to a slower section of the slope and looked back over my shoulder. Emma and Jemmons were way back and behind them rose the raging inferno of the Castle, belching out clouds of dense black smoke and sheets of flame.

As I picked up speed again, the wind became keener—and made me want to slow up. It flapped the sleeves and bottoms of my biggles and chilled me to the bone, but I was enjoying myself. It had been years since I'd been on a board and I was loving the sensation of effortless motion, controlled by the *merest* movement of my body. I even took on a few mounds and did some stunt stuff. But I was always slowing right down and looking back to check where Emma and Jemmons were. I saw Emma fall off once and waited to see her get safely back on her board again. Jemmons waited for her, too. He was taking good care of her. Good old Roger, I thought. I looked down the hillside—there was no sign of the Princess! How could I have been so stupid? It suddenly hit me—I'd been suckered! She had taken the key and thrown me off the scent by casting suspicion on Jemmons. I had taken my eye off the ball—I had my eye on the wrong ball—I should have been watching the Princess! I pushed off and shot after her, getting myself into my trademark skateboard crouch—the jetscreamer, as I used to call it. It consisted of one arm forward, one arm back, chin jutting, knees bent as low as they could go. I was really motoring down that hillside. The board was cutting the snow with a satisfying swishing noise as I travelled over it. And then, suddenly, the snow ran out, just vanished from under me, and I was sailing out and out into nothing but air. I looked down. I had just run right off a cliff.

Chapter 18

Many things go through your mind when you're about thirty or forty feet up in the air on a piece of wood no bigger than an ironing-board, and you don't know what's below. Your instinct is to bail. But I managed to keep my body shape in the classic Telemark stance and landed that board on a lower slope, with little more than a light jolt and the briefest of wobbles.

"Yes!" I exclaimed, punching the air.

It was the second precipice that did for me. The one I shot straight off moments after celebrating my perfect landing off the first one. Although I lost my balance and fell off, the height of the cliff was nowhere near as high as the first one and I only hurt my pride.

I picked myself up, stamped both feet, and knew I had been very lucky I hadn't broken any bones.

I could see the flat white mantle of ice spreading out all around me, and realized I was only a few yards from the foot of the knoll. I looked round to see where Emma and Jemmons were, but, of course, the two bluffs I had just come over obscured my view of the upper slopes—I couldn't even see the Castle, only smoke. I remembered my makeshift wheels and quickly fitted them on my board in the four slots. Then I walked down to the "shore" of the ice and pushed off. And did I shift! I only had to do a couple of good push-offs and I was up to maximum speed and running over that ice like a bowling ball. I headed round the little headland to my left, made by the lower bluff. And found the Princess and the Duck standing on the slope. The Duck looked a bit shaken. The Princess was supporting him.

"Hey!" I called.

I skidded in and bailed, running up the slope to them to stop myself.

"Stephen!" cried the Princess. "You have the key?"

"Er, no. I thought you had it."

"You see what I have to put up with?" said the Duck. "I told you he'd muck it up—he's a bloody idiot!"

"Normal service has been resumed I see."

"Stephen, why didn't you stay with Jemmons? I told you he had the key," said the Princess.

"I thought—well, what I thought was—it might be a double bluff."

"What're you on about—a double bluff?" quacked the Duck. "You've only left Emma up there with a bloody psychopath!"

"What?" I exclaimed.

"Jemmons has got the key—he's Corrective Measures! They've turned him!"

"Nobody tells me anything!"

"Where're you going?"

"Where do you think?"

I picked up my board and was about to set off in the direction from which I had just come.

"Wait!" cried the Princess. "I will go with you!"

"No!" said the Duck.

"You want me to stay, Sir Julian?" said the Princess.

"No. What I meant was: why don't you go the other way?" he pointed vaguely in the other direction. "Round there—they might come down that way."

"I could go that way," I said.

"No!" said the Duck, looking annoyed. "You go that way—stick to the way we decided—you're always chopping and changing your mind! You're so indecisive."

"I'm not."

"Don't argue!"

"I'll go this way," smiled the Princess. She ran off along the "shore" in the other direction.

"What the hell was all that about?" I said.

"Shh!" said the Duck. "Just go round there."

"Why? What're you playing at?"

"I've got the bloody key," said the Duck. "They'll be coming down round there—we've got to get away from her."

"Who?"

"Who? The Princess!"

"You've lost me."

He grabbed me by the front of my biggles. "Just do as you're told and leave everything to me. I'll explain later," he said, waving me away.

"Is Jemmons a murdering traitor or not?" I said.

"No—I only said that for her benefit—now get going, we haven't got much time—she'll twig in a minute. She's not bloody stupid—like some I could mention!"

"Up yours, Duckworth!"

I skated off towards the spur of land and quickly rounded it. To my delight and surprise, Jemmons and Emma were waiting for me just around the corner.

"Emma! Rog!"

"Get in here, Stevie!" said Jemmons.

I skated straight at them and bailed, falling into their arms.

"What going on? Everyone seems to know except—"

"Shh!" said Emma. "Can you hear anything, Roger?"

Jemmons listened intently and shook his head, while reaching inside my biggles.

"What're you doing?"

He pulled out the sparkling cranberry glass key like a magician.

"But?"

"Our Princess can read minds, matey," said Jemmons. "The Duck's trying to distract her—but we're not sure what her range is."

"I had the key all the time?" I said.

"No, I had the key," said Emma. "The Duck gave it to me on the wall."

"But I found it."

"I let you find it," corrected Emma.

"And then I picked your pocket and gave it back to the Duck," said Jemmons.

"But the Duck was unconscious."

"Playacting," said Jemmons.

"So, how did I end up with it?"

"Oh, Stephen, you are so dense," said Emma.

"You mean the Duck planted it back on me?"

"Now," said Jemmons. "Stand back. I'm not sure how this thing works."

Emma pulled me aside and I took the opportunity to kiss her cheek. She ruffled my hair.

Jemmons held the key aloft like the Statue of Liberty's torch. Nothing happened.

"What's it supposed to do?" I said.

"I reckon it's some sort of tracking device," said Jemmons. "A vibration or sound wave thingy."

"Or mind waves," I said. "Give it to me."

Jemmons handed it over. I put it to my forehead.

"What are you doing?" said Emma.

"I'm thinking about the Princess," I muttered.

"This is not the time to be indulging your erotic fantasies," said Emma.

"It's a mind device," I said. "Shh—I'm getting something!"

"Saints preserve us! Look out there!" exclaimed Jemmons.

"What? Where?" I said.

"It's gone again," said Jemmons. "There was a blue light flashing way out there on the ice, when you were doing your mind thingy."

"Did you see anything, Em?"

"No—do it again."

I pressed the glass cone to my forehead and repeated the trick.

"There 'tis! D'you see it, Emma?"

"Oh, yes! Yes! I see it!"

"Where?" I said.

"It's gone again," said Jemmons.

"Yes, it stops every time I stop thinking about her," I said. "That is the Princess' time machine—it's way out there on the ice somewhere."

"Very clever, Stephen!" said the Princess.

We all swung round to our right and looked up on the little headland. She was standing over the Duck, who was trussed up and kneeling on a snowboard at her feet. She gave the board a gentle kick with her foot and sent the Duck sliding down the slope towards us.

"Aaagh!" cried the Duck.

Jemmons rushed to catch him just as he reached the bottom and toppled over on his side. The Princess bounded down and was face to face with me in a matter of seconds.

"I'll take that, darling," she smiled. She plucked the glass key from my hand. And gestured the others over with a crooked finger. Jemmons finished untying the Duck and they came and joined us. "Now, here we all are, together again."

"Yes," I smiled. "All my wedding guests are assembled."

"You are funny, darling," said the Princess, indulgently.

"I don't think we're part of her plans, mate," said the Duck, rubbing his wrists where the straps had burnt his skin.

"All that switching the key round, Sir Julian—you made me feel quite dizzy," said the Princess. "And now, I'm afraid, I must say au revoir. I'm sure those nice policemen will be along any minute to pick you up and put you back in their nice warm prison." She gazed up at the Castle. "Even warmer now."

"Didn't I mean anything to you?" I said.

"Oh, I didn't mean you, darling—you're coming with me. We have new worlds to discover—and populate—but not this planet, I think—it's not my type."

"You prefer wet ones," said the Duck.

"Touché, Sir Julian—I shall truly miss that devious little mind of yours—my, my, what fun we have had—you ran me a close race. But we must not forget what you are—a loser."

"Don't leave us here, Your Highness," pleaded the Duck. "At least drop us off somewhere a bit safer—give us a sporting chance. Hey?"

She tilted her head on one side and blinked at him. "Oh, but, Sir Julian, you know how these things work—the winner takes all, the loser has to fall," she said with mock sadness. "Where is the fun in victory if the vanquished live to fight another day?"

"I had to ask," said the Duck. "Not for myself, you understand—I was thinking of the others."

"Of course you were. And now, Stephen, you will show me how this—this skateboard, as I think you call it, works and we will slide off into this icescape and consummate our everlasting love. Over and over and over again."

I swallowed hard.

The Duck kicked my foot. "Stall her!" he said, out of the corner of his mouth.

"Um? I've changed my mind," I said. "I don't want to marry you now."

Something wet and slimy lashed me across the face. It was so fast—none of the others even saw what happened.

"You promised to marry this creature?" exclaimed Emma.

"Well, no—that is, the Duck said—"

I felt another stinging slap across my face.

"Get on that board!" hissed the Princess.

"Did anyone see that? She—"

"You have sunk to some pretty low levels, Sloane," said Emma. "But this one really takes the limbo prize—even for you!"

"We are wasting time!" The Princess picked me up and stood me on the skateboard. And then stepped on behind me and threw her arms around my neck. "Go—out there! To that beacon!" She pointed to the flashing cranberry coloured light far out on the ice sheet.

"It won't work between us," I said. "I'm, um, impotent."

"Is that true?" said Emma.

"No—it is not," said the Princess. "I have given him a thorough, seventy-two-hour medical examination—to make sure he is fit to mate with me—and he passed with flying colours—he has a sperm count the size of—"

"—A small galaxy—yeah, I know," I said, "but they're not all top drawer, Your Highness, some are a little mean, in a cool, streetwise kind of way. I know the sort of (I cleared my throat) quantities I can offer are pretty impressive, but it's quality that counts, Your Highness. You can't be too choosy in your position—you've got the royal bloodline to think abouttttt!"

The Princess gave us an almighty push-off and we shot out across the ice like a marble on plate glass. The wind was rushing past my face so quickly it was peeling my gums back off my teeth. The Princess squeezed me and squealed with delight.

"Wowweee! This is so cooool!" she shouted, above the whoosh of the wind and the rattle of the wheels.

It was like hammering towards a giant white screen along a wide white highway—I kept thinking we were going to fly off the edge of the world, but we just kept going and going and going…

Suddenly, a grid of blue, green, and red lights lit up under the ice all around us. They reminded me of airport landing lights, but these were unbroken lines and they were actually inside the ice, more like those disco lights they put under the dance floor. The whole ice sea was criss-crossed with them.

"What are all these lights?" I shouted.

"It's called sectoring," said the Princess. "They're searching for us."

"Who?"

Loud organ music began playing—just like the start of an ice hockey end—only the music was more high church than high octane. It sounded like we had the entire hallelujah chorus out there on the ice with us.

She tapped me on the shoulder and pointed. I glanced to my right and saw seven wedding cake-type hovercrafts coming around the eastern end of the island, in a V formation. I looked back over my shoulder—and saw another skateboard coming after us! It was quite a way back, but I could count three people aboard it. I turned my head back quickly and pretended I hadn't seen anything.

"How much farther is it?" I said.

"Don't worry," said the Princess. "They won't catch up."

I glanced over at the squadron of hovercrafts. "No, I don't think they've even seen us yet," I said.

"I don't mean them—I mean the Duck and company," said the Princess. She nudged me. "As if you didn't know."

"I don't see why you're so dead set against my family and friends coming to the wedding," I said. "After all, dear, it's my day, too."

She giggled.

"It would make me so happy," I went on. "Can't you at least try to get along with my father?"

"Stop it—you're making me laugh," she said, giving my face a playful lash with something slimy.

"What is that thing you do?" I said, licking my lips and tasting salt.

"Soon we will be aboard my ship. Your father and the others will no doubt perish on the ice," she said. "I find that sad, yes, but it is in my nature to destroy inferior species like yours—though I admit your father is one of the most enlightened humans I have ever met. He was even prepared to sacrifice you to save his own miserable skin—I find that very moving. Do you know what I mean, darling?"

"I know exactly what you mean," I said. "He's moved me a lot!"

Suddenly, a red signal flare burst directly overhead, illuminating the area around us for miles in a bright crimson light.

"Oh, how tiresome—they've spotted us," sighed the Princess. "Now I'll have to exterminate them all."

"One skateboard against a fleet?" I said. "Oh, come on, not even you could—"

There was a loud slurp. My board lurched forward and felt lighter. A dark cloud passed over, casting a huge shadow across the ice.

"Er, Princess, what was—?"

I heard a fierce squawk, followed by what sounded like someone playing an enormous pair of castanets. I hung a one-eighty and looked up, as I still skidded backwards on two wheels and one foot.

The giant squid had just silently appeared on the ice and was towering over me, its tentacles lashing and writhing in anger.

"What the—how the hell did you get down here?" I exclaimed. "I thought you were tapas!"

It peered down at me with its enormous oily eyes and showed me its chattering beak. That's when I fell off my board and started sliding across the freezing ice on my butt. It was seeing that beak. That big bone-crunching beak. Man, what an overbite! The thing had obviously pecked the Princess up and swallowed her whole and was getting ready to do the same to me! I backed away on my backside, pushing frantically with my hands and feet. And then my spine bumped up against something big wet and slippery—a gigantic feeder tentacle engulfed me and plucked me up into the air—leaving my stomach forty feet below! It held me up close to its face and stared at me with its big black eyes. I thought that was it. Well, you would.

And then it swung me away and placed me out of harm's way on the ice floor, like a chess piece, so that it was between me and the rapidly approaching fleet. It was as though that squid was trying to protect me.

I could see the Duck clearly now—he, too, had swerved off in my direction to get on the safe side of the giant squid. Only he was coming towards me too fast and wouldn't be able to slow down in time, without a spill—so I figured he'd swerve around me to avoid a crash, because no one would be that stupid—I closed my eyes and screamed! I was skittled over and found myself flat on my back at the bottom of a rack of bodies, staring up into three faces—the Duck, Emma and Jemmons.

"Get-off-me!" I gasped.

They all rolled off and sat up.

"We are sitting ducks out here," said Jemmons.

For some reason we all looked round at the Duck.

"Don't look at me," he said. He scrambled to his feet and waddled off unsteadily in the direction of his skateboard. We all watched him mount it and kick off. I jumped to my feet and grabbed him as he tried to whizz past us.

"No you don't!"

I pulled him off and the board flipped up in the air and shot off across the ice.

"Your capacity for self-preservation is awesome," I said. "When the universe finally stops expanding and all the stars go out, there'll be a descendant of the Duck standing in the dark on the last asteroid, saying, anybody got a match?"

He shrugged me off. "What are you on about? We're fighting for our lives here—in case you hadn't noticed!"

"You're fighting for yours, you mean." I pointed at the giant squid. "That monster just saved mine." I looked round at Emma and Jemmons, and added: "But I'm afraid it ate the Princess."

The Duck gave me a shove. "What do you mean—ate the Princess? That is the bleeding Princess! She's a shape-changer!"

"You what?"

"Get down!" cried the Duck, pulling me face down on the ice.

A huge tentacle skimmed over our heads and slapped around one of the hovercrafts that had tried to come around its right flank. It picked it up and secured it with one of its great suckered arms, and then inverted it and began shaking it, like a kid emptying a moneybox. Only it wasn't coins falling out—it was the crew. I couldn't look and averted my eyes—and saw two of its other tentacles slapping the hell out of another vessel on its left flank. This time it wound the hovercraft up in its arm and flicked it across the ice as though it were playing ducks and drakes. The vessel span round and round, skipping chaotically towards the island, where it scored a direct hit and came to rest halfway up the slope.

The Duck tugged my sleeve. "Come on—that one over there's empty!" he quacked.

"Empty? What?"

I ran alongside him with the others. I had no idea where we were going. We were all just struggling to stay on our feet. I ran round to Emma's side and tried to grab onto her, but she handed me off like a rugby player.

"My father said if I didn't promise to marry the Princess, we'd never get off the island," I tried to explain, as we were slip-sliding along. "Do you really think I'd marry a fifty-foot squid?"

"I thought you liked tentacled women," she said.

"Oh, I get it," I said. I lowered my voice. "This is about those Japanese mangas I downloaded off the net, isn't it? I told you—that was for a linguini promotion Matt was working on."

"I think you've said enough, don't you?" she said, forcing a smile.

"I could never marry a woman with tentacles, Em."

She shoulder barged me like an ice hockey jock and I lost my balance and stumbled over.

"Em—Em, wait! You've got it all wrong! I hate sushi!"

The Duck was leading us towards the hovercraft our squid princess had been rattling. She had discarded it and the Duck clearly had a mind to board it. I gave up on Emma for the time being and ran to catch him up.

"You cannot be serious," I said.

"Got a better idea?" he puffed.

"It'll be full of guards."

"They'll all have headaches," he panted.

He had a point. The thing was just sitting there on the ice, showing no signs of going anywhere and no signs of life on board. Those crew members who had been shaken out of it were either lying on the ice injured or legging it across the ice. To our left, I could see the squadron had broken off the engagement and was speeding away to regroup. We kept running and reached the hull. There was no obvious way onboard.

"Now what?" I said.

"Round here, boys!" shouted Jemmons.

We dashed around the sleek white curve of the hull and found Jemmons jumping up and down, trying to reach a hatchway, but he couldn't quite make it.

"Allez up, Rog!" I called.

He stooped down and cupped his big hands. I ran to him and stirruped my foot and he hoisted me up. The small hull door was already ajar—presumably where the crew had abandoned ship—so I threw it open and peered in.

"All clear," I said. "Wait—there's a ladder."

I pulled myself in and fumbled with what looked like an emergency ladder attached to the inside of the hatch door. It was a telescopic contraption and I couldn't immediately figure out how it worked.

"Hurry up!" called Emma.

"Yeah, get a bleeding move on!" shouted the Duck, banging on the hull.

"What's Princess Squid doing?" I said, as I twiddled and fiddled.

"She's off after the fleet!" said Jemmons. "Look at those landlubbers go!"

I noticed a wire coming out of the hinge side of the door and followed the wall round to a box. I opened it and threw all the switches. The lights went out and a dim blue emergency light came on—the door hissed and the ladder extended down to the ice.

"About time," said Emma, being the first head to appear in the opening of the hatch.

I gave her a hand up.

"Welcome aboard, ma'am," I bowed.

"I haven't forgiven you yet, Sloane," she said, flashing her eyes at me.

Next, the Duck's head appeared.

"Here, this is nice—you'll find me on the bridge!"

He jumped aboard, waddled down the passageway, and vanished around a corner.

I pulled Roger in.

"Horatio Duck's on the bridge," I said.

"Is he now?" said Jemmons. "We'll soon see about that—I'm taking the wheel of this beauty."

"Good," I said. "Where're we headed exactly, skipper?"

"Ah? I shall have to have a look at the charts, matey."

Jemmons hurried away, leaving me to secure the hatch.

"Yeah. Well, don't take too long, mate!" I shouted after him.

Emma folded her arms, leant back against the wall, and watched me work.

"I wasn't jealous," she said.

"What about?" I said.

"You and the Princess."

"That was all the Duck's doing." I locked the hatch.

"I know. He did the same thing to me," she said.

"How do you mean?"

"With Travis."

I shook my head and looked dumb.

"Travis and the Princess are one and the same."

"You are kidding!"

She shivered. "No—it's true."

I took her in my arms and held her to me. "Oh, Em—I'm sorry—I had no idea—I'll kill her—him! No I won't—on second thoughts, I'll kill the Duck!"

"I don't think he had any choice. You can see what he's—I mean, she's capable of," said Emma.

"Yeah. But why did she do it—play us off against each other like that?"

"To get to you, of course," said Emma. "She was both your rival and your suitor."

"The Love Lives of a Shape Changer," I said.

"Hm. Complicated."

"But—all's well that ends well?" I said.

She smiled and we kissed, softly, romantically, lovingly... and the hovercraft rose up and started throbbing.

Emma withdrew her lips. I kept my eyes closed and lingered, enjoying the exquisite moment for just a little bit longer.

"But she'll be back," said Emma.

I opened my eyes. "Yeah, you're right and the Duck won't give up while there's still a chance of getting his hands on her machine—come on!" We held hands and ran together. "We've got to stop him—make him take us somewhere safe. I don't care where I live as long as we're together!"

Chapter 19

We arrived on the bridge—in the top tier of the hovercraft—through a central chute, a bit like a dumbwaiter, which brought us up into the hub of a round control room, via a clear plastic tube. Which didn't open for us. But we could see the Duck and Jemmons, chasing each other around. We laughed and I knocked on the thick plastic. The Duck shot us a glance and screamed something. But we were sealed in and couldn't hear what he was saying.

"What's he saying?"

Emma studied the Duck's lips for a moment. "He's—trying—to—kill—me!"

"All this over who's going to drive the ship," I said, developing a lopsided smile. I smacked my cheek—I didn't want to start looking like him! "Open this bloody—" I looked around at the doorless plastic tube we were in and tried to think of a word for it.

"Lift?" said Emma.

"Open this lift!" I yelled, hammering on it like mad. "Open the lift!" joined in Emma.

And then we watched in dumb horror as Jemmons caught the Duck and hurled him over a bank of computers and dived after him.

"He'll kill him!" I gasped. "What the hell's got into him?"

I shuffled round inside the tube and tried to find something to press or pull—I felt like a mime artist—but there was no way out, or even back down. We were trapped. All we could do was watch, although there wasn't much to see, because they were both still hidden behind the control desk.

"Don't worry," I said. "The Duck always gets out of these tight situations."

Suddenly both men rose up like puppets—and Jemmons was choking the Duck with a length of electrical flex!

"Do something!" cried Emma. "He's killing him!"

"So what?" I said. "I mean, so what can I do?"

Emma gave me a dark look and started beating her fists against the clear tube again.

"Let him go, Roger!" she screamed.

I banged with her. But I couldn't help thinking about the psychological metaphor I found myself in though. The tube, I mused, was like a fallopian tube and the flex Jemmons was strangling my father with represented the umbilical cord...it suddenly became clear to me: I wanted my father to be dead.

"Stephen!" screamed Emma. "Do something!"

"Let him go! Let him go!" I yelled.

The Duck was struggling for his life and there wasn't a damn thing I could do about it. And then the Duck managed to get his feet up on the console and started running along it, like a motorcyclist on a wall of death, smashing the controls about. The hovercraft lurched and roared, and rose up and down. Jemmons tried to restrain him, but the Duck was flipping himself about like a trout on a hook, kicking everything he could reach. Suddenly the chute hissed up and Emma and I tumbled into the control room.

I rolled back up onto my feet and charged over to jump on Jemmons's back. He swayed about and tried to shake me off, but he wouldn't let go of the plastic cord around the Duck's throat. By now the Duck had stopped kicking and was just twitching.

"Roger? Roger?" I cried. "Let go—you're killing him!"

"Kill the Duck, kill the Duck, kill the Duck..." Jemmons kept repeating.

"Yeah," I smiled, tilting my head on one side. "Kill the Duck...kill the Duck..."

Emma ran around to the other side of the control desk and climbed up to try and unlock Jemmons's hands.

"Steve!" she screamed.

"What?"

"Look at his eyes—they're dilated and staring—I think he's having a fit!" she cried.

"That's no fit," I said. "He's been brainwashed to kill the Duck—that replicant that attacked me in the attic was chanting the same mantra—I remember joining in."

"We've got to bring him out of it," cried Emma. "Roger, let Mr Duckworth go, he hasn't done you any harm, has he? What has Mr Duckworth ever done to you? Just ask yourself that, Roger."

But I could see the counselling stuff wasn't working, so I got off Jemmons's back, wrenched one of the monitors out of the control panel, and smashed it over his head. Jemmons and the Duck slumped to the floor. I dropped down on my knees, tugged Jemmons's fingers away, and untwisted the flex from the Duck's neck. The Duck took a huge gulp of air and then dozens more in quick succession. Emma climbed down off the desk and knelt down to see to Jemmons. I helped the Duck to his feet.

"Did you have to hit him so hard?" said Emma.

"Well, it was attempted murder," I said. I looked through the observation window and saw the giant squid being chased by eight or nine hovercrafts. "Anyway, that's the least of our worries—the navy's got Princess Squid on the run."

The Duck heard me—though he was still unable to speak—and stumbled over to the window to take a closer look.

"She's leading 'em straight to us," croaked the Duck.

"Why doesn't she just get in her time machine and escape?" I said.

"That's a point," said the Duck. "That's a good point."

"She loves a fight and hates to lose," I said.

"That's it!" said the Duck. "She's going to take them on! There's a chance!"

"A chance for what? Let's just get the hell out of here," I said. "She'll keep them busy for a while."

"Typical," nodded the Duck, rubbing his throat. "I've told you before—a true Duckworth never runs. You might be able to turn a blind eye, mate—but I expect to do my duty this day."

"Oh, don't start all that," I said. "You won't run because there's still a chance of getting your hands on that machine."

"I am not leaving that brave creature out there—who saved our lives not ten minutes ago—to face the enemy alone. It is not in me, sir!"

"She's a giant squid for heaven's sake—she can take care of herself!"

"She is a sensitive, fellow—whatsit of the universe," said the Duck.

"She's a dangerous alien shape-changer!"

"Well," said the Duck, "wouldn't you change your shape if you looked like a squid?"

"Emma, tell him," I said.

"He's got a point, Steve," said Emma. "Besides, I can't leave Roger—I think he's concussed. Is there a first aid kit on this ship?"

"First aid kit?" said the Duck. "There's a bleeding hospital down below with a fully equipped operating theatre."

"Have you forgotten what my father and that thing out there put us through?" I said. "He tried to marry us both off to the same alien—and it was a squid!"

"That's just the kind of planetal small-mindedness that's going to put the kybosh on humankind's colonisation of the cosmos," said the Duck, sticking one hand inside his biggles and gazing heroically out into space. "How can we boldly go where no man has gone before if we turn our noses up at the first sign of a tentacle?"

"You can boldly go there if you like, mate—leave me out!"

"Steve—see if you can find me some bandages and an aspirin—he's going to have the mother of all headaches when he wakes up," said

Emma, cradling Jemmons's head in her lap. He was right where I wanted to be.

I looked to the Duck, but he was already twiddling dials and sussing out the controls of the vessel, something I, I have to admit, would have been of absolutely no help to him in whatsoever.

"Duck, I'm going below—do the lift for me."

"You got it, man."

I stepped under the chute. The Duck hit a button and I shot up out of the hovercraft like a pea out of a peashooter—high into the freezing night air, screaming my head off all the way. And then I stopped in mid air high above the ice. I stopped screaming and looked round. All seemed still and calm for a moment. And then I was falling through the rushing air—towards the ice! I started screaming again. Suddenly, something soft and slimy splatted against my bottom and I began moving sideways, back towards the ship. I looked round and saw two enormous black eyes staring at me. I was on my former fiancée's tentacle again. It lowered me gently onto the second tier deck. I jumped off, gave her a quick salute, opened the first door I came to, and darted inside.

This time I decided to take the emergency stairs. I remembered the coloured line system painted on the floors of the passageways and followed the green one, because I just thought it might lead me to the ship's infirmary. I knew the white one led out on deck, because it was the first one I saw when I got inside the door. Then I changed my mind to the red one—red for red crosses, blood and hospitals, I thought. I opened a strongroom-type door somewhere in the bowels of level one and found hundreds of bombs. That wasn't it. I tracked the blue line and found myself in a dormitory, full of hundreds of hammocks, couchettes, and bunks. I followed the green one, which I should have stuck to in the first place—green crosses—and that brought me to a surgery. The doctor, or whoever he was, was slumped over his desk, out cold. I rifled through his cabinet and helped myself to as many bottles of tablets as I could carry and a box of bandages.

* * *

"Where have you been?" sighed Emma. "Roger's been bleeding."

"Didn't you see me shoot up?"

"You've been shooting up?" she exclaimed.

"No—in the air—oh, forget it. Here." I handed her the box and all the bottles from my pockets.

Roger was sitting up but still leaning against my girlfriend in a way that made me jealous—no, I mean, envious.

"How you doing, Rog?" I said. "Killed any ducks lately?"

Jemmons looked a bit sorry for himself and didn't answer

"Don't tease him," said Emma, unrolling a bandage around his head.

I went over to the Duck, who was sitting in the captain's swivel chair, stroking his wispy goatee beard thoughtfully. We were moving slowly over the ice. It was like being in a skybox—only we were in the game.

"Where's everyone gone?" I said, peering around the panoramic window at all the empty ice.

"The fleet are on the other side of the island," said the Duck. "Regrouping."

I scanned the horizon and spotted a plume of smoke in the distance, drifting from the top of the white knoll.

"Where's you know who then?" I said.

The Duck lifted his bottom off his chair and jabbed a finger downwards.

"Under the desk?" I said.

He gave me a lopsided smile. And pointed again. I stared down at the lower deck, but couldn't see what he meant.

"No, I'm not with you," I said.

"Can't you see the tentacles?" he said, in exasperation.

I spotted the end of a tentacle gripping a lower rail, directly below us—and then another a few yards farther around—and then another—and then another! They were all the way around.

"What's she doing—is she underneath us?"

"No—she's clinging on the side—like a buffer," said the Duck.

"What's she doing that for?"

"Well, I don't know, do I? Go and ask her."

"Ask who?" said a turbaned Jemmons, coming to join us.

The Duck looked round and up at him and jumped.

"Keep that maniac away from me!" he quacked, feeling his throat and laying on the croak in his voice a bit.

"I'm sorry I attacked you, Duck—I don't know what came over me," said Jemmons. "I heard a voice telling me to do it."

"Yeah," sneered the Duck. "That's what all the psychos say."

Emma came and stood next to me and we held hands down by our sides.

"It wasn't Roger's fault, Dad—someone brainwashed him," I said, giving Emma's hand a squeeze, and exchanging a loving look with her.

"Aye and I'd like to know who," said Jemmons.

"Well," said the Duck, "I don't think we have to look a million miles, do we?"

One of the tentacles unfurled itself from the rail and poked straight up in the air three or four times and then resumed its grip.

"I think she just gave you the bird," I said. "So, what are all those coloured lines of light under the ice for?"

"They're strategy vectors," said the Duck.

"Come again."

"They're for auto-battle mode. You vector in a colour and the ship follows that line only," explained the Duck.

"What's the point of that?"

"Well, it's complicated—it's for doing complex manoeuvres at full speed. Be too fast to steer. Think of it as speed chess for battleships."

"And you know how to do all this?" I said.

"I think I've got it sussed." The Duck took out his tin and started rolling a spliff.

"My confidence in you runneth over," I said.

"I'm sure your father knows what he's doing," said Emma.

"Yeah, well, he's not my idea of Captain Kirk."

"Fireships—that's the way to deal with a superior force," said Jemmons. "Why, when I had the honour to sail under Lord Horatio Nelson at the Battle of Copenhagen in—"

"Yeah, well, this ain't no Napoleonic War—this is high tech stuff, mate," said the Duck, sealing his spliff with one long lick. He lit up. "Gotta know what you're doing with this lot." He waved at all the winking lights, knobs and monitors.

"What does that pink one do?" I said.

"That one?" The Duck expelled a thick stream of aromatic smoke. "I think I know what that one is. Don't worry, I know enough to take on this lot."

"What lot?" I said.

"That lot," said the Duck.

The squadron had split into two groups and was coming around both sides of the island, heading directly for us. I took the spliff off him and inhaled.

"Do something," I spluttered.

Emma relieved me of the joint, took a quick drag, and handed it back to the Duck.

"Watch this," said the Duck. He chose a red button. "This is what you call smart warfare." And pressed.

Suddenly, we flashed to what seemed like twenty places at once and spun round to find ourselves facing three enemy wedding cakes.

"Oops!" said Emma.

All three vessels slowly started turning on the spot. The candle-like pom-pom guns mounted around their rails dropped a few degrees and commenced firing. About two hundred fiery brimstone bombs blasted over at us, from every tier.

Our squid figurehead reached up six or seven tentacles—it was too quick to count—and smacked them all back.

"Wonder what her batting average is," I said.

"Time to split," said the Duck, pressing another button. We shot away, made dozens of abrupt turns and straight sprints and came to a sudden halt. The ice was clear.

"Where'd they go?" said the Duck.

"I feel sick," said Jemmons.

We started moving very slowly over the ice again.

"They must be around here somewhere," I said.

"Perhaps we've won," said Emma.

We all turned and looked at her. I caught something out of the corner of my eye—right behind us—a line of huge battleships was following in our wake at a sedate pace, like gigantic carnival floats.

"We've got company," I said, in a sing-songy voice.

The Duck looked round and did a double take. "So, they wanna play follow the leader, do they?" he said. "Well, follow this!"

We accelerated and left them for dead. But they quickly fanned out and came after us. The Duck reached inside his biggles and pulled out a mini disc.

"Here, see if that Holy Roller jukebox over there'll play this," he said.

"What is it?"

"See Emily Play—classic Floyd, man."

"How do you switch this thing on?" I said, inserting the disc in the multi-player tray.

"The pink button, of course," laughed the Duck.

The throbbing strains of "See Emily Play" poured out of the P.A. system in a psychedelic swirl of sound. The Duck headbanged and steered one-handed, while he smoked his spliff with the other. We swerved and zigzagged all over the ice, dodging and weaving his way through and around our bewildered pursuers. Our course must have been so wild and unpredictable that they couldn't work it out. The Duck was laughing and rocking—he was as relaxed as some kid driving a dodgem car at the fair. Round and round the island we drove, until we met one coming the other way! But the Duck merely bumped into it and it rebounded off the squid clinging to our rail and was sent careering across the ice. And every time they fired their brimstone bombs at us, the squid batted them straight back and set them on fire. One by one, the Duck eliminated every enemy ship from the game. And then he span off across the empty playground of the ice doing crazy victory spins and slides, and laughing and quacking at the top of his voice. Until we were brought to an abrupt halt and everyone lurched forward and rocked backwards and fell down on the floor.

"What was that?" I said.

"That," said the Duck, "was our new braking system—we've been suckered—to the bleeding ice!"

We all scrambled to our feet and rushed to look out the forward observation window—the squid was gone.

"Damn it!" quacked the Duck. "She's lit out."

"Well, at least we're still alive," I said.

"I am not living in a bloody refrigerator!" said the Duck. "Where'd she go?" He ran around the panoramic window, looking for her. "There she goes—she's changed back! We're too late. Hang about—she's stopping."

I took the cranberry glass time machine key out of my inside pocket and held it up.

"She won't get far without this," I said.

The Duck leapt up in the air and jumped on me, kissing me all over. "When did you nick that? Oh, you little genius—you are so like me—it's uncanny! A true Duckworth through and through!"

I shoved him off me. "I took it when we were on the skateboard—she'll kill me," I said, suddenly realising that I could be in big trouble with the Princess. I handed it quickly to the Duck.

Suddenly, the lift chute hissed up and the Princess appeared inside the tube. When it didn't open for her, she simply punched it and it shattered. She stepped into the conning tower. This time I had learnt and kept my eye on that key—and I saw the Duck slip it into Jemmons's pocket.

"All breakages must be paid for," smiled the Duck.

"Have you got it, Sir Julian?"

"Got what, Your High—"

A tentacle shot out of the Princess' sleeve and hung him up by the neck, cutting off his air.

"I was going to leave this miserable ball of dung you call a world and return to civilisation," said the Princess. "I even helped you to defeat your pathetic little enemies—and in return, you steal my front door key—what kind of a people are you?"

She released the Duck and dumped him on the floor. Emma rushed to help him, bumping into Jemmons on the way.

"Oops, sorry, Roger."

Jemmons stepped aside for Emma but kept his eyes fixed on the Princess.

The Princess transferred her slimy tentacle to me and smoothed my cheek, then reached under my chin and lifted me up on my toes.

"Once I thought we could be an item, Stephen—but now I know that can never be—I have heard every crude, ignorant word you've thought and said about me."

"I never meant to hurt your feelings, it's just that I love—"

She put her tentacle to my lips. "Hush. The simple truth is you are too prejudiced to be my consort. I realize that now," she said. "Did you steal my key, darling?"

I shook my head and said, "Yes, yes, I did."

"You bloody idiot!" cried my father. "Now, we'll be stuck here for—"

The Princess shot out another tentacle and gagged him.

"Where is it?" she smiled, batting her eyelids.

"Roger's got it," I said.

Jemmons never flinched. The big Plymothian seaman straightened his back and stuck his chin out defiantly.

"Is this true, Roger?" asked the Princess, moving her tentacle slowly over to his shoulder and drawing it delicately down across his broad chest.

"You can go to hell," said Jemmons.

The tentacle quivered and blurred. In a nanosecond it was gripping his manhood and squeezing the colour out of his face. She came in close and eyeballed him.

"That's no way to speak to a lady, Roger," she said.

And then Jemmons did something I still can't believe he did to this day—he tilted his head back, as though in pain, and brought it forward with full force, like a striker rising to head a ball into the net. The veins in his neck stood out and his gnarled forehead struck her bang on the nose. Right on that sweet spot. Her eyes fluttered and she flopped to the floor— just as any human being would have—and keeled over. Her tentacles glowed Day-Glo green for a moment and slurped back inside her.

"Aunt bloody Nora!"

"And that, Your Lowness, was a Glasgow hello!" quacked the Duck.

Jemmons looked stupefied, hardly able to believe what he had just done.

"Quick—tie her up!" I said.

"Don't be daft," said the Duck. "Nothing's going to hold her when she comes round—we'd better peg it—and fast. Come on, Rog—you'll be the one she's after!"

"No," said Jemmons. "I'm not going to leave her till I know she's all right. I've never hit a woman in my life."

"Are you stark staring mad?" cried the Duck. "That's not a woman—that's an alien shape-changer—she's a vampire!"

"Vampire?" I exclaimed. "You never told me that! You were going to marry me off to a bloody vampire?"

"She's not a proper one—she's a shape-changer—they have to drink your blood to copy your DNA so they can do their shape-changing and see if you're compatible," explained the Duck. "That's all."

"Oh, well, that's all right then," I said. "You really are a piece of work, Dad."

Emma felt her throat. "Did he—I mean, she—drink my blood, too?" she said.

"No, of course she didn't," said the Duck, as though the very idea was ridiculous. "Drink your blood—what are you on about? Well, just a pint or two."

"Pints!" exclaimed Emma.

Emma and I held onto each other for protection and stared down at the creature on the floor in horror.

"Princess?" said Jemmons.

The Princess stirred and moaned.

"Give me that key before she wakes up!" cried the Duck. Jemmons searched his pockets. "I haven't got the blasted key," he said, turning his attention back to the Princess.

"You must have! Well, who's got it then?" he quacked.

"Don't look at me," I said.

Emma held up the key. The Duck tried to snatch it, but Emma held it out of his reach.

"Roger's right," said Emma. "We should make sure she's all right first—she saved our lives. In any case, if we steal her time machine, how is she going to get home?"

"How is she going to get home?" said the Duck. "What about us—how are we going to get home, you mean?"

"We are home," I said. "At least we're on our own planet."

"You're all mad!" cried the Duck. "We can't stay here—they'll skin us alive after what we did."

"We'll find somewhere," I said, smiling at Emma.

"Right, that's it—you leave me no choice—Jemmons, you'll have to marry her!" cried the Duck.

"How d'you work that one out?" said Jemmons.

"We've got to keep her sweet. Now, Roger, be honest, do you have a problem with that?"

"This is madness," I said. "You can't ask Roger to marry her—what if she fancies a post-nuptial snack in the night?"

"Stephen!" said Emma. "That is so cruel!"

"No, I can't marry her," said Jemmons, vigorously shaking his head.

"Look, Rog," said the Duck, "don't think of her as a squid pretending to be a woman, think of her as a woman who just happens to be capable of turning into a squid—once in a blue moon."

"Once every full moon more like," I said.

"No, it's not that," said Jemmons, shaking his head.

"All right, so she feels a bit slimy and tastes a bit salty—but give me one good reason why you won't marry her," said the Duck.

Jemmons opened his mouth to answer.

"I can give you eight," I said. "And they've all got suckers on."

"This is species discrimination!" cried the Duck. "I will not tolerate this outrageous prejudice!"

"You cannot expect a human being to mate with a—with a—"

"Go on, say it," said the Duck.

"Slimy alien vampire," I said.

"That's speciesist!" quacked the Duck. "So what if she looks a bit different from your usual bird, that's no reason to reject her out of hand."

"Er, shouldn't that be out of tentacle?"

The Duck looked genuinely—not that this means anything in his case—shocked at my quip.

"You disappoint me, Stephen, you really do," he sighed, slumping down in his captain's chair. "I never thought I'd live to see the day when a son of mine could utter such a—such a cruel, ignorant, racist remark. I would have been proud to see you married to this fine specimen of a—of a princess. I built you up. Princess, I said, Stephen is a baronet, that's above a knight, but below a baron, a sort of baron-knight, but I promise you, Your Highness, there won't be many of those where my son is concerned—I've seen to that, genetically speaking—you won't find him wanting in that department, I said—"

I interrupted him. "Save your speeches. I know where this is going—you know Jemmons won't marry her, so you're trying to make me feel guilty, so I offer to do it—well, it won't wash, because I love Emma and I'm marrying Emma. Period."

"Well, how else are we going to get out of here?"

"I know: why don't you marry her?" I said.

Before the Duck could open his mouth to protest, Jemmons spoke:

"I never said I wouldn't marry her," he said, with a shy shrug.

We all looked at him in astonishment.

"But you said you couldn't marry her," I said.

"Shut up—he's marrying her," said the Duck.

"For heaven's sake let him speak!" said Emma.

"I can't marry her, because she don't love me," said Jemmons.

This remark left the Duck and me speechless. But Emma immediately went to give Jemmons a hug.

"Oh, Roger, that is so sweet," she said.

"I would marry her if she'd have me—but I don't reckon she's too keen," he said.

"But you cannot be serious," I said. "She's a squid."

"Oh, I know she's not every man's idea of a catch."

"Only in a net," I said.

Emma shot me a scornful look.

"Well, you can joke, Stevie, but I've been a single-hander all my life—no woman ever looked twice at me—so maybe it is time I found myself a shipmate. I reckon this here woman is as good as any I'd find if I searched the seven seas over. So, I'm willing, if she's willing."

Emma smiled tearfully and gave him a little peck on the cheek.

"I'm sorry, Roger," I said. "You're right—she's quite a catch—woman."

The Duck patted Jemmons on the back and said, "It is a far better thing you do than—"

"—You've ever done!" I said.

"I'm not doing this for any of you. I'm doing it for me—if she'll have me," said Jemmons. "Now, I don't know if it's love I feel here in this lonely old heart of mine, but something's all a-flutter in there, like a fledgling attempting his first clumsy flight to freedom, his first jump into the new domain of air—"

"Yeah—all right, Rog, don't milk it, mate," I said.

"She's coming round!" said Emma. "Princess?"

The Princess' body glowed and throbbed with a fluorescent green light. Her eyelids fluttered. Strange gurgling noises emanated from deep within her, slowly turning into a blood-curdling scream!

We all—including her would-be suitor—ran for our lives. Emma and I took the emergency stairs. The Duck and Jemmons bolted for the chute. As we clattered down the metal stairs, we could hear ferocious shouts and crashes behind us—it sounded like the Princess was trashing the control room.

"Which way?" cried Emma, as we came to the foot of the stairs.

"I don't know—um—this door!" I grabbed her hand and dragged her inside. It was dark and cramped, but it felt safe.

"What's that smell?" whispered Emma.

I felt around the wall for a light switch, but there wasn't one.

"I don't know."

"If I'm going to die," said Emma, "I am not doing it in a smelly hole like this."

I moved to open the door and hit my head on a chain. I pulled it and a light came on. Emma screamed. I looked around. I screamed. We were in a store cupboard and the shelving looked like those pigeon holes you find in hotel receptions—only instead of room keys and letters, there was a decapitated head in each. But even worse—we recognised one of them! Emma buried her face in my chest.

"Oh, Steve—it's Jody."

"It must be the spare parts for the androids," I said. I peered more closely at Jody's head. The eyes were wide and staring. "Dear, dear, Jody," I said softly. "I knew her, Emma—I mean, I really knew her."

"Hi, Steve—Hi, Em!" said Jody. "How's it hanging, guys?"

Emma and I decided not to reply, but opted instead to vacate the cupboard as soon as possible. I know we were cowards, but you have to remember we were being chased by a fifty-foot squid, so our nerves were a little jangled.

Emma was first out the door—I couldn't stop her—but I turned back—to switch off the light and close the door with a kind of quiet respect.

Emma was gone—around the corner, I assumed.

"Emma?" I called.

"Steve?"

"Where are you?"

"Here!"

I spun round. Emma was standing just a few yards away.

"There you are—look, I've been thinking—what about those snowmobiles we saw on the lower deck. Think you could drive one?"

"No problem," she smiled.

"Steve?" said a voice, directly behind me. "Oh, my God!"

I turned round and did a double take—it was another Emma! I looked back at the other one. They were identical. I stood side on to them so that I could keep them both in the corners of my eyes and only had to turn my head slightly to face either of them.

"Steve?" said the first one, the one on my left. "It's me."

"I'm Emma, Steve," said the one on my right. "Don't listen to her—it's the Princess."

Chapter 20

I stared at her, looking for something Emmaesque to leap out at me. I was waiting for that sixth sense to kick in and give me the aura, that quintessence of the real Emma. I looked round at the other one. There was just no way of telling them apart.

"Ah!" I said. "I know which one's Emma."

"Me!" said the two Emmas.

I smiled. "You know it's kinda nice having two of you. I don't suppose we could come to some permanent arrangement—"

"No!" chorused the two Emmas, folding their arms.

"Oh, well, it was worth a try. Now, the real Emma will have the key. So show me the key," I said.

"I hid it," said the one on my right.

I looked to the one on my left. She was staring levelly at the other one.

"All right—where did I hide it then?" she said.

I turned back to the other one for the response.

"For heaven's sake, Steve—I'm not going to tell you—that's what she wants—she's reading our minds—she's waiting for me to think of the place I hid it," she said.

"Um—I know! What were you drinking in the cellar?"

"Bollie!" they both shouted.

"Erm."

"I told you, dipstick, she's reading my mind!" they chorused.

"Oh, yeah." I thought for a moment. "Got it! I think I could tell if I kissed you both."

The two Emmas walked towards me and leant against the wall, directly opposite me, with their arms folded and the same sick sceptical expression on their faces.

"It was just an idea," I said.

"Go ahead," they both said. They looked at each other and sighed impatiently.

I puckered my lips. "Okay, let's do it," I said. "Who's first?"

"After you," they both said.

"I know, I'll dip out," I said. "Eeny-meany-micker-acker-ear-eye-domin-acker-domin-acker-lolli-poppa-om-pom-push!"

I pointed to the left hand Emma. She smiled and stepped forward. I took her in my arms and we kissed. I opened my eyes and looked over her shoulder at the other one. It was a real turn on—twins! It felt good— and I was just beginning to get the distinct feeling that I was picking up the right Emma vibes—when I was suddenly wearing a full set of wrap-around tentacles.

"You idiot!" said the real Emma, backing away.

"Give me the key—or I will crush him," said the Princess, slowly changing back into her real self, right in front of my face. There was much slurping and erupting of flesh and I got splashes of slime all over me. I closed my eyes. She spun me around and held me in a stranglehold.

"Sorry, Em," I said, spitting some slime off my lips.

"It's in there," said Emma, pointing to the cupboard.

"Well, don't just stand there—go and get it," snapped the Princess. I don't think she cared much for Emma.

Emma gave me another disapproving look and disappeared into the storeroom.

A few moments later, the smiling head of Jody peeped round the door.

"Hello," she said. "Emma's fainted and says you must come and help her."

Emma stepped out, holding the head. She looked at it.

"Nice try, Jody, but I think you just gave it away."

"Oh, did I? Sorry, Em."

"You just needed more rehearsal, Jody," I said.

"Oh, hi, Steve—how's it hanging, baby?"

"Put that pathetic droid head back and give me the key," said the Princess.

Emma went back into the cupboard. As she came back out and closed the door, she placed her hand on it and paused.

"What's that?" she said. "Can you feel it?"

The Princess pushed me aside and laid her hand flat on the wall. I did the same.

"It's vibrating," I said. "Are we moving?"

"No," said the Princess. "There was no upthrust."

Suddenly, we all noticed a slight change in the light—it got dimmer.

"I know what it is!" I said.

"What?" said the Princess.

"It's a net—they've locked onto the coordinates of the ship and they're going to transport us through time to another place."

"Can they do that?"

"Oh, yes," I said. "How d'you think they brought me and Emma here in the first place? You watch—all the walls will turn black and everything'll go into red and blue outline—with bits of green in the shadows."

"Give me the key," said the Princess, rushing to Emma, to take it off her. Emma handed it over.

"You won't be able to get off," I said. "There's a force field or something."

"Temporal gravity," said the Princess. "I must hurry."

She began running up the corridor, but was soon slowed down to a walking pace by the force.

Faint hints of green started appearing in the shadows of the ship's superstructure. The throbbing increased, but it was still faint compared to the pounding pulse Emma and I had experienced in the latter stages of the transfer, when we were caught on the barge. The event was just beginning.

I reached Emma and took her hand. She slowly turned her head to look at me.

The light began to flicker a little. We watched the Princess' progress up the passageway and set off after her. Suddenly, the Princess fell and lumps started to swell up in her back.

"She's in trouble," I said.

The Princess rolled over slowly onto her back and beckoned us.

"What's wrong with her?" said Emma, trying to go faster, but we were really having to strain to pick up our feet. It was like trying to run directly into a very strong wind—only our clothes and hair were not being blown.

"I don't know—it must be the force." My voice was beginning to deepen. "It's much stronger than last time."

"Bigger ship," intoned Emma, in a kind of slow sexy drawl.

I gave her a slow glance. Our eyes met. She slowly covered her mouth and slowly looked embarrassed. I slowly grinned.

It seemed to take half an hour—though it must have been much less than that—to reach the Princess. There was still no sign of the blue and red outlining—the sort of X-ray effect the "netting" causes—presumably because, as Emma said, the hovercraft was a much bigger vessel than the barge and would, therefore, take more power to timeport, so I was hoping there was still a chance of us getting off—if we could only find a quick way out.

"Take her legs," I said.

Emma stooped down and seemed to take an age to lift the Princess' legs. I reached under her arms and lifted.

"We're going to get you off," said Emma.

I looked at her and did a double take—she sounded like a man!

"My God—you sound like Margaret Thatcher!"

"The force is getting stronger," said Emma.

"They must be putting too much testosterone in the mix," I said.

"She's heavy," said Emma. "Princess? Can you help us?"

The Princess was unable to respond. I assumed she had tried to change into her giant squid form to bust out of the ship, but the metamorphosis had been interrupted by the temporal gravity net. And now she was stuck in mid-transformation. It was not a pretty sight. Half her face was sort of melted away, revealing a peculiar white-textured skin beneath. And her fingers had developed a few small suckers. There was also quite a bit of slime. For all I knew the process could have been still going on in her body, but it was so slowed down, it was hard to detect.

We carried her with great effort to an open area, where I remembered there being an iron staircase, leading down to the loading bay and the snowmobile pool, somewhere nearby. If the vessel had the same layout as the one that had picked me and Emma up off the barge, the large hatchway we had been brought aboard through would be in the same place. That's what I was hoping anyway.

As we turned to go down the stairs, we saw the Duck and Jemmons struggling along an adjacent passageway. We met on the sort of landing area, where all the corridors converged on the emergency stairs. Jemmons waved. The Duck just concentrated on pushing himself along. Emma and I stopped so that they could catch up and give us a hand.

Now I began to see the beginnings of the strange red lines, sketching in the geometry of the ship's architecture. It really was just like a very finicky artist drawing an outline of the interior with fluorescent pens of red, blue, and green light.

The Duck and Jemmons had just about reached us.

"This is temporal netting," I intoned. By now my voice was beginning to sound rather like it was being played on vinyl at the wrong rpm, making it much more bassy and slower than normal.

The Duck ignored me and tried to get ahead.

"What's wrong with her?" said Jemmons.

He sounded like he could sing "Ol' Man River."

"She got stuck in mid-change—gruesome, isn't it?" I said. "I wonder what her menopause looks like. Give us a hand with her."

The Duck still ignored me and tried to walk past and head down the stairs. I grabbed the sleeve of his biggles and pulled.

"Help us," I said. "Take a leg."

"I'm not helping her—she would have left us to die," he said, in his normal voice.

"Your voice hasn't changed," I said.

"I had to have a bioelectronic voice box fitted when my voice never broke."

"That explains a lot. Take her foot—or I'll smack you," I said.

"Who's got the key?"

"She has."

He kept pulling against me, so I let him go and he fell down the stairs in slow motion. The rest of us picked up the Princess and started down slowly, like climbers returning from the summit, picking our steps carefully and checking with each other before making any deviation from the path. When we tried to skirt round the fallen figure of the Duck, who was finding it difficult to get back up, we had to co-ordinate our feet, because the Duck actually used the Princess' body to pull himself up, as we went by. I was just about to let go of my shoulder and reach out to hit him, when he took one of the Princess' feet from Emma and joined in.

"Good boy," I said.

By the time we got to the bottom of the stairs, we were all exhausted, but still had half the ship to walk, and carry the Princess. We could see the corridor curving away from us, but none of us had the spirit to be the first to tell the others to crack on.

"This is no good," said the Duck. "Wait here—I'll go."

I was too tired to argue. Jemmons looked in an even worse state than me. Emma looked fairly fresh.

"I'll go with you," she said.

The Duck cringed at the sound of her deep voice. Emma took his hand and they set off. Jemmons and I slumped down with the Princess and rested with our backs against the wall. As I watched Emma slowly trudge around the corner with the Duck, I wondered if it would be the last time I would ever see them again. Tears came into my eyes and stayed there. I looked around me—and would this be the last place I would ever see? It was like the inside of the Museum of Modern Art— with rivets. I noticed a red line going into the door I was leaning against. Red is for bombs, I thought. I hauled myself up and opened the door— bombs stretched away from me on hundreds of racks, aisle after aisle of bombs. I looked over at Jemmons. His eyes were closed. I crawled in. I found a trolley—presumably for transporting bombs around—and climbed on, and then I pulled myself along the aisle, rather like a surfer paddling out to meet the waves. I didn't have to go far before I found what I was looking for. It was a wooden crate—already opened and half empty—with the words: LAND MINES – TYPE: TIMER. I laughed ghoulishly to myself in my new horror movie voice, and lifted one out very carefully, placed it even more carefully down on the floor, and set the timer for fifteen minutes. Then I turned to haul myself back out on the trolley.

Suddenly, something gripped my ankle!

I turned my head in terror and saw what looked like a small robot— probably used to carry the bombs about. It looked a bit like a metal bulldog, with huge jaws.

"Let go, you little sod!" I said.

I attempted to shake him off. But his pneumatic mouth was firmly locked onto my leg. When I realized how heavy and strong the thing was, I panicked—I had visions of being trapped in the bomb store when my land mine blew up. Hoist by my own petard. Few before me could have used that metaphor more aptly. When all my efforts to kick my captor away with my other foot failed, I tried to reach it to turn the timer off. But the little metal munitions worker tugged me back each time. And then I saw that I could reach another bomb off the rack above us—a round one with the word BRIMSTONE printed on it in yellow paint.

"Here, boy!" I said. "Fetch!"

I threw the bomb and it clattered up the aisle and rolled along like a bowling ball. My captor immediately let me go and shuffled after it.

I dragged myself away on the trolley and pulled myself through the door.

Jemmons looked round just as I was bolting it behind me.

"Quick—help me put her on," I said.

I rolled off and we lifted the Princess onto the trolley.

"Come on," I said. "It doesn't look like they're coming back."

Jemmons nodded and we made our way to the front of the trolley, took the towing bar, and started pulling it very ponderously along the passageway. We made slow progress—the bend in the big wide corridor seemed never-ending. Twice Jemmons stumbled and fell and I had to stop and struggle to pull him back up on his feet. The second time he told me to leave him and go on, but I wouldn't, even though I wanted to leave them both and just save myself. All I could think about was getting off that vessel alive with Emma. That was all I cared about, but there was something else in me that wouldn't let me desert Jemmons and the Princess. I don't know what it was—a basic humanity, perhaps, or just the thought of what Emma would say when I tried to explain it to her.

It had begun to get much darker and I could see our invisible artist filling in more and more straight red lines, and shading in the shadowy recesses in green. Also the throbbing had increased and there was now quite a powerful thrum throughout the ship. In fact, it had suddenly become very loud. I panicked because I thought maybe the temporal net had speeded up and we had actually run out of time. The throbbing noise became alarmingly loud. Jemmons and I looked at each other wide-eyed and shook our heads. I think we were trying to say goodbye to each other.

At that moment, a huge snowmobile roared around the bend ahead and skidded to a halt, but with the powerful engine still left ticking over. The ski-suited, begoggled driver raised her goggles up and waved. It was Emma. She was alone.

"Thank God!" I said, sounding uncannily like Tom Waits by now.

She climbed down off the seat and came to give us a hand, in slow motion.

"Where's the Duck?" I intoned.

"Don't ask," she responded, in a deep dark voice.

We lifted the Princess off the trolley and carried her to the two-man snowmobile. There was enough room for me to share the driver's seat and for Jemmons to sit on the passenger seat, holding the Princess in front of him. The only problem was Emma found the snowmobile was too long to turn in the corridor, so she had to drive us all the way back down to the foot of the stairs—where we had started from—and use it as a turning area.

"So what happened with the Duck?"

"He has the key," she said.

"He has the key?"

"Didn't you see him pick her pocket when he asked you who had the key?"

"Damn. No, I didn't. I should have known—the little—"

"He said he would be back."

"Yeah. Right. I like your voice. You sound like Conan the Barbarian's sister."

As we drove, I noticed that the speedometer was up around the 60 clicks mark, but we were only moving at something a little faster than walking pace. I remembered my bomb, but was too embarrassed to mention it. It was a pretty stupid thing to do.

"Can't this thing go any faster?" I said.

"We're doing sixty," said Emma.

"Sixty what—zimmer frames an hour?"

And then we were entering the loading bay. The hatch was open and the ramp engaged.

"Hold on, everybody!" said Emma.

Jemmons grunted. Emma swung the big machine around and nosed it out—and then we were on the ramp and sailing through the freezing air, with the ice below us and the starry night above. But we were still being pulled by the temporal gravity from the ship. Suddenly we shot forward in a violent surge, as we escaped the force field, and then we were free—sailing off the end of the ramp and gliding, with the engine roaring and the skis squishing pleasantly over the ice.

"We did it!" exclaimed Emma, taking one hand off the steering wheel to punch the air.

"Brilliant, Em!" I cried. "Now put that other hand back."

Our voices were back to normal.

She braked in a wide arc and we looked back at the stricken ship, glowing and pulsing in the distance.

"So, what exactly did my wonderful father say before he deserted us?" I said.

Emma left the motor running as she spoke—I think she was enjoying dominating the big powerful beast. Or, maybe that was just me fantasizing.

"He said he would find the Princess' ship."

"I bet he did. And then what?"

"He said he was going to—" Emma's voice slowed down. But this time she was doing it herself. "And—come back to rescue us."

"A likely story."

The ship suddenly exploded into a billion pieces, lighting up the ice sheet for miles and miles around. Bits and pieces of debris spewed out high over our heads and the shock wave actually slid us back several yards and singed the tiny hairs on our faces. The whole explosion was assuming the shape of a giant jellyfish, expanding and spreading its orange tendrils in a perfect dome all around itself.

Emma opened the throttle and we were off, gliding ahead of the bouncing shrapnel and burning debris, which we could already see hitting the ice and hurtling towards us. And then hot shards from the ship's superstructure began flying by and skimming across the ice ahead of us, hissing as they came to rest, forming hot puddles, that steamed and glowed. It was an uncomfortable feeling, waiting for something hot and jagged to hit us, but miraculously nothing did, and we were soon beyond the last of the spitting puddles, running on clean ice. Emma was heading for the far side of the island, which was still a smoking volcano of snow. I cast my eyes to the left and watched it pass as Emma circled round. There were some figures on the lower slopes, and others straggling down from what was left of the wall.

"I hope your father wasn't in there," said Emma.

"Dad?" I swallowed hard and stared back at the roaring inferno.

"What do you think happened?" said Emma.

"Dunno," I said. "Er, meltdown?"

Suddenly another snowmobile zoomed out from a sheltered cove and headed towards us. There was a bespectacled character astride it.

"It's Dad!" I cried. "He's alive! It's my dad, Em! Dad! Dad!" I waved my arms about. I guess I must have been worried about him, subconsciously.

"Easy, junior," said Emma.

Jemmons, who must have been half asleep, stirred.

"Are you all right, Princess?"

"Yes. Yes, I think I am, Roger," she said drowsily.

We slowed down and the Duck pulled in alongside. There was a spliff in the corner of his mouth. Emma stopped and switched off the ignition. The Duck did the same and relit his spliff.

"Thank God, you're okay—we thought you might have been onboard," I said.

"What the heck happened?" he said, through a cloud of marijuana smoke.

"It just went," I said. "Didn't it, Em?"

"Yeah," she said. She made an explosive gesture with her hands. "It just went—boom."

The Duck looked sceptical.

"I could have been on there," he said.

"But you weren't, were you?" I said.

"That's not the point," he said. "I was going to come back and help, but I thought I'd give you a bit more time."

"A bit more time to do what—die?"

"I had a bit of trouble with me starting motor. I see you brought her," he said, doing one of his lopsided smiles. "What d'you bring her for?"

"Did you find her ship?" I said.

"Ship. There wasn't any bleeding ship," he said, in disgust.

"No ship?" I said. "But there must be."

"He means there is no actual vessel," said the Princess. "I used the term 'ship' loosely."

"So what did you mean?" I said.

"She means it's just a time portal back to her planet—I've been led right up the garden path—hers!" said the Duck.

"You've been there?" I said.

"Well, I had a quick look. There's nothing much to see—just a load of islands and lagoons."

"Sounds marvellous," said Emma.

"My world is rather like your Pacific Ocean, Emma."

"Yeah," said the Duck. "Only the water's petroleum green and the sky's tangerine with yellow bleeding clouds. I thought I was on acid."

"Oh, don't, Sir Julian," sighed the Princess. "You're making me homesick."

"Yeah, and you're welcome to it," said the Duck. He reached inside his biggles and pulled out the cranberry glass key. "Here. That was the crappiest planet I've ever been on."

The Princess took it and kissed it. "My key, my key," she said, breathlessly. "If only you knew what this means to me. The planet Mormagleea is my precious home planet, but it is only one of a thousand homes I own all over the galaxy. And this key opens them all."

"So how do we get home?" I said.

"Good bleeding question."

The Princess climbed off the snowmobile. Jemmons helped her down.

"Oh, poor, Sir Julian," she said. "He is such a little boy—he expected a fantastic time machine, with lots of new gadgets—all bells and whistles—something he could drive and show off to his friends on dull Sunday mornings. And all he got was a door into another world." She laughed and laughed.

"This is the thanks we get for saving her bleeding life—she's all right—she's got a home to go to—she's going to leave us here and swan off to her psychedelic fish tank," said the Duck.

"Oh, how divine it will be to immerse myself once more in the warm, perfumed waters of Mormagleea, and stretch my frozen tentacles to their full extent. Oh."

"Oh, I so want to bath," said Emma.

"And so you shall, dear Emma," said the Princess. "Do you really think I would abandon you here in this dreadful place after all you have done for me?" She turned to the Duck. "You see, Sir Julian, what you failed to discover was my key's secret properties. Like me, you see, it can transform!"

She held the key up and it changed into a remote handheld control, poxed with multicoloured buttons.

"Neat!" exclaimed the Duck.

"Now, take me to that beacon out there and I will show you just what my little box of tricks can do. Where would you like to go today—or tomorrow or yesterday?"

The Duck grinned and quacked, "I always knew you'd come up trumps, Your Highness. I knew you were class and that's why I wanted you to marry my son."

"Yes, yes," said the Princess. She gazed up at Jemmons.

"But I think now I shall go with my original choice—if the gentleman is as willing as I think he is. What do you say, Roger?"

Jemmons hesitated bashfully. Emma nudged him.

Jemmons dropped down on one knee. "Your Highness, will you marry me?" he blurted.

"Arise, my Prince!" cried the Princess. She pulled Jemmons up into her arms and kissed him.

We all applauded.

"Er, Your Highness," said my father, as we were all climbing back onto our snowmobiles. "Does our agreement still stand? After all I did introduce you to your intended. I did broker the union, so to speak."

The Princess smiled mischievously. "I'll give you the plans and mathematical formula, Sir Julian—and let you work it out for yourself."

"It's a deal," said the Duck. "I think I'm up for a bit of reverse engineering. Now, we've got to go to Bristol first to fetch Emily and then go and drag her old man out of that twenty-ninth century PLEASURE-Dome. Oh, and can you drop me off in 1740—there's some frost-damaged furniture going cheap."

"Oh, Sir Julian," said the Princess. "You make me sound like a taxi service."

"Wait!" I said. "I have something very important to say."

Everyone stopped in their tracks and looked round at me.

I dropped down on one knee.

"Emma, will you marry me?" I said.

"Marry you?" said Emma.

There was a long embarrassing pause.

"Love, I don't want to rush you, but I'm getting a stiff knee down here."

"Only if Sir Julian agrees to marry Emily and the Princess dear Roger—in a triple wedding at Duckworth Hall," said Emma.

I looked to the others for their answers.

"I'm game," grinned Jemmons.

"Oh, you dear, sweet, sentimental, young romantic you!" exclaimed the Princess, embracing Emma. "Of course, I agree—it's a most excellent idea."

"Sir Julian?" prompted Emma.

We all looked to the Duck.

"No bloody way!" he blurted. We all lurched towards him threateningly. He held up his hands and quacked with delight. "You should have seen your faces!"

We remounted our snowmobiles and vroomed off towards the twinkling violet-blue light on the horizon.

But the Duck's wouldn't start.

"Hey! Wait for me!" We heard him shouting. "It's conked out! Wait—it won't start! Come back!"

"We'd better go back for him," said Jemmons.

"Who?" I said.

And we all roared away with laughter.

END

www.ingramcontent.com/pod-product-compliance
Lightning Source LLC
Chambersburg PA
CBHW031112030726
47496CB00002BA/512